First published in 1996
by HEADLINE BOOK PUBLISHING

First published in 1997
by HEADLINE BOOK PUBLISHING

A HEADLINE FEATURE paperback

10 9 8 7 6 5 4 3 2 1

ISBN 0 7472 5552 0

Typeset by Palimpsest Book Production Limited,
Polmont, Stirlingshire
Printed in England by
Mackays of Chatham PLC, Chatham, Kent

HEADLINE BOOK PUBLISHING
A division of Hodder Headline PLC
338 Euston Road
London NW1 3BH

A former Head of News and Current Affairs, Keith
Baker is currently Chief Editorial Advisor for BBC
Northern Ireland. He lives in County Down.

Inheritan

Keith Baker

For Joan Harvey

Acknowledgements

It is more than two and a half years since I first approached my agent Carole Blake with the idea for this story. As the book took shape, she and Julian Friedmann helped me over many hurdles and were always there for advice, support and friendship. I also thank Bill Massey at Headline for his good-natured editorial wisdom. Most of all, I want to thank my family – Jo, Louise, Simon and Rose – for allowing me the time.

Prologue

Six so far. More if he did not manage to stop it.

Four of them had been shot, their bodies discarded like grotesque human refuse, each man with a bullet hole in the centre of the forehead and the back of the skull blown away. All of them would have known death was coming, would have had to face the gun raised and pointed at them.

A bomb had killed two others, a man and a woman blown to fragments in their car when the key that turned in the ignition triggered the device wired to it. The man had been the real target although the woman would have been something of an unexpected bonus. As it turned out, she had been no innocent bystander. She had done her bit, even served a prison sentence several years ago after a patrol had searched the pram she was pushing and found that the baby girl in it had been managing to sleep peacefully in spite of the discomfort of half a dozen timing devices packed under her thin little mattress.

The baby was nearly ten now, the eldest of four children suddenly become orphans, Miller thought angrily as he drove, more little pieces of debris left to drift in the currents of grief that coursed through this place. But no one would worry much; it was their hard luck. Think of the bereavement and loss their parents had caused. That was what people would say to ease their own consciences and after a while no one would think about them at all.

Miller closed the shutter on his mental image of their

1

bewildered faces. Emotion could not play a part in this. He glanced up from the road and adjusted the rearview mirror, catching himself unawares, for a moment seeing what others saw if they took the trouble to look: tired, haunted eyes, a face ageing quicker than it needed to. It was the job that did that, drove you night and day, enfolded you in a way that no one outside the force could understand.

But this – this was different. Why was he doing it? It was not the first time he had asked himself that question and felt cold inside. There was fear in the eyes that looked back from the mirror. Forget the whole thing, they said. Turn around and go home. But he could not, of course; he knew that. It had all gone too far. He had to finish it or else he would find himself looking over his shoulder for the rest of his days, waiting and wondering.

How would they do it? They seemed capable of anything. A convenient accident, perhaps? His gaze fell on the speedometer. No point in having one now. You're driving too quickly, he told himself. There's plenty of time. He will not get there before you.

There had been a contact this afternoon, rare and risky and out of the blue, because they had a strict rule: no unexpected calls, just the use of certain payphones at certain fixed times. Then they would meet, usually in one of three car parks, the multi-storey near the cinema, the big one along the river near the supermarket or the one at the railway station. On occasions when they needed to talk for longer, there was the car park of a pub on the road to Bangor. When they met, he would hear what his man had to say and then he would hand over the envelope. Sometimes the information was crap and not worth the money, even though it was only a measly fifty quid a throw, but sometimes it was gold and that made up for the dross.

Tonight would be neither. Tonight was about the camera.

This afternoon's call had not been pre-arranged. Miller had walked into the windowless nether world of the CID room, where day merged into night under fluorescent strips. A young duty officer, shirtsleeves, hair tousled, looking just awake, was trying to answer the phone through a mouthful of sandwich that could have been lunch or breakfast or just a sandwich.

'And who's calling?' His voice was wary. 'Just hold a minute.'

He pressed a button and frowned.

'It's a call for you, sir. A man. Won't say who it is. Will I take a message or what? Or maybe you want to take it?'

Miller paused on the way to his desk. 'What does he sound like?'

The young man shrugged. 'A bit odd. Hard to make out. It's certainly not the Chief Constable anyway.' He smiled at his own wit.

Miller laughed. 'Oh aye? How would you know? Does he ring you that often? Switch it through, for goodness sake.'

He picked up the phone. 'Hello?'

There was a pause and then the caller spoke.

'I think I can help you get what you're looking for.'

The voice was muffled, as if the man was holding something over his mouth.

Right to the point, Miller thought. No introductions. But then he did not need them. He knew the voice at once and was startled to hear it but he tried not to show his surprise. He put his hand over the receiver and whispered 'it's OK'. The duty officer nodded and went back to his sandwich and the *Sun* crossword. Miller slumped into his chair with his feet on the desk. He fumbled in his pocket for a cigarette and then remembered he had stopped. Damn.

'And what would that be then?'

His tone was cheery. Verbal back-slapping. Two old pals on the phone.

'Your camera. I'll be at the pub tonight. Half seven.'

Then he was gone and the line was dead.

Miller kept talking, his heart pounding, wanting to hear more but there was nothing more to hear.

'Aye . . . aye . . . really? You have? Oh, that might do the job very well. How many miles on it? Jesus, that's not bad – as long as the price matches.'

His voice was intentionally loud and he looked over towards the duty officer. He knew the young man had to be listening. They exchanged a knowing smile. Car dealers.

Miller stood up. 'Well, I'll need to get up to see it. I'll give you a shout tomorrow maybe. Brilliant,' he said into the lifeless receiver. 'All the best.' Then he had hung up.

'Wee car for the wife's birthday,' he said across the room and winked. 'Mate in the trade.' The younger officer had grinned, flattered at being drawn into his superior's benign little domestic conspiracy. And now, several hours later, hours that he had endured with increasing impatience, Miller was on his way.

But not to meet a man from the motor trade.

The camera had disappeared two days ago from the glove compartment of his car as it sat in the station yard. It was not so much the camera that concerned him but the pictures that were in it. The fact that they were gone had frightened him ever since. It meant he did not have much time left.

That was why he had decided to tell his wife. He had told her both what he knew and what he suspected so that if anything happened to him she would know why. She had always worried, had always feared for his safety. Every day, he knew, she contemplated what life would be like if he were suddenly taken from her. And now the fear and bewilderment were in her eyes as well and he wondered if he had done the right thing.

He passed the towering platforms that were Samson and Goliath, the giant yellow cranes which stood astride the Belfast shipyard and had become the city's most enduring landmark. Further on there was the oil storage depot and then the awning through which the harbour airport beckoned. It had rained with a drab greyness all day but it had stopped now. As he drove on up the hill past Holywood, he caught glimpses of blue sky arriving much too late, the sunlight cutting through the cloud and toasting the edges a watercolour pink. Where it touched Belfast Lough, the water shimmied in an autumn evening dance.

On the far side, you could just see the hill with the monument. It was there that the latest victim had been found this morning, bound with electrical cord and dumped like an informer, except that he had not been one. There had been no marks of torture because there had been no need for interrogation. Whoever had put the bullet in his head had already known everything.

There would be the usual funeral, of course. Adams and the other familiar Sinn Fein faces were practically on permanent coffin-carrying duty. This murder would grip the community, as the others had before it. Some people would be horrified, some would rub their hands with vengeful satisfaction. Others would run for cover.

These were no random assassinations drawn from the customary lottery of sectarian hate. All of the victims had at some time been directly responsible for the deaths of God alone knew how many others – soldiers, policemen, husbands, wives, children blown to bits in their fathers' cars. Some blamed the Loyalists, whose official spokesmen denied it, but then people wondered about the new groups rumoured to be emerging on that side of the fence now, new sets of initials to add to the terrorist list. Still, this work was too skilled, too clinically efficient to be the work of the boys with the earrings and tattoos and the drink on their breath, no matter how organised they were these days. The Republicans talked of security force death squads and Miller knew they were closer to the truth.

The pub appeared ahead, all fake tudor oak and cladding to make it look as if it had stood there for centuries. In fact, it had been there for less than ten years, built on the site of a bar which had been demolished using that unique Ulster method, a beer keg full of fertiliser explosive. What rustic exterior charm it had was being eroded gradually by the gaudy addition of more modern flourishes, like the pink electric signature of an American beer sign in the window.

Miller pulled into the big car park, his tyres scattering and crunching the rough gravel. There were one or two other vehicles, all of them near the road, so he drove to the back, up by the hedge, then reversed so that he was facing the entrance and no one could approach without being seen. He sat for a few minutes listening to soft rock on Radio Ulster. Thirteen days since he had had a cigarette. The Eagles told him to take it easy but there was not much chance of that. A few cars drove by on the main road beyond but no driver looked his way and no other car drove in.

He got out, locked up, then walked towards the pub. He pushed the door open and entered. Inside it was big, built for Friday and Saturday nights when the kids packed it with their designer beers out of the bottle and the music was way, way up. Tonight it was almost empty and the long-legged bar stools stood in an orderly row like a forgotten guard of honour on a deserted parade ground, unwanted except for one at the end where a tall man with a moustache sat, engrossed in a pint and the evening paper.

At a table in the corner, three men laughed at the punch line of a story which Miller could hear was about Ian Paisley going to heaven and meeting the Pope. He had heard it before. There were no new jokes, he thought sadly as he looked at the men. They were in their early thirties, double-breasted in Hugo Boss suits and wearing ties with floral patterns, all individual and all managing to look the same. He glanced at the coats strewn on spare chairs, at the briefcases and bulky satchels pregnant with laptop technology. A pit stop on the way home to the comfort of North Down.

Miller hated people like that. No, he did not hate them, he resented them, that was it. He resented the way they refused to allow the Troubles to touch them, as if what had been happening over the years was no concern of theirs, just a tiresome inconvenience that sometimes meant they had to make a detour on the way to work. What did they know of bodies in ditches, friends being murdered? But then, he thought as he eased himself onto a stool near the door, weren't they lucky? Maybe what he really felt was envy and what he resented was their ability to lead a normal life. Although it could never be entirely normal. Not one hundred per cent. Not in this place.

He ordered a Scotch and dry ginger. He could see the barman giving him a quick professional once-over as he rinsed a glass but he was used to that. All it took was a glance. He was conspicuous in his anonymity, a big man, a bit overweight and out of condition at forty-two, hair receding at the temples and a complexion that said too many long hours and smoky rooms and not enough sunlight and fresh air.

He was tired and he wondered what would happen when all this was over. Even though he knew that what he was doing was the right thing, there would be no prizes for it – but he was aware of that. He would just have to get out, get another job. It would all be made too uncomfortable for him. Oh, there might be some quiet recognition for his work but it would be superficial and short-lived. Backs would be turned, promotional opportunities would drift past him. He would be treated as if he did not exist.

He folded his raincoat and put it on the stool next to him. He bought a packet of nuts, something for him to do with his hands since he could not smoke, and he sipped his drink, positioning himself facing the bar so that he had his back to the room but still had a good view of it in the mirror behind the dispensers.

The door opened and a man came in. He was in his late twenties but he could have passed for forty. His fair hair was lank, the face below it puffy. He wore a leather bomber jacket that was taut over a problem waistline and black chinos that were baggy at the backside. Dessie Gillespie. In a relaxed moment once, Miller had kidded him that he sounded like an Irish jazz musician but Gillespie had looked blankly at him and he had decided not to try to explain. It would have taken too long.

Gillespie paused at the door for a moment and gazed round the bar as if he were looking for someone but then he seemed to decide that whoever it was was not there. He walked to the bar and ordered a pint which he took to a corner table under a window. He did not look at Miller who sat for a few minutes with his whisky, then stood up to put his coat on, taking his time, and said goodbye to the barman.

'Cheers.'

'All the best, sir. Mind how you go.' No one else paid any attention or noticed his departure.

Outside there was a dusty Ford Fiesta which had not been there before. Miller got into his own car and waited, drumming his fingers on the steering wheel and checking his watch. A few minutes later, the door of the pub opened and Gillespie came out, turning towards the car park and into a wind that had come from nowhere, bringing a sudden chill with it. He zipped the leather jacket up as far as it would go and kept his head down as he walked quickly to Miller's car and got in. No one saw him.

Miller kept his eyes straight ahead as the passenger door clunked shut.

The car was warm and the sudden temperature change made Gillespie shudder. 'You haven't got a fag, have you?' The voice was throaty, the accent East Belfast.

'I'm off them,' Miller grumbled, annoyed at being reminded. He turned to look at Gillespie. 'So tell me about the camera.'

'I think I know who's got it. Something somebody overheard.'

Miller studied him. Gillespie was agitated and perspiration was damp on his brow.

'Are you OK?'

'What do you think? You know what happened again last night. This could get me killed.'

8

'Believe me, it could get us both killed. So where's the camera?'

Gillespie licked dry lips but did not answer. Miller's skin prickled. This was wrong. He looked around the darkening car park but they were still alone.

'What the hell's going on, Gillespie?'

The door of the pub opened and someone came out. Miller saw it was the tall man who had been sitting down at the far end of the bar when he had arrived. They both paused and watched as he pulled his collar up, walked to a car and got in. They could hear the engine start.

Miller turned back to Gillespie. 'So tell me.'

'I can't tell you here. There's a problem.'

As he spoke, Miller saw a movement at the edge of his vision. The tall man was out of his car again and was striding across the gravel towards them. Miller swore at Gillespie and pushed his door open, wishing he had not put the damned raincoat on. He was reaching into his pocket and trying to get out of the car, all in one movement, when the first shot smashed the windscreen and hit him in the throat. The second one was higher and took part of his forehead away.

The gunman did not pause or break his stride. He was right at the car now and he pulled open the passenger door where Gillespie shook in terror, trying frantically to wipe blood and brain matter from his face, except that it was also on his sleeve and the back of his hand.

'You did well,' the tall man said and then shot him once in the side of the head. He moved quickly round to the driver's side where Miller's body had started to slide out. He pushed him back in and then checked his pockets. He found the envelope with the money but left it there. From his own inside pocket he pulled another gun, a nine-millimetre Hungarian automatic. He took Miller's right hand, clasped it round the weapon for a couple of seconds before opening the glove compartment and dropping it inside.

He walked quickly to his own car where it sat with its engine still running, then he drove out of the car park and away. It was just after 8 p.m. and it could not have taken much more than a minute.

In years to come, history would record that the murders he had just committed were one of the last violent acts of the conflict.

He did not know it but the Troubles were almost over.

Chapter One

20 YEARS LATER

It was just after 8 p.m. and it could not have taken much more than a minute. He did not know it but his troubles were just beginning.

Jack McCallan had walked into the bedroom, naked from the shower, his dark hair slicked back wet and glistening, to find her standing there, dressed in black and white like some *film noir* goddess, swinging the keyring around on her index finger. She had changed her hair and for a brief stupid moment he did not realise who it was.

He wondered how long she had been waiting in this contrived but effective pose. She wore a white silk jacket and a black skirt and she stood with her bare legs apart, slender black shoes emphasising their shape. The legs always had at least the hint of a tan, although it was certainly not the real thing at this time of the year, and the skirt was tight over her firm thighs.

It struck him suddenly that she had lost weight. If it was deliberate, then he hoped it was not the beginning of some unnecessary fad that would turn her soft contours into sharp angles. The hair was definitely a radical stylistic switch, no longer a golden confection tumbling to her shoulders but short and straight and curving in just below her ears. It was a little lighter than before, too, veering in the direction of ash, and he wondered why it was that some women of a certain age seemed to get blonder as they got older.

11

'You made me jump,' he said.

Julia Shriver arched an eyebrow and gave a lop-sided smile. She lowered her gaze.

'So I see.'

She came towards him as he felt himself stirring. She stood against him with her hands buried deep in her jacket pockets. He could smell her fragrance, feel her heat. She did not move as he began to open the buttons of her blouse. When it was undone, he reached in to free her breasts from the lacy flimsiness that held them. He bent his gleaming head to nuzzle her warmth and as he did so she moved, pushing him back suddenly so that he lost his balance and flopped on to the bed. He sprawled there in surprise.

Julia moved towards the bed and climbed on to it, straddling him and rolling the skirt quickly up over her thighs and hips. Underneath it she wore nothing.

She gave a sharp gasp as she lowered herself on to him abruptly, as if there were no time to spare. She bit her lower lip and closed her eyes as she rode him and then threw her head back with a shudder at the end. When the ripples had passed through her, she leaned towards him and kissed his wet hair softly.

'The taxi's waiting downstairs,' she said, her voice a warm groan in his ear. 'I'm afraid I told him we wouldn't be long.'

Reluctantly, she disengaged herself, took a pair of panties from her bag where it sat on a chair, then made her way to the bathroom. She had not even taken her shoes off, McCallan saw as he lay slowly dwindling on the bed. It had all been a bit frantic, even desperate, a quick sexual fix, totally unlike the Julia who normally liked their love-making to be languid and elaborate, and it made him wonder what was behind it.

'I like the hair,' he called out after her.

'Thank you,' she said softly for she was just outside the door, coming back in with a towel which she threw at him. 'I felt like doing something different.'

He did not know whether she meant the hair or the sex.

She took a lipstick from her bag and sat in front of the mirror at a dressing table which bore the flotsam of single manhood. There was loose change, aftershave, credit card receipts, all in a discarded jumble with a slight coating of dust.

'When are you going to tidy this place up? I thought you had a woman who comes in?'

'I did have. She quit. Moved out of the area and went to live with her daughter in Southwark. It's hardly worth getting someone else since I'm not here that often.' He smiled. 'The only woman who comes in now is you. Want to volunteer?'

It was an even sillier question than he had meant it to be. In the mirror she poked her tongue at him for a moment and then resumed the repairs to her make-up. He knew she hated this flat. The idea of her being anything other than an occasional visitor to his cramped domain was out of the question as things stood, but it was an issue they both knew they would have to face if their relationship was to go anywhere.

He watched her as he dressed. He had been out of London and had not seen her for over a week, right enough. Maybe that had a little to do with it but there was undoubtedly something different about her, not just the slight hollowness he could see now in her cheeks.

'Are you losing weight?' he asked.

'Just watching it,' she said. 'Some of us have to.'

At thirty-five, he was six years younger than she was and he had probably not put on more than a couple of pounds in ten years. He was naturally lean in build but the life he led had helped him stay that way. In the Army, fitness had been unavoidable but now that he was a civilian he still kept in shape.

'Don't overdo it,' he said. 'I'm not so sure about underweight women.' He waved his hand in a gesture of uncertainty.

'Oh yes, I forgot,' she smiled. 'You like them big, as I recall.'

He laughed. He knew what she meant.

*　　*　　*

Their paths had first crossed four months ago, on a mellow July evening, at a party in the North London home of one of McCallan's old college friends who now ran an art gallery. McCallan had not planned on being there that night, having driven to London from Northamptonshire in the late afternoon with nothing on the menu for the evening but something on a tray in front of the box. That was until he had found the invitation in the little pile of mail which the cleaning woman had left on the kitchen table.

Brian. He had not seen him for ages. He could see him fussing around, introducing people, calling everyone dear, his latest surly young man always a step behind. He had smiled to himself. Why not? It might be fun. Brian's parties usually were. Some hours later, when he found himself pinned in a corner beside the fireplace in what Brian liked to call his salon while a short, fat and breathless woman rambled on at him about some painter he had never heard of, he had concluded that this party was the exception.

'Of course, don't misunderstand me,' the woman droned in a Boston accent. Drooping eyelids oscillated with every syllable. 'I like his work enormously. I bought him early, after all. One of the first to do so. But at twenty-five grand he's gone a bit steep and anyway the colours don't suit my new walls. What about you? Are you a collector?'

The eyelids had stopped fluttering and the eyes beneath them had fixed him with an unsettling stare. It was then that he had looked over her shoulder to see a striking blonde woman watching his predicament with amusement.

'No, not really,' he had said, thinking about his tiny flat. 'I haven't got the space.' This was true, as far as it went, although he had not mentioned the fact that he did not have the money either.

It was time to escape. 'Would you excuse me for a moment?' he had said. 'There's someone here I just have to talk to.' He squeezed out of the way, aware that her stare followed him suspiciously, and walked the few feet to where the

14

other woman stood. It was a gamble but he would go for it.

'Hello. How nice to see you again. It's been ages,' he said a little loudly.

'Indeed it has,' she smiled. 'In fact, you could say it's been forever.'

The woman from Boston moved away. In a few seconds they could hear her from another part of the room, her drawl cutting through the party babble.

'Thanks,' McCallan said. 'I needed a lifeline. I was going down for the third time.'

'Glad to be of assistance.' She sipped from a glass of white wine, which gave him a chance to study her quickly. She had been willing to help his escape, there was a sense of humour, he had seen that already, and in the blue eyes that looked at him over the rim of her glass he saw curiosity, although nothing too eager. A diamond on her engagement finger dazzled beside a plain gold band and he wondered which of the other people in the room was her husband.

He held out his hand. 'Jack McCallan.'

She took the hand and held it. Hers was chilly from the glass but the grip was firm.

'Julia Shriver,' she said. 'Nice to meet you. Or should I say – nice to meet you again, just in case your friend's watching?'

'Oh, I think I'm safe now, thank goodness.'

'Are you a customer of Brian's? Most of the other people here seem to be?'

He was about to answer when Brian appeared at his elbow, as if summoned magically by the mere mention of his name. He wore a billowing blue silk shirt and glasses with colourfully dappled frames.

'Ah, good, Julia. You've met our war hero, I see.'

Her eyes widened. 'Really?'

McCallan opened his mouth to speak but Brian cut in first.

'Oh yes, quite a story. Tell her all about it, there's a love.

15

And look after her, won't you? She's here all by herself.' He patted them both on the shoulder and fluttered off.

Bloody Brian, landing him in it, McCallan thought, but at the same time he focused on those last few words and wondered why Julia Shriver was alone.

'Brian's an old friend from university. We keep in touch,' he said, then changed the subject. 'So we're both on our own tonight, are we? No husband keeping an eye on you?'

'Eh – no,' she said, a little awkwardly. 'Not this evening.'

He looked at her, waiting for her to volunteer more.

'He's away on business a lot.' It was all she chose to add.

McCallan nodded as if he understood. 'What line is he in?'

'Financial matters. Investments, that kind of thing.'

He could see at a glance that it paid off. There is something about the rich, he told himself, that sets them apart from the rest of us. It was not just the clothes or the quality of the jewellery; there was an aura about this woman, even a different sheen to her skin, it seemed, but at the same time he had a feeling that beneath the easy confidence there was something not quite so secure.

'So what's all this war hero stuff?' she asked. Her glass was empty and she held it out to him. 'Why don't you get us both a drink and you can tell me all about it.'

'Oh God,' he groaned. 'Do I have to?'

'No,' she said, 'but I'd like you to. I'm intrigued.'

And so he began to talk to her and as the evening went on he found it something that was very easy to do. Whether it was simply her, the way she allowed him to hold her interest, her eyes searching his face as he talked, or whether it was the wine, he did not know. At any rate, he felt comfortable in her presence.

With a fresh bottle of chardonnay, they had wandered into the kitchen and sat at the bleached pine table. First he had tried to find out more about her but she gave him very little. There was a house off Holland Park but there were

no children; that much he discovered. On the other hand, his
reticence about his own circumstances gradually disappeared
under her gentle persuasion. He had volunteered the headlines
of his life: the only child of a mother who had died when he
was fifteen and a father who had retired from the police in
Northern Ireland with a medal earned for his bravery in a
terrorist ambush. Born in Ulster, he had been educated in
England because it had been safer that way. When your father
was a potential IRA target, you just never knew. Bombs had a
way of claiming more victims than those for whom they were
intended.

'So now comes the ironic bit,' McCallan had told her. 'I
joined the Army and got shot.'

'Shot? But not in Northern Ireland, surely?'

'No, all that was over a long time ago. Part of history now,
really. No, I got shot in West Africa, not West Belfast.'

She poured some more wine into his glass and waited for
him to continue.

'We were a special forces group, a rapid reaction team, as
it's known, the sort of thing the UN calls in from time to time.
The Army's a very different occupation now. A lot of the old
regiments have gone, including my own, the Royal Irish, and
so instead you have groups of specialist units ready to go
anywhere at any time. Anyway, you remember the fighting
in Nigeria a few years ago?'

Julia nodded. It had been one of those tragedies which had
seemed to have no end and it had gradually slipped out of the
news headlines and out of international consciousness without
ever being entirely resolved.

'There was fierce fighting between rival tribes, if you recall.
Thousands being slaughtered, world-wide concern, children
starving, and so on. We went out there to lend a hand. One of
the last remnants of the Commonwealth and all that. It was a
big issue for HMG – sorry, the Government.'

Bloody irritating. He hated catching himself using phrases
like that. HMG. Little flecks of khaki embedded in his speech.

He doubted whether he would ever manage to dislodge them entirely.

'There was a Nigerian Army of sorts but it was no help at all. Their soldiers were all shooting each other anyway. There was lots of food and other aid being sent, medical supplies, but it wasn't getting to the people who needed it. So we got sent out to make sure it did. Certainly, all very humanitarian on the face of it but apart from that there were a lot of major British economic concerns and Britain was kind of keen on preserving them and keeping the government afloat.'

The kitchen was warm, even though the patio doors had been opened to the night air, so he took his jacket off and hung it over the back of a chair. 'Still, for whatever reason you like, there we were, up to our necks in it. Famine, drought, slaughter. All the things they don't tell you about in the career videos.'

He paused and his gaze went off into the middle distance somewhere.

'It's odd how vividly you remember some things. We were in this grubby little town with a couple of lorryloads of grain. I was in a Landrover in front. My driver and I had got a bit too far ahead and then we turned a wrong corner into a street that I remember thinking was strangely empty. Just dust and heat and shadowy doorways. Not an animal, not a beggar. Nothing moving. We stopped and I stood up in the Landrover and looked around. Bloody stupid. We were always taught to make ourselves hard targets, not to make things easy for the enemy. I'd have bollocked any of my men if he'd done that.'

He looked at Julia. 'You know that expression where they say you never hear the shot that gets you? Well, I heard that one. Loud and clear.'

He could not rely on memory for the rest of the story since he knew only what they had described to him afterwards: that the shot that hit him in the head had been a ricochet from a burst of automatic fire sprayed at them with more optimism than skill by a kid lying on a rooftop and that he was lucky it had not been a trained marksman with a Kalashnikov and a good eye.

They told him that his driver had put his foot to the floor to get him back to base hospital where the doctors had got him in time, in that all-important golden hour, operating with a speed and efficiency that had saved him. Days later he had been flown back to England, still unconscious, and then there had been more operations followed by the long wait to see if he would recover. When he had regained consciousness, the first thing he had seen was the anxious face of his father, who had once escaped such injury himself but had seen what high-velocity bullets could do to others and had never wanted to see such a thing happen to his own son.

'Anyway, four months later I was out of hospital and out of the Army and now here I am.'

'And you're OK?'

'Oh yes. Right as rain. Apart from—'

'Apart from what?'

'Well, I get these headaches every time there's a full moon. And then all this hair starts to grow and I get a bit of a cough, more like a bark, really—'

She dipped her fingers into her glass and flicked drops of wine at him. They both laughed.

'What on earth possessed you to join the Army in the first place? Surely you could have found a more peaceful career to pursue?'

'You might well ask.' She had got him in the eye and he dabbed it with a tissue. 'It seems a bit alien to me now but for as long as I can remember it was all I ever wanted to do. I don't know – the tradition appealed to me, I suppose. Something certain and orderly in a confusing world. A bit like boarding school had been. So after university, I went to Sandhurst and that was that. My shrink used to say that maybe I went into the Army because it saved me making any big decisions about my life. It was an enclosed existence that somebody else mapped out for you.'

'You have a shrink?'

'I had. Not any more. When I got out of hospital, it was quite difficult for a while, hard to adjust to what had happened. I also felt bad about the boy, the one who shot me. After I was hit, some of my men returned fire and they were rather more accurate about it than he was. When they got up to the rooftop, they found him. He was dead, of course, shot to pieces. He was only about thirteen, thin as a rake, probably hadn't had a decent meal in his life and nobody to look after him except whoever had given him the gun.'

He pushed his fingers into the thicket of his hair. 'Sometimes, in my quieter moments, I agonise about it. All the what-ifs, you know? If we hadn't been there, would he still be alive, that sort of thing. And I started to ask myself what the Army was all about, what good had come of any of the operations I'd ever been on. The doctors put it down to the trauma of my injury so they got me a psychiatrist.'

'I bet that did you a lot of good,' she said with obvious doubt.

'Yeah – well. He was a funny bloke. I think I just got over it myself, frankly. He used to ask me odd questions – whether I thought I had any homosexual leanings. Was there something about being surrounded by men all the time?'

'And?' she said with a mischievous smile, keen to have the answer. 'Was there?'

'Not always, no. But I still get a bit lonely sometimes when I'm having a shower. No one to scrub my back.'

'The psychiatrist might have done it for you if you'd asked him nicely.'

'He wasn't my type.'

'You're lucky to be alive,' Julia said, 'although I'm sure you're sick of people telling you.'

'Just a bit. Having a life is one thing. Doing something with it is another. You question what it's all for, you see how superficial most of it is, most of the things we do.' He gestured in the direction of the party noises in the next room. 'All this, for instance.'

After drifting around and running up a big overdraft, he had realised he had to get a job. He had tried his hand at a couple of things without much success and then he had met Tim Ewing, a friend from Sandhurst, who had just inherited the old family manor house in Northamptonshire and turned it into a management training centre.

'For the time being, that's what I'm doing, helping stressed-out business executives play outdoor games and stress themselves some more. I also know a bit about karate so I do that with them, the less dangerous stuff, needless to say, all about breathing and control when you're under pressure. It's a bit of fun and it gives me plenty of time to myself.'

'You mean there isn't someone waiting somewhere?'

'A woman, you mean?'

'A psychiatrist, for all I know.'

He laughed. 'No, nothing current. There hasn't been for a while.' He looked at her and for a moment lost himself in the fantasy that this was a woman who could change all that.

She was asking him about his father.

When the old Royal Ulster Constabulary had been disbanded and replaced by a new force, his father had retired. Since then he had fared rather well and had become a director in a business venture run by a successful old friend. It was a security company, armoured vans and so on at first, but developing later into computer systems and software protection. They had launched very successfully on the Stock Exchange about a year ago.

He had never thought of the police himself, he told her. 'Too many comparisons. Bob McCallan's wee boy, that sort of thing. But I suppose when I think about it now, you know, maybe I did want to get involved in something my father would have vaguely approved of. He cast a long shadow. Except he managed to get through twenty-five years of violence with hardly a scratch. Now he's comfortable in his retirement and I'm the one with the hole in the head.'

He began to pour more wine but Julia put her hand over the top of her glass so he concentrated on his own. He had had rather a lot by now but he was enjoying himself.

'Ever been to Northern Ireland?'

'Never.'

'Shame.' He raised his glass to her. 'I'll take you sometime,' he said cheekily.

'Oh will you indeed?' Her smile mocked him gently.

'Do you think we're going to have an affair?' he asked her suddenly.

As soon as the words were out, he wished he could have taken them back.

Jesus. He could not believe he had really said that.

'I'll tell you what,' she said calmly, standing up. 'I think it's time I went home.'

'Oh God, look, I'm dreadfully sorry.' He was on his feet, too.

'Yes, I'm sure you are,' she said.

'Can – can I drive you home?'

She gave him a look that told him not to be so stupid. 'No, I don't think that would be a very good idea. I'll get a cab. Anyway, I don't really think you should be driving, do you?'

He had unsettled and embarrassed her and spoiled everything and he cursed himself for it. They went back into the salon where she found Brian who dashed off outside to find a taxi. They waited in a pool of silence amid the cacophony of the party, neither of them knowing what to say. When Brian came back to show her out, she said goodbye to McCallan but at the door she turned and gave him a brief look of regret.

'What on earth did you do to Julia?' Brian asked when she had gone.

McCallan told him.

'Well, you're a very silly boy, aren't you, dear? I told

you to look after her, not try to throw your leg over her. Marvellous, bloody marvellous. Especially after everything she's been through.'

'I don't understand.'

'It's the husband, Daniel. He buggered off and left her about a month ago. Julia's been lying low and tonight was the first time she sort of emerged into the light. Not the happiest of experiences either, thanks to you.'

'Where's the husband now?'

'He's shacked up with some fashion model who's leading him around by the dick. Julia's well shot of him, frankly. Gorgeous but a bit of a brute, not averse to giving his lovely wife a slap across the kisser when he feels like it. And a wee bit of a question mark about some of his business dealings, too, from what I hear. One or two rather odd associates, rumour has it. Funny Arabs in dark glasses, that sort of thing.'

'Oh dear, Brian, I'm sorry. I feel very embarrassed.'

'And so you should be.'

'Look, let me have her phone number. I'll call her tomorrow to apologise, see how she is.'

'Well, don't blame me if she hangs up.'

He had made the call at about ten o'clock the next morning, his head muzzy and remorseful and his stomach in a knot of apprehension.

'Hello?'

'Julia, it's Jack McCallan.' There was silence. 'From last night?'

'Yes, I remember.' There was no trace of emotion in her voice and he wished he could see her face.

'Look, I'm ringing to apologise. I was out of line and I'm really sorry I upset you.'

'How did you get my number? From Brian?'

'Yes.'

'So he's probably filled you in then, about me?'

'Well – sort of. Yes. And that made me feel even more

embarrassed. Look, I just didn't want to leave it like that. I wanted to apologise properly. I—'

'You want me to think you're a nice man,' she said, 'not an arrogant prat.'

He gave a nervous laugh. 'Well, yes. I suppose so. Yes.'

There was no response from the other end. He kept going, desperate to fill the silence. 'Look, Brian's having an opening tomorrow night. I thought I might go and I wondered if you were thinking of coming along. I enjoyed talking to you very much and I'm afraid I made rather a hash of things. I thought we might have a drink afterwards – that's if you felt like it. Try to make up for my stupid behaviour last night.'

Brian's gallery would be safe territory where she might not feel threatened. He waited in agony for her to reply or to hear the click of the phone going down. He could not believe how much he wanted to see her again. The silence on the line seemed interminable and he was just about to ask if she was still there when she spoke.

'I can be there at seven thirty. How about you?'

'Perfect,' he said.

They had seen each other several times after that, tentative meetings at first over a coffee or a drink, and bit by bit she had begun to open up to him. Like McCallan, she was an only child. Her mother was English, her father an American who had packed his bags and disappeared without trace when Julia was about four. She had gone to university in Scotland and then into marketing with a publishing company which owned a string of magazines. She had worked on both sides of the Atlantic until the company had been bought over and restructured and she had found herself in her mid-thirties and out of a job.

At about the same time she had met Daniel Shriver. And now? Well, now it was a mess and she wanted a divorce. Daniel was still giving her a generous monthly allowance but she could not go on like this and she had asked her lawyer to start proceedings.

McCallan was a good listener and gradually he had become her confidant, her friend and finally, one night in the soft comfort of a Cotswolds hotel, her lover.

When the taxi reached the restaurant, McCallan paid the driver while Julia walked on in out of the cold. He liked coming here, mingling with the after-theatre crowd, and he took undisguised pleasure in the fact that there was always a chance you might see someone famous. Once had even glimpsed a fellow Ulsterman, Sir Kenneth Branagh, at a discreet table at the back.

McCallan felt relaxed in these surroundings although before he would not have. He put it down to Julia, being around her. He enjoyed going to parties and being the object of her friends' admiration and, in the case of the men, their envy. Their relationship was not a secret although they did not parade themselves in public either but, if he were being honest, the reason he had booked them into this rather conspicuous restaurant tonight was that every now and then he felt the need to tell the world – look what I can do.

Led by the head waiter, they weaved their way through the big open dining room to a comfortable corner table and it occurred to McCallan that she had not mentioned the progress of the divorce for a while. He would ask her when they were settled. As ever, the restaurant was alive with loud voices and waiters set in fast forward. Eyes glanced up at them as they passed.

There was a particularly noisy group of eight at a round table in the centre, clinking glasses as two more bottles of premier cru claret arrived to join those which already stood in empty faded grandeur. One member of the party was a very large man in a striped business suit, his eyes and face glistening. He got up from his seat and threw his soiled and crumpled napkin on to the table as they approached.

'Julia, darling!'

'Leonard! Lovely to see you,' she said, although it was not.

She leaned towards him so that the inevitable slobber would be on the cheek and not on the lips, which Leonard would naturally have preferred, and he gripped her shoulders in his sweaty palms.

'What brings you here?' he asked her, although his eyes had swivelled straight away to McCallan.

Julia made no attempt at introductions. 'Food, Leonard. Same as you.' Her arm made a sweeping gesture towards the bottles on the table and the rest of Leonard's party laughed.

'Bye,' she said and kept on moving. McCallan could feel the man's eyes on them until they had disappeared among the other diners and reached their table. They settled into the leather of the banquette and ordered a couple of gins and tonics while a waiter flourished menus the size of a tabloid newspaper.

'Who's that?' McCallan said.

'A business associate of Daniel's. I haven't seen him for a while. Horrible man.' The waiter came with the drinks and she took a stiff gulp of hers. Something was on her mind but he would leave it until they had ordered. He was ravenous and decided on lamb cutlets but she was not hungry at all and chose some steamed fish and salad. They opted for wine by the glass.

When the food arrived, she picked at it. 'What's the matter, Julia?' he asked.

'Sorry,' she said, 'just a bit down, that's all.'

'Well, then, I've got an idea, something I've been thinking about all week, actually.' He sat forward. 'I promised my father I'd go and see him next week. I haven't been over there for a while. But what about doing something this weekend to cheer you up? We could take off somewhere, go to the country or something. That place in the Cotswolds. Remember?'

She smiled. 'Of course, I remember. I'll always remember.' She looked tired and drawn. 'But I can't. Not this weekend. Not until I've sorted something out.'

'Daniel?' he asked cautiously.

She nodded. 'He wants me back.'

McCallan's heart sank. So that was the problem. She put her hand on his where it rested on the tablecloth. It felt cool and soft on his skin.

'It will be all right,' she said. 'He's been in New York all week, ringing me, pleading, begging. His woman has walked out on him, found somebody richer, I suspect, and I think there are business problems, too. He wants me back so that I can console him, no doubt. But he hasn't a hope. Not now that I have you.'

She squeezed his hand. McCallan could not speak for a moment.

'Why didn't you tell me?' he asked eventually.

'I didn't want you worrying. I was going to tell you tonight, though – but it's something I've got to sort out by myself.' She frowned slightly. 'I've agreed to see him. He's flying back from New York tonight.' She raised her eyes to the ceiling. 'In fact, he's probably somewhere up there as we speak.'

'Is this wise?' McCallan asked, hearing the strain in his own voice. He cleared his throat.

'It's the only way. I've got to settle it once and for all, make it clear to him that it's over, get the divorce sorted. Then I'll be shot of him. And after that?' She smiled. 'After that, I'm all yours.'

McCallan was elated and frightened at the same time. It was a moment he had wanted, a real commitment, but he wondered how on earth it was all going to work. And there was another fear: that Daniel Shriver would fly into one of his rages and harm her.

'He won't try to hurt you, will he, when you tell him?'

She shrugged. 'I don't know. He sounded very subdued. Very hangdog. I think I'll be all right.'

McCallan saw a figure in a striped suit meandering drunkenly towards them with a bottle of red wine in one hand and a half-full glass in the other. Julia saw him too.

'Oh God,' she groaned.

'Julia, darling,' Leonard said again. 'I thought I should come over and say hello to you and your young friend. You haven't introduced me properly. Mind if I sit down? Have a drink. Bloody fine stuff.'

He set the bottle and the glass on the table and was about to slither along the banquette beside Julia when McCallan stood up. People were watching. He smiled nicely and shook Leonard's hand, then bent towards his bloated face. Leonard was not Daniel Shriver but he would do.

'Why don't you just fuck away off, there's a good chap,' he said quietly.

Leonard recoiled and looked at McCallan. Drunk as he was, he could see danger behind the smile and he could certainly feel it in the strength of the hand gripping his. McCallan let him go.

'No need for that sort of thing,' Leonard muttered feebly, then rescued his wine and drifted off in the direction from which he had come.

McCallan sat down and Julia smiled at him.

'You have a way with words,' she said.

Chapter Two

They had both seen blood before but not like this.

'It must have been like striking oil in here,' the younger one said.

The dead man sat on the kitchen floor against a radiator. His hands were pulled up behind his head and tied to the bar that separated its two panels. The blood had come from the great black hole where his throat had been hacked open. It covered the tiled floor like a dark, sticky lake and glistened in the light from the overhead strip. As they moved around, they tried not to get any on their feet.

'Somebody's got a big knife,' the older man said.

'Jagged Edge,' said his companion.

'What?'

'Jagged Edge. You know, the old film. About somebody getting their throat cut. Jeff Bridges and – what was the woman's name?'

The older man glared at him. 'Don't be such a fucking idiot,' he said.

They looked at the body again. The man was somewhere in his late sixties. He wore pyjama bottoms and a satin dressing gown. He was a big man, fit and well-built at one time, but the body was flabby now, the stomach sagging, the muscles soft. He had a healthy, well-cut head of silver hair. Lifeless blue eyes stared back at them, cold.

The sound of a woman sobbing came from another room.

'We'd better go and talk to her,' the older man said. 'Get

this over with.'

They left the kitchen and went into the sitting room beside it. It was comfortable and casual, for private relaxation. There was a small fireplace with the ashes still in it, a settee and a well-used armchair. Newspapers and magazines were strewn on the floor. On a small table sat a selection of drinks and from the level in the bottles the whisky seemed to be the most popular. In the corner there was a computer console with dial-up facilities, video and monitor, hogging too much space, like an old radiogram from the fifties.

A small figure in a raincoat sat in the chair. She had locked her body into as compact a shape as possible. Knees together, elbows to her sides and her handbag in her lap, she rocked backwards and forwards, staring at the floor as she sobbed. A handkerchief was a sodden ball in her hands.

The younger man crouched on the floor beside the chair, looking up at her. She was in her late fifties. The tears flowed down tributaries etched in the grey flatlands of her face.

'He always knew,' she sobbed. 'He always knew something like this would happen.'

'What do you mean?' the man beside her asked.

'Because he used to tell me. He used to remind me every now and then. If anything strange ever happened, if anything ever happened to him, I was to ring you.'

She looked up at the man standing beside the fireplace. Inspector Michael Mattheson of the Police Service of Northern Ireland was heavily built. His sandy hair was cropped convict-short but that did not succeed in disguising the flecks of white scattered through it. Black eyes without expression were carved into worn granite. Like his companion, he had kept his raincoat on and it was still wet from the night outside. In spite of her distress, she was trying to be observant. She thought of the man lying dead in the kitchen, how he had often told her to note everything if she saw strangers near the house. 'Always important to register the detail,' he had said, which was why she noticed that the two men had kept their gloves on.

They were the sort used for driving, thin, snug, black leather. She wondered why they were the only police officers to have arrived. She had expected noise and bustle, flashing lights.

Mattheson was studying a couple of photographs on the mantelpiece. One was of a handsome woman in early middle age trying to relax on a chaise longue in the sort of awkward pose favoured by studio photographers because they think it looks casual. Her hair was neat, precise, and would probably have been stiff to the touch, fresh from a salon somewhere. There was a hollowness about her eyes that the lighting could not dispel. Beside it was a photograph of a young man in the uniform of a second lieutenant. Cap fitting snugly. Dark brows over dark eyes. A forced smile.

'You did right,' Mattheson said. 'Any other calls? Did you manage to contact anyone else?'

He gestured to the photograph. 'Him, for instance.'

She shook her head, a bit puzzled. 'Well, no. I thought if I rang you, you would see to all that.'

'Of course. Quite right,' he said. 'I just wondered. Did you call your husband? Any of your family?'

Her eyes registered a painful memory. 'My husband was killed in an explosion years ago. We never had any children and—'

'Oh I'm sorry. That was thoughtless.'

'It's all right,' she said.

The younger man spoke and she noticed his voice for the first time, an Ulster accent with slight traces of the north of England in it, or was it the other way round? So many people had made their home here, soldiers usually, who had married local girls and joined the police after the Troubles.

Sergeant Derek Tweed was not as tall as his companion but he was solid and broad-shouldered under the spacious raincoat. He had a pale complexion, wispy, thinning fair hair, and an almost transparent blond moustache. The blue eyes were restless, taking everything in. He chewed on a piece of gum which had long since ceased to have any flavour.

'Mrs Benson,' he said. 'I know it's painful for you but would you mind taking us through it? It's important for the investigation. I'm sure you understand. We've got to get the detail absolutely right. You know how it is.' He stood up. 'Can I get you anything? A cup of tea perhaps?'

'No!' she snapped. 'I don't want anything out of there.' She looked towards the kitchen. There was silence for a few moments until they could sense her softening again. She stared at the swirling patterned carpet on the floor and then began to tell them her story.

'I've been coming here twice a week for five years. Got my own key. He never bothers me. He lets me do things my own way, lets me come and go as I please. I keep the place nice for him, all his ironing and laundry and housework. He liked things in order, didn't like routines to be broken.'

Somehow she managed to find a usable corner of the handkerchief and she blew her nose on it. 'I tried to ring him last night, then I tried again this morning, to tell him that my sister had a hospital appointment today. We live together, you see. She's a widow, like me. She was a bit worried about getting the results of a test she had a couple of weeks ago and she wanted me to go with her. So I rang and rang and got no reply, not even the answering thing. He'll be wondering why I haven't turned up, I thought. I tried all day, on and off, and then I began to get a bit worried, you know?'

She looked towards Mattheson who nodded that he understood.

'After we'd been to the hospital, my sister had to go out in the car. She's a district nurse. So after she'd gone I just thought I'd cycle out, see if everything was all right and leave him a note if he wasn't in. I only live a couple of miles away and I'm used to these roads but they can be dangerous at night. I don't like cycling out here in the dark but there was nothing else for it. I couldn't leave it for another day and him maybe thinking I'd become unreliable all of a sudden. When I got here, it didn't look like there was anybody in. No lights or anything. I shouted up the stairs. No reply. I came in here and then I went into the kitchen.'

She stopped talking and shuddered at the vision that came to her. She looked up at Mattheson. 'Who would do a thing like that?'

'That's what we're here to find out, Mrs Benson,' he said. 'But we don't want to distress you any more. It's been a dreadful experience for you.'

She seemed not to hear him. 'He wrote the number down once. A long time ago. I always kept it in my bag. If anything funny ever happens to me, he always said, you ring him. He said you'd take care of everything.'

She looked round the room and then back at the two men as if something was missing. 'Where's the rest of them?'

'Rest of them?' Mattheson asked.

'I thought there'd be a whole crowd of you. All milling about here. That's the way you always see it on the TV.'

'That's right,' Mattheson said. 'They'll be here any minute, the fingerprint people and so on. We're a sort of advance party.' He turned to Tweed. 'You'd better be off.'

She saw them exchange a look, just for a second, saw something being transferred between them. Tweed smiled thinly at her and left the room. He went to the front door and stood outside for a few moments. It was still raining, a thick, wet blanket that covered the County Down farmland and the maze of twisting country roads that crisscrossed their way through it. The house sat in a cluster of dripping trees at the end of a long stony laneway that dipped down from a bend in the road. It was not a house you noticed as you drove by. Helpful, he thought, as he walked towards his car past a bicycle, sturdy and functional, which leaned against a front windowsill.

Mrs Benson heard him drive off. 'Where's he going?' she asked.

Mattheson came over and perched beside her on the side of the chair, putting his arm around her shoulder. If it was

33

meant to be comforting, it did not succeed. She did not like the feel of it or anything else about this man.

'He's gone to get some things we need,' he said. 'He has to contact a few people. In the meantime, we'll just wait for the others.'

She raised her eyebrows. 'But what's wrong with the phone? Why couldn't he—'

He moved the arm behind her so that one gloved hand supported the back of her head and he placed the other one under her chin. It was all done in one swift, co-ordinated movement. He gave a quick, firm jerk up and back, which was all it needed.

Forty minutes later her body lay under a rug on the back seat of an unmarked police car, a large grey Ford saloon. They had managed to fit her bicycle into the boot but they had had to tie the lid down to secure it. Tweed drove. They had taken off their coats and jackets and they wore overalls and plastic shoe covers which he had brought back with him. It was raining more heavily and as the wipers arced across the windscreen they left greasy smears behind. It was just the sort of night when you might fail to see a cyclist pedalling along an unlit country road.

'Here will do,' Mattheson said and they pulled in.

They switched the lights off and got out. There were no cars, no headlights approaching, but they could see a drizzly glow from curtained farmhouse windows not far away. The road surface where they stood was gravelly and fragile and it crumbled at the edges where it fell away sharply through a gap in a hawthorn hedge.

Tweed untied the rope at the back of the car. 'We'd better be quick,' he said.

He hauled Mrs Benson's bicycle awkwardly from inside the boot, then threw it off the side of the road and into the field, where it fell with its front wheel turned upwards. He opened the back door and took the blanket off the body then, holding her under the shoulders, he dragged her to the edge of the road. Her heels scraped along the wet gravel while her head sank into her chest and her arms hung loosely. When he got to the verge, he turned and let go of her and she tumbled into the ditch beside the bicycle, banging the side of her head on a pedal as she fell.

They did not pause for an inspection but got back into the car quickly. As Tweed put it into gear, he felt a hand on his arm.

'Wait,' Mattheson said, getting out. He opened the back door, reached inside and lifted Mrs Benson's handbag from the floor. He found her diary and flicked through it until he came to his own name and telephone number. Then he closed the handbag and threw it to where Mrs Benson and the bicycle lay. He got back into the car and waggled the diary in front of the younger man's nose before slipping it into the glove compartment.

'That was close.'

Tweed turned to him, beaming. 'Close,' he said. 'Glenn Close.'

'What?'

'The woman in Jagged Edge. Glenn Close.'

'Just drive,' Mattheson said.

Minutes later they were back at the house. Tweed had brought buckets and cloths and brushes and for a full hour they mopped and scrubbed in the kitchen and sweated under the overalls. They went over every crack and crevice until they were as satisfied as they could be that no blood remained. The place smelled strongly of the disinfectant they used but that would fade.

They had wrapped the body in a thick plastic sheet and left it on the cold concrete floor of the garage while they worked in the house. Now they opened the boot of the police car again, lifted the body awkwardly – God he was heavy – and placed it inside.

Tweed reversed the dead man's car out of the garage and

they closed the door behind them. They gave the house a final check, switching the telephone voice mail on in the process, then they took the overalls off and stuffed them into a plastic bag which Tweed placed in the boot of the second vehicle.

They drove off up the laneway, Mattheson leading in the police car. It was a strange, secret funeral procession and it had a long way to go.

Chapter Three

There was a stillness just before it happened. Then, when it came, it echoed around the hills and fanned out across the water in sheets of sound until it seemed as if the earth itself had exploded. There was the smashing of glass and the crack of metal being torn apart as the caravan erupted in a fireball and the flames leapt into the dark Donegal night, scorching the trees that had provided shelter.

In scattered farmhouses, people leaped from their beds with their hearts pounding and looked across the estuary to where the flames roared and lit up the sky. They could see what it was, what had happened, could see the fierce firelight throwing shadows on the shape of the house that was not quite finished yet and some of them crossed themselves at their windows and prayed to God that he was not there tonight. But then they saw the car parked alongside, its paintwork melting in the heat, and they knew their prayers were wasted.

Hours later, midway through the quiet Sunday morning, Jack McCallan was almost home. In front, Lough Neagh stretched across the horizon like an enormous inland sea edged by a complex patchwork of fields. As they came rapidly closer, he could see the detail. Farmhouses and haysheds, cattle grazing, unimpressed by the technological marvel descending on them. Just before the wheels touched the ground, McCallan turned his head away, as he always did. He did not mind being up but he never liked coming down.

He sat still at the window while other passengers groped into the overhead lockers and tugged their belongings out. McCallan knew he was not going anywhere until the man beside him moved and that would take some time. He was a good twenty stone and he was having trouble prising himself from the snug confines of the British Midland shuttle seat. He wore a shiny grey silk suit and a black shirt with a silver tie and he and several other men seated across the aisle had chattered endlessly in Italian throughout the flight. McCallan had amused himself with the thought that this was some sort of cheap weekend break for organised criminals. What would you call it? Getaway Tours. How about that? Then he had noticed in the sports pages of his newspaper that Northern Ireland were playing Italy in Belfast in a couple of days' time. Ah, the gentlemen of the Press, come to savour the atmosphere on the terraces and, by the looks of things, in the Italian restaurants along Great Victoria Street where they would find Italian spoken, if they found it spoken at all, with a pronounced Ulster accent.

The fat man was on his feet now, sweat breaking on his fleshy face as he hauled out his overnight bag and the PC on which he would fine-tune the purple prose. A stewardess with a rigid smile tried to help him but eventually gave up because there was no room. It would be two-nil to Italy, McCallan guessed, although football was not really his forte. His father was the soccer fan in the family.

When the fat man had gone, he shoved his papers under his arm and joined the few remaining passengers still filing off the aircraft. He was arriving sooner than he had originally planned. He had spoken to the old man a week ago and told him he would be with him about Tuesday or Wednesday. But now, in the new circumstances, what he really wanted to do next week was be with Julia. Still, he could not cancel altogether and let his father down, nor could he bear the thought of sitting around in London, wondering what was happening, waiting for Julia to call. So he had brought the trip forward and he would go back home on Monday. He had his mobile phone and he had left its number on the voice mail of the telephone at the flat so that she could reach him.

He was looking forward to seeing his father and he hoped he was all right. It was time he told him about Julia anyway and he wondered what he would think of her when they met eventually. He had tried to call him yesterday to tell him about the change of plan but he had just got the voice mail. Still, that was not exactly surprising. He was certain to be up in Donegal where he went every weekend since he had started building a house there. He had bought a piece of land about a year ago, very private, a secluded spot reached by a long rutted and muddy road, and it overlooked an estuary, the perfect retreat for him to indulge himself in his favourite hobby, bird-watching. At least McCallan hoped it was his favourite hobby. In the last few months he had noticed a fondness for drink becoming a rival enthusiasm.

The house was at the roofing stage and his father was anxious to have it completed before the winter set in and made outside work impossible. He had a caravan at the site. McCallan could see him, a big man in Barbour and tweed hat, binoculars dangling from his neck, walking along the edge of the estuary or in the slopes of the nearby hills, and then warming himself with the turf fire and the whiskey in Mrs Cassidy's pub.

When there had been no reply at home, he had tried to reach him on the carphone but it did not appear to be switched on. He would have forgotten again, as he often did these days. It worried McCallan that his father had started to become absent-minded and he wondered if it was anything to do with the drinking. It was not a good age for something like this to develop and he wondered why now, when the stress and the life-or-death anxieties had long since been lifted.

Bob McCallan had retired at the age of fifty with all the years of service he needed to qualify for a full pension. The force he had grown up with was being reorganised and he had seen that it was a good time to go. For political reasons, it was no longer to be the Royal Ulster Constabulary. Instead, the Police Service of Northern Ireland was created. They wanted new faces, new ideas, new attitudes, a bright shiny police force acceptable to all, untainted by the old wars and the old guard of which Bob McCallan was conspicuously a part. So he had smiled the smile of a man who knew that that was the way of the world and closed the door of his office behind him.

He had a new life and new prospects to look forward to and he had his friend Henry Lomax to thank for that. Lomax and Bob McCallan had grown up together, living side by side in a shabby terrace in a damp grey town in Tyrone. They had both gained places at the local grammar school but at the age of sixteen Lomax had dropped out and got a job with a firm of builders, itching to feel a pay packet in his palm, while Bob, like many young Protestant men of his generation and upbringing and traditionally right-wing views, had joined the police with thoughts of steady promotion, an orderly life, respect and position. All of that had looked possible for a couple of years, but then came 1969 and the beginning of the nightmare.

By the age of thirty, he was a very different kind of policeman from the one he had imagined himself becoming: he was an inspector with a special anti-terrorist unit, running informers, cracking IRA cells. By his own thirtieth birthday, Henry Lomax owned the building firm for which he had once worked, had moved his centre of operations from windswept Tyrone to Belfast and had started buying property, good sites going cheap in areas which had become derelict and dangerous, banking on a theory that the violence could not last forever.

And that was how it had turned out, so that when McCallan retired and the dust began to settle on the old conflicts, Lomax was well into his stride, controlling his world from the top floor of a dazzling glass tower with a wall-to-wall view over Belfast Lough. Not just a builder now, he was in banking and transport, among other things, and he owned prime chunks of a city ripe for development, a city which had seen better days and was about to do so again.

Lomax had a nose for a winner. He could sniff out a profitable prospect where lesser adventurers sensed nothing. One of his acquisitions had been a moribund freight company which he had bought for the cost of its bad debts. He changed its name to LOC, put his old friend McCallan in as a technical adviser with a directorship, then set about transforming it and its fortunes. First it was heavily armoured security vans driven by ex-policemen and soldiers, who were thick on the ground and eager to find work. Then, with McCallan's guidance, they added the development of customised security systems for businesses and private homes, everything from burglar alarms to electrified fences and lasers.

But the big breakthrough came when Lomax brought in a young managing director with a background in computer technology who had developed a new software system which seemed to be immune to viruses, with the effect that when LOC was launched on the Stock Exchange, it became an immediate hit and achieved world notice. Now Henry Lomax was in the comfortable position of sitting back watching the giant American software predators encircling his little company. One of them was already nibbling, McCallan had learned from his father. If the price was right, and it looked like it was, Lomax would allow LOC to be swallowed whole.

Or maybe LOC, stock and barrel, McCallan joked to himself, as he stood at the luggage carousel and watched it creak into action. LOC. It was a good name for a company like that. It was snappy and sounded secure. What it really stood for, of course, was Lomax Company, a thin veil of disguise that did not do much to hide the massive ego behind it. He smiled as he thought of Henry, pacing the floor in a cloud of energy and cigar smoke, a team of trained accountants going over the figures for him one more time. He would have suckered the Americans with his charm, slapped the

Tyrone blarney on with a trowel so that they thought they were dealing with some Irish buffoon, and then before they knew it he would have screwed down a price that would have left them sitting in the snow in their underwear.

If the deal with the Americans worked out, McCallan realised, his father would be out of the company. Not that he had much to do with it now as it was. It was only through sentiment that he was still connected at all, popping in two half-days a week to an office with a phone that nobody ever rang. LOC did not need his father's kind of expertise any more. It was like having Orville Wright as technical adviser to NASA. But there was his share-holding, he thought as he watched his case make its entrance stage left through the big rubber cat flaps at the end of the carousel. Business matters were not something on which he was expert, but he presumed the Americans would buy his father out and feather the retirement nest a little softer.

He snatched the case up swiftly before it went round for a lap of honour. He had taken the trouble of phoning ahead from London to order a hire car because his father was not around to pick him up, as he usually did. While he waited at the Hertz desk, he thought he would try his father's number again. He took out his pocket phone and dialled but there was still nothing, just the familiar recorded voice. Then he tried his own phone to see if there were any messages.

There was one. It was from Julia.

'Hello, Jack,' she said. He felt a prickling in the skin at the back of his neck. There was a deadness in her voice. 'I know this will be a shock to you, especially after our last conversation, but there's no other way to say it. I've been talking to Daniel. We're going to get back together again.'

McCallan's face drained. The words hit him with all the force of an electrical charge.

'I think it will be different this time, worth another chance. Daniel needs me and I think it's for the best. I'm sorry it has to be like this but it's better to get it over with. I can't say I won't miss you – but, well, there it is. We're going away for a little while so please don't try to contact me. There's no point.' She paused. 'Goodbye, Jack.'

There was a click and she was gone.

McCallan stood there with the phone to his ear, unable to put it down, feeling waves of shock tingling through him and then a foul acid bile that bit the back of his throat. His brow felt clammy. He wanted to turn, cancel the hire car, his father, everything, get the next plane back, burst into her home. What was going on? None of this could be true.

He redialled the number and listened to it all again. How could she be saying these things? It had to be some sort of a joke, somebody playing a trick, impersonating her. He looked around to see if anyone was watching him, waiting for a reaction, but that was nonsense too. No one was paying the slightest bit of notice. And the voice was real enough, even though the words were alien.

But this could not be possible. He would have to ring her. What was she playing at? Did she think this was funny? He punched at the number and then waited as it rang. He was disorientated by what happened next so he tried again. But over and over he heard the same thing: a computerised female voice telling him that the number he had just dialled had not been recognised.

Inquiries. They would sort it out. A lot of bloody nonsense. He rang and was answered by a flesh and blood female voice who put him on hold for a frustratingly long time.

'Sorry, caller,' she said eventually. 'That number is unobtainable.'

'But why?' he asked. 'Has it been changed or something?'

'Sorry, caller,' the operator said. 'I'm afraid I can't be of any further assistance.'

Another voice was speaking to him but he did not hear it.

In yesterday's early hours, he had woken with a start from a dream in which he had been standing in the blinding heat of an African street that was all too familiar. He had tried to walk but as he did the hard-caked roadway had turned into soft sand into which his feet sank until he was losing balance and somehow tipping slowly and helplessly forward towards a surface that seemed to keep falling away from him. He had sat up with a shout, staring blindly into the blackness of his bedroom, soaked in sweat and gulping for breath.

Julia had taken his face in the softness of her hands and smoothed the wet hair from his brow.

'It's all right, darling. It's over, whatever it was,' she had whispered, although she knew because he had told her what happened in these dreams. Then she had lain back on the pillow, talking to him softly, watching the terror subside. He had bent over and kissed her lightly but her mouth had opened for more and she had stretched her hand under the bedcovers and between his legs. Later, when he had woken again, less abruptly this time, she had gone.

That was the Julia he knew. Soft and sensual, soothing him. Not this.

The voice was speaking to him again.

'Mr McCallan, your car's ready for you, sir.'

He looked round and saw a dark-haired girl smiling up at him with a set of keys dangling from her finger. He frowned and snatched them from her without a word, then headed for the bar, leaving her standing there wondering what she had done.

Fifteen minutes later, he was driving out of the airport complex in a dark saloon that smelled of polish and pine air freshener while he exhaled the fumes of a large Remy Martin which had at least helped to unclench his stomach muscles but had not done a lot to unscramble his thoughts. He saw nothing as he drove except Julia. Where was she now? Sitting in the conservatory with Daniel and the Sunday papers, the smell of fresh coffee in the air, poised and perfect, the pair of them, as if nothing had happened, as if he did not exist? Or maybe they were on a plane for the Bahamas, sipping champagne.

If all this was true, what could have caused the change of heart? It was preposterous; this was not the woman he had been sharing his soul with for the past four months. He began to feel angry and humiliated. He would have to talk to her somehow, confront her, and to do so he would have to get back to London as soon as possible. So what the hell was he driving to Donegal for? He thumped his fist on the steering wheel and thought about turning.

He became aware of a light flashing somewhere and it brought his concentration back. Pay attention. The light was in his rearview mirror and he saw it was the headlights of a police car. God, what have I done? he wondered. Whatever it was, the smell of the brandy would not help.

The police car passed him, then pulled onto the verge just ahead and signalled for him to do the same. He pulled up slowly behind it, his window open already to let some air in. Two uniformed officers were getting out. They looked grave and he decided to get out himself. There was less chance of them noticing the brandy that way.

'Good morning, gentlemen,' he said as they approached. 'Is there a problem?

'Are you Mr Jack McCallan?'

'Well, yes I am but—'

'Could you show us some identification, please, sir? Sorry to have to ask.'

McCallan's wallet was in his hip pocket. He reached for it and pulled out his driving licence. One of the policemen glanced at it quickly and then handed it back, satisfied.

'Now what's all this about?' McCallan said. 'How do you know who I am?'

'We've been trying to track you down this morning, sir. Your local police in London called at your flat. One of your neighbours, a man who lives across the hall, was able to tell them where you'd gone.'

McCallan nodded. He had told the neighbour his whereabouts, just in case there was anything urgent.

'Then we just missed you at the airport,' the policeman said, 'but here we are. It's, well, I'm afraid we've got some bad news about your father.'

Chapter Four

The laneway down to the site had been turned into a quagmire with all the traffic that had been up and down it in the past hours. Apart from several police cars and an ambulance, there had been two fire tenders, one of which was still there. The firemen were packing up their hoses, which they had had to run a very long way to a water point. They had arrived too late, when the damage had been done, but it was doubtful if it would have made much difference if they had got there any earlier. From the way those living nearby had described it and from the total destruction they saw before them, he would have been gone in those first few ferocious moments.

McCallan stood in the cold and the wet and the stillness of shock. He had had the sense to bring all the right clothing for the robust Donegal weather but it was still packed in his case so at the moment he wore loafers which were being ruined by the mud that engulfed them. His feet felt soggy. Beside him, the substantial shape of Inspector Frank Dolan of the Letterkenny police was wrapped in a heavy wool coat which reached to the top of a pair of green wellingtons. He shifted from foot to foot to keep warm. He had cheeks like pouches and the icy bite in the air lit up the road system of broken veins that spread from the bridge of his nose. He felt ill at ease with McCallan's silence and had the urge to talk in order to fill it.

'I'm afraid they wouldn't have been able to save your father,' he said, gesturing to the firemen. 'They got here as quickly as they could but it's a hard place to get at. Everyone did their best, all the local people and everything, but there was nothing anyone could do, nothing at all.'

McCallan stared at the bizarrely twisted shapes of blackened and smouldering metal, which was all that was left of the caravan, top of the range, two bedrooms, nice little shower unit, good-sized living area. The whole fire site had been marked off by white tape beyond which no one could go except those directly involved in examining the scene. Several men in grey overalls and covers over their shoes moved around carefully, turning over pieces of wreckage, placing objects in plastic bags.

'When the forensic boys have had a look,' Dolan went on, 'we'll know better but at first glance, I'd say it was the gas. Probably a leak in the pipe, you know, a bad connection or something like that and the fire left on. Such a cold night.'

He took his blue peaked cap off as if he thought it was irreverent to have it on at a time like this. He scratched the back of his neck nervously. The wind caught his thin grey hair. He smoothed it down with a gloved hand and decided to put the cap back on again.

He lowered his voice. 'I don't think, you know, I don't think it was anything else. Certainly no sign of anything like, well . . .' He looked around in case he was being overheard.

'Like what?' McCallan turned to him although he knew precisely what the man was driving at.

Dolan was uncomfortable and did not want to have to spell it out. 'Well, your father's background, you know. The RUC and all that. It's something that always flashes through your mind, even after all this time. But he was very popular around here. I'm sure you know that yourself. Nobody around here would have harmed him.'

'Maybe it wasn't anyone from around here,' McCallan said.

'No, honestly, if there'd been a whisper of anything like that, we'd have known. Sure, when he was thinking of buying the site here, he asked us what we thought. We did some research for him, shall we say, and we advised him to go ahead. There's no problem here now for people from the North.'

It had always amused McCallan to hear people in Donegal, that most northerly corner of the island, talk about people from the east as coming from the north. The Irish compass seemed to have only two points, the north and the south. And maybe the west, if you were a tourist. Three.

His father used to come out with some of these geographical oddities as well, like talking about going down to Derry or up to Dublin, which displayed an eccentric sense of direction if your home was southeast of the one and directly north of the other. It was an occasional source of banter between them and it usually ended with his father blustering in frustration that he was only a bloody Englishman, the inaccurate insult he always drew on as a last resort, and so how the hell would he know?

A new shock wave went through McCallan suddenly. Christ, his father was dead. Dead. How could he be dead? It wasn't possible. There had been no warning of it. He had always assumed there would be some signals. A short illness, some sense of slipping away. Yet he would not have wanted anything lingering and malignant. No pain or drugs or anything like that. That would not have been bearable or just. But this was hard to take in, this suddenness, this snap of the fingers. It was abrupt and permanent and irrevocable, as Julia's phone call had been a few hours before. He felt immobilised, paralysed by loss, watching the things that were precious being snatched from his grasp to a place beyond his reach.

Inspector Dolan was still talking but McCallan had not been listening. 'We've got judges and everybody with their holiday homes here now, the way they used to before the Troubles started. There's no threat here, none at all. Anyone who might have been a danger is either dead or long since

49

living in America as part of the great rehabilitation scheme they came up with. You remember that?'

McCallan did, vaguely. When the Troubles had ended, one of the ways of ensuring their continued cessation had been to let the Republican prisoners out. The United States Government had provided the most politically irredeemable of them with passports and green cards so that they could start anew, away from their old haunts and temptations and the potentially bothersome combination of mischief and idle hands. When you were trying to rebuild a country, you did not need platoons of bomb-makers and snipers sitting around with nothing to do.

So the Land of the Free had embraced them and forgiven them and washed them clean in an attempt to give their lives a sense of purpose. And for some, particularly those with the most highly developed guerrilla skills, that had worked out just fine, since they had been snapped up quietly by the US Special Forces where their talents had been put to goodness-knows what use.

The wind brought a salty tang from the estuary. McCallan shivered. The Inspector could see he was very cold.

'Can I see him?' McCallan asked.

Dolan chose not to give a direct answer. 'Listen, there's no point in standing here, Mr McCallan. Let's talk about this somewhere else. Why don't we go where it's a bit warmer? Give you a chance to sit down for a while, have a cup of tea or something.'

McCallan nodded. He had had a snack on the plane hours before and then the police had taken him to Antrim police station where they had given him tea and quietly watched him absorb the shock of it all before making sure he was ready for the long drive ahead. They had asked if there was anyone he wanted to bring with him but he had said no, that he wanted to go alone. And so he had, stopping now and then in a lay-by when the tears had been too much and he could not see the road in front of him.

Cassidy's bar was half a mile away. From the fire in the big hearth there was the heavy smell of peat cut fresh from the bogs. Two men with red faces sat at it, glasses of Guinness on a little table between them, watching Dolan and McCallan cautiously as they entered. It was the same wary glance that people in this pub had given for the past hundred years to strangers coming into their midst. McCallan saw the look and returned it. What if it was not an accident? Could any of the people in here have had anything to do with it?

He had not been to Cassidy's for a while. He took in his surroundings, the familiar yellowing beer mat collection on the wall behind the bar, postcards shrivelled with heat and age jammed into the edges of the big mirror. Two of them were from Sydney 2000, which was quite a few Olympics ago. There were dangling shillelaghs because that was what the tourists expected to see and he could have been stepping back into any time in the twentieth century if it had not been for the oddity of the virtual reality game that blinked awkwardly from the back of the room.

Patricia Cassidy walked out from behind the bar to greet them. She was sixty, dressed with an elegant dignity in grey cardigan and jumper and a line of pearls at her neck. She came from a long line of publicans of the old school and since her father's death thirty years before, she had run this bar with genteel authority and pastoral care, ministering to her customers' needs and keeping a firm eye on some of her more errant charges. In return, they treated her with the kind of respect they gave to only two other people, the priest and the doctor, whose roles she sometimes felt she filled rather better than they did.

She ushered McCallan and the Inspector through the bar, away from the eyes of curiosity, and into what she called the back kitchen. The room was very warm from the heat of an old black range on top of which a pot of stew was mellowing. The windows were closed and steamed up and the change in atmosphere seemed to make Dolan breathless. He puffed and

51

took off his coat and draped it over the back of a chair. As they sat down at the kitchen table, their chair legs scraped on the stone flag floor. Without a word, Mrs Cassidy produced a bottle of Jameson and two glasses. She poured liberally for the men and they sipped. McCallan felt the whiskey catch in his throat as it went down and it brought tears to his eyes but in a few moments he felt its warmth spread slowly through him.

'This is an awful thing, Jack, awful,' Patricia Cassidy said. Her voice had soft and cultured Dublin tones, the lasting imprint of a boarding-school education. 'I didn't know your father was here at all this weekend. He would usually pop in for a few drinks if he was about. Mind you, I was in Derry for most of the day yesterday so I could have missed him. But nobody else seems to have seen him either. When did he come up?'

'I don't know,' McCallan said. 'He was expecting me during the week but I got a chance to come over early. I couldn't get him on the phone at home or in the car so I just assumed he'd be here, the way he always is. I thought I'd drive up and surprise him. I got as far as the airport and the police were waiting for me with the news.'

'Oh dear, dear. You poor man. And your poor father. It's dreadful, dreadful.'

She walked across the kitchen and took two generous bowls from the dresser, then ladled mounds of steaming stew into them from the pot. She set them on the table with two spoons.

'Here, you'll need this. You'll not think of eating unless someone thinks of it for you.' She took salt and pepper shakers from a cupboard and put them on the table. 'Now I'll let you two talk away here. Give me a shout in the bar if you need anything. And Jack, don't think about going back home tonight. There's a bed ready upstairs for you. One less thing for you to worry about.'

She went to the door and then turned. 'I know what's going

through your mind. You're wondering whether this was an accident or not. Am I right?'

She did not wait for an answer, nor did she expect one. 'There's a couple of things I have to tell you about that,' she said. 'First, your father had become very much part of the scenery around here. People were very fond of him. They're all very sorry to hear what happened. I don't think there's anyone who would have harmed a hair of his head. A big popular man he was, the life and soul of the bar some evenings. Sure you know that yourself. You've been in here with him.'

McCallan had, twice during the summer, sharing pints and stories with the regulars and sitting outside in the evening air that was still warm from the day, watching the deep red descent of the sun. Those had been nights to savour and when Cassidy's closed, long liquid hours after it was supposed to, he and his father had walked back to the caravan in the dark, laughing and unsteady.

Patricia Cassidy went on. 'But the other thing is – I must say that of late I've been a bit worried about him. He'd been hitting it a bit hard. A couple of times I got one of the boys to see him home, make sure he got into the caravan all right. Not that he ever thanked me for it. Very independent, your father. Did things his own way. But I worried about him, you know, when he got like that. I worried about an accident. Still,' she sighed, 'God rest him.'

She went out and closed the door. McCallan stared at it for a few moments, his eyes boring into its wood, thinking about what she had said. Then he turned to the Inspector again.

'So can I see him?'

'I don't know that you'd want to,' Dolan said. 'It was a shocking fire, a very fierce blaze. We've taken the remains to the mortuary in Letterkenny.' He paused and took a deep breath, then decided to give it to McCallan straight. 'Frankly, there was not much of him left. The heat must have been devastating. You just, well, you just wouldn't recognise anything.'

He put his hand in his pocket and took out a small clear plastic bag. 'We found this.'

McCallan took the bag. Inside it there was a signet ring, tarnished and twisted by the extreme heat to which it had been subjected, but McCallan could still see the shape of the compass and the angle, the symbols of Freemasonry. He turned it round, looking for what was on the underside. There were initials which he could just about recognise.

R.J. McC.

And then a childhood memory came to him. He saw himself as a small boy, standing beside the armchair, trying to twist the ring round his father's thick finger. He heard the voice. 'When I'm gone, although I'm not going anywhere yet, mind, you'll be able to wear it, if your hand's big enough.' Then his father had twisted the ring off his own hand, hung it on the boy's spindly finger, and laughed as it slid off.

McCallan looked down now at the piece of metal in his palm and he began to weep.

Chapter Five

He put his bag down in the hall and took the milk in from the front step. Three pints. Saturday, Sunday, Monday. His father must have forgotten to cancel it before he left. It was another indication of things slipping the old man's mind, not that it mattered now. On the other hand, McCallan thought, maybe it did. Maybe there had been signs there all the time, signs he would have seen if he had been here more often, all pointing to the fact that his father was not the force he once had been. Then there was the drinking, his own worries given voice by Mrs Cassidy. What had happened in the caravan that night?

He stood for a moment in the silence. It was eerie being in this house, impossible to think that his father would never be in it again, although his presence filled it, practically seeping out of the wallpaper. He waited for him to emerge from the kitchen, or the living room, or to come down the stairs. It would all have been a mistake. There would be a big smile and an arm round the shoulders and an explanation. But there was nothing. Just the silence and a slight odour of disinfectant.

He felt shattered. It had been a long, tense drive back from Donegal. On several occasions, he had found himself sitting forward against the steering wheel with his hands clenching it and he had forced himself to calm down by breathing deeply. He was stiff, as if there were a steel rod up through his back and neck. He reached an arm behind him and massaged the tightness in his shoulders.

Yesterday had taken on a momentum of its own. While death was the end of one chain of events, it was always the start of another and this one had added ramifications because of the circumstances. After he and Inspector Dolan had finished their stew and the Inspector had refilled their glasses enthusiastically, other people had begun to arrive. First there was the local Catholic priest, then the Church of Ireland minister from the tiny parish a few miles away. They had gone into a double act of commiseration and offers of assistance. McCallan had accepted the former but felt powerless at this stage about the latter.

After them came more police officers and a couple of the forensic people. Mrs Cassidy had made a huge pot of tea and dished out more stew and more whiskey for those who wanted it, which most of them did. As he had listened to the voices around him, McCallan had felt he was taking part in a strange hybrid event that was both a police investigation and a wake.

He was interested most of all in what the forensic men had to say. Not that they would stick their necks out, and certainly not before they had completed their report, but the whiskey helped to lubricate their resistance. And so they had explained to McCallan confidentially, and most definitely not officially, you understand, that the gas did not look as if it had been connected properly. His father may have tried to get the fire going, without success, but the gas would just have built up in the confined caravan space. They had found the remains of an oil heater as well and if he had lit that, well then, end of story, really.

He took the milk into the kitchen and noticed that the smell of disinfectant was stronger there. Somebody had been cleaning. The place was spotless, sink empty, surfaces gleaming, immaculate as usual, thanks to Mrs Benson, presumably. He opened the door of the fridge and put the milk inside. It would have to be cancelled, right enough, and he thought of all the other minutiae of his father's life that he would have to deal with. Did he have an account at the supermarket? A Sunday paper on order? What about electricity bills, that sort of thing? It was all going to take some time. But he had plenty of that.

The two Donegal clerics, on the other hand, had been pressed for time and had not stayed too long. They had stood up and had shared an awkward benediction and the strange little group in Patricia Cassidy's kitchen had fallen silent, reflecting on how brief life was and how suddenly it could leave you.

McCallan had felt desolate, his grief immeasurable. And there was no Julia to turn to either; she was part of his loss. He had sat for ages with his head in his hands and then Patricia Cassidy had come in from the bar to say there was a call for him on the line out there and she would put it through.

He picked up the phone. 'Hello?'

The familiar voice was deep and warm and there was a catch in it but just hearing it gave him a kind of reassurance and made him feel less isolated.

'Oh Jack, my boy. At last. Oh Jack, I don't know what to say. I just don't know what to say. I just can't believe it.'

'No, Henry,' McCallan said, 'neither can I.'

For the next ten minutes or so, he and Henry Lomax had shared their grief, reflecting on the last time they had seen him or spoken to him and how he had been in good health and good form, as if that somehow meant that he could not be dead now. Lomax endorsed the view of Inspector Dolan. McCallan did not need to see the body or what remained of it. There were other methods of identification, dental records, that sort of thing. Surely it would be best if he remembered his father the way he was.

He told McCallan he was not to worry about a thing, that he was there to help. Transport arrangements, the funeral – anything he wanted, he had only to ask. For a start, he would get on to a good undertaker and make arrangements to get the body back, once the authorities were ready to release it.

McCallan felt bombarded by good will but he decided to take the advice and not go to the mortuary. He did not need any more shocks. And he did not need any more whiskey.

What he needed now, he thought as he stood in his father's kitchen and filled the kettle, was a cup of coffee. Instant would do. He fetched it from the cupboard and he used milk from one of the bottles he had just brought in.

When the coffee was ready, he took it into the little sitting room and sat down in his father's armchair. The place was too quiet. He needed company of some kind. He lifted the remote control and flicked the video screen on, surfing idly through the channels. Cartoons, an old western, business news, a soap, pop videos, home shopping, the news channel, basketball, another news channel. This was no remedy for his loneliness and he turned it off rather than go any further.

He sipped his coffee and stared at one of the pictures on the mantelpiece. His mother looked the way he liked to remember her but he tried to see if there were any signs of what was to come. The face was a bit weary, perhaps, and he wondered how much she had been drinking then.

Apart from the holidays, his trips home from boarding school had been few: half-term, the occasional weekend, but eventually they had stopped altogether. 'Your mother's not herself,' his father had said to him on the phone. 'A few little health problems. Perhaps it's better if you don't come home for a bit. It might upset you and her. I'll try to come and see you instead.'

And so his father had turned up, erratically. Some weekends he would appear as planned, while on others McCallan would sit by the window, waiting for the taxi at first and then, when it was obviously not going to arrive, for the phone call of apology and explanation. It was always work, something that had happened unexpectedly, some security crisis or other.

On the subsequent visits, his father would try hard to make up for lost opportunities. They would head down to London, to the cinema or the theatre or, as often as not, to White

Hart Lane if Spurs were playing at home, where his father would bellow loudly in his conspicuous Ulster accent while McCallan sat quietly beside him, scarlet with shame. He smiled as he thought of it now, how easy it was to be embarrassed at that age, and he experienced a twinge of guilt at having felt that way.

During that time, he still wrote to his mother but she did not write back and he asked his father why, what was the matter with her, but his father had tried to dodge the issue. She had an illness, he would say, but it was hard to explain. Eventually, the boy could be kept away no longer and in the Christmas holidays he had come home to find his mother sick and raddled, her weight reduced horrifyingly, her skin like dried yellow paper and her breath sour with vodka or whatever it was that she had been able to get her hands on.

She spent that Christmas in bed, a tray of food untouched, while he and his father picked at their meal downstairs, each alone with his thoughts, their conversation reduced to pleasantries and requests to pass the salt. Early in the New Year, she had been taken into hospital but her liver was gone and there was little they could do. She went into a coma and died two days later. McCallan had been back at school when the call from his father had come.

Happy childhood memories, he thought wryly. They were memories he had always kept to himself, that he had not cared to communicate to anyone. But then he had never been able to share his feelings completely with another person. It had always been so far and no further, as if there was a part of him that was hidden from view, roped off like the private quarters in a stately home.

It was why he had always found long-term relationships difficult. There had been affairs of varying duration but he had never liked it when someone came too close and he would always wriggle out of the way rather than face a commitment. But with Julia it had been different. He had poured himself out to her, finding answers to his own internal mysteries in the process, secure in the intimacy they shared and their mutual need.

Trust, that was the word for it. A trust that had swept away his defensiveness and had carried him into her embrace. And now – now he felt robbed, as if she had broken into his heart and rifled among his emotions, scattering them around in pieces for him to try to reassemble, before vanishing, leaving him nothing to hold on to.

He thought of their last night together, her mood. Had her unease perhaps not been a nervousness about facing Daniel at all, but rather the knowledge that this was it – the last time? Had the decision already been made? Yet she had been so reassuring. God damn it, it was impossible to know, impossible, as he sat there, to distinguish between what was true and what was a lie. The only certainty, the only thing that was beyond doubt, was her final call and the brutal clarity of its message.

He looked at the mantelpiece and saw the picture of himself. There were none of his father, of course, not a trace of the person who had lived here. It was a security habit, a hangover from the old days when it was always felt prudent not to leave any clue to the identity and occupation of the householder in case you were fingered by the window cleaner or the man fixing the washing machine. In those days, when people asked him what his father did for a living, he always said that he was a civil servant. It was a code that eventually became so common in Northern Ireland that it backfired and anyone who gave their profession as civil servant was automatically assumed to be a policeman.

He went back into the kitchen, rinsed his empty cup and left it on the drainer beside the sink. Must keep the place tidy after all Mrs Benson's cleaning.

He froze suddenly where he stood.

Mrs Benson.

God, he hadn't contacted her. How could he have forgotten to do that? There had been a report of his father's death on the local radio news late last night and again early this morning. If she had heard it she would have got a dreadful shock. Stupid, stupid, stupid. How could he have overlooked her?

He went to the telephone in the hall. On the table where it stood, there were two pink tickets and he saw that they were for a play at the Grand Opera House in Belfast later in the week. His father must have had plans for a night out for the two of them. But he would never go anywhere with his father again. The thought hit him hard. Everywhere he turned, with everything he did, there was another sharp reminder that this was permanent.

He picked up the phone but the light was flashing to show that there were calls on the voice mail so he switched it on.

What he heard chilled him.

'Thank you for calling,' his father said. 'You're connected to my voice mail and if you'd like to leave a message, I'll try and return your call as soon as I can.'

McCallan stood and stared. There were a couple of clicks but there was no sound. People had obviously called and had rung off when they heard the voice. But there was one message. The screen on the phone dated it as Saturday. A woman was speaking. Not young. Hesitant. Something wrong.

'Mr McCallan,' she said. 'This is Grace Walker. I don't know if you remember me. I'm Beth Benson's sister.'

Chapter Six

McCallan sat on the settee in Mrs Benson's living room, nursing a cup of tea which someone had already refilled twice. He was dressed in trousers and a sweater and he felt conspicuous and disrespectful, surrounded as he was by people in their best Sunday suits, dark and Presbyterian.

Just when he had thought there were no more surprises, Grace Walker's message had brought fresh grief with the news that her sister had been killed in an accident. He had called Grace and explained what had happened to his father but she already knew because she had heard it on the radio. She had told him to come over and so he had arrived at the door to discover the house full of people who had come back there after the funeral.

He had forgotten how quickly funerals were held in this country and he would have to get moving and organise his father's. Henry Lomax had volunteered to find a good undertaker but he would also have to find a grave. A plot in the big public cemetery outside Lisburn seemed the obvious thing, but how did you go about that? Maybe undertakers looked after that sort of thing as well. He just did not know. There was not even his mother's grave to share. She had always wanted her ashes scattered along the shores of Strangford Lough, a place she had loved to visit when times had been better, and that is what he and his father had done one bright spring morning, ending with a seafood lunch in the hotel at Portaferry. It seemed a lifetime ago.

Grace sat beside him. She had already reminded him that they had met before, quite a while back, but to be honest he had no memory of it. She was not like her sister. Mrs Benson had been diminutive and nervously energetic; Grace, who was a little younger, was taller and sturdier and McCallan could only think of her as handsome. She sat upright on the edge of the settee with a cup and saucer in her lap.

The sisters came from farming stock and the family was completed by two brothers. McCallan could see into the tiny kitchen where they stood, substantial men with hands of rawhide, the whiskey glasses in them looking like thimbles. On the living-room table there was the remains of a big plate of triangular sandwiches, egg and onion, ham and tomato mostly, some of which had collapsed in a moist, buttery heap. Family and friends sat around the room, sad and subdued, remembering the departed in hushed tones. The air of quiet reverence had increased since he had arrived. Every so often, someone would glance at him, then look away again shyly when he caught their gaze.

In spite of her own loss, Grace Walker seemed more anxious about his. How was he coping? Was there anything she could do? There was a selfless inner strength about her and a genuine concern for his welfare that McCallan found humbling. He felt inwardly shamefaced about his own tendency towards self-pity, caused as much by the loss of Julia as the death of his father. No, he was fine, he told her. People were being very kind. It was just, well, it was all so extraordinary. That they should both be struck by tragedy at the same time was a bit uncanny.

'What happened?' he asked her.

'You'd think with me being a nurse I'd have a bit more sense,' she said, 'but it doesn't always work out that way. I'd been having tests, you see, although I won't afflict you with the gory details of what for, but anyway I got word that I had to go back to hospital to see the specialist and get the results. You always seem to be summoned to these things just the day before, don't you? I was a bit alarmed in case it was bad news and if it was I didn't want to be on my own when I got it so I asked Beth if she would come with me.'

She drank some tea from her cup. 'But it was her day for going out to your father's and she didn't want to let him down. She tried to call him to let him know what was happening.'

'When was this?' McCallan asked.

'She rang on Thursday night and then again on Friday morning but she didn't get a reply. She was a bit anxious that she couldn't reach him. The phone was just ringing and there was no voice mail on so she couldn't leave a message. But he must have put it on since then because I was able to leave one.'

McCallan frowned slightly as he tried in his mind to work out his father's movements.

Grace went on. 'When we got back from the hospital – oh, and the tests were fine, I'm glad to say—'

'Good,' McCallan smiled.

'When we got back, I had to go out to visit a woman and her baby whom I should have seen earlier in the day. I'm a district nurse, you see.'

McCallan was aware of that and he nodded. Grace paused. The story was getting harder to tell now and he could see her eyes becoming moist.

'She must have decided to cycle out to your father's house after I left. It was a dirty night, thick old drizzly rain, and it's hard to see on these roads at the best of times.'

She began to sob. She put her cup and saucer down and snatched a couple of tissues from a box on a coffee table.

'It's my fault,' she said. 'If I hadn't asked her to come with me for this stupid appointment, none of this would have happened. And there was no need for her to come at all, none.'

McCallan patted her hand. 'You can't blame yourself.'

She blew her nose and looked at him.

'Oh damn, this is awful of me. You have your own sorrows. You don't want to sit here listening to mine.'

'It's fine,' he said. 'Don't worry about me. I just can't believe all this has happened.'

When she had come back from her visit, she told him, it had been late and she had found the police waiting for her. Her sister's body and her bicycle had been discovered in a field by the side of the road. It looked as if she had died instantly. There was an injury to her head, probably sustained by the fall, but no sign of foul play, no sign of having been hit by a car or anything like that.

Grace was calm again, composed. 'I had to identify the body, down at the hospital. She looked perfectly normal, just the cut on the forehead, but it wasn't like she was sleeping. She was so still. Something had gone from her, you know? Her whole . . . essence.' She used her hands as if she were moulding the word.

But it was just a simple accidental death, she said, which would undoubtedly be the verdict at the inquest. McCallan had not thought about inquests. There would be one on his father as well but he would have to worry about that some other time.

'It's all so . . . so final,' she said. 'No other word for it. I keep thinking there must be something I can do to change what happened. I keep thinking they've all got it wrong, that it must be somebody else. Do you understand?'

'Yes,' McCallan said. He understood perfectly.

'There was something a bit peculiar, though,' she said, remembering. 'The next morning, long after the first lot of police had been and gone, two other men arrived. It was after I'd been to the mortuary. The doctor had come round to see me and had given me something to help me, if you know what I mean, so I'm afraid I wasn't much use to them and they didn't stay very long.'

'Who were they?' McCallan asked.

'I can't remember their names. Oh, they were genuine policemen all right. They had identification and everything. A bit more senior than the blokes who had been before. At any rate, what I do remember, and why I'm telling you all this, is that they seemed rather more interested in your father than Beth. Had she ever mentioned seeing anyone odd around the house, that sort of thing. I thought it was an odd line of inquiry, to say the least. I asked them about your father, told them that Beth had been trying to get hold of him the night she died. They said that as far as they were aware he was probably in Donegal but someone would get a message to him.'

She nodded in the direction of her brothers in the kitchen. 'They had a word with the boys as well and eventually they went away.'

'And your sister, had she ever mentioned anything unusual?'

'Not to me. It seems a funny thing for them to be asking, doesn't it?'

McCallan had to admit that it was. Nevertheless he did not want to dwell on it now, not sitting here with this woman and her grief.

'I wouldn't worry about it too much,' he said. 'You know what it's like here. Retired policemen living on their own. I suppose you can't be too careful.'

'No, I suppose not,' she said, although her expression told him she was not convinced.

A woman came past offering the teapot again but he raised his hand in polite refusal.

'No, honestly. I've had quite enough, thanks.' He stood up. 'I really mustn't intrude any longer.'

'You're not intruding,' Grace said. 'My sister was very fond of your father and he was very kind to her. They didn't know it, but they were kind of companions for each other over the past few years. And now they have departed together. It's so strange.'

She walked him to the door. 'By the way, there are some things of your father's here.'

'Really?'

'Yes, there's a suit that Beth was taking to the dry cleaners and a couple of shirts, I think. Do you want to get them some other time?'

'Yes,' he said. 'Some other time would be best.'

At the open door, he turned to her. 'Grace, I'm so sorry,' he said.

'So am I.' She took his hand in both of hers and smiled at him. He felt comforted by the gesture and it seemed as if a bond had grown from their mutual loss.

He got into his car and drove off. When he reached the house, there was a small Volkswagen outside it and a man was trying to put something through the letterbox.

Chapter Seven

He thanked the Reverend Nigel Rogers for his sympathy, picked up his calling card from the floor inside the front door and ushered him into the big sitting room. Rogers went straight to a painting on the wall at the far end of the room. It was a soft and gentle watercolour by the Ulster painter Tom Carr, and there was another example of his work in the hall.

'Tom Carr,' McCallan said. 'My father was fond of him.'

'Yes, I know,' Rogers said, turning towards him. 'I remember the day he bought this particular one. He called me and asked me to come over and see it. Frankly, I thought it would have looked better where the room was a little more brightly lit but he liked it where it is and, as you know, he was a difficult man to argue with sometimes when he had his mind set on something.'

'Indeed,' McCallan said, feeling a pinprick of indignation. He did not know this man from Adam, yet his words and his whole manner suggested that he had had some role in his father's life. If that was the case, then he certainly had not been aware of it. The clergyman was about McCallan's own age, perhaps a little younger even, with a schoolboy air about him. He was lightly built and wore glasses with heavy black frames that were too big for his face. Limp fair hair fell untidily towards one eye.

McCallan gestured to his visitor to sit down. He told him where he had been for the past hour and about Mrs Benson's accident. Rogers nodded; he had heard what had happened.

'Absolutely bizarre,' he said. 'But not one of my flock, I'm afraid. She was part of the Presbyterian congregation in Dromore, I understand.'

'Look,' McCallan said, 'You've got me at something of a disadvantage. I take it you're the local Church of Ireland man and it's obvious you seem to have known my father but to be frank, I've not heard him speak of you.'

'Ah,' said Rogers. 'I see. I'm sorry, I had assumed you knew who I was, which was wrong of me. Yes, you're quite right. I'm the local rector. My church is the little one up on the hill behind the trees, just out the road a bit.' He raised his arm towards the window. 'Do you know it?'

McCallan did and he nodded.

Rogers went on. 'It's normal, you'll understand, for me to visit the home of one of my parishioners who's passed away, always a sad occasion, but I have to say I feel this one particularly badly myself. I was tremendously fond of your father and we'd got to know each other quite well. He never mentioned me?' He seemed surprised and even a little hurt at the omission.

McCallan shook his head. 'No, he didn't.'

Rogers shrugged it off. 'Well, maybe that's not all that strange, in a way. I guess faith wasn't something he'd have talked to many people about. His was a quiet belief, a very personal one, and I think I was perhaps rather privileged to share it with him.'

McCallan was puzzled. 'Are we talking about the same Bob McCallan? I never thought of my father as being religious in any way. I know he was involved in the Masonic Order, if you could call that religious, but that was about the height of it.'

Apart from his mother's funeral, which had been a rather secular affair at the crematorium, he could not associate his father with the inside of a church at all, except for those occasions in the past when he had had to attend as part of a grim duty. Those had been the days of coffins draped with the Union Jack, a cap and gloves resting on top, the Royal

Ulster Constabulary Band playing the Dead March, the most familiar piece in its repertoire. Days like that, his father had always said, would put you off religion altogether. When you saw the grief of those widows and children, you wondered if there was a God at all and if there was, how he could let things like this happen.

Rogers laughed. 'Oh yes, we're talking about the same man all right. I've known your father for the best part of eighteen months, I suppose. I'd noticed him in the church a few times, always on his own, but I didn't know who he was. Then we got talking one Sunday after the service. He would come round to the rectory a lot after that. We had great conversations, great discussions about religion, very stimulating. The odd drink or two to keep us going. We talked about everything – mortality, the afterlife, whether there was one. We talked about repentance, atonement, what it means to forgive. We talked about you a lot, too.'

'Me?'

'Yes. I don't have to tell you how grateful to God he was that you were alive after what happened in Nigeria. You're a very lucky man and your father felt he was, too, because of it. But he often seemed to wonder what he had done to deserve such good fortune.'

McCallan stood up. Why did everyone think he was so bloody lucky? He certainly did not feel it. He looked at Rogers, unsettled. There were images of his father here that he did not recognise at all, not one bit.

'Listen, I'm going to have a drink. Would you like one?'

'That's kind,' Rogers said. 'What are you having?'

'Scotch.'

'Then that'll be fine for me, too.'

McCallan went to the sideboard and took out a bottle of malt.

'Ah,' Rogers said when he spotted the label. 'The house wine.'

'Sorry?'

'The house wine. The Macallan. That's what your father used to call it.'

'Did he?' It was a new one on him. Another one. He poured a splash into two crystal glasses and handed one to his guest. He sipped his own and thought that he did not know whether he liked this little man or not. He certainly did not like the fact that Rogers was so at ease in this house, so apparently intimate with his father, and he felt excluded and a little annoyed with the old man for having a friendship he knew nothing about.

'Yes, my father liked a drink, more so of late, maybe?' he asked, testing.

'Who doesn't?' Rogers said with a smile and for a moment McCallan thought he saw something in the man's eyes to confirm that there was more on the subject. If there was, Rogers chose not to add it.

'I would just love to know what condition he was in when it happened,' McCallan said, trying another approach.

'At least,' Rogers said, 'it would have been sudden and he wouldn't have known anything about it. Let's be thankful for that.'

'Frankly, if you don't mind me saying so, I'm not particularly thankful for anything at the moment. My father's dead and he shouldn't be and I don't find anything gratifying in that.'

He was irritated by the soothing tone and he did not care if Rogers knew it but the cleric did not shrink from the outburst.

'That's understandable,' he said. 'It's only natural you should be angry. It would be odd if you weren't. You've had someone you love taken away from you and it doesn't seem fair. It will take a long time to come to terms with it.' He drank from his glass. 'It's a very stressful time, death, funerals, but at least the fact that your father had the foresight to make all his own arrangements will take some of the strain out of the next few days.'

McCallan frowned. 'What do you mean?'

'He had his funeral planned, every detail. You didn't know?'

Feeling wrong-footed, especially because of his anger, McCallan shook his head and then listened to it all. There was a plot, already chosen, in the graveyard beside Rogers's church. It was right under a yew tree because Bob had liked the idea of the birds always being on the branches above him. He had even given Rogers instructions about the service, what hymns should be played, what pieces of scripture to be read. The undertakers had already been sorted out: McMullan's in Lisburn. The coffin was picked and paid for and there were to be no flowers, just donations to the Belfast hospice.

It was detailed and precise, leaving nothing to chance, and it was typical of the organised mind McCallan had known.

'I knew nothing of this,' he said. 'Why didn't he tell me?'

It struck him that Lomax could not be aware of any of it either and that he had better get hold of him in case there was a double booking.

'I'm sure he'd have got round to it.' Rogers said. 'That's all part of the tragedy, isn't it? He discussed it all with me just a few months ago and I rather expect that when he made the arrangements he didn't think he'd need them so soon.'

He put his glass down and looked at his watch. 'I'm afraid I'll have to go,' he said and stood up, 'but you have the card and you can call me at any time. Your father certainly used to. You'll need to get the arrangements into the paper, that sort of thing. I've already had a look at the diary so let's make the burial the day after tomorrow at noon, if that suits. Just talk to McMullan's. They'll handle everything. They're probably waiting for you to ring.'

He paused in the hall on his way to the door. 'One thing I have to say before I go. You're obviously very upset but please don't feel resentful of my friendship with your father. It didn't replace your relationship with him. It's just that sometimes we need people to talk to outside the immediate family circle and I think that's the way it was with him. He had a long and eventful life to reflect on. A lot of tragedy in the past, a lot of death. I was available. I didn't see all that much of him in church in the past few months, not since he started building the house in Donegal, but when he was there I always felt as if I was talking directly to him. Most people turn up on a Sunday because they like to be seen. They sit through the services and go home again and half an hour later they'd be hard pushed to tell you what the hymns were or what the sermon was about. But with him I always knew I would have one alert listener at least.'

He shook McCallan's hand. 'I just wish he could be listening the day after tomorrow.'

When he had gone, McCallan sat down with another whisky and thought about the images which had been presented to him. He could not see his father sitting dutifully in church, a regular member of the congregation. He could not see him engaged in intellectual debate with this man Rogers either but he had no reason to doubt that any of it was true. Rogers had left behind a very different picture of his father, a portrait he hardly recognised, and he wondered if there were any patches on the canvas which had yet to be filled in.

Chapter Eight

Henry Lomax gestured towards his guest's glass with the open palm of his hand and the butler came forward, bearing a wine bottle wrapped in white linen.

'Well, that's the damnedest thing,' Lomax said, 'your father turning into some sort of holy Joe.'

McCallan opened his mouth to correct him but decided not to bother. Earlier, while he had given him a run-down on his conversation with Rogers, Lomax had had a couple of large gins. Since then they had both savoured the meursault with the fish and the burgundy with the venison and now his host's imagination had gone into free fall. McCallan put his hand over the rim of his glass. He had had more than enough.

But Lomax was insistent. 'For Christ's sake, Jack, take it. You're not going to stay sober tonight. You and I are going to get as full as goats and then we'll go out into the night and howl at the moon if we want to. None of this bottling it up. There'll be no one to hear us and I wouldn't give a fuck if they did. So drink up.'

McCallan took his hand away and the butler poured what was left of the wine.

'Good man, Arthur,' Lomax said. 'Now you can bring us, eh – the armagnac, I think, and then you just take yourself off. We'll be all right here.'

'Certainly, Mr Lomax,' Arthur said. 'That's very kind.'

'On the other hand, you can stay here and get stuck in with us, if you want. Make a night of it?'

75

'No, thank you, sir, if you don't mind. Kind of you, all the same.'

Arthur was the genuine article. For more than twenty years he had seen service in Dublin and London with a branch of old Irish aristocracy before Lomax had lured him away with the offer of a ridiculously generous salary. But that sort of thing was not done, pinching someone's butler, and it was social suicide in the circles which Lomax wanted to break into but never really would.

After Rogers had departed this afternoon, McCallan had called Lomax to sort out the problem of the undertaker. While they talked, Lomax had invited him to come and have dinner with him at his home and to stay the night if he did not feel like spending it alone in his father's house. McCallan had been delighted to accept. He needed company.

'My dear boy,' Lomax had said. 'We can't have you rattling around there on your own. Not tonight. You must come down here. You know where we are.'

And so McCallan had got into his car and headed to Newcastle, which was about an hour's drive away. Lomax's home was a huge but austere-looking Victorian mansion set in several acres of ground off the coast road. It had been built by a linen baron out of granite cut from the Mourne mountains which loomed protectively behind it through a net curtain of drizzle. At the front were softly sloping gardens and the grey expanse of the Irish Sea with the Isle of Man a dim outline on the horizon when the weather was better.

McCallan and Lomax were in the private dining room sitting at opposite ends of an oval table which had been made in France in the early nineteenth century. There was another dining room, for more formal occasions, with a huge table which held twenty people down each side, but this was much more intimate although it was still big enough to serve as a sitting room as well. A log fire hissed in the hearth and two comfortable armchairs and a small settee were grouped around it. The room was lit softly, with pink candles on the table and hooded brass lights over the paintings on the walls.

Lomax lived alone. That is to say he was not married or otherwise accompanied, but his was a far from solitary existence. His use of the pronoun 'we' may have been a reference to his household which included the butler, the two maids in black uniforms, white aprons and white gloves who had served them dinner, and the cook, unseen, who had made it.

When McCallan had arrived, he and Lomax had embraced for ages at the door, crying without restraint into each other's shoulders. Theirs was a shared, deep-seated grief born of a lifetime's love for the father and the friend they had lost. But gradually their mutual attempts at consolation, helped along by generous amounts of drink, had eased into affectionate reflection and reminiscence. McCallan had then brought Lomax up to date, telling him about Mrs Benson's death and his visit to see Grace Walker and finally he came to the clergyman's story of his father's late-developing faith.

'Damnedest thing,' Lomax said again. 'I'm as surprised as you are. He never shared any of this with me either. It would make you wonder if you ever really know people, you know what I mean?'

It was a question which did not require an answer and instead of attempting to give one, McCallan sampled the brandy. The butler had given them glasses which were like goldfish bowls with stems and the level in them was way above the plimsoll line of sobriety.

He looked at his host. Lomax was not tall but he was solid and square-shouldered. He wore a black velvet jacket and an open-necked silk shirt covered his barrel chest and his bald head glistened in the warmth and the light. He was a powerhouse of a man, rarely sitting still, exuding an energy that was barely restrained. His was a huge personality, confident in any company, shifting effortlessly from the profane banter of a Tyrone building site to the antiquated manners of a Victorian drawing room, sometimes all in the one sentence. His charm could suffocate and his rages were chilling.

For all his wealth and success, one thing had always eluded Henry Lomax and it was doubtful if it would ever come his way now. In spite of all his efforts to be part of the establishment or, indeed, some said cynically, because of them, he had never achieved his dream of a 'K', of becoming Sir Henry Lomax. He brooded on it sometimes but then he looked around him and saw how much of Northern Ireland he owned and controlled in one way or another and said to himself 'Fuck them all.'

When the butler had gone, Lomax got up abruptly and crossed to the sideboard where he took two plump Havanas from a box. He tossed one to McCallan.

'I'm told I shouldn't be doing this,' he said. 'I should change my lifestyle, the doctors tell me. But I'll probably outlive them all anyway, so here goes. To hell with it.' He clipped the end of McCallan's cigar and lit it first, then his own. Twin blooms of smoke blossomed in the warmth of the room.

McCallan remembered the first time he had been to this house, the summer he had left school, when Lomax had moved in. There had been a charity fair in the grounds. He recalled the striped marquees on the lawn, the champagne and strawberries. There had been gorgeous girls in straw hats, the sound of a dixieland clarinet drifting in the warm summer breeze that came from the shore. It had been a wondrously impressive place at first sight and it was a house that made no less an impact on him now on an October evening grown chilly as they moved towards the fire and the two soft winged armchairs on either side of it.

McCallan felt uncomfortably uncouth. He thought of Julia and his evenings with her in expensive London restaurants. If she had deceived him, then he had also deceived himself, pretending to be someone he was not. So much for the urban sophisticate. Here he was, tucked away in a mansion in an obscure corner of the Irish coast in the company of a man who had left school at sixteen to go to work on a building site and yet it was he who felt like the hick from the sticks.

A painting on the wall behind Lomax's chair caught his eye and he got up to look at it. It showed two figures gazing thoughtfully from a window, a pretty girl with rosy cheeks and a white lace bonnet and an ugly man wearing a loose shirt and smoking a clay pipe.

Lomax answered the unspoken question without turning round. 'Dutch,' he said. 'Don't know the painter but it's somewhere around the mid-seventeenth century. Picked it up in Antwerp a few years ago. Not bad, is it?'

McCallan wondered what sort of price Brian from the gallery would put on it but it was probably a bit out of his normal league. Julia would like this room, he thought in an association of ideas, but it was not at all the affectionate reflection it should have been: there was a bitter tinge to it now.

'Actually, the best of them aren't here,' Lomax said. 'The Ulster Museum asked me for a loan of them so they have a stack on show at the moment. You should go and see them when all this is over.'

He paused. 'The Henry Lomax Collection,' he said in his best radio announcer's voice, startling McCallan with the change of accent. Then he cackled. 'Christ, who'd have thought it, eh?'

McCallan sat again, slumping wearily into the chair. 'I just can't get the hang of it, Henry. I just can't believe that he's dead.'

'Ah, well, he is, son,' Lomax grunted as he leaned forward, 'and we'd just better get used to it.' He took a log from a big wicker basket beside the hearth and threw it into the grate. A shower of sparks flew from the embers.

'I can't get the picture out of my mind, that maybe he was pissed and that none of this would have happened if he'd been sober. Had you noticed him hitting the bottle much? More than usual?'

Lomax thought. 'He always did like a drink. Nothing unusual in that.' He raised his glass. 'But, well, yes, he was hitting it a bit, to be honest. A couple of times when I called at his house, usually on my way back from Dublin, he was the worse for wear, I have to say. I got the feeling that's what he did most evenings, sat there on his own with a bottle of whisky, although he would never admit to it, always claimed he was busy in the evenings, social engagements. But I suspect it wasn't true. I think he'd got a bit lonely lately, you know.'

McCallan felt guilt stabbing at him. He thought of his phone calls to his father over the past weeks and months, the suspicion of a slight slur in the voice at the other end. Why had he not spent more time with him? But the knew the answer: it was because his mind and his body had been with someone else.

'Christ, I should have taken better care of him,' he muttered and held his head in his hands.

Lomax put his glass down and went over to him, putting his arm round his shoulders.

'Now here,' he said. 'We don't need any of that. You have nothing to blame yourself for. There's no way you could have watched over him. If anyone's at fault, it's me. I'm the one who spotted the signs.'

'No, we both did. I just didn't think it had got that serious. If I'd been with him more, maybe I'd have known different. I think the Reverend Rogers knew the score, too.'

'Oh, what did he say?'

'Nothing, really. But when I mentioned that I thought he'd been drinking too much, he didn't argue with me.'

He stared into the fire and the flames that were now licking round the new log. 'You know, at first I thought somebody might have killed him, that it had been a bomb.'

'So did I. It was the first thing that came into my head. And what do you think now?'

McCallan shook his head. He felt drunk and not entirely coherent.

'I don't know. I don't think so. No one else does, anyway, but I can't quite lose the doubt, you know? There's no evidence to suggest it was anything other than an accident. Funny, in a way I wish it had been a bomb. At least then I'd have someone else to blame.'

'Jesus, Jack, that's a terrible thing to say.'

'I know, I'm sorry. I'm tired and I'm pissed.'

Lomax got up and walked over to the sideboard. From a drawer, he took an old, worn photograph album. Several of the pages were hanging hazardously from the binding. He handed it to McCallan.

'Did you ever see this?'

McCallan had, many times, but he did not mind seeing it again.

He leafed through it carefully, pausing at a couple of the pictures in particular. There was a black and white snapshot, faded almost to brown, of two tiny boys with curly hair and grumpy chubby faces. They wore woolly cardigans and shorts that reached almost to their pudgy knees. A set of iron garden railings separated them as they frowned up to the camera. McCallan could just about see in them the men they would become.

Another picture showed the same two faces, a little bit older, grinning, one above the other, out of the opening of a tiny tent. Lomax wore a headband with a feather sticking out of it. In a third picture, there were the same two boys on the threshold of becoming young men, long trousers now, striped school blazers, hair slicked back at the sides and dangling across the forehead in oily curls.

McCallan tried to think of the old actor. From the fifties. Tony Curtis, that was it.

'Love the hair, Henry.'

'Christ, I wouldn't mind having some of it now.'

He took the album from him and looked through it himself, quietly. 'Me and your father,' he said, his voice catching. 'Better than brothers.'

He took a handkerchief from his pocket and blew his nose loudly. 'You should give yourself a good holiday when all this is over,' he said. 'I know I'm going to although I'll have to wait until I settle this LOC deal.'

'So it's happening, then? The takeover?'

'Of course it's happening. Next week, all being well. I've been licking the arses of a couple of the big American software boys for the past six months and one of them has finally come up with the goods. A great price, which I'm not going to divulge to you so you can go and fuck yourself. You'll hear all about it soon enough. No, they'll get the software stuff which is all they're really interested in and then we'll all get out with a bundle and they can do whatever they like with it after that.'

'I thought you liked that little company. You built it up yourself. Won't you miss it?'

'God, it's well seen you're not a businessman. Too bloody sentimental. No, I won't miss it. Of course not. It's served its purpose. Anyway, I'm not getting any younger. I'm heading towards seventy and what do I want all these business interests for? It's time for me to sit on a beach somewhere and watch the sun sink slowly below the horizon.'

McCallan gave a dismissive snort. 'Don't give me that, Henry. You'll never retire. Not while there's money to be made.'

'Don't you believe it, son. One of these days I might surprise you.'

McCallan yawned. His eyelids were heavy. The combination of the brandy and the fire and the emotional strain of everything that had happened was like a lead weight.

Lomax could see he was exhausted. 'Right. Time we were in bed,' he said.

He lurched out of his chair and grabbed McCallan by the hand, hauling him to his feet. They stood there a little unsteadily.

'I'll show you where you're sleeping,' Lomax said.

He led the way into the magnificent hall with its marble tiles, deep green walls and huge paintings that looked to McCallan's instinctive eye like Italian renaissance. There was deep green carpet on the staircase which led broad and straight to the upper rooms. Lomax had preserved the front section of the house with great taste and care for the period but at the back, away from passing glances, the twenty-first century had been allowed to encroach. There was a well-equipped office for Lomax himself and next to it a leisure area, complete with gymnasium, pool and sauna. It would be there, McCallan vowed as they made careful progress up the staircase, that he would steam away his hangover in the morning.

Lomax opened the door of a front-facing bedroom which was about the same size as McCallan's entire flat in London. The bed had a canopy and the covers were turned back invitingly.

'This is an awfully big house for one person, Henry,' McCallan said. 'Why did you never get married, have a family to fill it?'

He might not have asked the question had he been sober and he glimpsed a cloud flitting slowly across Lomax's face before he laughed.

'You know, they used to spread rumours about me, that I was queer. Living here all by myself, I had to be. That was the conclusion they all jumped to. But they were wrong.'

He sat on the bed which gave graciously under his weight. 'It's just – well, marriage was never on the agenda for me. I was always too busy to think about it.'

He looked up at McCallan. 'I always envied your father, you know, having you and your dear mother, God rest her.'

He reached out and squeezed McCallan's hand. 'I cried when your mother died, do you know that? She was a wonderful woman, wonderful woman. Unfortunately for me, I never managed to find the right one. Never had the time to look. Too fucking busy or vice versa.'

He gave an abrupt bellow of laughter.

'Aye, that was it. That was what your woman said. Too fucking busy or vice versa.'

'Dorothy Parker.'

'What's that?'

'Dorothy Parker. She said that.'

'Well, whoever. I've had them all, you know. Women. I have even fucked a member of the Royal Family in this very house. A very minor member she was but royalty nevertheless.'

His eyes sparkled suddenly. 'Although I have to say that at the time she didn't complain that my member was minor.'

There was a brief moment of silence and then they both burst out laughing with smutty juvenile glee, hugging each other drunkenly as McCallan collapsed beside Lomax on the bed. After a minute or so, they stopped, exhausted and out of breath.

'Jesus, that's a good one,' Lomax gasped, getting up and making his way to the door. 'I'd better go to bed. I'm wrecked.'

'Me, too. But listen, seriously, Henry,' McCallan said, the timbre of his voice falling as he tried to sound sober, 'seriously, I'm really grateful to you for having me over. I really am. I couldn't have got through tonight on my own. I just wish the circumstances were different.'

'I know. So do I. But there's not a lot we can do about that now. You've got the future to think of. And you'll have to start thinking about what you're going to do with your father's money. That's if he's left any of it to you.'

He smiled and winked and closed the door behind him.

McCallan sat on the edge of the bed as the significance of what Lomax had just said registered with him. He had been enveloped in the fact of his father's death and of Julia's sudden exit and he had not been thinking ahead at all, not beyond the funeral at any rate. It was all just beginning, he realised, and his life would never be the same again. There was his father's will to be dealt with, the whole question of his estate. And there would be the LOC deal to add to it, the sale of his father's holdings in that company.

Gradually it dawned on him that he was about to become seriously rich.

Chapter Nine

Gavin Pierce was coming to the end of his morning run. There was a misty drizzle which obscured his usual enjoyment of the Avon countryside but he did not mind too much because it was cool and refreshing on his face and all very different from the hot, lush private estate in Costa Rica where he had been taking his exercise over the past week. He turned left up the muddy laneway that led to the farm and as he reached the house, a Jack Russell terrier hurtled from somewhere round the back, barking irritably, then stopped and ran forward, its tail spinning with delight when it saw who it was.

Pierce came to a halt. He had covered five miles or so with a steady, even pace and he felt scarcely out of breath. Perhaps it took just a little longer for his heart rate to return to absolute normal but then he was fifty-five, not twenty-five, so what did you expect. He stretched forward with his legs apart, feeling the pull on his calf muscles, and the dog leapt up to lick his face. He ran almost every day, had done so for the best part of thirty years, and he hated those mornings when, for whatever reason, he could not. But today was not one of them. He patted the dog and went inside.

He was warm under his tracksuit and the heat of the house brought a flush to his face and made him sweat. He grabbed a towel from the cloakroom and wiped his face. He looked at himself in the mirror, saw the thin, hard features and the grey hair that was kept short and neat. He put a hand to the skin on his neck. Was he getting a bit scrawny? Maybe he could afford to put on a pound or two. But he had always been obsessed with weight and fitness and was unlikely to let himself go now.

He went into the kitchen. The house was several hundred years old but the kitchen was not. It had been recreated in a traditional style in an attempt to preserve an illusion of old-world charm and it looked like a page from a manufacturer's brochure, just too perfect. The pine cupboards that lined the walls were too new, as were the big table and chairs. Gleaming copper saucepans hung from a beam above the work surface. Everything was in its place, neat and orderly, the way Pierce liked his life to be.

He filled the kettle and put it on, then he flicked the remote control for the TV, leafing through the channels until he found business news. He took a china cup and saucer from a cupboard and put them on a tray, along with a small jug of milk and a silver sugar bowl. His wife would still be asleep and he would bring her tea in bed, as he always did, then he would shower and dress and drive to his office in Bristol.

He had always been a fastidious man and had entered the world of business rather later in life than most people but he had approached it with his customary care and had given things time to grow. As a result, he had this house, there was a white Mercedes parked in the garage next to his wife's BMW and money was never a problem, nor was it likely to be if things stayed the way they were.

Pierce's operation would never rate highly on the top ten list of glamorous business activities but that suited him fine because he preferred to be as low key as possible. He was an importer of coffee, which he sold and distributed under a number of brand names and labels throughout the UK. It was a business which kept him in robust financial health and provided him with a discreet camouflage that covered other activities in which he was a major, although not exclusive, player, the produce of which he distributed in transparent plastic bags which had no brand label at all.

Pierce was in the drugs trade. That, rather than the coffee, which was the front, should anyone inquire, was what had taken him to Costa Rica, from where he had returned only last night.

He took two Earl Grey tea bags from a box and plopped them into the white china pot that went with the cups and as he waited for the kettle to boil he looked out across the fields. The land looked grey and sullen in the rain and just this once it reminded him disconcertingly of the countryside he had known as a child in County Fermanagh. He had hated that place, had never appreciated the beauty that everyone said it possessed, and had been determined to take the fastest route out which, in his case, had been the Army.

It had provoked a family crisis but he had not cared. He had simply enlisted and that was that. If he had wanted to go into the Army, his father had said, why had he not thought of Sandhurst, of becoming an officer? Would that not be so much better? But he had not been interested in that, had no wish to mingle with the upper classes whom he considered to be his intellectual inferiors.

In the ranks, with the other squaddies, he had learned a lot about himself and his capabilities. Progress had been unavoidable, first to lance-corporal, then to corporal and eventually to sergeant. He had developed skills and a willingness to apply them that had led to a particular kind of soldiering and had brought him eventually into the SAS. He was a technician, good with his hands. They never trembled when he assembled or dismantled the delicate, intricate machinery of a bomb and he could use them to kill silently, which he did effortlessly and dispassionately on those occasions in troubled parts of the world when it was demanded of him.

But Pierce was not a team player: his own survival was more important than that of anyone else. When that characteristic was spotted by his superiors, his spell with the SAS was cut short and he was dispatched back to his parent regiment, finding himself patrolling the streets of Belfast, walking backwards and looking up at the buildings, waiting for the sniper shot that never came when you were expecting it.

This was not how he had wanted it to be and so, when his time was up, he had left the Army. There were other horizons and other armies, a lot of them in Africa where you made your services available at a price and were treated like a king. Parts of Central America were fruitful, too.

He had made enough money to buy himself a little house overlooking the sea in Donegal, to which he returned after each assignment, watching from a distance the continuing blood-letting across the border in the North. His travels had given him ideas and a lot of useful contacts for a future source of revenue. The control and supply of drugs was often at the root of some of the conflicts in which he had become involved. The jigsaw Donegal coast, with its hundreds of secluded inlets, was a perfect spot for unloading. From there he could supply the rest of Ireland, heading south to Dublin, east to Belfast and then beyond Irish shores.

He was pondering all of this in Donegal one summer afternoon in 1990, sitting on the garden seat and looking out towards the sea, when he saw a car coming. It was one of the reasons he had picked this place. It was difficult to approach without being seen, unless you crept down the grassy hill at the back. Otherwise, there was just the winding stony track, with the cliffs a sheer drop on one side, that led from the coast road. He saw the dust before he saw the car and by the time it had pulled up through his open gate there was a Browning pistol under a cushion beside him.

He recognised the two young men who got out of the car. Not that he knew them personally, but he recognised the type because he had served under young men just like them. They wore open-necked shirts and jeans and they were shadowy outlines with the shimmering sea and the sun behind them. They stood with their legs apart and their arms loosely by their sides to show that they were not armed but he could see their eyes flick briefly to his right hand where it rested on the cushion. All three of them knew that if there was a problem they would not make it to the gate alive.

But they had not come to cause him trouble. They did not introduce themselves by name but they established their credentials as officers of British military intelligence by giving him a complete history of himself that was alarmingly comprehensive and contained just the subtlest hint of blackmail, leaving him with the impression that perhaps life could become difficult for him if the authorities here in the Republic knew about his background. But it was half-hearted stuff which Pierce brushed aside. They needed him for something and he waited to hear what it was.

They had a proposition for him to consider. There was work which needed to be done and it was difficult to accomplish by conventional means but, as they pointed out, unconventional methods were nothing new to him. What they proposed was that he should carry out occasional assignments with which, for obvious political reasons, they could not afford to have themselves associated. The border, in particular, was a nuisance that got in the way.

They talked for a while and arranged to meet again, on which occasion they brought someone more senior with them, a man in his forties who chain-smoked. There was one more such meeting but before it a deposit of £5,000, a gesture, was paid into Pierce's bank in Letterkenny, having gone through several laundering accounts before reaching its final destination.

And so Pierce had gone to work for them although not until he had put a proposition of his own. He had business plans which were rather at the embryonic stage, he told his handler, involving the importation of certain goods. But it was an activity which might attract the attention of the police forces on both sides of the border. If their relationship proved to be fruitful, Pierce said, then he wanted the man to ensure that the gaze of the police did not fall directly on him. It would not be in their mutual interests if he were to be arrested.

The man nodded. Such an arrangement was possible but it would depend very much on the quality and reliability of Pierce's work.

But there were to prove to be no difficulties on that score. The subject of his first assignment had been a middle-aged building contractor who lived in County Monaghan. Pierce had no idea why they were so interested in him; that was not his concern. He watched the man for weeks, observing his routine, and had to confess to himself that he did not see anything unusual about it.

The builder's life seemed very ordinary and uneventful but it was destined to end abruptly on the Friday morning he set off for County Roscommon where he was due to have a meeting with a cement supplier. They found his car the next day, parked in a side road which it had no reason to be on, unlocked and with all his papers and belongings still in it. But there was no sign of the builder, nor was there the next day or ever again. Only one person, Gavin Pierce, would ever know about the soft pit in a forest glade, the unmarked grave where his body lay.

There was another cheque for £5,000 in the bank in Letterkenny after that, a reasonable going rate for that kind of work at that time, and over the next few years there were other disappearances, other cheques. In the long lulls in between, Pierce travelled abroad, particularly to South America, and put his drugs business together.

Then, at a routine meeting with his handler, he was told that their relationship had ceased: there would be no more need for his services. There was no explanation and it had made Pierce feel uneasy. He knew what the retirement plan was likely to be and so he had accepted an assignment with a government in Central America to keep out of the way. It was there that he had established a connection with a drugs baron who was also a legitimate coffee exporter.

The two men had agreed to combine the two endeavours, setting Pierce up first in the North of England and now at his current location. But when he had come back to Britain, he had found waiting for him a proposition that he use the old skills again. The targets had been identified, their routines studied, and it was an offer so lucrative that he had found it impossible to resist. He had done it and then it was over.

Pierce poured the tea. It was twenty years since he had killed anybody but he still knew how and he wondered if he would ever have to do so again.

His attention turned to the television screen. The business news channel was running a story that a big American software company, as yet unnamed, was thought to be about to acquire the Northern Ireland-based company, LOC. There was a brief history of the firm, illustrated by shots of sinister black vans with the logo in silver on the side, then footage of a long squat building with the same logo above the door. The reporter's commentary talked of how the firm had diversified from security to software, all of it attributed to the personal vision and the driving force of the Ulster business tycoon, Henry Lomax.

The script was such a promotional puff that Pierce wondered if the reporter was angling for a job as Lomax's PR. There was video of Lomax getting out of a car and walking towards the camera, wearing a dark double-breasted suit and a slightly smug smile. Then he swung through the revolving doors into a tall building with mirrored glass that reflected clouds and blue sky as the camera panned slowly up its eighteen floors. Pierce recognised the building. Situated along the Belfast waterfront, it was a familiar landmark. It had been built by Lomax and its top three floors were the base from which he ran his complex network of business activities.

Pierce frowned. It was not often that someone was able to put one over on him but Henry Lomax had and here was further evidence of it. Until almost a year ago, he had

had a substantial share-holding in LOC, shares which had come into his possession a long time before. Then Lomax had approached him and had bought him out with what at the time seemed a generous offer. Pierce had assumed that Lomax was increasing his share control in order to keep someone else at bay. The offer had been a good one, there were other things he could do with the money, and so he had said yes. There had been no mention at that time of an American suitor, one whose advances would be welcomed rather than spurned.

The screen flashed up the current LOC share price: almost twice what Lomax had paid him. Bastard. He saw what was behind it. There was not much Lomax did not know about his competitors or his collaborators in business. It was the drugs, that was it. It would not have mattered to Lomax until now. But if this American company was nibbling seriously, then they would put their bloodhounds on the case and if anything dubious came to light, even a whiff, they would be off like a shot. There was nothing anyone could prove but Pierce knew there were the rumours and that Lomax could not afford to have him associated with the company.

He carried the tray upstairs and pushed open the bedroom door. His wife was on her side with her back to him, still sleeping. He put the tray on the bedside table and bent over to kiss her gently on the neck. 'Tea,' he whispered and then left the room softly.

He went back down to the kitchen, poured himself a cup and had just taken the first sip when the phone rang. It was a little early for the office and he wondered who it might be.

It was a voice he had not expected to hear.

The conversation was short, he listened rather than saying very much and when the caller had gone he realised there had been a lot of things he should have said and had not. But the call and its unexpected message had thrown him completely.

He sat in thought for a while and to his great discomfort

he felt an emotion that was alien to him: it was what he could only describe as fear. He shivered as he picked up his cup again but, like himself, the tea had gone cold.

Chapter Ten

McCallan opened one eye and knew he would not feel any better when he opened the other one. There was a heavy fog in his head and his mouth felt as if someone had held a party in it. The cigar, that was what had done it. Always the killer punch. He blinked and it hurt. Never mind the wine and the brandy and everything else, why was it that you always blamed the cigar? He remembered his mother going to a wine and cheese party when they had such things years ago and not being well afterwards and blaming the cheese.

He fumbled for the watch beside the bed. Nine o'clock. Tuesday morning. He got out of bed, crossed to the window and opened the heavy brocade curtains. Outside, the rain was almost horizontal and the wind whipped the last tenacious leaves from the trees. Beyond, across the main road, the sea was a slate grey with flecks of white in the swell. It was a day that looked just the way he felt. He enveloped himself in a huge fluffy white towelling robe that someone had left thoughtfully on the end of the bed and went off on a journey of exploration to find the sauna.

Half an hour later, he felt a lot better, partly detoxified, the fog in his head reduced to a bearable mist. Dressed, he made his way to the breakfast room where a dark-eyed young woman in a maid's outfit shyly served him poached eggs, bacon and toast, which had been his choice when she had asked him, although he was well aware that he could have had porridge or scrambled eggs or kedgeree or anything else that took his fancy.

He was amazed how hungry he was. He ate alone, as he had expected to. Lomax would have been at his desk in Belfast by seven as usual but he would have been working long before then, firing out instructions and talking to people all over the world from the back of the car as he made his way in.

He scanned the papers, which had been left neatly on a table by the door, and reflected that he had stayed in worse five-star hotels. On an inside page in the Financial Times, he found a small story about LOC which talked of speculation that there was an imminent buyer. He turned to the share prices and ran his eye down the columns. He whistled softly when he saw what he was looking for.

After he had finished, McCallan found Arthur and gave him a message that he would ring Lomax later that evening. They had talked about what would happen next, the will and everything. Both Lomax and he were executors but he had not the foggiest idea of what it contained or what was involved.

As he drove through Newcastle in the rain, he wondered just how much his father was worth and what the hell he would do with it all. He tried to add it up. There was the house at Dromore but there was also a lot of land around it which was leased out to a couple of small farmers. Then just up the road there was the old farmhouse. He had forgotten about that. There was a woman renting that, wasn't there, a university lecturer or something? He had met her briefly once when he and his father had been out for a walk. There was Donegal, of course; he would want shot of that.

The thought of being suddenly wealthy and free to do whatever he wished gave him an excited tingle but it made him feel guilty at the same time. If he had a choice, he would much rather have his father back.

There was post in the hall when he returned, letters and cards of sympathy. That was just the beginning of them. He would have a lot of mail to reply to. He made a pot of coffee and sat with a pen and paper, listing the names and wondering who the half of them were.

The doorbell rang and he went to answer it. At first, he could not place the woman who stood there. She was in her early to mid fifties, strong-featured and striking, greying hair short and combed back. She wore a dark wool overcoat and she kept her hands in the pockets. Hazel eyes played with him as he struggled towards recognition.

It came to him as he looked beyond her, over her shoulder to where the big car sat, the engine idling almost inaudibly, two young dark-suited men in the front.

His eyes widened. 'Chief Constable,' he said. 'I'm so sorry. How good of you to come.'

Ned Rossiter was the caretaker of the Masonic building at Arthur Square in the centre of Belfast and he was getting too old for the stairs. Reluctantly, he admitted it to himself as he closed the big front door behind him and contemplated the long haul up four floors with a Marks & Spencer shopping bag in each hand.

It had been all right – when was it? – fifteen years ago, when he had got the job. The exercise had been good for him then, had forced him to keep in reasonable shape, but the relentless climb was a bit much for him now that he was nearly seventy. Time to retire. Again, he thought.

There was a lift, true enough, a goods lift which the caterers and others used when there were big installation dinners on the third floor but that was not much use to Ned. The flat was the problem, not that it was not comfortable and quite well fitted, which it was, although it had been a bit small when Ned's wife was alive, but it was the fact that it was at the very top of the building and he had to trudge all the way down and then back up again whenever anyone rang the front door bell.

Mind you, the old days must have been much worse, the early seventies, for example, when the IRA bombing campaign was at its height. Living in a flat at the top of a building in the empty heart of the city, being evacuated in the middle of the night into the cold, wet, dangerous streets, would not have been a bundle of laughs. Thank God all that had been over by the time Ned moved in. He would not have been interested in the job otherwise.

But he would have had to have found something, all the same. Ned was a Yorkshireman but had lived in Northern Ireland for nearly forty years, ever since he had been transferred from England by the engineering company that employed him. For some reason he had never risen above his fairly lowly rung on the management ladder. He had applied for promotion often enough but he never seemed to get anywhere and instead saw younger, less experienced people passing him by, until one day he was called into his boss's office and told he was being made redundant.

He had no savings worth a damn – keeping two daughters at university in England had seen to that – so he had sold his modest house and invested the money and taken this job as a caretaker. The fact that he was a Mason himself, of course, had helped him get it.

Ned paused on the third floor to get his breath. Nearly there. He put the bags down and looked around in the silence. This floor had all been done up a couple of years ago. He looked into the lodge room. It was empty now but it would be full tonight with whatever lodge, he had forgotten which one it was, performing its ancient ritual.

One of his daughters was actually living in Yorkshire now, not far from Leeds, his old home town, and here he was, on his own in Belfast. Life seemed to have moved in some kind of a strange circle. She had talked about him coming to live with them – her and her husband and their youngsters, a boy and a girl. He liked the grandchildren but he had dismissed the notion because he did not want to get in the way. She had mentioned it again recently, though, and maybe he should give it a bit of thought.

There was a room beside the lodge room. It had been an old dusty cloakroom once but in the refurbishment it had been turned into a bigger space, all nicely panelled, with a wall of wooden lockers, like something out of a public school, Ned thought. The lockers were for the provincial officers to use if they wished, somewhere for them to keep personal effects, such as their regalia.

Each rank was inscribed in gold-leaf paint on the locker door. Provincial Grand Master. Provincial Grand Treasurer. He stopped at the next one. Provincial Grand Secretary. He had forgotten. The poor man had died, that awful fire in Donegal. There was a son, wasn't there? He should really clear the locker and take the contents up to the flat for safe-keeping. Then he would contact the young fellow to make arrangements about collecting it.

He put his hand in his coat pocket and took out a bunch of keys, selected one and opened the locker door. There was a small tan case inside, almost like the sort of thing that would have held a pair of duelling pistols. He checked to see if it was locked. It was not. Ned paused. He really should not open this but he was curious.

There was an apron, neatly folded, plus all the usual bits and pieces, including a couple of small books, like hymnals, with Masonic regulations. At the bottom of the case there was a large manilla envelope with the flap taped shut. Ned turned it over in his hand. There was nothing written on it. It was bulky and it felt as if there might be another, slightly smaller envelope inside.

He made a face to himself. Odd. He put everything back in the case and turned the key in the locker. He would come back for it later. First he had to get this shopping upstairs.

McCallan was flustered and embarrassed at not recognising her. Dorothy Taylor, Chief Constable of the Police Service of Northern Ireland, was one of his father's oldest friends, but it was a long time since he had seen her. She waved his apologies aside and instead leaned forward and kissed him on the cheek before walking on in.

'Jack, I'm so sorry, so very sorry. I was devastated when I heard the news. I couldn't come any sooner, I'm afraid. I tried to reach you last night, left a message on your voice mail. Did you get it?'

'Oh no. Damn. I'm sorry. I haven't checked this morning. I wasn't here. I spent the night down in Newcastle with Henry Lomax and I've just got back.'

'Ah, I see. Henry Lomax. So you'll be nursing a sore head, then?'

'Actually, it could be worse. And to tell you the truth it was until I stewed myself in his sauna and then had a good breakfast.'

'Yes, I hear he's got quite a place down there.'

'He certainly has. Haven't you been? You must know him?'

'Yes, I do, but I've never been to his house. I first met him years ago through your father, of course, since they're such old friends, but I see him from time to time now professionally. He's on various committees and so on. Institute of Directors, that kind of thing. I'm giving a speech to them next week.'

McCallan ushered her into the living room and she explained that she had been visiting the regional police headquarters in Lisburn and had decided to call while she was in the area. She was relieved to find him in because it had been troubling her that they had not spoken.

As they talked, McCallan studied her. She took her coat off and threw it carelessly over the back of a chair. Underneath, there was a well-cut grey suit, civilian clothes but a touch formal, he thought, a uniform of sorts. He left her for a few minutes while he went to the kitchen to make coffee and when he came back he found her at ease in an armchair with her elegant legs crossed and her hands cupped across one knee.

She had been a young officer in the RUC when the Troubles had come to an end. She had been a rather rare specimen, a woman at the sharp end of anti-terrorist work, operating alongside men like Bob McCallan, but it had been her brain and her wits which had earned her that role and had made an impression on everyone who worked with her. When the force was reformed and a lot of the old guard, including his father, had retired, she had found herself in the right place at the right time, a woman on the way up.

She had undoubted ability, she was tough, and her gender was certainly not going to harm the image of a new force with opportunities for all. Promotion had followed by degrees and then transfer to head up one of the big new regional crime squads covering the West of England. Her public profile had grown, the Sunday papers wrote colourful features about her and she sometimes popped up on television discussions. She had been Chief Constable for the past three years.

She had the confidence that came with power. Her manner was engaging, the charm seductive, but McCallan sensed from her the ruthlessness that lay beneath it all and just for a moment he wondered if there had ever been anything more than a professional relationship between her and his father.

'Jack,' she said, leaning forward with the coffee cupped in her hand, 'how are you coping? Is there anything I can do, anything at all? You know you only have to ask.'

McCallan smiled his gratitude. 'Yes, I know. Everyone has been so kind.'

'I don't need to tell you how wonderful your father was, what he meant to me. He was a great man, a great help to me when I was a young policewoman just learning the ropes and great support over the years. Even after he retired, I often turned to him for advice.'

The thought about her and his father was there again and he could not quite shake it. She had never married, right enough. His own situation came to mind: unattached, having an affair with a married woman.

'Yes,' he said, 'he talked about you a lot. He was very proud of your success, always knew you would do well.

And he wasn't a bit ashamed about taking some of the credit for it.'

He smiled. 'But he was a bit old-fashioned, though. Women had their place, I suspect, although he would never have put it quite like that. I think even he was surprised when you actually became the Chief Constable, if you don't mind me saying so.'

She laughed. 'Well he only had himself to blame. He obviously trained me far too well.'

They talked on, their thoughts turning to how McCallan's father had died, and the conversation became more muted.

'You always wonder, don't you,' she said, 'when something like this happens. Was it just an accident? Have you been wondering? I bet you have.'

He nodded, relieved to find her broaching the subject instead of him.

'I wondered myself,' she said, 'so I did something I shouldn't do. I got on to the Guards personally. Not the sort of thing the Chief Constable should be up to, exactly. A bit high on the Richter scale of not terribly good diplomatic behaviour, I'm afraid, but what the hell, I couldn't just sit around. Your father was too dear to me for that. So I found out that they've got the forensic results now. They moved quite quickly on it, really, it has to be said.'

She sipped her coffee. 'Well, anyway, it does seem as if it was a genuine accident all right and confirms everything you were probably told at the scene. And I suppose that's a relief in a way although it doesn't make the shock of your father's death any easier. But at least there's no question of anything, well, sinister.'

McCallan thanked her and then he told her about Mrs Benson's death and the policemen who had called with Grace Walker.

'God,' she said, 'isn't that tragic? What a dreadful coincidence. That poor woman. As for her police visitors, I wouldn't have a clue. Could be anybody but it sounds a bit strange in the circumstances. I can always get someone to check with Lisburn, if it'll ease your mind, find out who they were and what they were on about.'

'Thank you,' McCallan said. 'You're very reassuring.'

She gazed over his shoulder and into the past somewhere. 'We all went through a lot. Some horrible things. It's a wonder we kept our sanity, never mind our lives. You can't imagine.'

She had forgotten, obviously. She was right in that he had never been a policeman in Northern Ireland and could not know what that had been like. He was also part of a generation for whom the Troubles were a swiftly fading memory. But one thing he did know, one experience he did share with a great many people: he knew what being shot was like.

'No,' he said. 'I can't.'

She had not really heard him, was still off somewhere else. 'You pause for thought at a time like this. You start to think about your own life, what you've done with it, your experiences.'

She turned her attention back to him. 'Did your father talk about the past much?'

She did not wait for his answer. 'You know, some people left the force because they actually missed the Troubles. Could you believe that? They missed the buzz, the excitement of the unknown, of being close to danger. Couldn't handle all this boring peacetime policing. Amazing, isn't it?'

It occurred to McCallan that she might be talking about herself but he did not say so.

'Maybe Dad might have been like that if he'd stayed,' he said. 'Who knows? But he didn't stay and, as far as I can recall, there were a lot of people like him who didn't have the option, did they?'

She looked at him. 'You're being a bit harsh, don't you think? All big organisations have to change to survive and we were certainly not any different. We had to do it bloody quickly because of the new political circumstances. It was only right to give people the opportunity to choose, to decide whether they felt they could be part of the new environment. If they felt it didn't suit them, then we let them go with dignity and a good financial deal, upgraded pensions, the lot. Only right and proper. We owed them everything. Your father never complained, did he?'

She had all the management patter. Wrapped in veils of euphemism, it meant that those whose faces did not fit were shown the door. But she was right. His father had not complained, nor, of course, had he waited around to become one of the compulsory volunteers.

'No, he made the right decision at the right time and it all worked out very well for him. A new life entirely.'

He thought for a moment. 'As for the past, when I think about it, there wasn't much in the line of reminiscence. The odd snippet now and again. I suppose he viewed it as something of a closed book, really.'

It was a book, he reminded her, which might have ended a lot earlier, in 1975, to be exact, on a bright spring day in County Armagh, roads lined on either side by pink apple blossom, when the Landrover in front of Bob McCallan had disintegrated in an explosion which had lifted his own armoured vehicle and blown it into the ditch. By that time, of the eight people in the police patrol, only four were still alive and as they had scrambled out, the shooting had started.

Two more had died at that point, shot in the chest by an expert sniper. Bob McCallan had grabbed an M1 carbine and crawled behind an apple tree for cover and until the Army helicopters arrived he had kept firing at the hillside from which the attack had come. By that time the terrorists had gone only he and one constable with serious wounds had survived. Out of that incident had come a British Empire Medal for his gallantry.

'Remarkable,' the Chief Constable said, remembering, 'remarkable.'

'It seemed as if he preferred to keep past history very much to himself,' McCallan said. 'Anyway, I used to think a lot of his reticence had as much to do with him not wanting to be reminded about my mother's death as much as anything.'

'Yes, well, you're probably right. And I suppose that if being secretive is part of your job and your way of life, then it's hard to be anything else. The need-to-know principle, we used to call it. You become a bit uncommunicative, reluctant to answer questions, always suspicious about why they're being asked.'

She looked at her watch and stood up. 'I have to go but may I ask you a question before I do?'

'Sure, anything.'

'May I say a few words at the funeral?'

Embarrassment hit him again and he kicked himself mentally for not having thought of it first.

'Oh, Chief Constable—'

'I think we'd both feel a lot more comfortable if you called me Dorothy, don't you? After all this time.'

'Dorothy. Of course. I'd be delighted if you said something. So bloody thoughtless of me not to ask.'

From her pocket she took a small white card with a phone number on it. 'That's my home. When all this is over and before you go back to London, you must come and have a drink. Just call me.'

'Thank you. I'd like that very much.'

They walked to the front door and as he reached across to open it he brushed against her accidentally. But she did not draw back from his touch.

In that brief awkward second, he felt the shape of her, firm under the fitted suit. His eyes met hers for a moment but he tried to pretend they had not and he busied himself with the doorknob as if there were a problem with it. Then she was out of the door and into the car and away up the drive and he stood there with his heart beating.

Chapter Eleven

'This is a waste of bloody time,' Tweed sighed.

'Can you think of anything better?' Mattheson asked him.

They were in the car at the side of the road just down from the church, watching the mourners arrive. They kept the engine running and the de-mister on so that the windscreen was clear and they could see who turned up. Anything that might give them a clue.

'Well, Christ, what do you expect?' Tweed said. 'Someone to appear with a placard saying "I did it"? Written in blood, maybe?'

Mattheson did not answer. He took a cloth and wiped condensation from the passenger window. Tweed was right: it was a bit pointless. But there was just the chance they might see someone or something that might take them further on than they were now, which was not very far at all.

They had been busy in the days since McCallan's death and the accident they had rigged at the caravan but they had been quiet about it, discreet, because they were investigating a murder of which the world was not aware. They had to find the killer quickly. Their job now was disposal, erasing all traces of the crime and the criminal. The housekeeper had been the first part of that task.

'Do you think we did the right thing talking to that woman Walker?' Mattheson asked. 'It didn't get us anywhere. What if she gets suspicious and starts asking questions?'

Tweed looked at him. It was not like him to be uncertain,

not Mattheson who could break an elderly woman's neck without a qualm. Maybe it was his own neck he was worrying about now.

He made a face. 'I suppose it was worth a try. She might have known something. It was just a pity she didn't. Anyway, I think she was too upset to think about us for too long.'

'What if Mrs Benson hadn't called us first and the local police had got in on the act instead?' Mattheson wondered. 'Where would they have started looking?'

'Well, they wouldn't have been able to get much further than we have, except they'd have been able to make more of a noise about it. There was no sign of a break-in or anything. No sign of a struggle. Whoever killed him must have talked his way in. Someone he knew or a plausible caller of some kind. Maybe it was about money. You get plenty of examples every day of old people being beaten and robbed in their homes.'

'No evidence of that here,' Mattheson said. 'No indication that anything was taken.'

'Well, then, maybe it all went too far. Maybe the killer hadn't meant to top him, so he fled in panic.'

Mattheson looked at him with distaste. 'Don't be ridiculous. His whole fucking head was practically hacked off. What sort of an accident was that?'

He turned away. He was getting rattled. They were groping about in the dark and it was the dark he was worried about, the darkness of the past. He wiped the window again. Whoever it was, they were out there somewhere and they would know that the murder had been covered up and they would be wondering why.

The day could not have been worse. Even though the little church sat in the shelter of a semicircle of evergreens, a bitter wind still managed to cut through and whipped the rain into the faces of all those who had been forced to stand outside. The church was full. There was no gallery, just the ground floor pews, all of them packed tightly with men and women, but men mostly, wearing bulky overcoats. The hard-pressed

verger had found some folding chairs with which he had lined
the aisle and anyone who could not get a seat stood around
against the cold stone walls. Those outside had turned up too
late for even that.

McCallan found it difficult to take his eyes off the coffin
in front of him. It had arrived at the end of its journey from
Donegal late yesterday afternoon and had lain in the musty
silence of the church through the night. He sat up at the
front in the pew reserved for the immediate family. There
were always some clothes of his in a wardrobe at his father's
house and he had dug out a suit which he had not worn for
a couple of years. It was dark grey and although it was not
exactly the sort of thing he would choose to wear these days,
it still fitted. With it he wore the black tie which his father
always wore to funerals. But not today.

Beside him sat Henry Lomax, the nearest thing he had to a
relative if you did not count a cousin of his father's who lived
in Australia and whom neither he nor the old man had seen
for many years. He had tried to call her several times with no
success and yesterday evening he had written. But perhaps
tonight he would try the phone again.

He looked around. A woman was standing at the back and
he saw that it was Grace Walker. The verger came past and
McCallan caught his arm. 'That lady standing over there,' he
whispered. 'Tell her I would like her to be with me here at
the front.'

A few moments later, McCallan was moving up the pew to
let her sit down. He smiled at her. 'Thank you for coming.'

She looked at him sympathetically. 'It was the least I
could do.'

Wearing a surplice that was dazzlingly clean, the Reverend
Nigel Rogers emerged from the vestry at the side and the
funeral service began. They sang a hymn, Praise My Soul
The King of Heaven, its lyric printed on a sheet which bore
the words 'A service of thanksgiving for the life of Robert
John McCallan BEM.' After the hymn, there were prayers

111

and a Bible reading delivered by the Rector. McCallan found it increasingly difficult to believe that this was what his father had ordered.

When Rogers had finished, the congregation sat down and there was the rustle of people settling themselves, with sporadic coughing from the back. As it subsided, McCallan heard footsteps on the stone flag floor as Dorothy Taylor made her way to the front of the church.

Her uniform was a deep charcoal version of the dark grey worn by the rest of her force. Silver buttons gleamed and she wore a white shirt and a black tie. It was the uniform of a modern western European police force and a far cry from the dark green she had first worn as an officer in the Royal Ulster Constabulary on patrol in South Armagh with body armour to match and a .38 Ruger pistol at her side.

She stood in front of the pulpit and scanned the faces turned towards her. Her gaze finally settled on McCallan and she smiled softly. He wondered if she was thinking about the same thing he was, that moment at the door. It made him uncomfortable and he felt intimidated by her and the directness of her gaze.

She began to speak. She did so effortlessly, without a text, without even a note, and she did it with the confident assurance of someone well used to addressing an audience. It was prepared carefully but sounded off-the-cuff. There were anecdotes about his father, some of them humorous, involving dubious escapades and dodgy characters, and they relieved the solemn mood, producing a ripple of laughter from the congregation, many of whom recognised familiar experiences in the stories. Other chapters, about colleagues blown to pieces, families destroyed by violence, narrow escapes from bombs and bullets, were a much more grim and harrowing recollection.

She had them in the palm of her hand. McCallan could see why she had become Chief Constable and what it was that had earned her the respect of the Northern Ireland community.

She was a skilful manipulator, an engaging blend of authority and charm.

She was coming to the end of the eulogy. 'For many of us, Bob McCallan was a guide, a mentor, an inspiring officer to whom we, all of us in this country, owe a great deal. Without men like Bob, without their sense of duty, their self-sacrifice, their sense of what was right, ideals which I know all of us here today hold dear, without all of that, Northern Ireland could have slipped further and further into the abyss and we would not be enjoying the quality of life, the normality, that we have today and that, happily, Bob McCallan lived to share and enjoy.'

In the body of the church, heads were nodding in agreement. 'Bob McCallan was a man of his time,' she went on, 'a man who did not hesitate to do what had to be done in the pursuit of order in this community. Although the force in which he served with honour has gone, it was men like Bob McCallan who paved the way for the kind of police force we have now and which I am proud to lead.'

She paused and looked straight at McCallan. 'Jack, although your father's death leaves a great void for us, that is nothing to the loss which you have suffered. Our prayers and our thoughts are with you today.'

McCallan was moved. He nodded an acknowledgement and mouthed a silent thank you, although he could hardly see her through the mist in his eyes. Beside him, Lomax blew his nose loudly in a large white handkerchief.

Dorothy stepped down from the pulpit and made her way back to her seat, putting her hand firmly on McCallan's shoulder as she passed. There was another hymn and a prayer, after which Rogers announced that McCallan had arranged refreshments at a local hotel after the service and would be delighted if people could join him there.

Then McCallan and Lomax put their arms across each other's shoulders to form a support to carry the coffin on its last journey. Two of the undertaker's men bore the weight at the other end. They took the winding narrow path to the graveside, the wind and the rain lashing at them mercilessly. Rogers walked ahead, reading the funeral rites, his surplice billowing like a sail. 'Man that is born of woman hath but a short time to live and is full of misery. He cometh up and is cut down like a flower. He fleeth as it were a shadow and never continueth in one stay.'

A huge mound of wet, congealed clay stood beside the open grave. Two gravediggers in wellingtons came forward and relieved McCallan and Lomax who was beginning to breathe heavily, McCallan noticed. There was a thin sheen of sweat as well as rain on his ruddy face. Gently, the gravediggers and the undertakers laid the coffin down on top of a wooden platform, then laced two black ropes through the brass handles.

Rogers continued to read, apparently unaffected by the brutality of the elements, seeming to savour every syllable of the archaic text. 'In the midst of life we are in death. Of whom may we seek for succour but of thee, O Lord, who for our sins art justly displeased? Yet, O Lord God most holy, O Lord most mighty, O holy and most merciful Saviour, deliver us not into the bitter pains of eternal death.'

Lomax's driver had come forward with a large black umbrella and McCallan and Lomax sheltered under it, listening to Rogers's voice rising and falling with the wind. 'Thou knowest, Lord, the secrets of our hearts. Shut not thy merciful ears to our prayers but spare us, Lord most holy, O God most mighty, O holy and merciful Saviour, thou most worthy judge eternal, suffer us not, at our last hour, for any pains of death, to fall from thee.'

The ground was soft under McCallan's feet and he looked down at the mess being made of his carefully polished black shoes. He thought of the field in Donegal, the muddy laneway, the cold and the rain that had not seemed to let up since he had arrived. There was a dampness that got right into the bones.

Rogers's surplice was stainless no more. Wet brown streaks of mud sullied its edges.

'For as much as it hath pleased almighty God to take unto himself the soul of our dear brother here departed, we therefore commit his body to the ground.'

The undertakers had hold of the ropes and lowered the coffin slowly down with the aid of them. When it reached the bottom, they pulled the ropes away again with swift, expert tugs.

'Earth to earth, ashes to ashes, dust to dust.' There was a dull thud as a moist clump of soil fell on the coffin. There was the Lord's Prayer and a benediction and with a final amen it was over. People began to look up from the ground and then at each other and after a pause they began to drift over to where McCallan stood. It was a full fifteen minutes before he had finished shaking hands and he and Lomax could make their way to where Lomax's Daimler stood warm and waiting.

As a result, they were the last of the mourners to reach the hotel. The room McCallan had hired for the occasion turned out to be a small function room with a dance floor. To his horror, there were disco lights mounted on tracks along the ceiling but, mercifully, they were not on. As he walked down the couple of carpeted steps into the room, he spotted a few familiar faces, among them Grace Walker and Dorothy Taylor, but he was relieved to see that only about thirty people had taken up his offer. He did not know what he would have done if they had all decided to come.

There were sandwiches and sausage rolls on a big central table. Some people stood with cups of tea, others with something warmer and more spirited. A waiter came forward with a tray that held glasses of mineral water or whisky. Both McCallan and Lomax chose the latter and then began to mingle.

As McCallan did so, a tall, elderly man in a smart grey three-piece suit came towards him. He had a full head of white hair, a soft white crescent of a moustache and eybrows that looked like tufts of cotton wool. Unlike most of the men in the room, he did not wear a plain dark tie. Although technically his was black, it also had a thin diagonal gold stripe and tiny gold crowns and it was a tie which denoted that he was an old boy of one of Northern Ireland's most historic schools. He was also the chairman of its Board of Governors. A gold watch chain hung across his waistcoat but Jack's eyes were drawn to the little gold emblem in his lapel. It was of a square and a compass and he thought of the signet ring that had been handed to him in Mrs Cassidy's kitchen.

The man shook his hand and McCallan could feel the pressure of the thumb between the knuckles. At the graveside there are had been quite a few such handshakes, accompanied by inquiring looks.

'David Reith,' he said and McCallan could not help thinking it was an ironic name on such a day. 'I was a good friend of your father's. It's a sad occasion.'

'Yes, it is,' McCallan agreed. 'Thank you very much for coming.'

'Not at all, not at all. As I'm sure you probably know, your father was a prominent member of the Masonic Institution. Provincial Grand Secretary of the Province of Down, as a matter of fact. I'm the Provincial Grand Master. Quite a few of our members are here.'

'I see.'

'Yes. He'll be quite a loss to us, quite a loss.' He leaned his head to one side and looked at McCallan quizzically. 'You're not a member yourself, I take it?'

'No,' McCallan said and smiled apologetically. 'I'm afraid I've never been much of a joiner, you might say. The drama society at school was about the height of it.'

'Well, you should think about it. Your father was a very conscientious Mason, very good at organising charity events, that sort of thing. It's a fine organisation and you can't believe all that nonsense about secret societies and so on.'

Even though his father had often praised its fraternal attributes, McCallan had no intention of joining some silly boys' club where they gave themselves grandiose titles. But he did not want to hurt this man's feelings. 'No, it's not that,' he said. 'I just don't believe in being involved in something if I can't give it proper time and attention.'

Reith stood back and looked at him, then he nodded. 'That's admirable. I quite understand. But if you ever did think about joining, I'm sure your father's mother lodge would be only too keen to have you. To carry on the family tradition, you know. There'd be no trouble getting someone to propose you.'

He took a card out of his waistcoat pocket and gave it to him. 'If you ever change your mind, just let me know.'

'Thanks,' McCallan said. 'That's very kind of you.'

Reith backed away almost theatrically with more expressions of condolence. McCallan looked around. Grace was over in a corner talking to a couple of people. She smiled at him and he raised his glass in a kind of salute and then started to cross the room towards her but as he did, a man stepped in front of him.

'Mr McCallan—'

'Jack.'

'Jack,' the man repeated. He was somewhere in his sixties with wiry grey hair that had gone a bit unkempt, like a bramble thicket. He looked fit and fresh for his age and his skin had a healthy glow, as if he spent a lot of time out of doors, but he carried a blackthorn walking stick and McCallan noticed that he stood a little awkwardly.

He shifted the stick from his right to his left and shook McCallan's hand. McCallan felt the familiar pressure of the thumb. 'Alfie Hutchinson,' the man said. There was a slight rasp in his voice as if he needed to clear his throat. 'I knew your father very well. I'm an ex-policeman myself. I dropped you a note because I didn't think I'd be able to get here today but I managed it all the same. I was very sorry to hear about Bob, very sorry indeed.'

'That's kind of you,' McCallan said. 'Very much appreciated.'

117

He tried to move on but Hutchinson was not finished. 'He was quite a man, your father. One of the old school. There's not many of them today who have a clue what it was like. That's how I got this.' He put his right hand behind him and pressed his back as if it ached.

McCallan could see that Hutchinson was waiting for him to ask what he meant and that once he did he would be here for a while. It was probably not often that he had the opportunity to tell his story, whatever it was, to someone who had not heard it before. McCallan finished his drink and waved to the waiter.

'You'll have something?' he said to Hutchinson.

'Whisky would be good, thanks.'

McCallan took two glasses and handed him one. 'An old injury, then?' he said.

'Bullet in the back. Just at the base of the spine. A fraction of an inch more and I'd have been paralysed for life, so I suppose I've got something to be thankful for.'

'How did it happen?'

'I was taking my daughter to school. 1989 it was. I was in Special Branch then. I got out of the car to see her across the road. I took her over and then came back and turned to wave. The next thing I knew I was on my face in the street and she was screaming "Daddy, daddy!" I can hear her to this day.' He drank deeply from his glass. 'IRA bastards. They shot me from a car. It had followed me. They never did get the guy responsible, at least not for that particular incident.'

There was a pause for silent reflection until McCallan interrupted it. 'Did you work with my father?' he asked.

'No, not really. I really only got to know him after we both retired. Through the Masonic, you know. Our paths crossed a few times and I got friendly with him that way. I saw a fair bit of him lately, one way or another. He had a narrow escape himself once. But I'm sure you know all about it.'

'Yes, he did. He was very lucky. Unlike the people who were with him at the time.'

'That's right. They're dead and buried and forgotten by most people now.' He shook his head. 'But some of us never can forget that kind of thing, all the bombings and the murders. Those IRA scum. It makes me sick to this day when I think that their . . . their spawn is sitting round the table up there at Stormont running this country.'

'Well, that's not exactly the case, surely?' McCallan said unwisely.

A fire lit in Hutchinson's eyes. 'Of course, it's the case. For the last twenty years we've been kow-towing to these bastards. All this Irish identity, cultural diversity crap. Dublin telling London what to do. Sometimes I think old Paisley's lying there spinning in his grave, saying "I told you so." Look what happened to the RUC. Where is it now? Gone. If you tell anyone you were once in the RUC they look at you as if you had some sort of disease. It's the way the Americans used to treat the Vietnam veterans. Total embarrassment. Hide them away somewhere and eventually they'll die off.'

He stopped suddenly and looked at McCallan and his eyes widened in horror at his own insensitivity. 'Oh, Jesus, I'm sorry, I'm sorry. What the hell's got into me? That was a terrible thing to say.'

McCallan put his hand on his shoulder. 'Don't worry about it. I expect that if my father were here he would be agreeing with you.'

'Nonetheless, I shouldn't have said that. I'm sorry.'

'You're OK.' He altered the steering of the conversation a few degrees. 'So what happened after the . . . the incident? How long did it take you to recover?'

'Months. I couldn't go back to Special Branch and I didn't want to leave the force. I was only forty-one. So they offered me a job with the department that looked after welfare, widows' pensions, that sort of thing. I did that for a few years and then the violence petered out and they were looking for volunteers and I got out with a good deal. It's only in the past

119

ten years or so that the back's got bad. A touch of arthritis doesn't help, either.'

'You look in good health, if I may say so.'

'The doctor advises me to do a lot of walking, if I can. And there's the garden.' He winked. 'Although with a bad back, I get the wife to do the hard stuff.'

He took a sip of his whisky. 'Listen,' he said, 'I'm keeping you back. You've got a lot of people to talk to. I just wanted to say I was sorry about your father. And I'm sorry about the outburst. It's just – at times like this . . .' He gestured round the room at all the other ex-policemen.

'I know. I understand,' McCallan said. 'Something like this brings it all back.'

Hutchinson moved away and Grace Walker came towards him. 'I'm afraid it's hello and goodbye,' she said. 'I've got to go.'

'Oh, that's a pity. I really appreciated your being here today, especially after all you've been through yourself. It must have been agony for you in the church.'

'No, you made it easier for me, inviting me up to the front pew and all that. It was a wonderful service, very moving.'

She looked over to where Dorothy Taylor stood calm and patient, encircled by a handful of elderly men, old warriors eager to tell her how to run her police force, to make it more like the way it used to be. 'She's brilliant, isn't she?'

'Yes, she makes quite an impression.'

She looked at him. 'You don't sound very impressed.'

'I'm sorry,' he said. 'I just wonder about people who are, well . . . professionally sincere is the only way I can put it.'

Grace looked taken aback. 'She said some very nice things about your father.'

He nodded. 'Yes, she did. That's quite true and I was very touched by what she had to say. You're right. It's wrong of me to be critical.'

'What are your plans?' she asked. 'Now that it's all over?'

'Well, it's not all over yet. There'll be the will and the

estate to be settled. After that, who knows? Back to London, I think.'

'Well, if there's anything I can do, you know where I am.' She looked just beyond his shoulder. 'I think someone else wants to talk to you. I'd better go. Bye.'

He said goodbye abruptly and then turned to see Nigel Rogers with a woman who looked faintly familiar. She was tall; in heels, as tall as he was himself and she wore a fitted dark blue suit that fitted her slim form perfectly. Her auburn hair was shoulder-length but it was tied back. Her face was lean, too, carefully sculpted, the nose fine and straight, the cheeks a soft hollow. She was about his own age, he guessed. She wore glasses with frames that did not seem to have a colour but the eyes that met his were indisputably green.

Beside her, Rogers was a diminutive figure. He had discarded the surplice which was probably in the wash basket at the rectory by now, awaiting restoration.

'Jack,' he said, 'have you met Ann Reilly?'

'I'm . . . not sure.'

She smiled. 'You have, actually. A few months ago. We met when you and your father were out for a walk along the road. I rent the farmhouse.' Her voice had depth and the accent was from Dublin or thereabouts.

He remembered. 'Of course. I knew the face was familiar but I couldn't place you. I'm sorry.'

'Not at all. You only met me the once and the circumstances were, well . . . rather different.'

Rogers excused himself and went to talk to Henry Lomax. 'Yes,' McCallan said, 'very different indeed. Listen, it was really very good of you to come.'

'Not at all. I was terribly shocked when I heard what happened. I was down at home in Waterford for the weekend and I just couldn't believe it.'

McCallan nodded. 'Well,' he said resignedly, 'it's something we're just going to have to accept.' He frowned briefly. 'Forgive me, I've forgotten what it is that you do. My Dad said you're a university lecturer or something, isn't that it?'

She laughed and shook her head. 'No, I'm not. I'm . . . well, it's all a bit complicated. I'm involved in an academic study, right enough. But . . . maybe I'll explain it properly to you some time. It would take too long just now.'

'Fine. I'm sorry. I obviously picked my father up wrongly.'

'It doesn't matter.' She brushed back a strand of hair that had come adrift and fallen across her left eye. 'Your father was a lovely man. I kind of got to know him better over the last wee while and he really was rather sweet.' She smiled. 'I couldn't have wished for a nicer landlord. He'd drop by for a cup of tea and a chat every now and then. In fact, we were talking about the theatre recently and we'd agreed to go out together tomorrow night, to the play at the Grand Opera House.'

McCallan was startled. The tickets on the hall table. They were not for him and his father at all: they were for his father and this woman. He felt a variety of feelings colliding inside, shock and resentment among them, and he wondered what had been going on in his father's mind.

'Yes, I noticed the tickets,' he said. 'I wondered why he'd got them. Look, why don't I drop them in to you? I don't see why you shouldn't have them anyway.'

'No, thanks. I'd rather not. It was a nice idea of your father's and I'd rather leave it like that, if you don't mind.'

'Of course. Whatever you think.' There was an awkward pause. 'Listen,' he sighed, 'I . . . eh . . . when all this is over I've got a lot of thinking to do, the future and all that. We could have a proper chat in a day or two.'

She smiled and nodded. 'I'd appreciate that. I know it's not the time and place now but I'll have to know soon whether I'm still going to have a roof over my head or not.'

They shook hands and he thanked her again for coming as she made her farewells. Others were doing the same and the room was thinning out. Lomax was the last to leave, with a crushing embrace. Afterwards, McCallan went in search of the manager, a young man who bustled about with an illusion of efficiency that was not matched by the quality of the hotel. He offered to pay the bill but the manager said he would send it on to him after he had made it up, which McCallan thought was precisely what he would do.

Lomax had taken the Daimler but had left another car and a driver to take McCallan home. As they left the hotel car park, they were watched by the occupants of a large dark Ford saloon who had observed everyone going in and out of the hotel, just as they had watched everyone going in and out of the church.

'That's that,' Tweed said. 'What's next on the agenda?'

Mattheson shook his head. 'I wish I bloody knew.'

Chapter Twelve

'I'm sorry I kept you waiting. I was held up with another client.'

Andrew Morris's voice was an authoritative baritone. He entered the room behind where McCallan and Lomax sat in front of his desk and as McCallan turned he was taken aback to see that the voice did not go with its owner. It should have belonged to someone substantial, not to this weedy young man in his late twenties in clothes which looked as if they were owned by someone a size bigger.

Morris crossed the carpeted floor with swift, silent strides and went round to his side of the desk. His hair was short and oily and parted at the side and he had a thin moustache and a chinstrap beard in an attempt to give his appearance some sort of maturity. He reached across and offered McCallan a hand that was rather dainty, although the handshake was firm enough and confident. Not Masonic, either, McCallan noticed.

'I was very sorry about your father,' he said and then he shook Lomax's hand as well. 'That was quite a funeral yesterday. A very fitting tribute.'

'You were there?' McCallan asked.

'Yes. At the service, although I had to leave as soon as it was over.' He sat down. 'Can I get you anything? Coffee? Tea?'

The two men declined. 'I have another appointment, I'm afraid,' Lomax said, 'so I hope we can get through this fairly quickly.'

'Fine,' Morris said. 'It shouldn't take long.'

The streets off Chichester Street in Belfast, leading down to the law courts, were a legal ghetto where, at virtually every doorway, a brass plaque announced that there was a solicitor's office within. The firm of McCaughey and Granleese was one such practice, long-established in this part of the city. No one named either McCaughey or Granleese had anything to do with it now but Andrew Morris was a nephew of the late Wesley Granleese so, however obliquely, it was still a family firm. The outer offices were bright and airy and open-plan. Receptionists sat at computer screens and there was music from speakers built into the ceiling. But Morris had kept his own office as a haven of tradition, aloof from modern trends. Antique glass-fronted bookcases held leather-bound legal tomes and on the walls there were monochrome photographs of his predecessors, stern men with rimless spectacles and ties with tiny knots. The desk he sat behind was an imposing slab of carved walnut and, like the voice, it did not match its owner.

Morris opened a drawer, took out a file and undid the ribbon that secured it. 'Your father gave me instructions that he wanted his will handled like this, with both of you here as executors for the reading. I could simply have notified you both of the contents and sent you a copy but he was adamant that he wanted some sort of formal meeting. I hope you don't mind.'

'No, not at all,' McCallan said.

'All right.' Morris glanced at the open file, as if reminding himself of what was in it. McCallan felt his heart racing and there was nothing he could do to slow it. He sat in eager anticipation and he hoped his excitement did not show. Everything that had happened since the weekend, Julia, his father's death, had altered his life immeasurably and he knew that what Andrew Morris was about to tell him would to so again.

The solicitor leaned his arms flat on the desk and locked

his fingers. He looked McCallan in the eyes. 'In a nutshell, with the exception of a couple of smaller bequests, you, Mr McCallan, are the substantive beneficiary of your father's will. The lion's share of his estate goes to you.'

McCallan cleared his throat and nodded. 'I see,' he said hoarsely.

'Let me give you the details,' Morris said. 'The first bequest goes to Mrs Beth Benson, your father's housekeeper. He has left her £10,000, although I understand that rather tragically she has also died?'

'That's right,' Lomax said. 'Presumably, in that case, the money goes to her estate and will be subject to whatever provisions she has made in her own will?'

'Correct. If she has one.'

'Yes, if she has one,' Lomax echoed.

'Let me tell you what he wanted to say about her,' Morris went on and began to read. 'For many years she has been my housekeeper, constant, reliable, trustworthy, selfless. I hope she will enjoy this small gift and that she will spend it on herself shamelessly.' He smiled ruefully at the two men. 'A pity she won't be able to do so, isn't it?'

'Yes, it is,' McCallan said.

'The second bequest is to the Reverend Nigel Rogers. Your father says of him. "For some time he has been a confidant and a tremendous source of comfort to me. Through him, I have achieved a greater understanding of life and its meaning, a greater sense of self-awareness. I leave him £50,000 to do with as he pleases."'

McCallan's eyes widened. £50,000 to Rogers. He had not warmed to the cleric on their first meeting and he felt no better disposed towards him now. Could Roger have known about this, that he was going to benefit? Had his father dropped him any hint? Had he somehow wormed his way into his father's confidence in the hope of profiting from the relationship? But it was useless to think about that, annoying though it might be. What would he do about the matter? Nothing. It would seem uncharitable and dreadfully petty to betray even a hint of his thoughts.

'The third bequest,' Morris went on, 'is to you, Mr Lomax.'

Lomax started and seemed genuinely surprised. 'Me?'

'Yes. Mr McCallan says of you. "Henry Lomax has been my lifelong friend. No one will ever know the depth of the bonds that unite us. My life and his have been entwined inseparably. I can leave Henry Lomax nothing of any monetary value that can in any way make any material difference to him, such is the extent of his own wealth, but I leave him my two Tom Carr paintings, knowing his love of art and hoping that they will be a constant reminder of our friendship."'

Lomax took out his handkerchief and wiped a tear away. Then he blew his nose loudly. 'That's lovely,' he said quietly. 'Very nice indeed.'

'And finally,' Morris said, 'Mr McCallan says he leaves the rest of his estate, and I quote, "to my dear son Jack whose very life is a deeply precious thing to me. May it be a long and happy one, free from anguish and anxiety."' Morris stopped reading and looked up. 'And that's that,' he said.

'So, eh, forgive me.' McCallan's mouth was dry. 'What exactly does that mean?'

'It means that everything else is yours,' Morris said. 'Since I was in the position of looking after your father's affairs anyway, I was able to do a rough inventory for you. There's the house in Dromore, of course, and the area around it, the farmland and the old farmhouse and so on. Then there's the site in Donegal which is worth quite a bit. On top of that, your father had a number of shareholdings, the most substantial of which, of course, is his interest in LOC, one of Mr Lomax's companies. I've done a calculation of what the shares are worth at today's prices and I've made a stab at the value of the properties, plus, of course, there's what your father has on deposit in his account at the Ulster Bank and various securities. In all, even after the State has taken its share, I'd say you are about four million pounds better off.'

He sat back, looking like a small boy in a grown-up's chair, and waited for a reaction. McCallan could feel his face flushed. He stared at Morris, blinking stupidly, with those last words hanging in the air like smoke. Four million pounds better off.

Lomax leaned over and squeezed his shoulder. 'Congratulations, Jack, congratulations,' he said. 'I know it's very difficult for you. I know you'd rather the circumstances were different and so would I but . . . well, congratulations anyway.'

'Yes,' Morris said, 'it's quite a substantial inheritance. Now, the next question is, although it's not necessarily one we need to sort out today – what do you plan to do? There are one or two things that will need a bit of attention because other people are involved. The house in Donegal, for instance. Do you want the builder to continue? He'll certainly want to know what's happening so you'll have a bit of negotiation to do there. And what about Dromore? Are you going to live there? And if not, what happens if you sell? There are farmers leasing the land there as well as the woman renting the old farmhouse. They'll need to know.'

McCallan thought about his brief conversation with Ann Reilly after the funeral. Morris was right. He had decisions to make but he had a feeling he might have made them already.

'Jesus,' Lomax said to Morris. 'Don't bombard the poor fellow. This is a lot to take in.'

'No,' McCallan said, 'it's OK. It's best to sort all this out as soon as possible. Actually, I have been thinking about it, in the back of my mind somewhere. I think the answer to your question is: no, I won't be living at Dromore. I don't know what the future holds for me but I guess at least I'll be lucky enough to be in a position to choose. I certainly wouldn't choose to live there. It's not a house I was ever particularly fond of so I'll probably sell it. As for Donegal, the same thing. That was my father's idea, his little dream.

Maybe I'll try and do a deal with the builder to buy the whole property from me. Or better still, you could do it.'

Morris nodded. 'I could try.'

'Are you sure about all of this?' Lomax asked.

'As sure as I can be, Henry. This place isn't my home. I don't live here. With my father dead, what is there to keep me? The simplest thing is to get Mr Morris to handle my affairs and dispose of the property for me. It's the best thing all round, I think.'

Even as he said it, he knew what it would sound like to the other two men. It was as if, with insensitive haste, he were disposing of the last traces of his father, exchanging him for hard cash. All Morris had meant to do was leave him with some questions to think about, not to come up with answers straight away. But he had gone with his first instinct, which was to put all this behind him and bring the curtain down on everything that had happened in the past few days.

And then what?

He asked himself that later, back in Dromore, gazing out across the fields as the afternoon gloom and his doubts began to gather. In theory, he could now look forward – but what had he to look forward to? In his relationship with Julia, his lack of money had always niggled away at him and he had wondered how he could ever provide her with any kind of financial well-being. Now he had all the money he would ever need but there was no Julia. He felt anger stirring within him.

What was there for him back in England? An empty flat. Bitter memories. He knew for certain that he did not want to go back to management training in Northamptonshire so what would he have to occupy him? Maybe he would buy a new house. It would do no harm to have a look around, anyway, see what was on the market.

He stood up. Damn it, was that it? All there was? His father dead and buried and parcelled up, Julia consigned to the waste bin of experiences never to be repeated? It just could not be so . . . so neat and tidy.

He paced up and down the room. It felt unfinished. Somehow there had to be more.

He glanced at the table. There was a growing pile of letters of condolence, more of which had arrived today. He would have to get round to replying but not just yet, not this evening. He wanted first to skim through his father's papers. Maybe that would help him purge whatever it was from his system.

Down the hall was a little study. There would presumably be some things in the office at LOC but not much, he suspected. Most, if not all, of his father's documents would be in the desk in this study. He went through each drawer. It seemed to be all there: bank statements, share certificates, receipts going back years. His father had been a meticulous man. It would take him ages going through everything and he suddenly felt tired and not up to it tonight.

The bottom left-hand drawer of the desk was locked and it was a minute or two before he located the key, hidden at the bottom of a bowl containing paper clips and drawing pins.

The first thing he saw when he slid the drawer open was the gun.

It was a shiny black .22 automatic in a clip-on holster and there was a box of ammunition to go with it. Carefully, as if it were some rare and delicate museum exhibit, he took it out. It was in good working order and it contained a full clip of bullets.

When he put it back into the holster, he noticed that folded beside it was a piece of paper which, when opened out, revealed itself to be a firearms certificate authorising Robert McCallan to be the legal holder of this weapon. A personal protection weapon. Even now, in the stillness of this room, there were the faint vibrations of the past.

But why, after all this time, had his father felt he still needed a gun, one that he obviously kept well-maintained, not some wartime relic? It was a recognised entitlement, he supposed, but surely it was doubtful whether everyone in his father's position was similarly armed. Or was there an artillery of handguns out there, stored away in old policemen's bottom drawers?

A sudden image of the smouldering caravan flickered briefly in his mind's eye, almost subliminally. At that moment he admitted to himself that those doubts were still there, too. The existence of this gun, which he now replaced in the drawer, did nothing to dispel them.

Next he lifted out a grey folder. It contained several newspaper cuttings relating to terrorist incidents and police operations in the 1970s and 1980s. One report was about an IRA attack on a police patrol in South Armagh, an ambush in which all the members of the patrol were killed except for one policeman who had held the terrorists at bay until the Army arrived to relieve him. As ever in such reports, the police officer, for security reasons, was anonymous. But McCallan knew who it was and, as if to prove the point, in the drawer he also found a little hinged box which contained the gleaming British Empire Medal that his father had been awarded for his heroism that day.

He was about to put the folder back when he saw a cutting that he had almost missed. There was a photograph in it, faded and smudged, and he hardly recognised his mother from it. It was her obituary, taken from one of the local weekly papers, five short paragraphs, the summary recognition of a life. McCallan looked at the picture for a long time, trying to will from it, as he often did with the photograph on the mantelpiece in the living room, some sign of the personality beyond. But with every passing day it became more difficult to do so. Each day, his memories of his mother became that little bit more smudged and faded, just like this picture, and he wondered whether the same thing would eventually happen with his memories of his father.

In a cardboard box he found a collection of old snapshots. First there was his father as a young man at a passing-out parade, then with flak jacket and sub-machinegun in front of an armoured Landrover, but mostly they were pictures of him at work and play with various colleagues.

McCallan's attention was drawn to a woman in one of them. She was younger, certainly, but her identity was unmistakable. In the picture, Dorothy Taylor, his father and another man, all three in shirtsleeves, sat at a bar table crowded with glasses and beer bottles. Their faces were flushed and shining, lit up by the flash from the camera. Dorothy sat in the middle and the two men each had an arm round her shoulders. It would have been difficult for them to keep their hands off her, McCallan thought. She would have been a sexual magnet.

Behind them people were dancing. An RUC social evening of some kind. His father was thinner and fitter-looking, his dark hair showing just a trace of the silver that would distinguish him in later life. McCallan did not recognise the other man. He was more heavily built, fairish hair receding, and there was a cigarette in the hand that was not round Dorothy's shoulder.

He put the photograph back with the others and replaced everything he had taken out, feeling somehow that this drawer held more than just its material contents. He wondered how often his father had looked in here and what he saw when he did.

The only thing McCallan did not put back was the medal in its little case. Instead, he took it back down the hall into the sitting room where he opened it and put it on the mantelpiece between the pictures of himself and his mother. In a day or two he would return to London, to do what, he was not certain, but he would take the pictures with him, to display them somewhere in his flat. And he would take the medal, too. It had been hard earned and it would no longer be hidden away.

Chapter Thirteen

Nigel Rogers flung open the door of the rectory as soon as he saw McCallan park his car at the side of the kerb and start up the garden path. 'Come in, come in,' he said eagerly and beckoned McCallan inside.

Rogers wore jeans and track shoes and a sloppy sweater and in discarding his clerical garb he seemed also to have divested himself of the slightly patronising manner that McCallan had found so hard to take when they had first met. The rectory was a two-storey red brick house with old and undistinguished furniture that went with the premises rather than with the current tenant. There was a slightly fusty air but the smell of coffee, freshly brewed, cut through it invitingly.

'Come into the kitchen,' Rogers said, leading the way. 'You'll have coffee?'

'I'd love some,' McCallan said.

There was a woman drying her hands at the sink.

'It's all ready to pour so I'll leave you both to it,' she said.

She turned and smiled at McCallan. She was in her late twenties, dark curls to her shoulders, brown eyes in a face that was a little chubby. Like the rector, she wore jeans and a sweater.

'Jill Brown – Jack McCallan. Jill's my fiancée,' Rogers explained.

'Pleased to meet you,' she said and shook McCallan's hand. 'I'm sorry to hear about your father.'

'Thank you very much.'

She lifted a set of car keys from the kitchen table, then turned and kissed Rogers on the cheek. They hugged each other for a moment.

'The cups are on the work surface and there are biscuits in the cupboard if you want some. I'll be back about five. Bye.'

The kitchen door slammed behind her. 'Nice girl,' McCallan said.

'She's more than that. She's wonderful.'

McCallan looked at him a little quizzically.

'She doesn't live here, if that's what you're wondering,' Rogers said and then laughed. 'I think that would be a little too modern for the good parishioners of Dromore, not to mention the Select Vestry. They'd have me out on my ear if there were any remote suggestion of impropriety. The lace curtains would be throbbing with indignation. But we're getting married in the New Year, which is not too far away now, and we'll both be very relieved, I can tell you.'

He pulled a chair out from the kitchen table and motioned McCallan to sit down, then he poured two cups of coffee and placed a jug of milk and a sugar bowl on the table between them.

'Look,' he said, 'I rang you because I thought we should have a chat, clear up a few things. I got quite a shock when that solicitor called me yesterday and told me about your father's will. I just couldn't believe it. Then I started to wonder about how you would feel.'

He poured milk into his cup and sipped. It was very hot and he sucked air in to cool it. 'Let's be honest. For whatever reason, we didn't exactly hit it off the other day. You feel a bit of resentment about my friendship with your father and that's understandable. But when I heard about the £50,000 I knew it would make matters worse. I just wish he hadn't done that, I really do.'

McCallan looked at him, thrown off course. It was not just the matter of Rogers's frankness: it was the girl. He had come with preconceived notions of the sort of person he thought

Rogers was but he had not expected to find a fiancée, nor such a natural and relaxed display of affection as he had seen between them. It gave him a new perspective on the rector. There was a warmth about the man that would have been easy for his father to respond to. But there was anxiety in his eyes and McCallan could see that it was important to him that he should not be misunderstood, that his integrity should not be doubted. And if Rogers were prepared to put his cards on the table, then so was he.

'You're right,' he said. 'I wasn't too ecstatic about it either, to say the least. And since we're being honest, I did wonder about your motives, befriending a lonely old man, that sort of thing. But—' he raised his right hand as if taking an oath to dismiss the thought, now that he had uttered it – 'I'm prepared to say that it was wrong of me to think that. Had I known you better, it would probably not have crossed my mind. And I don't think a disagreement or a misunderstanding between us is at all desirable. It's not what my father would have wanted, I suspect.'

Rogers smiled and sighed with visible relief, then held out his hand. McCallan took it and the two men shook as if making a new start.

'Thank you,' Rogers said. 'You've no idea how much better that makes me feel. As for the money, let me tell you what's in my mind.'

'There's no need. It's yours to do whatever you want.'

'But I do need to tell you, you see. It's important to me that you know. I've been talking to some of the Select Vestry this morning and the Bishop as well, who was rather surprised to hear from me, out of the blue. I was more surprised that he even knew who I was, actually. Look, you've been in the church, Jack. You know how cold it is. For a long time we've wanted to put new heating in but there hasn't been any money. Now there is, thanks to your father's generous legacy to me.'

'I see. Well, if that's what you want—'

'It's what I want. And I think it's something your father would have approved of.'

He got up and brought the coffee pot over to refill their cups.

'Look,' he said with a worried frown, 'there's something else on my mind, something I've got to ask you.'

'Go ahead,' McCallan said, puzzled.

'Did you ever hear of a man named George Miller?'

'Well, I don't know. In what context exactly?'

'I'm not sure. Someone your father may have known?'

McCallan pondered for a moment and then shook his head. 'No, not that I can think of.'

Rogers sat down. 'I've got to level with you,' he said. 'Something was troubling your father deeply and the better I got to know him, the more I came to see it. Now, I don't know exactly what it was, he always held something back, but it was very disturbing for him. And I have to confess it was a bit disturbing for me as well.'

'What do you mean?' McCallan asked. He had begun to relax in Rogers's company but now he felt tense.

'He used to ring me at odd hours. You wondered the other day about his drinking. I didn't want to say. But sometimes when he rang he'd had far too much, that was obvious, and he'd – well – ramble on, is the only way I can put it, about something or other that had happened in the past. Whatever it was, he was absolutely consumed with pain about it and I gradually came to the conclusion that there was some connection between these . . . these inebriated outpourings and his rather recently found faith and fascination with religious belief.'

McCallan racked his own brain swiftly, although pointlessly, since the exercise turned up no clues to his father's distress.

'So where does this man Miller come in?'

Rogers drank and then nodded. 'I'm coming to that. One night, quite a few months ago, he rang me, very late on, quite clearly the worse for wear. I could hardly make out what he was saying, in fact. He wanted me to come over. I was very alarmed and I didn't feel I ought to ignore him but I couldn't leave straight away.'

He blushed slightly and McCallan suddenly had a vision of him and Miss Jill Brown locked in furtive, whispered passion somewhere upstairs.

'By the time I managed to get there, he seemed to be even more drunk. I went in through the kitchen and found him sitting at the table with a bottle of whisky on the floor, empty, and another one heading that way. But what was even more disturbing was the fact that he had a gun.'

'A gun?'

'Yes. It was a small automatic, I think. Quite a neat object, I recall, but it frightened the life out of me.'

'I came across it in a drawer yesterday. They issue them to some people for personal protection, just in case. The eternal hangover of the Troubles. But I never knew my father still had one.'

'Well, on this occasion he was in no state to be in charge of it, that's for sure. Frankly, I didn't think either of us were going to survive the night. He was muttering to himself and I could see he was completely gone with drink and didn't even realise I was there. I sat down at the table beside him and tried to talk to him gently but he didn't seem to notice. I wanted to get the gun away from him but I didn't want to do anything to alarm him in case he shot me.'

'This is dreadful,' McCallan said.

'Yes and it got worse, I'm afraid. All of a sudden he sat upright with the gun in his hand and put it to his head. He said something like. "One of these days we're all going to go like poor old George Miller." Those were roughly his words but I do remember the name very distinctly – George Miller. But then, to my horror, he pulled the trigger. The gun was pointed at his head and he pulled the damn trigger. There was just a click – no bullet, thank God – and I thought. 'To hell with it', and grabbed the thing from him before he did it again.'

Rogers scratched his forehead and ran his fingers through his hair. 'As soon as I got it away from him, he burst into tears. He just collapsed on to the table with his head in his hands. Somehow, I managed to manoeuvre him to his feet after a while and get him up the stairs to his room. God knows how I did it. The effort nearly killed me. When he hit the bed, he fell unconscious, thank goodness.'

'What happened then?'

'Well, I didn't think he'd wake up but I couldn't bet on it so I decided to stay the night to keep an eye on him. I thought I wouldn't be able to sleep, anyway. I was too hyped up by what had happened. I stuck the gun in a kitchen drawer and then I bunked down on the settee. I lay awake for hours but I must have dropped off eventually because the next thing I knew it was broad daylight and your father was standing there staring at me.'

He looked at McCallan and shook his head in disbelief as he relived the moment. 'I'll never forget it. He looked as fresh as a daisy. He was washed, dressed, the hair immaculate as usual, and the aftershave would have knocked you over. And of course, on the other hand, I felt as if I'd been run over by a bus.

'I remember that when he saw I was awake he held out his hand and there was the gun in the palm of it. 'I found it,' he said. "You hid it in the most obvious place." Then he smiled and said "Not a word about this to anyone – otherwise I might have to use this on you." After that he turned with a laugh and left the room and I could hear him opening and closing a drawer down the hall somewhere. I suppose he meant the remark as a joke but I can tell you I didn't find it funny. I felt chilled by it. And by the way, I haven't told anyone, not until now.'

He sat back in the chair. 'So there you have it. I feel bad about adding to your distress, as if you didn't have enough, but I really did think it was something you should know about. Quite honestly, when I heard your father had been killed, I wondered if he had committed suicide. But that wasn't the case.'

'No,' McCallan said. His voice was drained and empty as he tried to cope with this vision of his father lurching around on the edge of sanity.

'And you have no idea at all who George Miller might be?' Rogers asked.

'No,' McCallan said, and then a thought came to him. 'But I have an idea how I might find out.'

Chapter Fourteen

As soon as McCallan pushed the buzzer, the big wooden gates swung open slowly with a subtle electronic hum. He got back into his car and drove up the short, steep driveway. There would be security cameras somewhere but he could not spot them. Dorothy Taylor's sprawling bungalow could not be seen from the road. It was on a hill overlooking Belfast Lough and shielded from casual observation by tiers of other comfortable residences with picture windows, all of them competing for the best wide-screen view. But this house won hands down, McCallan thought, because of the added bit of height.

Exterior lights came on as he parked at the front and took in what was spread before him. On the far side was the County Antrim shore: miles and miles of strung-out lights, flickering and pulsating in the calm night air. To his left, there was the jewelled tiara of the city itself and the glittering diamonds and glowing opals of the waterfront where the tallest, newest buildings congregated and displayed their finery. But mostly there was the Lough, its soft black emptiness broken only by the flashing of marker buoys.

He rang the bell at the same moment Dorothy Taylor opened the door.

'How wonderful to see you,' she said, squeezing his shoulders in both hands and kissing him on the cheek. He could sense a potent blend of Givenchy and Glenfiddich. It was just after seven and she could not have been home all that long. She was still in her uniform although she had discarded the jacket and was in skirt and white shirt. She led the way down the hall and he was aware of the sound of her movement, the soft swish of shirt against skin, skirt against tights.

There was Scotch in the glass she had left in the living room when she had gone to open the door and a fire, not long going, blazed in the hearth. She lived on her own, there were no encumbrances such as husband or children, and he wondered if she had lit the fire herself, which he could not envisage somehow, or if there was someone else around to do that. A constable from the housework division of the Police Service, perhaps? Or would that be Home Affairs?

The room was comfortable if a little ordinary, with a deep carpet, voluptuous brocaded armchairs and framed prints of old Belfast on the walls. But the panorama from the big front window was all the décor it needed.

She walked over to the sideboard where there was an array of bottles like a miniature Manhattan skyline.

'Drink?'

'Scotch would be nice.'

She tilted a generous slug into a heavy crystal glass and handed it to him. They sat in front of the fire and she slid deeply into the softness of her chair, her right arm and the glass in her hand dangling carelessly over the side. Her eyes assessed him and he could see she was both relaxed and predatory, a lioness in her lair, and that the drink she now lifted to her lips was not her first.

'You're very like your father, you know. You've got the same bones, the same – I don't know – same manner about you. You remind me of him quite a lot, of when he was younger.'

The thought about her and his father was in his mind once more and he wondered if that was what she was trying to tell him. There was always the possibility, of course, that what she saw in him was a chance to make up for something which she had not been able to fulfil with Bob McCallan. She almost stretched out in the chair and he knew that if he put down his glass and went to her she would not resist him. It was there in her eyes, both an invitation and a challenge, and to his discomfort he felt himself beginning to become aroused.

He shifted his position and concentrated on why he had come, to tell her about his conversation with Nigel Rogers earlier in the day. While he spoke, he could see her mood change. She sat up as a wave seemed to flow through her, restoring the familiar poise that she had allowed to fall from her shoulders. She listened to him attentively for several minutes without saying a word.

'And so I wondered if the name George Miller would mean anything to you?' he asked at the end.

She still did not speak but got up and went to the sideboard, then brought back the bottle and splashed more whisky into their glasses.

She sat down again. 'George Miller,' she said. 'Yes, it does. It does mean something to me.' She drank and then stared into the fire. 'It's a name I haven't heard for quite a while. It's a bit of a shock to hear it again, out of the blue like that.'

She turned her gaze to him. 'George Miller was a detective in the RUC. Anti-terrorist work. A bit like me and your father. Twenty years ago it must have been, just before the Troubles ended for good, he was found shot dead in the car park of a pub – not very far from here, actually – along with a man who turned out to be a well-known Loyalist hood but also one of our informants or, at least, one of Miller's.'

She paused for thought. 'It was a very dirty business, very painful. You probably won't remember – you would have been quite young at the time – but the end took rather a long time coming. When were the ceasefires? 1995? No, 1994. Ran for about eighteen months, then the IRA got fed up with the British Government pushing them to hand in their weapons and set off a bomb at Canary Wharf in London. Two people were killed.

'People couldn't believe it, you know. Just couldn't believe they could go back to it. We'd even had President Clinton turning on the Belfast Christmas lights just a couple of months before. It was like VE day, thousands of people laughing and celebrating. Then it started again, like a bad dream.

'Anyway, it concentrated a few minds, one way or another. Politics got moving, there were hasty elections to a peace forum to pave the way for talks involving all parties, a way of bringing Sinn Fein and the Loyalists into some sort of electoral process. But still the Provos weren't handing in any weapons. They saw it as defeat, you see, a surrender, and there was no chance of them talking about a ceasefire again.

'And then – then the bodies starting turning up, all of them people who were leading figures in the IRA campaign. Not household names, exactly, but people who would have had a say on whether there was a ceasefire or not. Over a period of weeks, four were found shot dead and one was blown up in his car along with his wife.'

She got up from her chair and walked towards the window where she stood cradling her glass and looking out at the Lough. The faint spectre of her reflection gazed back at her. Far beyond, there were the lights of the ferry heading out of Belfast on its way to Liverpool.

'It was a hell of a thing,' she went on. 'Sinn Fein started ranting about Loyalist death squads and collusion with the Army, the usual stuff, but beneath all the bluster they had to be afraid, not knowing who would be next. In the climate of the time, though, a lot of people in the community didn't mind a bit. Revenge and recrimination were very much in the air. People had seen peace and prosperity snatched from before their eyes and they were angry about it.'

She turned from the window. 'There were a couple more bomb attacks, some in London and one in Belfast, shots fired at policemen, that kind of thing, as the IRA began to retaliate, and then came George Miller's murder. A gun was found in his car. Not the standard police issue. When it was examined by the ballistics people it was found to be the weapon that had been used in four of the murders.'

McCallan nodded. He had a vague memory of all of this although it was almost impossible for someone of his generation to be sure. The events that led to eventual peace seemed to be a violent blur.

Taylor went on: 'Then the BBC received a claim of responsibility from the IRA, apparently authentic, saying they had executed Miller and his informant and alleging they'd been the leaders of a murder conspiracy involving Loyalist terrorists and the security forces. Big headline news for that one, of course. But then confusion reigned when there was a second statement – again apparently authentic and from the IRA – saying they hadn't issued the first one and claiming Miller and his friend had been shot as part of an internal Loyalist feud. To make matters even more complicated, there were a couple of conflicting statements from the Loyalist side, one saying they'd been responsible for the whole assassination campaign and the other saying they hadn't. Curiouser and curiouser.'

She walked back across the room and sat down again. 'In the end, no one knew what to believe, other than that someone was stirring the shit in a big way. Some people even claimed that the whole thing, from start to finish, was part of some sort of bizarre MI5 plot. And I must confess I wondered about that myself. Had the dirty tricks department been mixed up in it all somehow? I don't think we'll ever know.'

'At any rate,' she said and drank from her glass, 'after Miller's death there were no more assassinations and the IRA eased off again, too. Then the business about the gun was leaked before the Chief Constable had had a chance to review the investigation into Miller's death and make a statement about it. Somehow one of the papers got hold of the information and you can imagine the fall-out. Accusations of cover-up, calls for the Chief's resignation, the lot.

'At the end of it all, when the dust settled, there was the inescapable conclusion that George Miller had been behind the murders, setting the victims up, using security force intelligence files – some documents about certain individuals were actually found in his desk – and getting Loyalist hitmen to do the job.'

A hot coal fell onto the hearth tiles and startled them both. Taylor bent forward with a pair of fire tongs and dropped it back in.

'But,' she said, 'it would seem that it had the desired effect. There never was another IRA ceasefire, not officially, nor was there any formal decommissioning of weapons either, but it was clear that the appetite for what was inevitably going to be an endless cycle of violence had gone. The Provos reckoned that if they could be hit like this once, it could happen again, and their families had had enough, I suppose.

'It wasn't long before the first weapons started turning up. Tip-offs to the police in the South. Underground bunkers full of AK-47s and Semtex being discovered. After that, the whole political process started gathering pace. There was a huge momentum for change and for real peace, something that would last longer than a year or eighteen months.

'A big focus of attention was the question of how Northern Ireland was to be policed. The RUC had been a seriously flawed organisation for a long time in the minds of a great many people. The Miller affair could be added to a list of other misdemeanours that had gone before it and so it was really only a matter of time before it would be replaced by another force, more acceptable to all. And, eventually, after a few years, that's what happened.'

When she had finished, they sat in silence for a few moments, allowing the ripples of history to subside. But McCallan's mind was on the more recent past.

'Why on earth, after everything that's happened since, would this man Miller be on my father's mind now? And why did he still feel the need to keep a weapon at home? It all started me thinking again. About how he died – you know?'

'Oh, Jack, don't torture yourself about the accident. Believe me, we have to accept that that's what it was. It makes us all uncomfortable, of course, because of the way it happened. Maybe it could have been avoided if . . . well . . .'

'If he'd been sober, you mean?'

She shrugged uneasily and then moved on. 'As for the gun, I wouldn't read anything into that. We've started pruning back now. The personal protection licences come up annually and a lot of them aren't being renewed any more. We need to wean some of the old veterans off the notion that they're still under some kind of threat. We obviously hadn't got round to your father yet.'

She paused. 'By the way, to answer your question. George Miller and your dad were colleagues once. Did you know that?'

He shook his head. 'No, I didn't.'

'Well, they were,' she said. 'Your dad was very fond of Miller, I remember. He was very cut up about his death, both the fact that it had happened and what he'd been up to. It was a big blow to a lot of people.'

She sighed. 'You don't always see the pain. It lasts long and runs deep. He'd obviously had rather a lot to drink that night and all the old anguish was coming out and there was no one he could talk to who would understand or care. You don't live through an era like that without its leaving scars, Jack. Believe me, I know.'

'Did you know Miller?'

'Only vaguely. We overlapped very briefly as part of the same unit before he moved on somewhere else. I don't really recall him all that well.'

She offered him another drink but he declined with a smile. 'Not a very good idea,' he said. 'I don't want to get stopped by the police.'

'So what did the clergyman, your friend Rogers, make of it all?' she asked. 'Had George Miller's name ever come up before?'

'I don't think so. That's what made this all the more

unusual. He found it very frightening, naturally enough, sitting there with a drunk man waving a gun about.'

'I'll bet. Mind you, I'm not sure he should have mentioned it to you. Your father's death is distressing enough for you without that.'

'No, he was right to let me know. I'm finding out a lot of things – about his state of mind, the drinking and so on. It's not a pretty picture exactly but I think I'd rather people didn't leave me under any illusions. I don't like the idea of anyone knowing something and me being totally in the dark about it. I only wish – it's funny – I only wish I could talk to my dad and try to straighten it all out. But that won't be possible.'

'I doubt if it would be possible even if he were still alive. Forgive the amateur psychoanalysis, but it was probably a combination of things. Rogers may just have seen a symptom of it. It was life, really, the past – all those years of living with the fear of violence, either to himself or to others, the fact that he'd survived whereas a lot of his colleagues hadn't. Perhaps in his darker moments he felt guilty about that.'

McCallan looked at her. What she said made sense, based as it was on her knowledge of his father and the way life was here, but it did not make him feel any more at ease. And as he left the house and her goodbye wave at the door and slowly weaved his way down the winding hill towards the main road, he could not rid his mind of the picture it held of his father at the table with the gun.

Chapter Fifteen

McCallan opened his eyes and saw the dusty paper shade dangling from the ceiling. For a fraction of a second he did not know where he was and then he remembered. It was Sunday morning and he was in his flat.

He had flown back last night with a lot to think about, including a meeting with Tim Ewing over dinner tonight. He had found Heathrow unusually busy and noisy and London was grimy and miserable with air that left a sulphurous taste at the back of his throat.

He rolled over and his head touched the pillow beside him. There was the faint hint of perfume on it, fleeting, a last echo of Julia dying away.

This is the real reason you have come back, he thought, sitting up abruptly and clasping his arms round his knees. Your anger has brought you here.

He got out of bed and went to the bathroom, then came back and got dressed, feeling agitated. He went into his kitchen, which was really just an alcove off the living room, and made coffee. God, this place was tiny. The flat was in a fairly modern block in a warren of streets in Earls Court. There was a little enclosed central courtyard and as he drank his coffee he looked down on it, at the handful of bedraggled shrubs and the grimy little pond that the architect had placed there as an environmental gesture, and he felt a growing claustrophobia as he compared this to his surroundings of the past week. This was no match for the raw beauty of Donegal or the open sweep of the County Down countryside, even allowing for the cold and the damp which had got to him so much.

He needed to get out. He threw the remains of his coffee down the sink and grabbed his keys. A matter of minutes later he had retrieved his car from the lock-up garage where he kept it and was driving up Holland Park, virtually around the corner from where he lived but a whole world away.

He found the road he was seeking. There was no traffic on it. Rain had begun to fall, a thin drizzle that left an irritating film on the windscreen as he peered out, looking along the white-painted terrace for the house he wanted. Each one was a minor mansion with dignified pillars and some had colourful doors in defiant reds and pinks. Round the windows knotted wisteria hibernated until the spring but none of the houses showed any sign of life, nor gave any clue to who lived inside.

He located the number he was looking for and parked opposite. Even in surroundings of such privacy, this house was particularly anonymous. There were heavy curtains across all the windows and in the downstairs rooms the shutters had been closed. The place looked sealed and he wondered where she and her husband had gone.

He sat and looked at the building for a few minutes, feeling even more empty and abandoned than before, trying to picture its elegant interior. He had been in the house only twice in the past few months but had not lingered. They had certainly not made love there, feeling uncomfortable about being together under the roof which Daniel Shriver had provided.

He was distracted from his thoughts by the sound of a door opening and closing. An elderly man in hat and raincoat came out of the next house with an energetic West Highland terrier on a lead. As he passed, he put his collar up and gave the car and its occupant a curious stare.

He will wonder what I am doing here, McCallan thought.

It was a good question. He turned the ignition, put the car into gear and drove off. There was nothing for him here. Nothing at all.

And that, although he left out any reference to Julia or his visit to Holland Park, was what he told Tim Ewing over dinner several hours later. On the other hand, there were things in Northern Ireland that did need his attention. And so he had decided that, rather than abandoning everything, taking the money and leaving it all to the solicitor to sort out, he would deal with his father's affairs himself and he would seek Henry Lomax's help as a financial adviser. There was no one better.

Next day he packed a couple of suitcases into his car, had all his calls redirected to his father's number in County Down and set off for the ferry terminal at Stranraer in Scotland and the late afternoon crossing to Belfast.

It was a bracing voyage through a grey swell in the gathering dusk. He had brought some of his father's bank papers to London with him and as he sat at a table in the sparsely occupied coffee lounge, he began to go over them, making notes when he found anything that had to be checked, looking through the statements for various standing orders that would need to be sorted out. But he found it hard to take his eyes off the figures in the balance: solid, black, substantial and now his.

He lifted his coffee at the same moment as the ferry lurched heavily. He swore as he spilled it on the table and the papers he had spread out, leaving them soggy and steaming. He got a cloth from the waitress at the coffee bar and began to mop the mess up carefully. As he dabbed at a bank statement, he saw one line that he had not noticed before, the withdrawal several months ago of £100,000.

He wondered where the money had gone or what it was for. It was an unusually large sum. Perhaps it might have something to do with the building work in Donegal, a stage payment of some kind. If so, it was certainly quite a lot.

But he had already decided that tomorrow he would seek an appointment with his father's bank manager. It would be another thing to ask him about.

It was evening and dark by the time the vessel docked. McCallan drove into Belfast and on out towards his part of County Down. The village of Dromore was quiet and closed for the evening as he went through it and on up the road towards his father's place.

Passing the old farmhouse, he saw a light in the curtained kitchen window and he remembered Ann Reilly. It occurred to him that he really should tell her what was happening. Not that he had totally made up his mind, but it was likely he would sell the whole property, the farmhouse and farmland, and put the money to good use by investing it. He smiled to himself. It was like playing Monopoly.

McCallan looked at his watch and decided it was not too late to call. He stopped at a gateway, reversed and turned, then drove back and up the farmhouse lane. At the end of it, he parked behind a small Japanese four-wheel drive. Getting out, he thought he heard music and as he walked towards the front door he knew he had. The voice of an operatic tenor came loudly from the house. Verdi or Puccini. He was not sure which.

There was no bell so he rapped the door but did not get a reply, just the continuing melodrama of the opera. He tried again and after waiting for a while, decided to go round the back to the kitchen door. The music was louder there and he could also hear the sound of someone moving about inside, rattling dishes. He knocked loudly but still he could not compete.

He turned the handle and as he opened the door, the voice of the tenor burst out past him into the dark night air. Ann Reilly was over at the work surface, half facing away, and as she turned she started at the shock of seeing him standing there. She had a mug of tea in her hand and it fell from her grasp, smashing on the tiled floor.

It was an awful mess. He tried to shout his apologies over the noise coming from the CD player on a table in the corner. Ann went over and turned it off and they both looked at each other in an awkward moment of silence.

McCallan spoke first. 'God, I didn't mean to frighten you like that. I . . . well, I was passing so I thought I'd call and say hello.'

'Well then – hello.' She smiled.

'Here,' he said, 'let me clear it up.'

They both did in the end, he picking up fragments of enamel, she finishing off the exercise with a mop and bucket. He apologised some more but she told him not to be so silly, it was an accident, and when they had cleaned everything up she poured two more mugs of tea, still hot, out of the spacious pot from which the first one had come.

They sat down at the table and it reminded him with a jolt that this was like the first conversation he had had with Julia, when they had sat with a bottle of wine at that party all those months ago. But Ann Reilly was not like Julia Shriver. There was not the soft allure although she was undeniably attractive, with an easy, long-limbed physical grace. She was dressed in a loose grey jogging suit and well-worn track shoes. Her hair seemed slightly damp and hung loose, softening the contours of her face.

She was not wearing her glasses and he was immediately taken by the emerald green of her eyes and the assured way she held his gaze. She kicked off her shoes and pulled her feet on to the chair, folding her legs up to her chin. She looked very fit and he told her so.

'I try to keep in shape,' she said. 'These roads are good for running. Plenty of hills to test the cardio-vascular system.'

'You want to be careful at night, though,' he said, 'especially in the rain. My father's housekeeper was killed along this road just the day before he was. She fell off her bicycle and broke her neck, poor woman.'

'Yes, I heard. It was a strange thing to happen. Both of

them, you know – so close together. But don't worry about me. I can take care of myself.'

'Except when you have the music on too loud and don't hear people sneaking up on you.'

She gave a wry smile. 'Point taken. I'll keep it low.'

'Or else lock the door.'

He looked around the room. There was a fragrance in the air and on the mantelpiece he saw a candle under an aromatic burner. The kitchen, which doubled as a sitting room, was spacious but cluttered. A worn bed settee and two uncomfortable-looking wooden armchairs were arranged around an old solid-fuel range which had seen better days, a great many of them, but the heat that spread from it was relaxing. There were books and papers on the floor and on the long table where the CD player sat there was a computer terminal with its screen saver creating a pattern of coloured waves. Notebooks and printed pages were littered alongside.

Ann got up abruptly and went over to the player. In a moment, the sound of Chopin came from it, much more muted than the opera had been.

She sat down again. 'Maybe that's a bit more suitable. Opera's something you need to concentrate on. But I have to have music all the time, no matter what I'm doing. Working, whatever. It keeps me company.'

He nodded towards the computer. 'Have you been working tonight?'

'Yes, just tidying up some notes.' She remembered something and her eyes widened. 'Oh yes. You asked me what I did and I said I'd explain it to you sometime. Oh well, I'd better do that now, hadn't I?'

She pulled her chair closer to the table and sat forward towards him. 'First thing to clear up. I'm not a university lecturer, as you seemed to think, although I am involved in something academic, that's true. Actually, I'm a lawyer. Not in private practice, or anything. My full-time job's with the Department of Justice in Dublin but at the moment I'm on a career break which will take me up until the end of this year.'

'So what's the connection here?'

'Prisons.'

'Prisons?'

'Prisons. I've always been fascinated by the penal system in this country and what we do with people when we lock them up. I did some research on it as part of a social science module when I was at university – God, that seems a long time ago now, I can tell you – but I always wanted to pick it up again. It's such an interesting subject, well, to me anyway – the different approach in the two parts of the island, the whole legacy of the terrorist years. We've got some of the best-equipped prisons in Europe as a result of the Troubles, particularly here in the North, and a much more enlightened and liberal approach to educating and reforming the offender.'

'I see,' McCallan said politely.

Ann smiled. 'No, not yet you don't. I put my thoughts down on paper, how I'd like to do a comparison of the system, North and South, and I applied for a grant to the International Institute for Irish Studies. Lo and behold, they said yes, told me they liked the idea and would publish it when I had it finished. Shall I make more tea?'

'Not for me, thanks. I'm fine.'

'The reason I'm here, in County Down, is that there's a prison not far away – Maghaberry. You've been past it, I'm sure?'

McCallan nodded. In the early days of the conflict, the Government had introduced internment without trial, a brief and ill-judged piece of policy that had stiffened Republican support and resolve rather than diminishing it. One early morning in 1971, hundreds of suspects had been rounded up by the Army and herded off to a prison camp constructed on the flat fields at Long Kesh outside Lisburn. When internment ended, Long Kesh remained, refurbished and renamed the

Maze prison, until gradually, over the years, its inmates were either released back into the community when they had served their time or transferred to a new jail which had been built at Maghaberry, a few miles away. A revamped and reconstructed Maghaberry was still much in use, a very model of a modern penal institution, although many of the drug-dealers, murderers and criminals of various kinds who languished inside it were the offspring of the terrorist inhabitants of the past.

'I wanted to base myself somewhere near it,' she went on. 'I've already done half the research, at Portlaoise prison down south, and when I was doing that I rented somewhere nearby. It was a good idea and I wanted to do the same thing here. Part of what I want to write about is the effect these prisons have, socially and economically, on the rural communities in which they're built. You get great, big posh housing developments springing up, for example, all full of prison officers forming a sort of community of their own. I wanted to talk to the prison staff as well as the prisoners, visit them at work and in their homes.'

McCallan studied her as she paused to sip from her cup. She used her hands a lot as she spoke, her long, thin fingers outstretched and taut. There was a remarkable intensity in her demeanour.

'Anyway,' she said, 'I had this flat in Lisburn which was too expensive for me, much more than my budget could afford, but I really wanted to be out in the countryside. One day I was having my car looked at by the dealer in Dromore and we got talking and he told me about this place. I had a look at it and then rather brazenly knocked on your father's door one day and asked him if he would like to rent it. He was a bit reluctant and said he'd think about it, that it wasn't in very good repair. I told him I didn't mind as long he didn't charge me too much.'

She laughed. 'I think he thought I was a bit cheeky but I didn't care. About a week later I called again and he told me to ring his solicitor who would fix everything up.

I've got an agreement until December 31st. The rent's dirt cheap, thank goodness, the place will do me for a while and so here I am.'

McCallan could see why the rent was low. He could feel a draught from the windows which undoubtedly needed to be replaced. There was no central heating and the rest of the house was probably freezing, damp as well, most likely, but in here she had managed to make maximum use of what cosy charm the place had. He felt uncomfortable about talking of selling but, on the other hand, if she was going back to Dublin at the end of the year, it might not make any difference.

'That's fascinating,' he said. 'I'd love to see what you've written when you've finished.'

'No, you wouldn't,' she told him. 'You're just saying that to be nice. You'd find it dry and boring.'

'Well then, I won't bother.'

'Very sensible. So tell me what's happening. Do I still have a roof over my head or are you going to chuck me out on my ear?'

She was direct, that was for sure, and he could not sidestep the topic now.

'Not if you're planning to leave at the end of the year anyway. Actually, I did want to talk about that. It's really why I called, to be honest, to put you in the picture. I think I am going to sell the place but now that you explained your timetable I'll wait until you've gone.'

'That's thoughtful.'

He shrugged. 'Practical, too. It's one thing less to have to think about just at the moment. My father's death has rather altered my centre of gravity. He was generous enough to leave me with considerable financial security but I can't duck the responsibilities that go with it.'

She frowned slightly. 'I suppose not.'

'I haven't always been sensible about money matters but I think I owe it to him to be a little bit more level-headed, try to have a bit more sense of purpose than I've had for a while.'

'You could be forgiven for not wanting to take life too seriously.'

'What do you mean?'

'Your father told me what happened to you. Getting shot in Nigeria. I think if it were me and I'd come through something like that, I'd be inclined not to give a toss about anything.'

'That's all right for a while but now I reckon it's time I started to grow up again.'

He thought for a moment. 'So you'd been talking about me?'

'Sshh,' she said, holding her hand up abruptly to stop him saying any more. She closed her eyes as she waited for a familiar virtuoso passage in the music. She smiled sensuously as she listened and when the moment had passed she opened her eyes again and came back.

'I love that bit. Yes,' she said, 'he used to drop in every now and then for a cup of coffee and a chat. I think he got a bit lonely sometimes. He talked about you a lot. I got the impression of a very devoted and grateful father.'

She frowned. 'I was so sorry to hear he had died. It was an awful thing to have happened.'

He realised as she spoke that he was glad she had been at hand for the old man. He would have been quite taken by her, the theatre tickets were ample evidence of that, but he was also aware of being drawn to her himself.

He looked at his watch. 'God, it's late. I'd better go.'

'Stay as long as you like.'

'No – it's time I left. I've got a call to make anyway.'

He stood up and she walked with him to the door. When she opened it she turned and to his surprise gave him a quick hug.

'What's that for?'

She shrugged. 'I dunno. I just thought you might need it.'

They looked at each other.

'Look . . . Do you think we might, you know, go out

or something?' he asked, fumbling uncharacteristically for words.

'That would be nice.'

'Well, then, what—'

'Why don't I ring you or maybe call by the house and see how you're getting on?'

'Great. If you're sure.'

She smiled confidently. 'I'm sure.'

Chapter Sixteen

In the morning, McCallan called his father's bank and asked to speak to the manager. He reached a secretary who stonewalled for a bit and then the manager came to the phone eagerly.

'Mr McCallan,' he said. 'So sorry about your father. What can I do for you?'

'I wondered if we could have a talk.'

'Of course. When? I'm free now, if it suits you.'

Half an hour later, he was ushered into a compact office at the back of the Ulster Bank in Lisburn. God, they were all so young, part of a whole new generation that seemed to be running this country. First Andrew Morris, the solicitor, now this man, coming round the desk enthusiastically to shake his hand.

McCallan put him at about thirty and he was obviously going places if he was in charge of such a big branch at that tender age. He was long and thin in a dark double-breasted suit and he had soft fair hair which was swept straight back from his face. He motioned McCallan towards a small two-seater settee.

They settled themselves awkwardly, two tall men in an inadequate space, and as they did so, McCallan glanced at the nameplate on the desk although it was a name which had already imprinted itself on his brain from the conversation on the phone. Darryl Paisley.

The young manager saw the look and recognised it.

'No, no relation,' he declared with mock firmness.

'I'm sorry. Was it that obvious?'

'Most people ask and if they don't I know they want to so I try to get it out of the way early.'

The exchange broke the ice and after a little more small talk, McCallan filled Paisley in on the details of his father's will. There were still formalities to be gone through, of course, but once that was done, he said, he wanted to transfer his father's funds to an account which he would open in his own name. Such an arrangement would suit him, at least for the time being.

Paisley expressed his delight, relishing the prospect of holding on to such valuable business.

'If there's anything at all I can do, anything, you know you only have to ask.'

'Well, there is one thing,' McCallan said, unzipping the document case he had brought with him and taking out the bank statement, stiff with coffee stains. 'I wonder what this is.'

His finger pointed to the line showing the £100,000 withdrawal.

Paisley raised an eyebrow as he looked at the page. He did not know offhand but strictly speaking it was none of McCallan's business; it was a regular, proper transaction which had taken place long before his father's death. Still, you did not risk losing such a client by telling him to get lost.

'Let's see,' he said, getting up and going over to the computer terminal on his desk. The keyboard rattled under his fingertips.

'There we are.' There was a click and the soft rhythm of the printer and then Paisley passed over a sheet of paper.

McCallan stared at it. The sum of £100,000 had been paid by cheque to the firm of McCaughey and Granleese, solicitors.

The evening flight from Bristol was due into Belfast Harbour airport at six thirty but it was almost seven by the time the automatic doors parted and Gavin Pierce strode out of the terminal into the cool air. There was one of those hit-and-run breezes that whipped round the corner of the building and he remembered that it had been a night like that when he had last stood on Northern Ireland soil, a long, long time ago.

Waiting in his mac beside the car, Mattheson watched Pierce approach and took in the dark wool Italian overcoat he wore and the soft leather hold-all he carried. They had not met before but there was a mutual, instant recognition, almost as if they had caught each other's scent in the wind.

He opened the rear door and Pierce slid in.

'Good flight?' Tweed asked as they moved off. He was driving as usual.

Pierce did not answer him but looked towards Mattheson in the passenger seat.

'What did you get?'

'It's on the floor beside you.'

Pierce reached down and lifted a plastic carrier bag. From it, he took a pistol lodged in a clip-on holster. The gun was of Czech manufacture and could be used single shot or rapid fire. It was fully loaded but there were a couple of cartons of ammunition to go with it.

'It's clean,' Mattheson said. 'No previous CV to worry about.'

Pierce clipped the gun to his belt and slipped the ammunition into his hold-all. Then he sat back in his seat and looked out of the window on to a Belfast he hardly recognised.

Half an hour later, Jack McCallan put his raincoat on, closed the front door behind him and stepped into the back of the silver Daimler that had been sent for him.

After leaving Ann Reilly last night, he had called Lomax to tell him he was back in Northern Ireland and that he had decided to try to take care of his father's affairs himself. Lomax had sounded surprised but rather pleased, then suggested having dinner and said he would provide a car. McCallan had agreed, since it would allow him to have a few drinks without having to worry about driving.

'But this time,' he had said, 'I'm paying. I can afford it now.'

As the Daimler sped quietly along the road towards the Belfast motorway, he settled into its leathery softness and thought about the events of the day. Paisley had been helpful but limited; he had been able to show where the £100,000 had gone but not why. So when he had left the bank, McCallan had called McCaughey and Granleese and asked for Mr Morris, who was away, his secretary said, and would not be back until tomorrow. Whether this was true or not, McCallan had no way of knowing but he had made an appointment to see Morris the following morning.

He looked thoughtfully out of the car window, wondering whether he should mention any of this to Lomax. He decided not to. Whatever this was, it was personal business of his father's. Anyway, he had other things to tell Henry about.

They had reached the city but had by-passed the centre by cutting along the West Link and now they were on the Lagan Bridge heading east. Below them, the blue lights of the weir were reflected in the ripple of the river as it made its way out to where it merged into Belfast Lough, which was just a little too far away to be seen in the dark.

The Daimler left the bridge and turned towards what had once been part of the docks until with the coming of peace it had gradually been transformed. Now, as the car travelled along, it passed languid waterfront apartment houses, colourful bistros and elegant shops which sold designer clothes.

It stopped outside a restaurant with frosted glass windows which seemed to glow. There was no sign above the door. Inside, the furniture was period chrome and leather, what used to be known as hi-tech, and the floor was polished black wood. The walls were stark and white and on them hung several abstract paintings that were a violent splash of colour.

Lomax was at a table at the back where a huge window looked out on to the river and provided a view of the waterfront that made Belfast look like a bonsai New York. He stood when he saw McCallan come in, then hugged him vigorously before they sat and got down to the important business of the menu.

Almost at the same time, Tweed switched to sidelights and turned slowly down the laneway to McCallan's house. McCallan's own car was parked at the front so he reversed gently into the deep shadows at the side, then turned the engine and the lights off.

For five minutes, the three men sat still, listening and watching for any hint that there might be someone in the house, even though it was dark and unlit. Then Mattheson and Tweed put on the thin leather gloves they had worn the last time they were here and got out. Pierce stayed where he was. Tweed took a small briefcase from the boot and they walked round to the front of the house.

'Talkative bastard, isn't he?' he said. 'What the hell do we have to have him tagging along for anyway?'

'Somebody else's idea. An extra precaution. Ours not to reason why.'

Tweed shivered. 'He gives me the creeps.'

Mattheson took a set of keys from his pocket and opened the door.

When they were inside, Pierce got out of the car. He walked round the outside of the house, peering at it in the gloom. Not bad, he reflected, but nothing like his own place, not nearly as impressive.

There was the sound of a car engine. Lights were coming down the lane.

He pressed himself into the bushes as a Japanese four-wheel drive swung confidently up to the front door. There was nothing he could do to warn the men in the house but they would have heard the noise anyway. They would freeze where they were and wait for the visitor to go away.

But there was the police car. Big and black and looking every inch what it was.

Someone got out of the vehicle. A woman. He could hear the muffled ring of the doorbell inside the house. Then he heard the sound of the back door opening and closing softly.

But not softly enough. Not clever, Pierce thought.

The woman had heard the noise as well. She turned away from the front door and began to walk round the side.

She stopped in her tracks when she saw the big car sitting there, then started to walk slowly towards it.

She had her back to Pierce and he could not afford to let her see any more.

He stepped forward swiftly and used his right hand to give a short, sharp sideways chop to the carotid artery.

McCallan found that when it came to it he did not feel much like drinking although Lomax made up for him, replenishing his own wine glass liberally throughout the meal. McCallan brought him up to date about why he had decided to stay for a while, although he was not entirely clear about his reasons himself, other than feeling the need to do something responsible. Then he told him about his conversation with Nigel Rogers and the horror story of his father and the gun.

'Do you remember the George Miller business?' he asked.

While McCallan had been talking, Lomax's face seemed to have become darker, whether from the drink or blood pressure he was not sure, but he looked brooding and a little dangerous and the good cheer had gone from him.

'Oh, I remember him all right, poor bastard. Murdered and then disgraced for doing what a lot of people thought should have been done a long time ago. Yes sir, I remember him.'

'I never ever heard my father mention his name,' McCallan said. 'Don't you think that's a bit odd?'

'Why should it be odd? Your father wasn't a man to dwell on the past, especially on those things which hit him badly. I dare say he didn't talk much about your mother, either.'

McCallan nodded. That was true. Her name had rarely been mentioned over the past few years and when it had, usually by McCallan himself, his father had got rid of the topic as quickly as possible, answering in monosyllables as if it made him uncomfortable.

'Look out there,' Lomax said, pointing towards the glitter of the city. It looked confident and secure, the glass towers of the business houses beacons of prosperity. Lomax's own building seemed to stand out from the rest, lit in a distinctive electric blue. It was not the World Trade Center exactly but it was the centre of his world, his trade.

He went on. 'We wouldn't have any of that if people hadn't been prepared to take risks, stayed firm, stood up to these bastards and shown them they couldn't win, that the only bit of Ireland they were going to end up with was six foot deep and the dimensions of a coffin. Maybe if they'd been faced up to before, we wouldn't have had to wait so long, gone through so much bloodshed.'

'But, Henry, you can't condone what Miller did. You can't condone murder.'

'It was war. A lot of people didn't think about it as murder, still don't. Have you ever killed anyone?'

'What?' He looked round the room to see if any of the other diners were listening but they were not paying any attention.

'You heard me. Have you ever killed anyone?'

McCallan paused thoughtfully. 'I think so.'

'What do you mean – you think so?'

'I mean I think so,' he said, a little indignantly. 'I was involved in various operations in my time, where there was shooting. I returned fire and saw people go down, that's all.'

'And did you think of it as murder?'

'No, of course not. But that was different. It was a question of survival.'

'And so was this. Men like George Miller died so that this place could survive – survive and grow to be the way it is. It's just a pity they couldn't live to see it.'

He drank from his glass, almost a signal that the conversation was at an end, and McCallan decided it was time to go. It was not the first occasion he had heard Lomax on this topic and had had to listen to the old bitterness – indeed, he had been hearing it for most of his life – but he still marvelled at how Henry, who was probably the richest man in Northern Ireland, sometimes managed to make it sound as if fate had dealt him a bad hand.

The Daimler was warm when he got back into it and he was asleep before they had reached the other side of the city. He knew nothing more until someone spoke and woke him.

It was the driver. 'There's something happening, sir,' he said.

McCallan sat up and blinked. They were creeping down the laneway to his house where there were flashing blue lights and policemen looking in their direction.

Chapter Seventeen

McCallan stood with his hands on his hips and looked round the living room once more. Everything seemed to be in place. The Tom Carr paintings were still on the walls and nothing had been moved or disturbed. He and the two policemen beside him had switched on all the lights in the house and gone through each room but the story was the same: it was exactly as he had left it, apart from the fact that Ann Reilly's four-wheel drive was parked at the door.

One of the officers was explaining what had happened.

'She must have disturbed them,' he said. 'She saw your car and rang the doorbell but there was no reply and then she thought she heard a door closing at the back, although it appears to be locked so she might have been mistaken about that. It could be that what she heard was someone trying to get in. We've dusted the windows and doors for fingerprints but there's not much likelihood of picking anything up.

'Apparently she started round the side of the house and noticed a car parked there and then someone hit her on the back of the head. When she came to, the car was gone but she has a phone in her own vehicle and she called for help.'

'Which hospital has she been taken to?'

'The Lagan Valley in Lisburn. I think she cut her knee when she fell. Nothing too serious, though. She seems to have got off lightly, to be honest. God knows what might have happened to her.'

McCallan frowned as he closed the door on the departing

policemen. He had questions. If someone had been in the house, how had they got in? And what had Ann being doing here? He would get the answer to that himself when he went to the hospital in a couple of minutes. The rest was not so easy.

There was no evidence of a break-in at all and if Ann had not come on the scene, he would not have known anyone had been here. She must have interrupted them before they got started.

He walked into the kitchen. She had to be wrong about the back door. He had locked it before going out and it was locked now.

But if she was right? He stood and looked at it.

If she was right, it could mean that someone else had a key.

As far as he was aware, the only person apart from himself who had one was Grace Walker; she would have her sister's, of course. But that was stupid. What would she be doing snooping around here at night?

Ann's story suggested more than one person, anyway. And there was another thing. How had they known there was no one in? Had they been watching the house and seen him go out?

Each question in his mind led to another, all of them impossible to resolve. House-breaking was rife in this part of the world, the police had told him before they left, and remote properties like this were done over on a regular basis, often in broad daylight with people driving vans up to the door when the owners were out and even loading the furniture in.

But somehow McCallan felt this incident was different. There were now too many things that were not quite right. Each one on its own – no problem. But coming together – that was another matter. There was his father's odd behaviour and his very death itself. There was Beth Benson's accident, too. What were the odds of those happening more or less simultaneously? And now there was this, the break-in that wasn't.

He felt uneasy, as if there were ghosts watching him. He needed to talk to Ann but first he would have another quick look round to see if there was anything he had missed.

The gun. Damn it, he had forgotten that.

He hurried to the study but the desk was still locked and the key was where he had left it. He opened the drawer. It was all there, the gun, the ammunition, the firearms certificate and the other bits and pieces. It was time he handed it in. But perhaps he would not do so for a day or two, just in case.

He drove to the hospital in Ann's vehicle, purely out of curiosity. It was nippy and responsive and he quite liked the feel of it on these country roads. She kept the interior very clean and tidy, no back-seat litter. The only touch of personality was the CD that began to play as soon as he switched on the ignition. He found the box in the glove compartment. Richard Strauss. He listened as he drove but turned it off after a while. It was a bit too intense for his taste.

She was lying on a bed in a cubicle in the casualty unit. A nursing assistant showed him to her and then went off to get the doctor on duty. Ann began to sit up.

'No, no,' he said. 'Stay where you are. Take it easy.'

Her skirt was pulled up, revealing the firm curve of her long legs, and a plaster had been taped to her knee. She looked pale, with shadows like bruises under her eyes.

'You know what happened?' she asked.

'Yes, the police told me. Are you OK?'

'I'll live.'

'Where did he hit you?'

'Side of the neck.' She rubbed it gingerly. 'Feels like he knew what he was doing.'

'How come you were at the house anyway?'

'I told you I'd drop by sometime. Last night. Remember? I was a bit bored and I wondered if you were in, saw your car and thought you were. I'd have driven off again if I hadn't heard the door closing at the back.'

'You're sure about that? Only . . . the back door was still locked when we checked the house.'

'Fairly sure,' she said, although there was a tinge of doubt, 'but I suppose I could have been mistaken.'

'Did you get a look at the car?'

'Not really. I'd just noticed it, seen it for a second, and then somebody came up behind me. I don't know how long I was unconscious but the car was gone when I came round. Was anything stolen?'

'Nope, nothing. No sign that anyone was in the house at all. Strange business. Have you made a statement?'

'Tomorrow. They said if I was up to it I should drop by the station in Lisburn in the morning.'

'Then I shall take you there, save you having to drive.'

The cubicle curtain was swished aside to usher in Dr Sue Lee, a small, rather stern woman with oval Malaysian eyes behind black-rimmed glasses.

'And how are you feeling now, Miss Reilly?'

'A bit better, doctor.' She held her hand out straight. 'I've stopped shaking anyway.'

'Good,' the doctor said. She stood over Ann and shone a pencil light into each of her eyes in turn. 'Mmm. I think you're OK.' She turned to McCallan. 'Are you a relative?'

'No, just a friend. I thought I'd take the patient home if you were ready to let her go.'

'Yes, I think that will be all right. Would you like me to give you something to help you sleep, just in case?'

'No,' Ann said. 'I'll be fine.'

'In that case—' She helped Ann to her feet. McCallan took his raincoat off and put it over her shoulders.

On the way home she shivered a couple of times and clutched the coat more tightly round her even though he had turned the heat up. It was probably a touch of delayed shock. He had seen it in the Army in the aftermath of unexpected violent incidents: soldiers, no matter how seasoned, going quiet when the realisation of their sudden proximity to death or serious injury had sunk in.

The kitchen of her house was not as warm as it had been the previous evening. He found whisky in the cupboard to which she directed him and he poured two glasses. She drank from hers and shuddered again as it went down. He opened the door of the range to let the heat out and threw a shovelful of coal on. She stood silently in the middle of the room with a dazed look in her eyes.

'You look tired,' he said.

'Listen, I . . . look, would you stay? Would you stay here tonight? There's a bed settee in here and . . . well . . . I'd rather not be on my own.'

Her eyes were pleading.

'Of course,' he said, 'if that's what you want.'

She went off and came back with pillows and blankets and she showed him how to convert the settee. Then she said goodnight and left him to it. He undressed down to his briefs, turned the light off and settled down, or at least he tossed and turned and tried to but it was difficult with everything that was in his thoughts.

The range was warm and he kept its door open. The flames flickered and cast glowing shadows across the room.

He had just dropped off when some instinct woke him.

Ann was standing beside the bed wearing a long cotton nightshirt. She looked down at him silently and then, still without a word, she pulled back the covers and got in. She nestled into the crook of his arm and in a few moments she was asleep.

Chapter Eighteen

He woke first, having hardly slept at all. He had lain awake for ages, feeling the pressure and the heat of her body against his, hearing her breathing, smelling her warm fragrance until he had turned gingerly away from her, afraid that he would wake her and she would discover how aroused he was.

He looked down at her face. It had a distinctive angular beauty and he could see her eyelids flickering in sleep. There was a soft scent from her hair. As he bent his head towards her she woke up suddenly, her eyes ensnaring him. For a moment they were both absolutely still and then they were kissing and her tongue was lithe in his mouth and his briefs had gone somehow and she raised her arms over her head so that he could pull her nightshirt off. He rolled on top of her and then he was inside her, smoothly and easily, and she wrapped her long legs round him, pushing herself up, forcing him in deeper. He straightened his arms and looked down at her and saw a wildness in her eyes and their pace increased as she urged him on, harder, to come inside her and he did with a gasp and then fell across her.

After a moment she chuckled and nibbled the lobe of his ear. He shivered.

'I knew you'd be a wonderful lover,' she said.

'Oh? What made you think that?'

'Instinct. Just something about you. When you were here the other night, I could have happily had you there and then.'

He looked at her, surprised by her frankness, just as the forcefulness of the sex itself had been unexpected. She had come to his bed, ensuring that it would happen. He had not resisted, nor had he wanted to, because there was a hunger in him, although he recognised that his willing participation was in part fuelled by his anger with Julia. But if sex with Ann was a way of getting back at her then it was a bit pointless since she would never find out and probably would not care.

He fumbled in the bedclothes for his pants and she laughed as he tried to put them on discreetly. She threw the bedclothes back and walked across the room with long strides. Her body was strong and joyously feminine: the firm curve of her buttocks, the nipples tightening in the cold air of the room.

'I'm going to the bathroom,' she said, 'and then, O wicked landlord, now that you've had your evil way with me, you can take me to the police station.'

There was a police station in Dromore but because of budget cuts and a reduction in manpower over the years it now opened only for limited periods. Instead, Ann had arranged to give her statement at the regional headquarters, a sprawling red brick complex on a hill overlooking Lisburn from where last night's officers had come. High fencing surrounded it, there were slits where there should have been big windows and it looked like a fortress built to withstand assault from hostile tribes, which was not far off the mark.

It had been constructed in the days when the IRA bombing campaign was in full cry, when rocket and mortar attacks on police stations were almost routine and terrorists sometimes drove huge containers loaded with thousands of pounds of explosive right up to their front doors. Over the years, many police personnel had died in such onslaughts.

If they ever move out it could be a tourist attraction, McCallan thought as he drove up. People would wander around as if it were a medieval castle. Maybe the National Trust could take it over.

They told the men at the front desk why Ann had come and then someone took her off down a corridor. McCallan sat down to wait, leafing through the morning paper. Human traffic flowed past but no one paid him any attention until a bulky man in a raincoat came in. He passed McCallan, then turned and came back.

'You're Jack McCallan, aren't you?' he said. 'Bob McCallan's son?'

McCallan looked up. The face peering down at him had a pleasant smile. The man was about his own age, with curly hair that was disappearing at the front and a chin that was beginning to duplicate itself.

'I'm Barry Toner,' he said, holding out his hand. 'I'm a Detective Inspector. I knew your father vaguely. Met him at a couple of retirement dinners, that sort of thing. I was at the funeral the other day with a few other people from headquarters. We said hello at the graveside but I wouldn't expect you to remember.'

'Oh, right,' McCallan said as he stood to shake Toner's hand.

'What brings you here?'

McCallan explained. 'Oh, I see,' Toner said. 'Interesting. Look, I'm sure she won't be long but why don't you come and wait in my office. We'll get you a cup of coffee or something and leave a message where you are.'

McCallan thanked him and then followed. They went along several corridors with Toner being greeted politely by a number of the people they passed and then they were in what was obviously the main operations room. It was strangely empty with just two people sitting in front of computers at the front of it.

'All out fighting crime?' McCallan asked as they walked through.

'Probably,' Toner said and shot him a glance over his shoulder. 'There's a lot of it about.'

His office was through a door at the far end of the room

and he shared it with two other detectives, neither of whom was in. Abandoned clutter covered the desks. Toner took off his coat and hung it up and as he stretched, McCallan noticed the expanding waistline. He motioned McCallan to a seat, then picked up the phone and ordered two coffees from someone. He raised his eyebrows. 'Milk, sugar?' McCallan shook his head.

Toner pointed behind where McCallan sat. 'Have a look at that.'

On the wall was a big white board written on in black marker pen. There were names and dates. 'Some of the things we're working on,' Toner said. 'The first one is the case of an eleven-year-old girl whose body was found in the Lagan near Drumbo about six weeks ago. She'd been sexually assaulted and strangled. There's a lot of pressure out there over that one and we haven't got very far yet. The next one's a drug-dealer who was shot dead on the outskirts of Dunmurry. Eighteen bullets in him. Sub-machinegun. We know perfectly well who did it but proving it's another matter.'

The door opened and a uniformed officer came in with two steaming styrofoam cups. Toner thanked him and then waited until he had gone before turning to the next item on the list. He went through them all in turn, a depressing litany of lawlessness.

'It's getting pretty tough,' he said. 'A lot of violent crime and we don't have anything like the manpower we used to have.' He opened a sugar sachet and tipped it into his coffee, then stirred it thoroughly with a plastic stick which emerged twisted by the heat. He flicked it into a waste bin. 'What line are you in yourself? Oh, I remember. Army isn't it?'

'Used to be,' McCallan said, then explained why it was not his line any more.

'Lucky man,' Toner said, 'or is that the sort of stupid thing people always say?'

'Depends on your definition of luck.'

Toner shook his head. 'I couldn't imagine why anyone

would want to join the Army. I saw too much of those poor bastards when I was a kid in West Belfast, patrols wandering along looking petrified. That was when they weren't breaking down people's doors and kicking the shit out of them.'

It suddenly occurred to McCallan that Toner was a Catholic. It was the name, of course; it was a giveaway. Then it struck him, for the same reason, that Ann probably was, too. God, what was it about this place that made you put people into sectarian pigeonholes? Still, a Catholic Detective Inspector in the regional police headquarters would have been a rare bird in his father's time.

'I wouldn't have thought the police was exactly in the great West Belfast tradition, either,' McCallan said.

'True enough. I'd have thought it was something you might have considered yourself, since it runs in the family.'

'No thanks. Not for me. I'm sure my father would have been pleased if I'd thought of making a career of it but he never ever suggested it, never pushed me in any direction, really. He seemed happy enough when I told him I wanted to go into the Army. He was very supportive. How did your family react when you joined the police?'

'My father laughed.'

'He laughed?'

'Yes. He saw the joke. You see, he was once in the IRA.'

He noticed the shock in McCallan's eyes and gave a smile.

'It was a long time ago. When he was seventeen. Cannon fodder for the movement. He got eight years for his part in bombing a big social security office. Typical IRA strategy. You bomb the building, then people can't get their money and they blame the Brits for it.

'My father got sent to the Maze and served half his sentence. When he came out he was completely disillusioned with the cause, as they used to call it. Refused to have anything more to do with them. He managed to get a job as a barman, got married and had children – me and three sisters – and then he got involved in one of the reconciliation groups that were springing up.

'He began to get known, appearing on television discussions, giving talks, campaigning against terrorism. Then one night, three lads with masks came to our house in Andersonstown and took him off to an entry near the Gaelic football ground. They beat him with baseball bats and then they shot him in the legs.

'It's what you used to read about as a punishment beating or a knee-capping. People who weren't involved never saw the final results. My father spent the rest of his life in a wheelchair but it never stopped the work he'd become involved in, never.'

He stopped, the anger and the grief rekindled in his eyes, and sipped his coffee.

'That's . . . that's a remarkable story,' McCallan said. 'I take it from the way you referred to him that he's . . . well . . .'

'Died two years ago.'

'I'm sorry. It must all have been very difficult for you – for your family.'

'Oh, you don't have to scratch very far below the surface to find the pain in this place.'

'So why the police? Anything to do with what happened?'

'Oh, I suppose so. I sometimes reflect on that myself, whether it was some sort of gesture, a very conspicuous tearing-away from that whole West Belfast background. But – I'm sorry – no harm to your own father and the others who served in the old RUC – but we do have a different force now, one that by and large has the confidence of the whole community. I've got a family, three children. A real stake in the place. For years things were always somebody else's fault, somebody else's responsibility. But we all have a part to play. When the police force was reorganised, I thought that would make a difference for a start and I wanted to be involved, help to make things better. All very noble, don't you think?'

He laughed and waved his hand at the white board again. 'Some improvement, eh?'

The door opened and Ann came in with a policewoman. They stood and McCallan introduced them. Toner and she shook hands.

'All done?' Toner said.

'Yes,' Ann said. 'I'm afraid I haven't been a lot of help.'

'Oh, you never know. Even though nothing seems to have happened on this occasion, at least we know there might be someone operating around that area, looking over houses and so on.' He smiled comfortingly. 'You might have been more help than you think.'

McCallan wondered if he should share any of his unease about the incident. He had a feeling Toner was a man he could talk to. But perhaps not here, not now.

'Let's have a drink some time,' he said at the door. 'Continue the conversation.'

'I'd like that,' Toner told him. 'Call me here any time and if I'm not around I can be reached with a message.'

McCallan paused as a thought struck him.

'I've just remembered,' he said. 'My father's housekeeper, Mrs Benson, died in an accident just a short time before he did.'

'I heard about that. People were talking about it at the funeral.'

'Her sister, Grace Walker, was a bit curious about a couple of policemen who came to see her, plainclothes men. They seemed to be more interested in Mrs Benson's connection with my father than anything else, wondering if she'd mentioned anything unusual lately.'

'Like what?'

'I don't know. But now with this incident last night—'

'Did she get their names?'

'They told her but she doesn't remember. She was still very shocked at the time. I just wondered if you could shed any light on it.'

Toner made a face. 'Odd,' he said. 'It doesn't sound like anyone from here but I'll ask and if I find out I'll let you know.'

Outside the police station, Ann and McCallan walked to where they had parked his car.

'I've got to go to Belfast to see my solicitor,' he said. 'I'll drop you back home first.'

'No, you don't have to do that. I've some things to get in Lisburn. I don't mind taking the bus.'

'You sure?'

'Of course.'

He looked at her, feeling awkward, not knowing how to part company. She smiled at him, then took his hand and squeezed it.

'Call me later,' she said and strode off down the street.

As he drove down the motorway to Belfast, he wondered what he was getting himself into. Having just been abandoned by Julia, surely to God he was not going to let himself get caught up in another relationship? But this morning had happened; there was no altering that. It would be very easy to be captivated by this woman, her air of unpredictability. You are in a delicate emotional state, he warned himself. Be careful.

Forty minutes later he was in the reception area at McCaughey and Granleese, looking through a paper he had already read once today. When he had phoned yesterday to get an appointment he had been told that Mr Morris could probably squeeze him in at about 11.30, although he might have to wait a few minutes, and he had said that was fine. But by 12.05 when Morris eventually came to get him, his patience had worn a bit thin.

The solicitor ushered him into his office, full of apologies, and said it was a pleasure, although a bit of a surprise, to see him again so soon.

'What can I do for you?' he asked. He did not sit but stood in front of his desk, leaning back against it, which McCallan took as an indication that he intended this to be a short visit. McCallan sat down, although he had not been invited to do so, and took the bank document from his inside pocket. It was beginning to look like a piece of ancient parchment.

'I was going through my father's things and I came across this, showing the sum of £100,000 withdrawn several months ago. There's no apparent explanation for it so I asked at the bank and they tell me it was a cheque paid by my father to you. I was just curious, that's all. Can you tell me what it was for?'

Morris pushed himself away from the desk and went round and sat in the chair behind it. The smile had gone. He did not look at McCallan but instead scanned the faces in the photographs on the wall, as if he were consulting them. McCallan wondered what he had stumbled into.

Morris turned to him. 'All right,' he said, as if he had made a decision. 'Strictly speaking, that was then and this is now. It was business conducted legally and properly between me and your father and I don't have to explain it to you. Client confidentiality and all that. But if I don't tell you, it will leave an air of suspicion and mistrust between us and you'll have doubts about my honesty. I don't want that.'

McCallan said nothing. He had expected to be told it was something to do with the property in Donegal, for example, or maybe some sort of a tax matter, but he had a feeling he was about to be handed a can with worms crawling over the side.

'About six months or so ago,' Morris said, 'your father came to see me and said he wanted to give someone £100,000. I said it was his money and he could do what he liked with it but he said it was a bit more complicated than that. He said he wanted to give it to someone and he did not want the person to know where it came from. He wanted me to write to them and say they had been left the money in the will of someone who wanted to remain anonymous.'

'Who was the person?' McCallan asked.

'The name he gave me was that of a woman called Eileen Keane with an address at Malahide, just outside Dublin.'

McCallan was baffled. The name meant nothing to him.

'Who is she?'

Morris shrugged. 'I don't know. He wouldn't say and I didn't ask him. None of my business. The only thing he told me about her was her address and the number of her bank account.'

'He knew that?'

'Yes, he did. I was a bit edgy about the whole business. I felt there was something, well, not quite ethical about it, sending someone a letter containing statements which I knew to be untrue, under our firm's letter heading, and so on, but he was very reassuring. He promised me there was nothing illegal or suspect about it. He could quite easily leave the money in his will, he said, but he wanted to make sure she got it while they were both still alive.'

'What did you do?'

'What he asked me to. I wrote to her and I paid the money into her bank with your father's funds which I'd already transferred to our own account.' He turned to his computer terminal and McCallan could hear the mouse clicking. 'I'll give you a copy of the letter I sent.'

McCallan waited for it to be printed and then Morris handed it to him.

'Dear Eileen Keane,' he read, 'I am required to inform you that under the terms of the will of a client, recently deceased, of our firm, McCaughey and Granleese, you have inherited the sum of £100,000. The sum has been bequeathed to you from our client's estate without condition other than the stipulation that our client wished to remain anonymous. The amount concerned has already been transferred to your account with the Allied Irish Bank at Malahide, Co. Dublin.

'If there is anything you wish to clarify, please contact me at this office but I must emphasise that we cannot jeopardise the terms of this bequest by acceding to any inquiry which might seek to establish the identity of our late client.'

Underneath was a thin scrawl which purported to be Andrew Morris's signature.

'Did anyone contact you?' McCallan asked when he had finished reading.

'No, no one. Mind you, the letter might have scared her off. All that stuff about jeopardising the bequest. She might have thought that saying nothing was the best way to hold on to the money.'

McCallan had more questions, all of them revolving around Eileen Keane, whoever she was, but, like Paisley the bank manager yesterday, Morris's help was limited. He seemed relieved to have shared the secret with someone at last and it was as if he were passing McCallan the responsibility for the mystery, absolving himself from any further involvement with it.

McCallan left the office, baffled and a bit embarrassed. Who was this woman and what had she meant to his father? Morris would have been wondering, too, damn it, dreaming up God-knows-what sort of permutations.

There was a coffee shop nearby and he went in. It was somewhere to sit for a while and collect his thoughts. He ordered a coffee and a bagel which turned out to be cinnamon which he did not like.

Like everything else lately, he thought as he pushed the plate away. Full of surprises you could do without.

Chapter Nineteen

He tooted the horn and Ann came running out of the house, closing the door forcefully behind her. She wore a brown zip-up cord jacket, jeans and sandy-coloured boots. Over her shoulder she carried a canvas satchel which she threw into the back of the car as soon as she slipped into the passenger seat.

'Ready?' he said.

'Ready.'

He put the car into gear and drove off.

He had spent the previous afternoon and evening roaming the house restlessly. He had gone through every drawer, every old file and folder, particularly those in his father's desk. He had even climbed up into the roof space where he knew some things were kept and had rummaged through several dusty boxes, but all he had found were old school reports and homework books, magazines and newspapers kept for obscure reasons, random family memorabilia.

Of this woman Eileen Keane there was nothing, not a clue.

He thought about the sum involved, £100,000. It was not as much as it might have been a few years ago at, say, the turn of the century, but it was a substantial amount nevertheless, a hell of a lot more than just a token gesture, like, for example, the gift to the unfortunate Mrs Benson.

He could always just drive down there, of course, down to Malahide. He had the address and he could knock the door but he did not know what or who he would find and he needed some hint, some indication of what part this woman had played in his father's life before he did anything else.

In the late afternoon Morris had called him to say that the builder had been on the phone, wondering what he wanted to do about the house in Donegal. McCallan had seized on the opportunity. He needed time and space to think, a diversion, so he had asked Morris to arrange for the builder to be at the site the following afternoon and he would drive up to see him.

Then this morning he had woken up feeling clear-headed and energetic and full of the joys of spring, if this had not been October. Perhaps it was something to do with the sparrows he heard chattering in the hedge outside when he woke or the sunny, piercingly bright day that was revealed when he pulled the curtains. Whatever the cause, he felt alive and he had phoned Ann, acting on impulse, and asked her if she would like to go to Donegal with him.

'When are you going?' she asked.

'Now. Twenty minutes.'

'Make it half an hour and you're on.'

It was a glorious day for the drive, a defiant last-ditch burst before the onset of winter. He filled the car with music from one of the pop stations and they chatted over it. They were in no hurry as they drove from County Down into part of Armagh and then deep into Tyrone. Just before noon they found themselves at a country inn on the outskirts of Omagh so they decided to stop for an early lunch.

They both ordered lasagne and salad and took their plates outside to the tables on the terrace. Ann took her jacket off, revealing the tight-fitting sweater underneath. The sun was warm on their faces and the sky was a vivid blue, the only cloud an occasional brush stroke added as an afterthought. As they ate, they looked down at the green river valley tumbling away below them.

They had made love once, briefly and energetically, but he

really did not know any more about this woman than that first night in her kitchen. On the way up in the car, they had talked about everything except personal matters. He knew what was behind his own reluctance but not hers. He was curious.

'So tell me,' he said. 'Is there a man in your life?'

'No. I don't go in for complicated attachments.'

She was probably right. He had once felt like that himself.

'Neither do I,' he said.

He looked at her. She was withdrawing from him; he could see it in her face.

'What is it?'

'Nothing. It doesn't matter.'

He touched her arm gently.

'It's . . . well . . . I lost someone dear to me once,' she said. She glanced at him and gave an awkward smile as if she did not understand why she was telling him this. 'It's not something I often talk about.'

She turned away from him and looked out towards the fields.

'I was a student in Dublin. I was twenty, a virgin, believe it or not. I never could connect at all with boys my own age. They seemed so empty and puerile, always trying it on, but I wanted something more than that. I don't know – something more fulfilling.'

A fly landed on the edge of her plate and she flicked it away angrily with her napkin.

'Then I met someone. His name was Dermot Farrelly. He was older than me, thirty-five – about the same age we are now, I suppose. He was a lecturer and historian, quite well known in Ireland, and he wrote a lot in the papers about Irish politics. I'd never met anyone like him. We became lovers and I adored him.'

A waitress came by and removed their plates. McCallan asked her for some coffee and the bill.

'You said you lost him?' he asked softly when she had gone. 'What happened?'

'One night he was walking home. He had a flat just off Stephen's Green. It was late and he'd been out for a drink with a few colleagues. At the door of his building, there was someone waiting. Dublin's drugs problems are horrendous, junkies everywhere. This one was desperate for a fix, would have robbed anyone. He had a knife. According to some people on the other side of the street, there was a struggle. Dermot was stabbed several times and the junkie ran off. The police caught him a few streets away, though, and found the knife on him. It took ages for an ambulance to come and by the time they got Dermot to hospital he was dead.'

'I'm sorry,' McCallan said.

'Oh, you learn to cope and you get over it,' she said. 'The murderer got life and got his throat cut in a fight in prison a year later. So I suppose there was some sort of justice in that.'

The waitress arrived with the coffee. Ann sipped hers, then made a face.

'Oh, for God's sake!'

She put her cup down. 'Excuse me. Miss?'

The waitress turned.

'I don't remember that we actually asked for our coffee to be cold,' she said. 'Is it too much to expect it to be hot?'

The waitress took their cups. 'Sorry,' she said. 'I'll get some more.'

'Look, it doesn't matter now. I couldn't be bothered. How about you?'

She turned to McCallan. He shrugged.

'Maybe we should hit the road,' he said, surprised and a little embarrassed by the sudden outburst.

They drove in silence for a while.

'I'm sorry about that,' she said eventually. 'I can't stand that sort of thing. Bad service.'

'Don't worry about it,' he said. It was a lot of fuss to make over a cup of coffee but he was sure that had not really been the cause and that the revival of difficult memories probably had more to do with it. For the next few miles, he thought about everything that had been happening in his own life: Julia's disappearance, his father's mental state and now this woman Eileen Keane. And there was Ann herself.

'You look a bit thoughtful,' she said. 'What's on your mind?'

What would he say? Not that he was wondering about her. Not about Julia either. He decided that he would tell her about the £100,000 gift and its unknown beneficiary. Why not?

She studied the road ahead while he recounted his conversation with Andrew Morris.

'So what are you going to do?' she asked.

'I don't know but it's going to nag away at me until I find out who she is and why he gave her all that money.'

'Maybe it's something you don't want to know about.'

'Oh, I've thought of all that. What if it's a mistress he kept all these years, that sort of thing. I even began to toy with the idea that maybe my mother wasn't my real mother at all and that this woman is.'

'In that case, I rather imagine she'd have got a lot more than £100,000.'

'That's true enough,' he agreed, 'but I can't leave it alone. Could you?'

She thought for a moment. 'Probably not. But so what if your father had secrets? We all do. Maybe it's best if you let them die with him. I think you should wrestle with yourself for a little while longer before you take any rash decisions.'

'Believe me,' he said, 'that's just what I'm doing.'

They were in Donegal by now and were reaching their destination sooner than he had thought they would. With the end of the journey coming nearer he felt his heart sink as all the horror of his last visit came flooding in.

They turned off the road and down the track that led to the site. The afternoon sunlight was gentler and the area was quiet and peaceful but the scars were still there. The remains of the car and the caravan had gone and where they had stood the grass was a huge patch of black stubble. The tall beech tree which had sheltered the caravan looked crippled, one side of it stripped and scorched from the flames which had coursed up its flanks. And there was the shell of the house, standing like a grey brick mausoleum.

They got out of the car almost reverently. The tide was out and the smell of the shore was sharp. Knots and dunlins skittered about on the wet sand and among the slippery green rocks.

Ann took his hand. 'This must be very painful for you,' she said.

He did not answer because he could not explain to her. It was all there in his mind now, all the doubt, all the wondering, the helplessness of not being able to know for sure.

There was no one about, no sign of the builder, although they were a little early, so they went for a walk along the shore, crunching over the dried seaweed and kicking at shells. Half an hour later there was still no sign of him so they got back into the car and drove the half-mile to Patricia Cassidy's pub.

She was the only person in the bar when they walked in. She was bent over the big fire, lighting it so that the place would be warm for tonight's customers. She turned when she heard the door open and smiled when she saw who it was. She hugged him, trying not to get coal dust on his shoulders from the rubber household gloves she wore.

McCallan introduced Ann and then asked if the builders had been around. 'No,' she said. 'I haven't seen any of them since – since the accident.'

McCallan went to the phone in the back room while Mrs Cassidy made a pot of tea for three. When he came back he was scowling. 'Well, that's marvellous,' he said. 'Just bloody marvellous. They got the day wrong. They thought I meant tomorrow afternoon and the damn builder's in Derry all day and won't be back until tonight.'

'What are you going to do?' Ann asked and he smiled.

*　　*　　*

An hour later, they drove up the long tree-lined drive to the subdued elegance of the big country house with its perfect view over Lough Swilly and the soft colours of the hills on the far side. There was, he had said back at the pub, no earthly point in wasting the journey. He did not want to come traipsing back up here some other day and since the builder could see him tomorrow, why not stay the night? Would that suit her or had she anything pressing tomorrow morning?

'No,' she had said, 'that suits me fine. I might have to make a phone call to sort something out but that's all.'

'Good. That's settled then. I know just the place where we can stay, if they can take us.'

He had phoned the hotel and found that they were in luck. Business was quiet, they were about to close down as usual for the winter months, and he had no trouble booking a room. He had done so discreetly, from Mrs Cassidy's living room, so that she would not hear that he was booking one room instead of two and he had been amazed to find his heart beating harder with the illicit thrill of it.

They reached the end of the drive, parked and got out. Ann stood for a moment and took a deep breath as she looked around. The light was fading and there was a quickening breeze coming in off the sea, bringing a tang with it. A raiding party of oystercatchers screeched low along the shoreline, otherwise there was not a sound to be heard.

'God, this is so lovely,' she said.

They walked across the gravel to the hotel, feeling awkwardly empty-handed, but McCallan had already explained to the manager on the phone what the problem was so there were no difficult questions about luggage.

'We may need one or two things,' McCallan said. 'Shaving gear for me, toothpaste, that sort of thing.'

'That'll be no problem, sir,' the manager assured him.

'Don't worry about me,' Ann told McCallan and patted her satchel. 'I've come prepared.'

The room into which they were shown had them both grinning idiotically. It was huge and simply gorgeous. The wallpaper was in yellow, a delicately flowered disciple of William Morris, and there were several pieces of good period furniture, placed strategically. In front of the window and its postcard view of the darkening lough sat a long pink settee. It looked comfortable and inviting but not as inviting as the bed, which was wide and wonderful. There was no duvet here but real blankets and crisp linen sheets, turned back and beckoning.

The manager walked through the room and at the far end he opened the door to the bathroom. The floor was dark polished wood and on it stood an enormous deep tub with ancient brass taps. There were dried flower arrangements and the room smelled of lavender. Ann lifted a bar of soap from the wash basin and sniffed it appreciatively.

'Will there be anything else, sir?' the manager wondered. 'Anything else I can get you?'

'No,' McCallan said. 'This is terrific. Thank you.'

The manager gestured to the phone by the bed. 'Just ring down if you need anything.' He looked at his watch. 'Dinner's from seven and the bar's in the cellar downstairs.'

He left the room and the door closed behind him. McCallan sat down in an armchair. It was comfortable and he felt relaxed. Ann came out of the bathroom. She had taken her boots off and her feet were bare. She took her jacket off too and threw it on the bed. Her eyes were on him, with a sense of purpose. As he watched, she pulled the sweater over her head and dropped it to the floor, then she unbuttoned her jeans and stepped out of them.

For a moment she just stood there until she reached behind and unclasped her bra, letting it fall. Her breasts were full, the nipples a deep red. She hooked her thumbs into the sides of her white pants, eased them down her thighs, then kicked them away.

She walked to where he was sitting and knelt in front of

him. Her gaze never left his eyes as she unbuckled his belt, unfastened his trousers and drew them slowly down over his hips.

Then she bent her head and took him into her mouth. He closed his eyes.

Forty five minutes later, McCallan descended the stone steps to the cellar bar. He had showered and shaved and tidied himself up as best he could but he needed a drink. When he had stuck his head round the bathroom door to tell Ann where he would be, he had found her stepping into the bath, submerging herself in the suds with a sensual smile.

There was no one about. He peered over the bar but did not see any sign of life. He walked on in towards the fire, which was a huge hole in the wall with great ingots of turf smouldering on it. There were wooden chairs and the tables were polished wooden casks.

'Yes, sir,' a voice said and he turned to see the barman, small and elderly and standing behind the bar with a look that defied McCallan to suggest that he had not been there all the time.

'Oh, hello,' McCallan said. 'I'll have a pint of Guinness, please.' The drink was a turmoil in the glass as the barman poured it and when it had settled McCallan took it over to a seat by the fire along with a copy of that morning's *Irish Times* which he found on the counter.

He sat and savoured the cool, smooth bitterness. He felt mellow for the moment, in spite of his various worries. He browsed through the paper. Since it was published in Dublin, much of it contained exclusively Irish news. The front page had a picture of the Irish Prime Minister and his large, smiling family going into a big rock concert.

He was about to put the paper down when something caught his eye.

It was at the bottom of a long column on a page devoted to UK news. It was a short item and it said that police in London had taken a number of the directors of a small Middle Eastern bank in for questioning about certain aspects of the bank's operations in Britain.

But there was one director for whom they were still looking. The name was in ten point type like everything else in the story but it leaped out of the page at McCallan as if it were in letters ten feet high.

Daniel Shriver.

As he read on, he discovered that the police had searched the offices of Shriver's financial consultancy company, taking away boxes of papers for examination, and they had been to Shriver's home in Holland Park but there was no sign of him or his wife Julia, neither of whom had been seen for at least a week.

That was it. There was nothing else. McCallan read the few short paragraphs again, struggling to get something further out of it but the story did not tell him anything it had not told him the first time.

In his head he heard Julia's voice. We're going away for a little while.

Her call began to take on a new perspective. Had she known any of this when she had made it? He wondered where she was – and how she was. Anxiety began to take the place of the anger. Somehow he would have to find out more.

'Hi.'

Ann was standing beside him. He had not heard her come into the bar and suddenly he did not want her to be there. It was all wrong. Her smile vanished when she saw the trouble in his face.

He showed her the newspaper. 'Read that,' he said. 'I'll explain over dinner.'

The dining room was a huge conservatory with warm lamplight. The only other occupants were three elderly women attacking their meals at a big table in the centre of the room. McCallan and Ann sat by the window. She ordered duck and ate slowly while he picked at a seafood dish.

He told her about Julia, the break-up of her marriage and then the shock of the phone call on the same day he had heard about his father. And now – now he did not know what to think.

'But you want to think that somehow she didn't really mean it – that it was all something to do with this swindle. Her husband's idea, not hers. Am I right?'

'I suppose so. Yes,' he said.

'Well, I wouldn't count on it too much. Life's not like that.'

He said nothing.

'You're in a bit of a state, aren't you?' she said.

'Look, I'm sorry if I misled you about anything.'

'Misled me? How? A trip to Donegal? Or because you let me fuck you?'

There was a hard edge in her voice. She laughed.

'That's how it was, remember. I fucked you. You just made yourself available.' She shook her head in disbelief. 'Why do men always have to think it's such a big deal?'

They sat there quietly for a while after that, feeling uncomfortable.

'Look,' she said at last, her voice softer. 'I'm tired and I'm going to bed. Why don't you sit here for a bit, have a drink. You've got a lot to think about.'

'You don't mind?'

'Why the hell should I mind?' She smiled and put her hand on his thigh under the table. 'It's just a pity. I could have gone another round.'

He sat in the library with a brandy, relieved to be alone. It felt like she was teasing him and she made him feel uneasy. But then what did he expect – blurting out everything about Julia to a woman he had been screwing about an hour before – sympathy? He rubbed his forehead in his hands. God, this was a mess.

When he got to the bedroom there were no lights and he could hear from the deepness of her breathing that she was asleep. The moon was full and she had not pulled the curtains and a pale, almost spiritual, light lay across the floor like a tide. He crossed the room quietly and sat down on the settee at the window, looking out at gems of light in the hillsides, the sleeping stillness of Donegal. His eyes were heavy and he put his head back to rest for a moment.

Chapter Twenty

The moment he woke he remembered the dream. In it, Ann and Julia had merged into one person, then separated and merged again so that when he was talking to one, she became the other.

A nightmare, he thought, then realised that that was indeed what it had been.

His shoulder was practically numb, whatever way he had been lying, and he rubbed it as he stood up. The bed was empty but there was a note on the pillow.

'See you at breakfast,' it said.

He washed and shaved, feeling stale in clothes which were on their second day, and went downstairs. She was at last night's table, looking fresh and rested, and she grinned at him as he came in. There was an empty plate in front of her with a couple of bacon rinds on it.

'I had the works,' she said. 'Bacon, egg, sausage, tomato, the lot. I'd recommend it. Did you sleep all right?'

'Not really,' he muttered, rubbing his shoulder again.

'You should have got into bed with me,' she said, biting into a piece of toast. 'I wouldn't have molested you.'

He looked at her, seeing a flash of mischief in the green eyes. A waitress came by and he ordered poached egg and toast and coffee. He was on his second cup when a girl came in and said there was someone at reception to see him. He got up from the table and Ann went with him.

A man in a crumpled suit stood in the hall, fidgeting with his hat.

'Mr McCallan?' he said. 'I'm Willie Drumm, the builder.'

'Oh yes,' Ann said. 'The man who doesn't know what day it is.'

McCallan looked sharply at her.

'Sorry,' she said. 'I'll go upstairs and freshen up. Leave you to it.'

McCallan's conversation with the builder was brief. He had more important matters on his mind than the house but it was the whole field on which it stood that interested Mr Drumm. McCallan could see what was in his head. Looking at the site yesterday, he had realised you could build two or perhaps even three small holiday homes there instead of one, provided planning permission was not a problem, which he did not expect it would be.

He told Drumm he would think about it. When he got back, he would talk to Andrew Morris and Henry Lomax and make sure that if he did sell, it was at the right price.

When Drumm had gone, Ann came down the stairs with her satchel on her shoulder and her jacket zipped up, ready for the journey. McCallan paid the bill and they set off.

The drive back was a lot quieter than the previous day's trip had been and he found a speech station on the radio to fill the gaps in the conversation. After a while, Ann put her head back and began to doze. They turned on to the motorway outside Dungannon and were about ten miles along it when she spoke.

'It's hot in here,' she said, unzipping her jacket slowly.

McCallan looked at her and started. She had nothing on underneath.

He was in the overtaking lane, doing almost eighty and passing a heavy container lorry, when she eased the jacket off her left breast. She rubbed her right forefinger slowly round the nipple and it began to stiffen.

'What the hell are you doing?' he said.

'Taking your mind off your troubles,' she murmured, closing her eyes. 'And mine.'

He passed the lorry, wondering if the driver could see anything from his high cab, and pulled into the inside lane, reducing speed. Other cars passed him and he glanced nervously at them.

She moaned and he turned to look at her. She had spread her legs and opened the fly of her jeans and her hand had disappeared into the crotch. He could see the shape of it, moving rhythmically, and he could feel his own arousal as he watched.

He had picked up speed again without noticing. There was a small Renault in front of him, going much slower, and he was almost on top of it before he realised. With a swerve, he pulled into the passing lane.

'Jesus!'

Lights in his mirror were blinding him. A petrol tanker was bearing down from behind and he lurched into the inside again, cutting abruptly in front of the Renault which sounded its horn in indignation.

Beside him Ann's rhythm beat faster. His mouth was dry and his hands were clammy on the steering wheel. If they had been on any other road, he would have had to turn off somewhere. But they were on the M1 and he could not pull in.

Then she would be aware of that, too. She had started this just after they had got to the motorway, knowing that it would cause him maximum discomfort. She was tormenting him, making him suffer.

The groaning was louder as she began to climax.

On the radio, Woman's Hour was just beginning.

She came with a sharp cry and a shudder, raising her pelvis up off the seat, then subsided with a soft moan.

He flicked his indicator and passed a car pulling a caravan.

'Feeling better?'

'Mmm,' she said, biting her lower lip. 'Much.' Then she zipped her jacket up and closed her eyes again.

They were outside the farmhouse in about twenty minutes. She fastened her jeans and lifted her satchel from the back seat.

'Do you want to come in?'

A sunny smile, as if nothing had happened.

'I don't think so. Things to do.' He sounded a little grumpy and she was amused.

'Oh, I see. Well, look, I've got to go to Waterford for a few days. Why don't you call me when I get back?'

'I'll think about it.'

She gave a little laugh. 'I'll bet you will.'

When he got to his own house, the voice mail light was flashing on the phone. There were three calls on it, all from the night before and all from the same person.

'Jack dear,' the last message said, a little despairingly. 'Where the bloody hell are you? Don't tell me you've buggered off when I've come all this way to look for you.'

He frowned. What on earth was Brian doing in Belfast?

Chapter Twenty-one

The lounge bar of the waterfront hotel was on the first floor and he saw him as soon as he walked in. He was in a blue suit with a buttercup shirt and he was at a seat over by the window, although his eyes were not on the view but on the Filipino waiter who was approaching him with a Bloody Mary on a tray.

He waved as soon as he saw McCallan who joined him and ordered a mineral water. Brian's gaze followed the waiter as he went to fetch it.

'Heavenly creature,' he sighed.

'What's this about, Brian?'

'Dear boy, I had to come. I'm so glad I've found you. I tried the flat and discovered you'd redirected the number but I couldn't get you so I decided to come in person. What's been going on?'

McCallan told him about his father's death.

'Oh, that's so awful. No wonder you've been hard to track down. Have you read the papers?'

'About Shriver? Yes. I stumbled on it yesterday.'

'That's why I have to talk to you.'

The waiter set McCallan's drink down and Brian waited until he had gone.

'I know about Julia's farewell message.'

'How?'

'Because she told me about it.' He stirred his drink and took a mouthful. 'I got a strange phone call from her the other day, very early in the morning. She wouldn't say where she was calling from but there was noise in the background, announcements. Sounded like an airport somewhere.

'It was all a bit hurried but she said it was the first chance she'd had to phone anyone. Shriver was watching her like a hawk, apparently. She'd tried to call you again but you weren't there so she'd called me instead.

'I didn't know what the hell was happening because I didn't know she'd given you the brush-off, you see. Then she told me about her plan to confront him that weekend about the divorce but she said he was hyped, all fired up. Slapped her about a bit. She thought she'd seen him at his worst but she'd never seen him like that. He told her he was in big trouble, the shit was going to hit the fan and the police would be looking for him. He had to get away and he wanted her to go with him.

'She refused, of course, and that was when he threatened to have you killed.'

'He did what?'

'He was serious, she said. She was convinced of it. In the state he was in, he was capable of anything. He claimed he'd had people following you, that he knew everything about you – where you lived, where you worked, what you'd been doing together – everything.

'And that was why she made the call to you – with Mr Shriver standing at her shoulder. She couldn't risk anything happening. She told me she was going with him – she hadn't a clue where – but that she was going to get away from him if she could. She wanted you to know she was sorry, wanted you to understand why it had happened. I tried to ask her a couple of questions but she rang off quickly. And then I saw the papers. Frankly, I wasn't a bit surprised.'

McCallan sat back in his chair, letting it all sink in. He could kill Daniel Shriver. What was he doing to her? But in the midst of his fear for Julia was his own guilt. His heart sank when he thought of Ann, the things they had done.

'Are you all right?' Brian asked.

'I've been better.'

They talked for a bit about what they would do if Julia phoned again, how Brian might get a message to McCallan. There was no hint that she would do so but it was worth hoping she might.

'What time's your flight back?' McCallan asked.

'Oh, any time. I've got an open shuttle ticket, although I don't want to be home too late.'

'Then let's get out of here for a while.'

They walked through Belfast aimlessly. It was Brian's first time in the city and he admired its well-ordered streets while McCallan told him some of the things that had happened since his father's death, although he did not tell him about the legacy to Eileen Keane and he left out any reference to the episodes with Ann. He felt too ashamed to mention that.

Then he had an idea that would be the perfect way to kill a couple of hours and something that Brian might appreciate.

They retrieved his car from the hotel car park and drove to the Stranmillis Road in the south of the city. He found a space right beside the Ulster Museum.

The Henry Lomax Collection was in the spacious gallery at the top of the building. McCallan had to admit his surprise at the extent of it and as they walked around Brian practically purred with each new discovery. There was a heavy concentration on Irish art, particularly those painters with a strong Ulster connection, but it was a collection to rival the museum's own. There was Lavery, then Conor, right through to Shawcross and up to some of the newer artists. But there were other schools, too: French Impressionists, Dutch paintings like the one he had admired in Henry's home.

McCallan wandered off into another gallery and suddenly found himself faced with work of an entirely different kind. On these canvases there were burnt-out cars and hollow-eyed children, policemen with shields charging petrol-bombers. This was the museum's permanent Troubles exhibition. He could feel the violence reverberating from the walls.

But it was a bronze sculpture in the centre of the room that held him. It was of a woman being thrown violently backwards by the force of an explosion, her arms and legs outstretched, frozen forever at the moment of the blast. McCallan wondered why the sculptor had chosen a woman as the subject rather than a man. Was it because they seemed more helpless, more vulnerable? He remembered it being said once that they were the real victims of the Troubles, the wives and the mothers who had had to live with the pain.

By the time he had seen Brian off at the airport and got home in the late afternoon, there were two more letters of sympathy in the hall. He was really going to have to tackle them. Tomorrow. Definitely tomorrow. A look in the fridge and the kitchen cupboards told him he had shopping to do as well.

The following morning, he went to the supermarket and stocked up. He bought nothing too complicated: freezer food, things that were handy for the microwave. Then he went to a stationery shop and bought a couple of writing pads and two bundles of envelopes. By 11 a.m. he was sitting at the kitchen table, pen in hand, writing to people he had never heard of to thank them for being so thoughtful.

He looked through all the signatures, searching for one in particular, but the name Eileen Keane was not among them.

And then he came across a name he seemed to recognise. Alfie Hutchinson. Why was that familiar?

Yes, of course, the old policeman at the funeral, the one who had been wounded. And as he remembered, something else came to him. Hutchinson's old job. Pensions and welfare.

He went out into the living room and picked up the phone book.

Chapter Twenty-two

It occurred to him that this was the second Sunday morning in succession on which he had driven around looking for somebody's house. However, this was nothing like Holland Park.

Alfie Hutchinson lived off the Castlereagh Road on the east side of Belfast in a modest avenue of red brick post-war semis. McCallan parked the car and got out. The morning was dry and bright but cold. Number 22 looked like all the rest: small family saloon parked at the side, handkerchief garden at the front. It struck McCallan immediately how different this policeman's fortunes in retirement were from those which his father had enjoyed.

He had finally got hold of Hutchinson last night, said he wanted to talk to him about something he did not want to explain on the phone, and had been invited to come over this morning. As he rang the doorbell, he heard the shrill yapping of a dog inside but there was no human response. He tried again.

'I'm round the back.'

He turned to see Hutchinson standing at the side of the house. He wore dark grey overalls under which a white shirt and striped tie looked oddly formal.

'I'm putting some stuff on the fence,' he said with a smile and held up brown-smeared hands as if surrendering. 'Come on round. The wife's at church and that bloody wee dog would take the leg off you when she's not here to keep it under control.'

He led the way. 'So how have you been keeping since the funeral?'

McCallan noticed the awkwardness of Hutchinson's gait.

'Oh, I'm fine. It takes time to get over these things but there's a lot of bits and pieces to sort out. Keeps me occupied.'

The back garden was a good bit bigger than the front. There was a small lawn and a paved path at the side of it and neat, well-tended flower beds which would mean a colourful view from the kitchen for Hutchinson and his wife in the spring and summer. Their garden was separated from their next-door neighbour's by a chest-high wooden fence. Beside it sat a tin of wood preservative and a paintbrush.

'Thought I'd do this while the weather's dry,' Hutchinson said. 'Keep the bloody thing from rotting. Except there's no guarantee that your man next door will bother his arse doing his side.' He picked the brush up and dipped it into the tin. 'I hope you don't mind if I keep going.'

'No, not at all,' McCallan said. 'Don't let me interrupt you. You're not at church yourself, then?'

Hutchinson made a long horizontal stroke with the brush. 'No thanks. Don't believe in it, really. The churches haven't done very much for us over the years, have they?'

McCallan thought of his father's recent interests. 'That's certainly a point of view,' he said.

'So what can I do for you?'

McCallan sighed. 'Something's been on my mind, kind of rattling around in it, and I wondered if you could help.' He paused. 'What do you remember of the George Miller case?'

Hutchinson seemed to freeze in mid-stroke, then turned to look at him. He put the brush down. 'Why do you want to know?' he asked.

Here it was again. Someone reacting to the name as if they had been slapped in the face.

'I can't go into it in detail,' McCallan said, 'but I have good reason to think that George Miller's death may have been disturbing my father towards the end of his life. Something was on his mind, troubling him a lot.'

Hutchinson picked up a grimy rag and wiped his hands. 'You know about the Miller case?'

McCallan nodded. 'I started wondering yesterday. Did Miller have a wife and if so what happened to her after he was killed? It occurred to me last night that because of your connections, your old job in pensions, you might know.'

Hutchinson was silent for what seemed a very long time as he busied himself cleaning his hands. Then he raised his head again and looked at the younger man, searching his face, his eyebrows knotted in a question McCallan could not read.

There was the sound of someone rapping on a window and he turned to see a grey-haired woman waving and smiling from the kitchen.

'Church is over,' Hutchinson said, waving back. 'It's safe to go in now.' He put his hand on McCallan's arm. 'It's getting a bit cold out here, too. Why don't we go inside and get a cup of tea?'

Mrs Hutchinson was a small, fussy woman and he worried about hurting her bony little hand as he shook it. She flitted about the kitchen, turning on the kettle, finding cups, somehow managing not to trip over the Yorkshire terrier which darted in and out of her legs.

'I'll just go upstairs and wash my hands properly and get out of these overalls,' Hutchinson said.

'Please do,' his wife called after him. 'That stuff stinks. And don't leave those overalls lying on the floor.' She turned to McCallan. 'I'm always picking up after him.' She smiled and he could see that she did not really mind at all.

They went into the front room which McCallan presumed was reserved for visitors since it had that not-much-used feel about it. She switched on the electric fire in the hearth and he took the chance to look around. Young couples with children smiled from golden picture frames.

'Your grandchildren?' he asked.

'Yes. Aren't they lovely?' She pointed to one photograph. 'That's my daughter and her family. We're going over to them for lunch.'

'Oh, then, I'm keeping you back,' McCallan said.

'No, you're not,' Hutchinson said, coming into the room carrying a tea tray. 'We don't usually eat with them on a Sunday until about three. It's like Christmas Day. I keep waiting for the King's Speech.'

They all laughed. Hutchinson winked at his wife and she smiled back. There was an easy warmth between them. McCallan could see that even after so many years of marriage they still enjoyed each other and he contrasted their happy relationship with the solitary existence his father had led and, indeed, with his own confused and unsettled emotional state.

Mrs Hutchinson said she would leave them to it because she had things to do in the kitchen. When she had gone, Hutchinson poured. It was the good china, a rosebud pattern with a trimming of gold leaf. McCallan took the cup and saucer which were handed to him.

'You took me by surprise,' Hutchinson said. His voice had become serious. 'You saw that.'

It was a statement of fact rather than a question.

'Yes,' McCallan said.

Hutchinson sat back in his chair, stirring his cup, looking towards the window with its venetian blind but seeing much further than that.

'Bear with me while I try to tell you this in my own way and maybe it will make sense.' He put the spoon down on the saucer. 'Our day is long since over. You see that very clearly when someone like your father dies. We all turn out, to be honest, as much to see which of us are still alive as to pay our respects to the deceased. We're vague echoes now, the old warriors, a bit of an embarrassment in the new Ulster. That funeral the other day – it was a performance, like a state occasion, a remembrance of things past.'

He lifted his cup and sipped his tea. 'At first it's the old

212

nostalgia, how much we miss the comradeship we all had then, the bond we had during the Troubles that united us through dreadful times. But then other thoughts come into your mind. The realities.'

He looked at McCallan. 'Let me tell you about your father.'

He leaned forward and put his cup and saucer down on the tray which he had left on the rug in front of the fire. 'There's a rosy glow that settles on us all with age but when I wipe it away I remember things a bit differently, how they really were. I remember a man who wasn't universally loved by the people who worked with him. I remember a man about whom there were, well, let's say, some doubts.'

McCallan could feel indignation beginning, a reddening at his neck that was not caused by the dry heat from the fire. But he calmed himself because he needed to hear what Hutchinson had to say.

'What do you mean?'

'Your father was very tough. He had a reputation as a hard man.'

'Hardly a failing in his line of work, I would have thought.'

'Oh sure. But he had a reputation for being ruthless at getting the results he wanted. He didn't appear to mind cutting a few corners and things may not always have been done by the book. I never worked directly alongside him, of course, but we all heard the rumours.'

He saw the anxiety in McCallan's face and tried to inject a note of understanding.

'But Christ, what do we expect from people who've seen their colleagues blown to pieces before their eyes? A thing like that – it burns your soul.'

'Rumours,' McCallan said. 'What sort of rumours?'

Hutchinson sighed uncomfortably but he could not retreat now.

'There were people who might have been arrested but weren't. A couple of terrorist operations that were blown by informers in advance but the volunteers ended up dead anyway. And then – and then there was the George Miller business. Many of us were a bit surprised to find Miller involved in something like that. It wouldn't have been his style, exactly.'

'Miller and my father were in the same unit.'

'Yes. And so was Dorothy Taylor, as a matter of interest.'

'I know. But not at the same time.'

'Oh yes, they were.'

McCallan's eyes widened. 'But I thought – are you sure? Would they all have worked together?'

'Absolutely. Miller joined the unit about six months before he died. Taylor and your father were in it then.'

'How come you're so certain? As you say yourself, you didn't work with them.'

'Because it's fresh in my mind for reasons I'll come to in a moment.'

McCallan frowned. If what Hutchinson said was true, why had Taylor glossed over her connection with Miller? Why pretend she did not really know him?

'Mind you,' Hutchinson went on, 'not many of us shed any tears for the people who were taken out. IRA scum, the lot of them. A lot of people thought that was the best way to settle all of this, just dispose of them, not pissing around with a half-baked security policy that had us pretending we were a normal police force when we obviously weren't. And I'm not just talking about the Loyalists either. I mean respectable middle-class people who'd already seen this place starting to return to normal and wanted to see the IRA beaten so that it could stay that way.'

This was the Henry Lomax school of political science and he had heard it all before. How glad he was that Alfie Hutchinson was right: his days were over. But he had a question, one he did not really want to ask.

'Do you think my father could have been involved with George Miller?'

214

Hutchinson put his hands up defensively. 'Please,' he said, 'let me go on first.'

McCallan nodded. He would have to be patient.

'Like I say, I didn't know your father all that well when we were in the force but since we retired, both of us, I got to know him better. Nothing to do with the old RUC, really, but we are – or were—' he fumbled with the tenses – both keen Masons. Your dad became quite important in the Order, Provincial Grand Secretary. I began to meet him at functions and found him a lot more pleasant than the legend. His new life seemed to be agreeing with him. He was great company, full of brilliant stories, certainly enjoyed a drink.'

The room was getting hot so Hutchinson bent over to the fire and turned one of the bars off.

'Then one day he rang here and asked if he could see me, that there was something he wanted to talk to me about. I said OK and we arranged to meet the next afternoon in the bar at the Stormont Hotel, just up the road. He was there when I arrived and he'd already had a few, as I recall. He told me he'd been writing things down, things about the old days. I asked him if it was his memoirs but he said no, it wasn't, nothing like that. He said he wanted to get things off his chest, to put something down on paper. He said he had it all written now and he was keeping it somewhere safe but some day someone would read it and they would understand.'

'How long ago was this?'

'Oh, it must have been the best part of a year ago, I suppose. We had another drink and then he explained why he wanted to talk to me. He said he wanted to find an address for George Miller's widow. He thought I might know – just as you did. Where did her pension payments go? He wouldn't tell me why he wanted to know, just that it was a personal matter, something he wanted to find out discreetly, and he didn't want to start trying to make inquiries himself.

'So I found out for him. I still have contacts in the old department, some people still remember me. While I was at it, I managed to get someone to check, just out of curiosity, on how long your father and Miller worked together. That's how I know Dorothy Taylor was there, too. And now you come along asking about George's widow as well and you can see why your question out there caught me unawares. I won't ask you why you want to know but I'll tell you what I told your father.'

Somewhere in the house the dog barked again and they could hear Mrs Hutchinson telling it to keep quiet. Her husband paused until silence had been restored.

'After Miller was killed, things became very difficult for his widow. There was a lot of aggravation, all centred on the police, suspicions about what we were up to. Collusion with Loyalist terrorists, all that sort of thing. She started getting nasty phone calls, obscene messages, threats, and not all from the Republican side of the house either, I would suspect. Other wives didn't want to see their husbands' jobs going down the swanee because of what had happened. Then there were a couple of stones through her windows and after that she couldn't stand it any more, the poor woman.

'And so she was forced to move away. She had a sister just outside Dublin and she went to live with her. Things were a lot better down there and then after a couple of years she remarried. A school headmaster, apparently. A man called Eamonn Keane.'

Eamonn Keane. Eileen Keane. Eileen Miller.

McCallan thought of the sculpture he had seen in the Ulster Museum. The pain of the women.

He tried to grasp the implications of what he had been told. Hutchinson had not replied directly to the question about his father's possible involvement with Miller, yet McCallan thought he had the answer all the same. Whatever his father's tie-up with Miller, it had certainly been significant enough for him to send Miller's widow £100,000 and conceal where it came from. And where was this document his father had been writing? There was certainly no sign of it in the house.

He came out of his thoughts and saw that he was being studied anxiously.

'Sorry,' he said with a weak smile. 'I was miles away there.'

He looked at Hutchinson. He owed this man some explanation. He could not just get up and say thank you very much, that was all very interesting, sorry to have troubled you, and leave. Hutchinson had been candid with him; it had taken courage to be so honest. If he was any good at reading human nature at all, this was a man he could talk to with frankness.

For the next fifteen minutes, he told him everything, every detail: the gift to Eileen Keane and how it was handled, the incident with the gun that Nigel Rogers had witnessed, his own conversation with Dorothy Taylor and how it would seem that she knew Miller rather better than she had admitted. Then he described the episode at the house when Ann was attacked and finally he gave voice to his tortured thoughts about his father's death itself.

Afterwards Hutchinson said nothing but there was worry bordering on alarm in his eyes.

'All finished?' Mrs Hutchinson chirped as she came round the door to take the tray away.

McCallan stood. 'I really must be going,' he said when she had left again. 'It's been very good of you to listen but it wasn't fair of me. I just didn't know—'

'Wait,' Hutchinson said, gripping his arm firmly. 'What are you going to do about all of this?'

'I don't know. I really don't.'

'If you want my advice, don't do anything. Let it drop.' He was whispering as if someone might be listening. 'Go about your life as if this hadn't happened. You don't need to know any more than you know now. You're a wealthy young man with a great future. Leave the past where it is.'

At the front door, McCallan turned. 'Would you?'

Hutchinson did not give him an answer but as he closed the door behind him he knew what it was.

Chapter Twenty-three

Hutchinson drove into the multi-storey car park in High Street, eased his Toyota gingerly into a space for disabled drivers and admitted that there was not a hope in hell that young McCallan would take his advice. There would be too much of his father's spirit in him for that and he would do what he felt he had to do.

He locked up and made his way stiffly down three flights of stone stairs and into the street. It was five thirty and he was early because the traffic had been a lot lighter than he had expected. His Masonic meeting started at six fifteen and the hall was just a few hundred yards away, round the corner in Arthur Square. He had not actually planned on going to this one. Now that he no longer held any office in his lodge and had retired to the back benches, it was not compulsory for him to be there, but he needed a bit of a distraction, something to take his mind off Jack McCallan and yesterday's conversation.

Carrying the little case containing his regalia, he walked slowly against the steady stream of people, all heading towards buses and trains and car parks, glad that Monday was over at last. At the door of the hall he rang the bell, three short bursts that would indicate that he was not a stranger. After a minute or so, the door opened.

Ned Rossiter was a little breathless. 'Mr Hutchinson,' he said. 'You're the first. I've just finished getting the hall ready.'

'Evening, Ned. Yes, I know I'm a bit early. Sorry to take you by surprise.'

He started up the stairs while the caretaker closed the door behind him. Ned would station himself in the entrance hall until all the members were in and then he would go up and get the drinks ready for the refreshment which always followed the meeting. This was not a temperance lodge.

In the spacious locker room, Hutchinson took his coat off and hung it up, then sat down with the case on his knee and looked around him. They had done a good job fitting this place out. All these splendid lockers, much better than the dusty old cubbyhole it had been before.

He saw the one with Provincial Grand Secretary written on it. That was Bob McCallan's old office and he wondered who would replace him. There were a couple of likely choices. It might be—

Jesus! He stood up abruptly with the force of the thought that had struck him.

The case fell to the floor with a thud. He stared at the locker and rubbed his hand over his mouth. It was possible, just possible.

He looked at his watch. Twenty to six, so there was a bit of time.

'Ned!' he called out and hurried back down the stairs.

Rossiter was looking up as he reached the hall. 'Mr Hutchinson? Anything wrong?'

'No, not at all.' He tried not to sound too excited. 'Bob McCallan, the Provincial Grand Secretary—'

'Ah yes, Mr McCallan, poor man. Nice man he was, too. Actually, Mr Hutchinson, you've just reminded me of something. I took the liberty of clearing out his locker the other day. I brought all his things up to the flat and I meant to contact his son about collecting them. It went clean out of my head until now. Stupid of me.'

'As a matter of fact,' Hutchinson said, 'that's what I was going to mention to you. I was talking to young McCallan yesterday and he asked me if I could pick up his father's belongings for him. Would it be all right with you if I took them?'

'Certainly. Of course, it'll be all right. Will you get them after the meeting?'

'Well, if it's all the same to you, I wouldn't mind having them now. I might forget afterwards and there's still a bit of time before anyone else gets here.'

Rossiter gave him a weary look. 'All right,' he said. 'Come on with me.'

Five minutes later, Hutchinson was back in the locker room with a case which was almost identical to his own. He tried it and found it was not locked and as he lifted the lid he saw a large envelope. He stared at it for a second, then closed the case again sharply.

God, now what would he do? He certainly could not stay here and sit through a Masonic meeting, that was for sure.

He put his coat on, stuck one case under his arm and took the other in his hand. As he bustled down the stairs, he heard the bell ring in the hall. Rossiter opened the door to let two elderly men in but Hutchinson brushed past them abruptly.

'Alfie?' one said. 'You not staying?'

'No. Something's cropped up. Have to rush.' He smiled back at them but before he disappeared round the corner into Ann Street he saw Rossiter give him a puzzled stare.

He was walking quickly but he was aware that he limped a bit more when he did and that was likely to attract attention. But attention from whom? There was nobody following him, for God's sake. He calmed himself, slowed down and made his way back to where he had left his car.

The level on which he had parked was almost empty now that the daytime traffic had gone. He got in and opened the case. The envelope was still there. For some reason he had half expected it would not be, that he would have imagined it. He picked it up, feeling its bulk, telling himself he was being stupid to be so apprehensive; it was probably something entirely innocuous.

He opened it and saw that there was another envelope inside, sealed tightly with sticky tape. He tore it open and found a sheaf of A4 pages, hand-written. He did not know the writing but he assumed it was Bob McCallan's.

He started to read. He did so rapidly for about twenty minutes and at the end there was a pounding in his head and his mouth had dried up.

A car swept by with a squeal of rubber and he gasped aloud.

It parked in a bay just opposite him and a young man and a girl got out. They slammed their doors, the sound loud, reverberating off the concrete walls, then there was the squeak of the electronic lock and they hurried off hand in hand. They had not even noticed he was there.

He was alone again with this envelope and what it contained and he did not want it near him. There was no indication that anyone else knew of its existence but he wished he had not read it. Could he just destroy it? Take it home and burn it? But that would mean bringing it into his house and he did not want to do that.

In a few moments, it came to him what he should do. He put it all back in the big envelope and into Bob McCallan's case, then he got out of the car and locked it again. There was a public phone on the ground floor and he needed to make a call. After that, he would head home but he would have to make a stop along the way.

While Alfie Hutchinson was on the phone, Jack McCallan was crawling home down the motorway, embedded in the teatime commuter traffic and seeing none of it because his mind was elsewhere. But tonight it was focused and he felt strangely calm.

He had a feeling things were starting to fit into place.

That morning he had woken with an idea and had driven into the city to the offices of the *Belfast Telegraph*. For a small charge, their archive material was available to anyone who wanted to trawl through it. They still kept copies of the original newspapers, stored away in a warehouse somewhere, but the archive was also on CD-rom which made browsing an easier and less inky activity.

He had sat down in front of the screen with a cup of coffee from a vending machine and had looked for the events which had led to Miller's killing. First there were the shootings. Four victims, all men, all shot in the head, all apparently executed with some degree of formality. Then a car had blown up, killing the man driving it and the woman with him.

All of the victims had had strong IRA connections. Safe in the fact that the dead could not be libelled, the security correspondents had had free rein to give details of the terrorist operations in which at least five of the six had been known to have been involved.

To the paper's readers, the deaths would have had the appearance of, in the one instance, a bombing mission gone wrong or, in the case of the others, internal terrorist justice at work. There was also speculation about whether Loyalist terrorists might have been involved and there were reports, less prominent, of the familiar and fairly routine Sinn Fein allegations about what they always referred to as British Army death squads.

Next McCallan had found the date of Miller's murder but he had selected the paper for the following day when the story would have been reported first, since the *Telegraph* was an evening newspaper.

Staring from the front page was the face of George Miller, his eyes almost seeming to lock with McCallan's.

Far from being unfamiliar, it was a face he had seen before.

It was the face of the man in the photograph in the desk drawer, the man with his father and Dorothy Taylor. So much for casual acquaintance.

He had flicked on through several editions, seeing the story unfold, the claims and counter-claims. In the midst of it all, he had come upon a report of Miller's funeral. There was a big front page picture showing the widow, the woman who was now Eileen Keane, crying painfully while walking behind the hearse. There were arms around her, supporting her, the arms of a teenage girl with long tousled hair, her head bowed. And underneath there was the abbreviated prose of the caption:

'Daughter Laura comforts her mother Eileen at George Miller's funeral today.'

A daughter. It was the first time there had been any mention of a family. Hutchinson had not referred to one. Andrew Morris, the solicitor, would not have known.

He had moved on, seeing Miller's murder disappear gradually, then re-emerge with the revelations about the gun found in his car and its link with the dead terrorists. Bit by bit the story changed. He read about elections and other political developments, proposals to change the police force, stores of terrorist weapons being uncovered, and as he had skimmed, he had seen that the pace of change, the pace of history itself, which must have seemed slow then, had actually been rapid.

But why had that been the case? What had brought it about after such a long period of stalemate? The answer, as he weighed up the words of the columnists and the pundits and the leader-writers, was that the IRA had always held the key to peace, one way or another. The ease with which so many of their key players had been killed had taken away the last remains of their appetite for war.

It was as Dorothy Taylor had summed it up, although the sculpture in the museum came to his mind again and he wondered how much of a part the Republican women would have taken in the decision to end it. The mothers wondering if their sons were coming home, wives crying over dead husbands, daughters not understanding why daddy had been taken away.

He had turned once more to the picture of Miller's funeral. There she was. Eileen Keane.

What does she look like now? he had said to himself, turning round with embarrassment when he realised he had actually muttered the thought aloud. But there was no one in the room except the librarian who was busy at a bookshelf at the far end and had not heard.

When he had turned back, it was to see something in the picture that he had not noticed before. And as he had stared at the screen, he had begun to wonder.

A car behind blared his horn at him.

The vehicle in front had sped ahead and he had not noticed. He moved on quickly. Once off the motorway, the traffic was thinner and he made it to Dromore quite quickly. He passed Ann's farmhouse, unlit and gloomy, but he was not surprised because she had said she would not be there. He parked outside his own house and lifted a plastic bag from the seat beside him. Once inside, he turned on the television set and the video recorder in the living room and from the bag he took a video disc which he put into the machine.

He had bought it this afternoon from the archive sales office at Ulster Television. He had resisted the temptation to view it there and then because he wanted to be alone when he did so. Somehow he knew it would be an important moment.

He sat down in his father's chair with the remote control in his hand and played it through. It was short, just a couple of minutes, but he was gripped by what he saw on the screen. He played it over and over again, slowing it down and freezing it in places; the impact on him just as strong every time.

He rubbed his head where there was a tightening at his temples, then turned the video off. He switched to the local television news while he got up and poured himself a much-needed whisky. There was a story about some political meeting which had taken place today, there was a big road accident somewhere in which a couple of people had been killed and then came a special investigation by one of the station's reporters about the rising crime rate.

He sat down with his drink to watch it. The reporter had filmed a pay-off standing at the gates of Police Service headquarters. 'Tomorrow,' she said, 'our growing crime problems are expected to be brought into sharp focus once again when the Chief Constable, Dorothy Taylor, makes a lunchtime speech to the Institute of Directors. The text of what she will say has not yet been released but I understand she is expected to attack inadequate Government funding and call for more resources to do the job. We'll have a full report on *Newstime* tomorrow evening but we hope to bring you some of the speech live on our lunchtime news.'

'No thanks,' McCallan said. 'I think I'll give that one a miss.'

Unbidden, a sudden image of Julia rushed into his mind and he flicked to the text service, zapping hurriedly through it. But there was nothing new, no fresh information about the investigation into the Middle Eastern bank and the missing Daniel Shriver.

He needed to talk to someone. But who? He could not involve poor old Alfie Hutchinson again; things had moved on too far since yesterday. He topped up his drink and then had an idea. He found the telephone book, looked up the number he wanted and dialled it.

'Inspector Toner's office, please,' he said, then waited. He wondered how Toner would react to all this, unexpectedly. He had liked him when they had first met and he had a feeling he could trust him. But Toner had gone for the day and was not there. Instead, McCallan got the duty officer to whom he gave his name and number, asking if he would contact Toner and get him to ring him at home.

'It's quite important,' he said.

As he rang off, he noticed that the little voice mail light was flashing and he did not know how he had missed it. He dialled in and found that there was one message.

The voice was a rasp, almost a whisper.

'Jack, it's Alfie Hutchinson. I've found what your father was writing. It was in a locker at the Masonic hall. But I . . . I can't hold on to it. I'll be at home inside the next half-hour. Call me there. I'll wait.'

McCallan checked the time of the call on the phone display.

An hour and a half ago. He had written Hutchinson's number down somewhere. Where was it? On the table with the letters he had not finished, that was it. He found the piece of paper and dialled.

'Hello?' It was a woman's voice.

'Mrs Hutchinson?'

'Yes?'

'It's Jack McCallan here.'

'Oh – yes?' She sounded a bit hesitant. 'Is everything all right?'

'Yes, thank you. Is your husband there?'

'Well, no . . . no, he's not. He's . . . he's gone to meet you.'

'To meet me?'

'Why, yes. He'd gone out to his Masonic meeting and then – well, then, you rang here and said you'd got his message and you'd meet him at a pub down in Holywood. He came home a while ago and I told him and then he left again.'

The skin on the back of his neck tingled. 'How long ago was this?'

'Must be about an hour ago. Look, would you mind telling me what's happening? I'm a bit confused.'

'Oh, it's nothing,' he said, trying to sound soothing, 'just a bit of a mix-up. My fault. Do you know the name of the pub, by any chance?'

She told him. It was down by the seashore and she gave him directions to it. Then he asked her for the number and make of her husband's car.

'Just in case I see him on the road,' he said. 'Listen, Mrs Hutchinson, don't worry about anything. Alfie and I have got our wires crossed a bit, that's all. I'll try and catch up with him and if he comes in in the meantime, tell him I'll call later.'

He rang off. He had lost a lot of time and would have to move quickly. Whatever was going on, he had to get to Alfie. But there was something he could bring with him.

He went to his father's desk drawer and unlocked it.

227

The gun was gone.

He rummaged through the drawer hastily, just in case it was beneath all the other things, but it was not. Then he saw that one of the boxes of ammunition was missing, too.

Someone had been in the house – but when? Not the night Ann was attacked; he had seen the gun then himself.

But this was a problem that would have to wait.

Chapter Twenty-four

He drove furiously, watching out for police cars, squeezing through traffic lights as they changed to red, but he was in luck and he was not caught. Half an hour after he left his house, he turned under the railway bridge in Holywood and along the walled seafront road that led to the pub. The sea was on his right, lit by the amber glow of street lamps, and it lapped hungrily at the protective boulders that prevented it from tugging the wall in.

The pub had coach lamps outside and cobbled glass in the windows to give it that fishing village look. There were not many customers and Alfie Hutchinson was not among them. The barman was wiping a table and clearing away some of the empties. He was young, kitted out in a striped waistcoat and bow tie, and McCallan could see that the neck of his white shirt was grubby.

'Hi,' the barman said. 'What can I get you?'

'Nothing for the moment. Actually, I was looking for someone. You didn't see an elderly man in here a while ago on his own. Wiry hair, very curly. Walks a bit funny.'

'I did. Except he wasn't on his own.'

'Really? You sure?'

'Certain. He came in on his own, right enough. Ordered a half of lager. Then another bloke came in and sat with him for a while. Didn't order anything. After a couple of minutes, the two of them left. The old fellow didn't finish his drink.'

'Do you know how long ago this was?'

The barman thought. 'Oh, half an hour ago, easily.'

'Do you remember what the other man was like?'

'Let's think. Tall, about fifty. Grey moustache. He had a nice coat on, I remember. Looked like it had cost a bob or two. When he came I thought he was a peeler, you know, a policeman, the way he looked around. Like you did. But he was a bit well-dressed for that. Are you one? You look it.'

'No, I'm not. Just trying to track down a friend.'

He went outside to the car park. There were six cars in it, none of them a Toyota, and then he saw it away in the darkness, beyond the pub lights. He approached it slowly and then walked round it. It appeared normal. There was nothing and no one inside. He bent down and looked underneath. No strange devices. What was he doing that for? Was he going mad? He tried the driver's door but it was locked. Wherever Alfie had gone and whoever he was with, he was either on foot or in someone else's car.

He got into his own vehicle and drove back up the road to Belfast. He was outside the Hutchinson house in twenty minutes and he sat for a moment, trying to settle himself so that Mrs Hutchinson would not think he was alarmed, but when he got to the door he could see that she was distressed enough for both of them.

He sat her down in the kitchen and put the kettle on. The Yorkshire terrier growled tentatively at him but he ignored it.

'What should we do?' Mrs Hutchinson said. There were tears in her eyes and she was trying not to let them spill out.

'I think we should call the police, just in case,' McCallan said. 'I'm sure Alfie'll turn up but we might as well err on the safe side and let them keep a look out for him.'

He went out to the hall where they kept the phone. The old tradition, just like his father. In a few minutes he came back and made tea, then sat at the kitchen table beside her.

'That's that done,' he said. 'They'll have someone here in a few minutes.'

'God, the neighbours will be wondering what's going on when they see a police car. You can't do anything here without everybody noticing.'

'One thing puzzles me. Why did you think it was me on the phone?'

'Because of the accent. English. Like yours. And the voice said "It's Jack here."'

Someone was listening in on his phone. It was the only way they could have known that Hutchinson had left him a message. He thought of the night of the intruders at the house. What if they had not been taking anything out, but had been putting something in?

He had been right. Someone had a key.

They talked on until the doorbell rang and the dog started to bark. Mrs Hutchinson told it to keep quiet and McCallan went to let the police in. They were in uniform, two constables, a man and a woman. He brought them into the living room, told them Mrs Hutchinson was too distressed to talk for the moment and filled them in on Alfie's disappearance. He did not want her to hear the things he was leaving out, like the details of the bogus call she had received.

He told them instead that he had arranged to meet Hutchinson in Holywood but that he had been late and had learned from the barman that he had left with someone. Then he had found his car still in the car park, all locked up. It was a bit peculiar, he said, and he did not like to think that anything had happened to his friend.

The police took the details and on McCallan's advice said they would come back and talk to Mrs Hutchinson later.

'In the meantime,' the woman said, 'we'll get someone to have a look at the car and ask around at the pub. There's probably nothing sinister about it. I'm sure Mr Hutchinson will turn up.'

'I'm sure you're right,' McCallan said. But he was not sure at all. Not if Alfie Hutchinson had his father's document, his real last testament.

He left shortly after the police had gone, telling Mrs Hutchinson that he would call later to see if there was any news. When he got home, he crept into the house, feeling like a burglar, aware that someone might be listening. He stood in the hall and stared at the phone, then took off his jacket and went out into the garage where his father kept his tools. He found a box of screwdrivers and brought them back into the house.

He selected one small enough to cope with the little screws. His father had never adjusted to the age of the cordless telephone. He had this one in the hall and an extension in the bedroom and that was it. When he had taken it apart, he could see nothing. It all looked perfectly normal, no strange electronic growths on its internal mechanism. He screwed it back together again, frowning. Someone had to be listening to his calls, unless they had been able to eavesdrop on Hutchinson from wherever he had telephoned.

There was a chair in the hall and he sat down on it, feeling discomfort in the silence of the house. He looked at the lead from the phone and his eye followed it to where the junction box was attached to the wall.

The same screwdriver would do. He knelt and took the plastic housing away gently and there it was, clipped into the wiring where it could not be seen, a minute metal disc, someone's ears into this house.

He left it in place and then he sat in the chair and looked at it for a moment or two until he felt enraged all of a sudden and leaned forward, yanking it from the wiring and throwing it on to the floor. Now they would know what he had discovered but he did not give a damn.

He picked up the phone and rang Mrs Hutchinson again but the call was answered by a woman's voice which he did not recognise. It was her daughter. He explained who he was.

'How's your mother?' he asked.

'Very worried. We all are. She asked me to come over. The police haven't come back yet. We're waiting to hear from them.' There was a voice in the background and he could hear Mrs Hutchinson wondering who was on the phone.

'Don't trouble her,' McCallan said. 'I just wanted to see if there were any developments. I'll be at this number if you need me.'

He hung up and wondered if Toner had called but the voice mail was not flashing. He was thinking about phoning him again when the doorbell rang, making him jump. He had to stand for a moment to let his thumping heart subside and as he did, the bell rang again.

There were two men at the door. One was tall and grey-faced with dark, hollowed eyes, the other was smaller and broader with wispy fair hair and a moustache.

'Mr McCallan?' the taller man asked.

'Yes?'

He put his hand into his inside pocket and pulled out a Police Service warrant card.

'I'm Inspector Mattheson. This is Sergeant Tweed.'

The fair-haired man nodded and muttered a greeting.

'What can I do for you?' McCallan asked.

'It's about your friend Mr Hutchinson. There's some news and I'm afraid it's not altogether good. He's been found in an alleyway down in Holywood, rather badly beaten up. He'll live, I'm glad to say, but he's been taken to the Ulster Hospital at Dundonald and he's in intensive care. Do you know where the hospital is?'

'No.' McCallan said, shocked.

'Well, apparently he's been asking for you, saying there's something he has to tell you, and the hospital thought it might be helpful if you were with him. Since you might have trouble finding the place, we'll take you there and bring you back again.'

Jesus. Poor Alfie. Who had done this to him? He thought of his call to the Hutchinson house. Obviously the family did not know.

'Sir?' Inspector Mattheson was looking quizzically at him.

'What? Oh, right, yes,' McCallan said. 'I'll get my jacket.'

Their car, a large dark saloon, was parked beside his own. 'I'll sit in the back, if you don't mind,' Mattheson said.

'Yes, why don't you sit in the front beside me, sir,' Tweed said, speaking for the first time and holding the passenger door open for him. McCallan noticed he had a slight English accent.

No one spoke as they drove off up the lane. McCallan was beginning to come to his senses again and there was something about these two men, a silent sense of purpose that made him feel uncomfortable. Once he had seen the warrant card, he had accepted what they had to say all too readily. But when he thought about it now, now that it was too late and he was in the car – a detective inspector and his sergeant. Were they not a bit senior to have come on an errand like this? He looked round at Tweed for some sign that he was right to be suspicious but his eyes were fixed on the road ahead as he drove.

They came down the hill into Dromore, through the winding little town and out on to the dual carriageway that would take them to the M1 and Belfast. McCallan broke the silence.

'Any idea what Alfie's injuries are?'

Mattheson leaned forward. 'None at all, sir. Just that he was quite seriously injured. And with his age – well, he's not a young man.'

'Of course. Any idea what might have happened? Who did it?'

'I'm afraid I can't help there, either. But these days,' he sighed, 'this sort of thing's not uncommon, I'm sorry to have to say.'

'No, indeed,' McCallan said, looking out the window. The countryside was hidden in the darkness. His mind was racing. He did not like the smell of these two. But surely he must be wrong. They were genuine policemen and this was a genuine police car. Look – there was the police radio, right in front of him under the dashboard.

But then he thought of the two policemen who had called with Grace Walker. They were genuine enough as well yet no one appeared to know anything about them. He thought of the listening device lying on the floor of the hall where he had thrown it. There had been a dark car, like this one, the night Ann had been hit on the head. His father's gun was gone, too. And a man with an English accent had phoned Mrs Hutchinson.

'How has Mrs Hutchinson taken the news?' he asked.

'She's very distressed, of course,' Mattheson said. 'She was with him at the hospital when they asked us to come for you.'

McCallan felt a sudden, paralysing chill which was replaced very quickly by the calmness that he remembered from his days in the Army when an operation was in difficulties and they had to get out of it. First take in your surroundings, see what use you could make of them, how much trouble you were in. They had placed him well, Tweed driving, Mattheson behind in the back seat, ready to shoot him in the head if he made a false move. The one advantage McCallan had was that they were not aware that he knew. But he was finished if he gave any hint of it.

While they drove, he talked affectionately about what a nice old fellow Alfie Hutchinson was and what a delightful wife he had and how awful this was for both of them. Lovely family, too. Gorgeous grandchildren. All the time, he familiarised himself with the car, where the door catch was, how to get out of the seat belt.

They were approaching the roundabout outside Hillsborough. There was a rumble strip on the road and Tweed began to ease back on the accelerator. McCallan finished what he was saying and stopped talking altogether. As quietly and unobtrusively as he could, he took long, deep breaths to prepare himself, just as he had always shown his business clients, to help them cope with their stress.

There was traffic on the roundabout. Tweed did not have

the right of way and he would have to slow way down. McCallan eased his left hand under his right elbow where it could not be seen and slowly slipped the safety belt out of its catch. He glanced at Tweed but he had not noticed; there were too many other things demanding his concentration.

They were almost at the white line now, almost at a standstill. This was as slow as they were going to get. As Tweed slipped the car up into first gear again, McCallan brought his right arm across to the left side of his face, then swept it back sharply and violently away from him.

The rigid edge of his hand smashed Tweed's nose which folded with a crunch. Tweed yelped with the pain and brought his hands up to his face. McCallan flicked the passenger door open with his left hand and hurled himself backwards out of the car. His shoulders hit the ground hard and painfully and to his horror his right foot had caught in the safety strap, but then the car swerved sharply because Tweed had abandoned control of it and his foot was suddenly free and he was out and away and running for the safety of the darkness.

He needed to get off the road and into the fields as quickly as possible. There was an embankment covered with gorse at the roundabout but it was much too steep and he would never climb up it before they caught him so he ran down the hard shoulder as fast as he could, back in the direction from which they had driven. An oncoming car blinded him for a few seconds and behind him he heard violent braking, the sound of car horns and the slamming of doors.

Then there was another sound, the sharp crack of an automatic weapon, followed by two more shots. He ducked instinctively although he knew he was away from the light and he doubted if they could see him. But he had to be certain. There was wooden fencing along the side of the road. He did not stop to climb it carefully but hurled himself at it without slowing his pace.

He did not see the long, sharp nail that protruded angrily from the top.

He cleared the fence on his belly and, as the nail ripped into his side, it brought a sudden agonising pain that made him gasp. He fell into the muddy field with a groan, feeling nausea sweep over him. But he had to get up and keep going. In the darkness behind, he could hear more horns blaring and then the sound of a police car roaring off somewhere with its siren wailing.

He ran on for another few hundred yards, holding his side, his feet sinking into the muddy earth, and then he stepped into a pothole and fell again. He got up and looked back. The night was dark but the sky was clear and in the moonlight it did not appear that anyone was following him.

His side hurt a lot and the hand that held it was covered in blood. He had no idea how badly he was bleeding but he had to try to stem it. He took his jacket off and ripped his shirt apart, shivering from shock and the cold night air. Then he put the jacket back on and stumbled forward, holding the crumpled shirt over the wound, hoping he would not pass out from loss of blood before he got to where he was going.

Chapter Twenty-five

Grace Walker was about to slam the door and ring the police when she realised who it was. At the same time she saw the blood. Before he could speak to explain she hurried him inside.

'You'll have to get out of those clothes,' she said. 'Where are you hurt?'

'My side,' he gasped. He was covered in slimy wet mud and he appeared to have fallen in more than that. A pungent stench filled the hall. He kicked off his sodden shoes and she led him upstairs to the bathroom. He undressed in the shower and washed some of the dirt away while Grace went to fetch her nurse's bag. She did not ask him what had happened; there would be time for that later. When she came back he was wrapped in a towel which was stained with blood where he held it to his wound.

'You better come in here,' she said, showing him into her bedroom.

He lay down on the bed while she looked at the injury. It was nasty but fortunately not that deep and the bleeding seemed to have almost stopped. All the blood had made it look worse than it was. She bathed it in a disinfectant solution and he winced with the pain. Then she took some sutures from her bag to stitch it up and gave him an injection in case of infection.

She opened a drawer and took out a white sheet. 'I haven't got any proper bandages, I'm afraid,' she said, as she ripped it into strips.

When she had wrapped it around him securely she went into the bathroom and came back with a soft blue towelling robe. 'It's mine and it's probably a bit on the small side,' she said, 'but put it on anyway and come downstairs.'

The robe did not fit too badly since Grace was not a small woman. He sat in the kitchen and watched her open a tin of chicken broth which she put on to heat. He was aware that she had not asked him anything, leaving him to explain in his own good time.

'I'm sorry about this,' he said. 'I was in pain and you were the only person I could turn to.'

'I'm glad you did. That cut could have turned really nasty. You seem to have got into a bit of bother.'

It was the understatement of the century and he told her so. He hesitated. The last person he had confided in was Alfie Hutchinson who had now disappeared. He did not want anything happening to Grace as well, although no one knew he was here and as soon as possible he would get out of her house and away.

But he would have to tell her what had been going on. It was unavoidable and if anything further happened to him, well then, she would know. He gave her the whole story, right back as far as the legacy to Eileen Keane. He told her about his father with the gun, the files he had seen today, Alfie Hutchinson, the bug in his phone.

She listened wide-eyed as he described his escape from Mattheson and Tweed and how he had crisscrossed the country roads for hours, ducking in and out of hedges when cars appeared, losing his way several times before he managed to get to her house.

'It's them. Definitely them,' she said when he gave a description of the two men. 'They're the two who came to see me after my sister was killed. No doubt about it.'

McCallan took a spoonful of the soup. 'Then who the hell are they and who are they working for? What's it about, Grace?'

'This Inspector Toner you mentioned. Is it worth while trying to contact him again?'

He shook his head sadly. 'How can I? These two men, Mattheson and Tweed, if they're real police officers, then who can I trust? How do I know that Toner isn't mixed up with them? I just can't take the chance.'

There was a scratching at the kitchen door and it startled him. 'It's all right,' Grace said. She got up and opened it and a large black cat walked in confidently, its tail erect and curling. She turned the key in the lock and then secured a bolt that was fitted at the top.

'God, Grace, I'm sorry,' McCallan said when he saw what she was doing.

'What for?'

'Here I am putting you in danger. If they knew I was here. But I had nowhere else to go.'

'I told you. You did the right thing.' She presented a brave front but he knew that inside she was frightened.

'I've got to get away. Leave you in peace.' He stood up but he felt weak and light-headed all of a sudden and flopped back into the chair again.

Grace laughed. 'Don't be ridiculous. Where would you go? And more to the point, what in? My bathrobe? No, you're going to have to stay here tonight and we'll sort it all out in the morning. No one will come here anyway; they won't think of that.'

She leaned forward and took his face in her strong hands. 'Jack, I'll help you all I can. Whatever you suspect may have happened in the past, your father was kind and generous to my sister. Even in death, he was good to her. I can't overlook that nor would I want to. Now let's get you upstairs so that you can have some rest. You can have my bed tonight. I'll make one up in the spare room.'

He was much too exhausted to protest so he went up the stairs with her, slipped gently under the duvet and drifted into sleep.

In the room next to him, with the light off and the curtains open, Grace pulled a chair to the window and watched the occasional car go past.

Chapter Twenty-six

Inspector Barry Toner set out for the office from his home in Banbridge, just twenty minutes south of Lisburn. It was seven thirty. He was slightly early and very angry.

That idiot in the duty office had not given him the message last night that Jack McCallan had called. Only when Toner had phoned in this morning had someone else found a note and mentioned it. Jesus, some people were thick. That clown would be on report as soon as he got in. He had tried McCallan's number already although for some reason there was no answer, just the voice mail message, but Dromore was on his way to work, more or less, and he would drop by.

The day was hardly light yet and there was a soft, damp mist that clung to the branches along the winding back roads. He had not been to the McCallan house before but he had got the address from the office where it had been on file with a report of the incident there the previous week. He found it eventually and drove down the sloping laneway. There was a car outside, McCallan's apparently, judging by the English registration. He got out and rang the doorbell, then stepped back and looked up at the house. The curtains were all open but there were no lights, no sign of life. He tried the bell again. Still no response. He would go round the back and try there. He knocked on the kitchen door, then turned the handle. Locked. He cupped his hands over his eyes and peered in through the window.

There was someone sitting in a chair at the table and there appeared to be something lying on the floor.

It took a moment for him to register what he was seeing.

Just a mile and a half away, McCallan was getting up. He felt stiff and his side was still sore but it did not appear to have started bleeding again.

He went into the bathroom where he found his socks, underpants, jacket and trousers drying on a radiator. She had tried to clean them as best she could but they were a crumpled mess. The shirt was just a bloody rag, beyond redemption. The trousers were still a little damp but he put them on anyway, as well as the socks and underpants, and went downstairs, bare-chested. Grace was grilling bacon and the smell was irresistible. The cat was standing beside her, rubbing itself possessively against her legs. She turned when he came in and for a moment he saw her eyes linger on his body. He doubted if she saw too many semi-naked men in her kitchen. Then the look passed and she smiled.

'Toast? Tea? Fried egg?'

'Everything,' he said. 'I'm ravenous.'

When it was ready, she set a plate in front of him and he started into it. While he ate, he told her what he had been thinking.

'My best bet is to get across the border, right out of the jurisdiction for a time. That's the only way I can be sure every policeman I see isn't part of this, whatever it is, and isn't going to kill me. Forgive me if I sound a bit paranoid but I think I've got good reason.'

She did not disagree. 'How do you propose to get there? Or can I guess?'

He looked at her with a coy smile. 'Well, I was wondering. Your car. Could I borrow it? I can't very well go and get my own. The house is probably being watched.'

She shook her head. 'Sorry, Jack. I knew that's what you were going to say. Can't do it, I'm afraid.' She got up and fetched the teapot from the work surface and refilled both their cups. 'It's a sensible idea all right but I can't help. I've got to go to a meeting in Newry Hospital this morning. I can't miss it because I'm giving a talk at it and I've no other way of getting there in time. I can't cry off and if I don't turn up, the meeting will be a disaster and people will be a bit anxious and start wondering where I am.'

She sat down again and the cat jumped up into her lap. She lifted it gently and set it on the floor. 'On the other hand,' she said, 'I could take you with me. When you get to Newry you're almost there. Right on the border. I could drive you across.'

He thought for a moment. 'Even better, if I'm in Newry I could get a train, a train to Dublin. Why don't I go there? There's a lot more I still have to find out and I know that's where some of the answers are.'

She frowned. 'Are you sure that's what you want to do?'

'It's what I have to do, isn't it? I certainly can't hang around here making us both a target.'

She nodded and patted his knee. 'OK. Now let's fix you up.'

She left him in the kitchen and he heard her go up the stairs. When she came back she was carrying a dark double-breasted grey suit and a white shirt. 'I'd almost forgotten about these,' she said. 'They're your father's. I mentioned them to you on the day of Beth's funeral, if you remember. Think they'll fit?'

His father had been slightly taller, broader, too, but he must have had a smaller collar size. The shirt was a bit tight at the neck, although he could leave it open, and the suit was slightly roomy but it would do. He retrieved his wallet from his own grubby jacket.

'Shoes?' he wondered suddenly.

'I did my best,' Grace said, holding up the pair he had worn through the fields last night. They had more or less dried out and she had tried to polish them but they would go into the nearest bin as soon as they could be replaced. He felt strange, a bit self-conscious, in these expensive but rather drab clothes. The jacket had a faint but familiar smell, a fading mixture of cologne and cigar smoke, and it made his father's presence seem very strong all of a sudden.

Grace interrupted the moment. She had her coat on and her bag in her hand.

'Time to go.'

They left the house and drove towards the dual carriageway, taking a tortuous route that led them away from the vicinity of McCallan's home. As a result, they were long gone by the time the stream of police cars from Lisburn and Banbridge screamed into the area. And when the security cordon was being set up, the vehicle checkpoints, the diversion signs, they were well on their way.

Chapter Twenty-seven

Barry Toner stood in the hall looking into the kitchen as the scenes-of-crime team padded around. They wore white sterile overalls and operating-theatre overshoes and were equipped with all the trappings of modern forensic science. They spoke hardly a word. The routine had taken over and each of them had gone into his or her role. Nothing in the kitchen would escape examination. Every surface, every crack, every crevice would be subjected to it to see what story it could tell.

The two dead men would not be saying much.

The police doctor was finishing with them. The older of the two was in the chair, his head right back and his arms dangling at his sides. There was a black hole in his forehead, not quite at the centre, and his blank eyes stared at the ceiling. His mouth was wide open and Toner could see all the metal fillings in his back teeth. The other man, the fair-haired one, was on the floor beside him, next to an upturned chair, lying on the right side of his face. There was a gaping hole where his left eye had been. In addition, his nose had been all smashed up and a blood-sodden handkerchief lay on the floor beside him. He was a mess.

A search of their pockets had identified who they were: an Inspector Mattheson and a Sergeant Tweed. A double police murder. A computer check had shown that it was even worse than that. They were both members of the Chief Constable's own headquarters staff, her inner circle, the team she described as her secretariat. She was on her way here now and although the bodies could be taken away at any time they would not be moved until she arrived.

She would not be on her own, either. Trevor Wyatt, the Divisional Commander, was coming and so was the Head of the Regional Crime Squad, Denis McIvor. Toner did not like McIvor and McIvor did not like him. He would never make Chief while that man was around. McIvor was a God-fearing Protestant, a lay preacher in some kind of evangelical sect, and his father and grandfather had both been in the old RUC. Toner knew that McIvor found his own background and his West Belfast origins hard to take. However, he should not take his eye off the ball just because of all the hassle McIvor would bring with him. There were questions to be asked. For a start, what the hell had Mattheson and Tweed been doing here?

'How long do you think they've been dead, doctor?' he asked.

She was a short woman in her forties, plump in her white overalls. She straightened up a little stiffly from bending over Tweed.

'Not long. Matter of hours. They're not that cold. I'd say – oh, somewhere around midnight or either side of it.'

After McCallan's call, anyway. Damn it, where had he disappeared to? That young man was in deep shit.

'No prizes for guessing the cause of death?' he asked.

'Only for guessing what kind of gun was used, I suppose. You won't know that until the pathologist digs the bullets out of their brains. Not their own guns anyway. I see they're still safely anchored. These boys would have had a big surprise.'

She pointed to Tweed. 'This one's been in a fight, too. Mightn't have happened here, though, from the way things look. Didn't win it, either.'

Toner went back up the hall to the front of the house. Police vehicles were backed all the way up the lane with their roof lights flashing. The van from the morgue had arrived and was having trouble getting in, as would the Chief Constable and her entourage when she turned up.

He found a uniformed sergeant. 'Let's get a bit of traffic control going here,' he said. 'Clear all these bloody cars back up on to the road. Jesus, this is a shambles.' As he said it, he knew he did not mean just the parking problem.

The main road above had been sealed for several hundred yards at either end. There was white tape across it and police cars positioned to stop anyone unauthorised getting through. At one end, Constable Gary Irvine stood beside his vehicle and watched a Post Office van drive cautiously towards him.

'What's up?' the driver said, getting out.

'Police operation. You'll have to take one of the other roads, I'm afraid. This one's closed.'

The postman held up a handful of letters. 'But I've got post for that house down there.' He pointed in the direction of the McCallan home. 'What am I going to do with it?'

'Better give it to me,' Irvine said and took the bundle. There were three letters. Two were in small brown envelopes and looked like bills and the third was large and bulky with the name and address scrawled on the front.

He looked up and, over the postman's shoulder, he saw a large van coming up the road, fast. It had a big aerial and an array of other electronic attachments and UTV in bright yellow and blue lettering on the side. Christ, how had they got on to this so quickly? He threw the letters into the back seat of the car, sent the postman on his way, then stepped forward with his hand raised.

Back down at the house they were going through everything, not just the kitchen, and in a desk drawer they had found a firearms certificate authorising the late Bob McCallan to carry a personal protection weapon. There was some ammunition but no sign of the gun to go with it. There would be a central record of its markings and you did not have to be a genius to come up with the idea of comparing them to the bullets which the pathologist would extract from the dead men.

'Something here, sir,' one of the team in the kitchen called to Toner. He stood at the doorway but did not enter. The man was kneeling on the floor over at the radiator, away from the bodies. He was using a surgical instrument to scrape something from the edge of the floor tiles and put it into a sterile container.

'Traces of what seems to be blood all along the edge here,' he said. 'You wouldn't see it unless you were looking. And I would say it's definitely not recent. Nothing to do with these two.'

Toner frowned. What had been happening here?

He heard car doors slamming and then there was a commotion at the front of the house and he turned to see the Chief Constable, the Divisional Commander and Denis McIvor. The three of them were looking at him as if all of this were his fault, particularly McIvor, a dry-faced man with a tight mouth.

They marched forward purposefully towards the kitchen but as politely as he could he stepped in front of the doorway to block their path.

'Ah – sorry, everyone. Crime scene. We don't want it violated.'

They were taken aback by his quiet authority and they stopped in their tracks.

'This is Inspector Toner, ma'am,' McIvor said with distaste. 'He found the bodies.'

Taylor nodded to him and he explained the circumstances which had led to his being there. As he spoke, the three senior officers stood at the door of the kitchen and looked but did not go in. Divisional Commander Wyatt was behind McIvor and the Chief Constable, peering over their shoulders. He was very tall, about six foot five, and just a few years older than Toner. A Londoner, he was a product of the police academic fast track, one of Taylor's bright young things, and was said to be destined for a Chief Constable's position back across the water before too long.

The horror they saw gripped them but Toner broke the spell.

'Have you any idea what they might have been doing here, ma'am?'

Wyatt swung round to him. 'You're not proposing to interview the Chief Constable, are you?'

'Well, no. I just thought—'

'It's all right, Trevor,' Dorothy Taylor said, turning away and moving back into the hall. She looked a bit agitated and upset, which was understandable, but as she moved on into the house, first into the small living room, then into the bigger room and back into the hall again, she glanced around furtively and Toner could not shake the thought that she was looking for something.

'I've no idea why they were here,' she said eventually, 'or what Jack McCallan's role is in this, either. Do you know where he is?' She looked at Toner and he could see the distress in her eyes.

'No, ma'am. But we've discovered that his father's personal protection weapon's missing.' He was going to mention the blood traces but he changed his mind; it might always be a false alarm.

'They were good men,' Taylor said, addressing no one in particular. 'They'd been part of my staff when I was in the west of England – Mike Mattheson was from here originally, of course – and I found positions for them here when I was appointed. You need good men around you, people you can trust, especially when you move into a new environment. They've been with me ever since. Good officers.'

Toner remembered her address at the funeral. 'You know Jack McCallan, ma'am,' he said, 'and you knew his father very well, of course. Were you aware of any connection between him and Inspector Mattheson and Sergeant Tweed, anything at all that would explain their presence?'

'I think that will be enough,' Wyatt said sharply. He stepped forward in front of Toner and glowered down at him. 'This has been quite a shock for the Chief Constable, as it has for all of us. But I think that in view of your own rather unusual involvement in this case, Inspector, it's better if someone else takes charge of it.'

'I'm sorry, sir?' Toner asked.

'Well, you were the first person on the scene, weren't you? You'll have to give a statement about what you found and how you came to be here. I think it would be rather peculiar if you were involved in the investigation in any other way, don't you?'

Toner began to speak but changed his mind. There was no point; no answer was required. How could someone as young as Wyatt be such a pompous asshole? Was Dorothy Taylor impressed by this sort of thing?

'In view of those circumstances and in view of the seriousness of the crimes which have been committed, I'm asking Mr McIvor to take personal charge of the case and to put a senior team on it,' Wyatt said. 'Obviously, he'll draw on your help, if he needs it.'

Toner looked at McIvor smiling smugly and he knew that that was highly unlikely.

Wyatt turned to the Chief Constable. 'What about your speech today, ma'am? The Institute of Directors. Will you still go ahead with it?'

'Of course,' Taylor said firmly. 'I've got to. More to the point, I want to. It's an important speech and a lot of people are waiting to hear what I have to say. And it will give me an opportunity to mention something in public about this dreadful loss.'

The back door opened and they looked towards the sound. Two men wearing overalls came in and laid body bags down on the floor.

Chapter Twenty-eight

It was coming up to one o'clock and the banqueting hall of the hotel was packed. They were catering for four hundred today, round tables for eight or ten with white linen and flower arrangements. Most people were hungry but they would have to be patient a bit longer. In order to satisfy the appetite of the lunchtime news programmes first, Dorothy Taylor's speech would be given before they ate, not after. The businessmen waited and consoled themselves with the wine and hoped that she would not speak for too long, in spite of what had happened this morning.

Nevertheless, it had subdued them. For many, the murders of two policemen had a resonance of the past, of the bad old days which they had hoped were forgotten. Not that this was anything like that, of course, but it was nonetheless nasty and when policemen were killed you always thought back.

The hotel was built above sloping lawns leading down to Belfast Lough. The view was ever changing and never dull, a version of what Taylor saw from her own front window. Indeed, she could have walked here from her home in a matter of minutes. The long top table from where she would speak was along the windows, on a slightly raised platform so that everyone in the room could see, especially the television crews in a cramped clutch at one end, corralled out of the way, waiting to bring her address to the viewers at home.

Rather unexpectedly, one of those viewers would be the

President of the Institute, Henry Lomax, if he was well enough to look in. The Deputy President had taken his place and had already apologised to the gathering, explaining that Lomax had been taken ill and was unable to attend. His absence was almost as much of a talking point as the murders. 'Not like him to be unwell,' someone said. 'Chest pains, apparently. Sounds like ticker trouble.'

It was just after one now. The news bulletins had started and the television producers watching down the line from their studios in Belfast were drumming their fingers nervously. But they smiled and half-relaxed as they saw the big doors at the end of the room open and Taylor and two of her aides walk in. The room rose gradually in applause as people woke up to the fact that she had arrived. By the time she reached the top table and the place where the toastmaster had set her lectern, it was a full-scale standing ovation. She surveyed the room, her face drawn. She nodded in acknowledgement for a few moments, then sat.

Her audience settled down to wait and then the Deputy President rose. He was a young man in his late twenties who, after a lack-lustre education, had become a brilliant entrepreneur, making an outstanding success of his family's rather dreary printing firm. But public speaking was not his forte, especially not on a day like today when he found himself pitched into it.

With fluttering hands he clutched the lectern as if he thought it would prevent him from falling. 'Ladies and gentlemen,' he said, then tapped the microphone unnecessarily. 'I'm sure you don't need me to tell you that we are gathered here today in rather unexpected and tragic circumstances. We are therefore all the more grateful to have our guest . . . to have the guest we have here today. So without further ado, it gives me great pleasure to introduce Dorothy Taylor, the Chief Constable of the Police Service of Northern Ireland.'

He sat, visibly relieved, and Taylor rose to renewed applause.

When it had faded, she turned to her host. 'Mr Deputy President, ladies and gentlemen,' she began and took a sip from a glass of water.

There was the flash first, brief, erasing everything with its white light.

And there was the roar, devastating and shattering, as the world and the room and the people in it were torn to pieces. Then came the dust, thick clouds, blinding, choking, and the screams of the injured and the dying.

Sir Iain Crichton, the Secretary of State for Northern Ireland, was at home in Gloucestershire, congratulating himself that he had done a good morning's work at his constituency clinic. He had listened with all the concern he could muster to complaints about rights of way, poor water pressure and road repairs not completed, while his private secretary, Miles Beardsley, a pale young man with windswept fair hair, sat and took detailed notes. This was not his proper job, strictly speaking, but he was ambitious and eager to please.

They had moved on to the Ram's Head for lunch and had been joined by Sir Iain's estate manager for a discussion over a pint about rather more private business involving sheep prices and the estimates for repairs to some of Sir Iain's farmworkers' cottages. Their lunch had just arrived, hotpot for three.

The mobile phone rang in Beardsley's pocket.

Within minutes the car was at the door and they were away, leaving the food untouched and steaming on the table. They used several phones at once as they sped along the country roads. The driver was talking to the nearest RAF base. A regular flight from Heathrow to Belfast was out of the question because they needed to get there quicker than that. Crichton was telling his wife why he had to leave all of a sudden and Beardsley was trying to get patched through to Crete where the Prime Minister was attending a European summit conference.

The moment he reached him, Crichton took the phone,

hearing the eerie reverberation of his own voice as it spanned the miles from earth to space and back down again, hardly able to believe what he was saying himself.

In the affluent suburb of Ballsbridge, on the south side of Dublin, an unmarked police car with two watchful men in it sat in the grounds of a dignified Georgian mansion which had long ago been turned into several superior flats.

The radio squawked a message to them.

In the topmost and smallest apartment, the Prime Minister of the Republic of Ireland, an office which rejoiced in the traditional Gaelic title of An Taoiseach, the chieftain, was also engaged in a little private business but it was an activity which would have taken a great many of the good people of Ireland by surprise had they known about it.

The Taoiseach was a man who stood solidly for the values of the family and set great store by his own, parading them for the cameras at every opportunity. He had five children from eight to eighteen, three girls and two boys, and his wife was still undeniably glamorous in late middle age. But at the very moment the radio message was being delivered to the car waiting below, he was sitting on the edge of a brass bed, wearing nothing but a silk robe, fondling the penis of a naked young man from the Department of Public Affairs.

He stood and let the robe fall to the floor, just as the two men ran from the car and into the building.

Half an hour later, McCallan's train was nearing Dublin. At last. When he had got to Newry with Grace he had discovered he had missed the express and that he would have a long time to hang around for another one. It had been her idea that he should go to Dundalk instead and try to get one of the district trains from there. It was just a few miles away and at least he would be across the border. So he had made his way to the bus station from where there was a regular commuter service.

But when he had arrived in Dundalk, he had found he had a little time to wait there, too, before the next train came, so he had gone up the street and into the first reasonable-looking man's shop he had come across to get something to replace his father's shirt. He had not had a lot of time to browse and he had opted for a thin black roll-neck jumper which he reckoned would be anonymous and warm and after he had tried it for size he had kept it on.

Next he had gone into a shoe shop where the young male assistant had been roused momentarily from boredom by the sight of McCallan's current footwear.

'That's what you get for standing around on a building site in the wrong sort of shoes,' McCallan had said ruefully, by way of explanation. The assistant had given a watery smile and had resumed his normal indifferent state, tossing a shoe horn idly from hand to hand.

A pair of black casual shoes with heavy rubber soles looked like they would do. They did not exactly go with the formality of the suit but they would be comfortable and easy to wear in. He also bought a small sports bag and on the way back to the station had stopped off at a chemist's to buy a hairbrush, shaving gear, soap, a toothbrush and toothpaste. He had dropped his old shoes into a litter bin and made it back to the station just as the train was pulling in. As it set off again, he had squeezed into the grubby toilet with his purchases and had re-emerged, feeling cleaner and less conspicuous.

The train was bringing him to Dublin all right but it had stopped at every halt and hole in the hedge, places he had never heard of before and probably never would again. They were pulling into another little station now. He looked out and to his surprise saw the name Malahide coming closer. East coast geography was not his strong point and he had not realised Malahide was one of the stops along the way. That would save him going to Dublin and hiring a car.

But he would need a car anyway, he thought as he stepped on to the platform. He stopped at the ticket office on his way out and asked the woman behind the glass where he might be able to get one. She seemed uncertain.

'Hertz? Avis? Anything like that?' he asked.

'Oh, I don't think you'll find any of those around here, unless you go into Dublin or the airport. But there's a garage down the street. They sell second-hand cars and they might be able to do something for you.'

He thanked her and walked out of the station, turning left into the busy main street. It was an active little town which appeared to him more English than Irish and it had the feel of old money about it. Interior design and deliberately quaint bookshops mingled with the butcher and the greengrocer. Cars seemed to be able to park wherever they liked and he did not notice too many Skodas among them. There were tennis courts and a substantial clubhouse with a sign proclaiming it as the Malahide lawn tennis and croquet club. To his left there was the road to the harbour and a well-kept Georgian terrace with doors in bright colours.

He saw the garage ahead of him on the other side of the street. It was festooned with fluttering bunting and cars sat in the forecourt with fluorescent price tags on their windscreens. A small flight of steps led up to a glass-fronted office, outside which a middle-aged man in a suit was talking with apparent authority to a mechanic in overalls. This was the boss, by the look of it. McCallan explained what he was looking for.

'Sure,' the man said, coming down the steps. 'We'll be able to help you out. How long would you be wanting the car for?'

'Oh, no more than twenty-four hours.'

'There's my son's car here,' the man suggested, walking over to a compact Volkswagen. 'He's away in England at the moment, due back the day after tomorrow. Why don't I let you have that?'

'Fine.'

'Then we'd better go up to the office and fill out a few forms.'

They were walking back towards the building when a young man came bursting out.

'Quick! The news is coming on again!'

'Right,' the man said and began to hurry.

'What's all the excitement?' McCallan asked.

'Haven't you heard? The Chief Constable's been killed up in the North. Blown to bits by a bomb.'

The wind from Belfast Lough was hard in the jogger's face and he felt he had suffered enough. He had done four miles along the sea path and if he cut up into the country park and began to double back he would at least have the shelter of the trees, although the steep hill would be a bastard. Come on. A young fellow like you. You can handle it.

He veered off to his right and up the sharp incline that led to the woodland, already feeling the pull on his calf muscles and the pressure on his breathing, but he kept his head down, watching for awkward rocks and threatening roots, and did not slacken his pace. Only when he was among the trees did he raise his head, seeking out the contrours of the path in front. The ground all around him was covered in long grass and thick brown ferns and the branches above swayed and creaked as they took the force of the wind. A blackbird half flew, half scurried across the path ahead, shrieking its alarm.

His eyes followed where it went and then saw something else, in among the bushes. He looked away and ran on. Don't stop. It's nothing. Just your imagination.

He kept running, another two hundred yards or so, and then he knew he could go no further. He stood, breathing hard, bent forward with his hands on his thighs, before he turned. He had to go back and see.

He ran lightly, more slowly, as he tried to find the spot. Was that it? No – yes, there it was. He stopped and looked around to see if there was anyone else about but he was alone. He stepped cautiously off the path and into the undergrowth. It

was like a big bundle, really, like a parcel of old clothes, but
. . . oh God.

He was looking at the body of an elderly man. When he
got right up close he could also see what someone had done
to him before they had shot him neatly in the centre of the
forehead.

He turned suddenly and threw up all over one of his
new Nikes.

Chapter Twenty-nine

McCallan drove out of the forecourt and turned right towards the coastal road. He needed to get away from that garage, the excitement round the television set, and go somewhere to collect his thoughts for a few minutes. He had the address on a slip of paper in his wallet and first he stopped at a newsagents to ask for directions. To his relief he discovered that at least he was heading the right way.

He drove on out of the town, past a sign that thanked him for keeping Malahide tidy, and about a mile further on he pulled into a deserted picnic area with damp wooden tables. Two ragged crows poking in an overflowing litter basket flew off as he drove up. The tide was out, leaving silver pools trapped in the undulating wet sand, and a small fishing boat with flaking paint lay high and dry on a bank.

It was incredible. Dorothy Taylor was dead. She had taken the full force of the blast and in his former life he had seen what that could do. They would find bits of her clothing, unidentifiable pieces of flesh, that was all. God knows how many others were dead. At least six, the news had said, but it was bound to be much more than that. McCallan's heart sank with the thought that Henry Lomax might be among them.

But he had himself to worry about, too. Last night he had been a target for murder; now he was a suspect. The news bulletin had reported on the other murders of the day, two of the Chief Constable's staff officers found shot in a house at Dromore, and he had seen the footage of the front of his own home with all the police activity outside it. Now the world was looking for him but he had got across the border in time.

One or two of the reporters were beginning to suggest that there was perhaps a link between the Chief Constable's death and the killing of Mattheson and Tweed. Either that or it was one hell of a coincidence, that was for sure. People were even beginning to wonder if some new terrorist group had been let loose.

He had stood in the garage in utter disbelief, watching the Head of the Regional Crime Squad giving an interview and saying they wanted to talk to Mr McCallan in order to eliminate him from their inquiries. But everyone knew what that meant. They did not appear to have a photograph of him yet, which was helpful, but he had paid for the car rental with a credit card and he had also had to produce his driving licence. The garage owner had been preoccupied with what was on television and had left McCallan with the office assistant who had not been paying enough attention to notice the name. But it was only a matter of time before one of them did.

He started the engine again and turned back on to the road, thinking about Lomax. He would have been beside Taylor at that lunch. As President of the Institute he would have introduced her. There was no way he could have escaped the blast.

He switched on the radio and found that all normal programmes had been ditched in order to provide extended news coverage. They reckoned a couple of pounds of high explosive had been used, placed under the table among the electrical wiring, or perhaps hidden in the base of the microphone itself, and activated by a timing device. There were more names for the dead now, all well-known Ulster business people, among them the Institute's young deputy president. The estimate of six fatalities had now risen to ten, with sixty-eight injuries, thirty of them serious. But why was there no mention of Henry?

And all of a sudden there it was. He caught the name 'Lomax' and turned the volume up.

'Apparently he had been taken ill and had been unable to attend today's lunch,' the presenter was saying, 'but a short time ago Mr Lomax spoke to one of our reporters from his home outside Newcastle.'

Lomax's voice came down a phone line. 'I'm deeply, deeply shocked and saddened,' he said. He sounded hesitant and his speech was a bit slurred. McCallan wondered if it was medication or if he had been drinking. Either was possible. 'I have lost so many good friends in this appalling outrage. It's dreadful, dreadful.'

'Do you feel lucky that you weren't there yourself?' the reporter piped in.

'I don't think luck comes into it. I am fortunate not to have been there, of course, but that pales into . . . into insignificance compared to these awful events and the loss of so many good lives and the grief . . . the grief that their poor families will be suffering.'

The interview ended and the programme switched to a politician in the studio. Thank God. At least Henry was safe but he sounded old and ill. He hoped he was all right.

A housing development was coming up ahead and he wondered if this could be it. Not all of Malahide wore the dignity of centuries. There were more modern, less distinguished properties but the people who lived proudly in them could still boast the address. These particular houses were detached four-bedroomed villas and when he came nearer he saw that there were rows and rows of them, all set unhappily close to each other.

It took him a minute or two and a couple of wrong turns before he found the one he wanted. There was a For Sale sign outside it.

Barry Toner turned into the McCallan laneway and acknowledged the cursory salute from the uniformed constable who stood at the head of it. The road had been reopened but the house itself was still under quarantine. The scenes of crime team had long gone and would be in their labs now, poring over their discoveries, of which there had been many since Toner had looked through the kitchen window this morning.

At the morgue, the bullets had been removed from Mattheson and Tweed. On examination, they had been found to be a perfect match for Bob McCallan's missing gun, as Toner had expected they would be.

Then there was the matter of the bug.

It was after all the top brass had departed and the hall was empty again that it had been spotted lying on the carpet underneath the table near the loosened cover of the telephone junction box. Someone had been listening to McCallan's calls and he had found out about it.

Half an hour later, when they discovered Mattheson and Tweed's car a few miles away, they knew who the eavesdroppers had been. A very surprised farmer had found the vehicle hidden in a semi-derelict hayshed into which his dog had gone sniffing out of curiosity. It was intact, locked up, but when they had got into it they had found a small receiver plumbed into the glove compartment.

There had been something else in there as well, an odd discovery which worried Toner when he heard about it: a diary which belonged to Bob McCallan's housekeeper.

At police headquarters, they had got into the office the two men had used. It was tucked away down a corridor where old records were kept, away from the hustle and bustle of the main thoroughfares. No one seemed to know precisely what brief Mattheson and Tweed had. They had always reported directly to the Chief Constable, and she was not around to ask.

Their computer files provided the best hope although for a while they had had trouble getting past the security codes. But now they were in and gazing in amazement at a treasure chest of secrets. It included personal and in some cases damning dossiers on prominent politicians. Several of them, it was noted, had been Taylor's early critics but were now among her most ardent supporters. There were surveillance files on some of her senior officers as well as on members of the Northern Ireland Police Authority. Taylor, it would seem, had been keen on being a step ahead of her enemies, real or imaginary. It reminded Toner of books he had read at school about J. Edgar Hoover.

None of this information was known to him officially, of course, since he had been moved off the case, but he was damned if he was just going to sit on his hands and watch it all going on around him and he had friends at headquarters who were keeping him up to date. He had also made a call to a contact in the West of England Regional Crime Squad, an inspector like himself.

Mattheson was RUC originally, enough miles on the clock to retire any time he liked. Tweed and he had been a double act for a long time, working in serious crime.

'Very unpleasant gentlemen,' his friend had said. 'Taylor whipped them away from the coal face after a while and into her office. They were always around her after that. There was a rumour that she had something on them. Something nasty she'd found out. Maybe that they'd been on the take, you know?'

Whatever it was, it had been enough to buy their loyalty, Toner thought as he parked the car and went into the house. But it was a secret which all three would take to their graves.

After all this morning's activity, the house was strangely still. He stood at the kitchen door but could not bring himself to go in. He knew now that something had happened in here, not just the murders of Mattheson and Tweed, but something else. The traces found along the edge of the wall near the radiator had been blood all right and had been there for weeks at least. It was blood group O, the same as Bob McCallan's.

Toner turned back towards the small living room. He could not let this go, which was why he had decided to come here and sniff around by himself. He would not be caught in the act by McIvor or anyone else, not while the shit was hitting the fan elsewhere. They had all been called to police headquarters for a meeting with the Deputy Chief Constable, Peter O'Brien, who found himself unexpectedly in charge now that Taylor was dead. In Toner's opinion, he was making a complete and absolute balls of things, from which they would all be lucky to recover.

O'Brien's expertise was in finance and management structures, not in operational matters, but after the explosion at the hotel he had swung into action like a wartime general, as if to prove himself. He had mobilised every available police officer, had requested that garrison troops be put on stand-by as back-up, and had swamped West Belfast, raiding houses, arresting suspects. Toner had groaned when he had heard.

Even a couple of grey-haired Sinn Fein councillors in their sixties had been rounded up, as a result of what information, Toner did not know. Taylor had had a lot of enemies in West Belfast; that was true. She had turned her attention, with occasional good effect, to the criminal gangs which operated from there, many of which had evolved from the expertise of the IRA, but this was no way to go about it, as had been proved this afternoon. There had been scuffles in one street in Andersonstown, stones thrown at the police. Then someone had thrown a petrol bomb at a Landrover which had swerved to avoid it and killed a six-year-old girl.

News travelled fast in that part of the world, rumour fed rumour, and now they were hijacking cars and burning buses and police had unearthed the tear gas and the plastic bullets from somewhere. It was like turning the clock back forty years.

As for Jack McCallan, he seemed to have disappeared off the face of the earth. Even based on the flimsy experience of their one and only meeting, Toner found it hard to think of him as a killer, yet he was the only real suspect they had. And there was the other murder victim now, poor old Alfie Hutchinson. Someone had beaten him to a pulp and had even chopped one of his fingers off before shooting him and dumping him in the bushes at Crawfordsburn Country Park. And would you believe it, Jack McCallan was a link there, too.

Taylor had definitely behaved oddly this morning. A bit wired. Surely it had not been his imagination that she had seemed to be looking for something, but what was it? He went into the living room and sat down, his hands bunched into the pockets of his raincoat. The chair was soft and comfortable. How normal it all was, cosy. Yet awful things had happened in this house.

There was something in his coat pocket and he took it out. It was a photograph. He had forgotten about it. It had been in the drawer with the firearms certificate and things and he had taken it with him. It showed a young Dorothy Taylor, Bob McCallan and another man, obviously a policeman too, whose face was vaguely familiar but he could not place it.

He looked towards the television and the video in the corner. The stand-by light on the video was on. There was a box for a video-disc on top of it and he wondered what McCallan had been watching. He picked the box up. It had UTV's logo on it but it was the writing on the label that intrigued him.

He turned the video on and sat down to watch. It was interesting but he could not see the connection. He played it again.

The third time he saw what McCallan had seen.

'Oh, my God,' he whispered in the emptiness of the room.

McCallan retreated down the path and turned to look back at the house. There was no sign of anyone being at home. He had rung the doorbell several times without success but he would try it just once more. From the corner of his eye, he noticed a movement at the window next door. A woman was peering at him through the lace curtains. Just as he was about to ring the bell again, he heard her.

'If you're looking for Mr Keane, Father, you won't get him yet for a while.'

He turned to see a small elderly woman with her hair in a bun and eyes clenched behind thick glasses. Father? Why had she called him that? Then he caught a glimpse of his own reflection in the window and saw the sombre clothing, the dark suit and the black roll-neck sweater which could easily be mistaken for the uniform of a priest.

'Actually,' he said, 'I was rather hoping I could talk to Mrs Keane.'

The woman put her hand to her mouth and her dull eyes widened. 'Oh, Lord, Father, don't you know? She . . . she died.'

'No,' he said, 'I didn't know. I'm sorry.' He felt deflated, a bit cheated.

'Must have been about six months ago now.'

'How did it happen? Had she been ill?'

'Leukaemia, poor woman. Very sad.'

'Yes,' he said thoughtfully, 'it is.' He looked at the wooden sign rooted awkwardly in a flower bed. 'So how long has the house been for sale?'

'About the past three months. He's looking for somewhere smaller, he says, now that he's on his own, but there's a lot of houses on the market in this area at the moment and you could take your pick. I reckon it's going to be hard to shift. There haven't been many viewers. I see people coming and going, you understand.' She began to look at McCallan with a little more curiosity. 'I don't think I've seen you before.'

'No, I'm visiting from England. Mr and Mrs Keane are old acquaintances. I found myself in Dublin and decided to call and see them, give them a surprise. I'm afraid I hadn't expected anything like this. It's quite a shock.'

'Yes. Poor Mr Keane.'

'Have you any idea where I might find him?'

'He's where he always is at this time of day. He has a long walk in the afternoon after lunch and then he goes down to the church for a while. That's where he'll be. It's not too far.'

She gave him directions. 'Bless you for being so helpful,' he said instinctively, then realised as he walked away how appropriate that was.

The church was easy to find, as she had said it would be. There was no one inside and he took a pew in a corner at the back so that he could observe whoever entered without immediately being seen himself. It was cold and gloomy, a place of eternal dusk. A fragrant hint of incense lingered in the air and heavenly figures with outstretched arms looked down on him with suspicion from the stained glass windows.

He waited for almost half an hour, rubbing his hands to keep warm, his nose and ears nipped, and he was beginning to conclude that he had missed Eamonn Keane altogether when the door creaked open. A tall man with a slight stoop entered in a waft of cold air, stood for a second, then walked with heavy footsteps down the centre aisle. He wore a wool coat with a scarf knotted at the neck and he carried a tweed cap in one hand. He looked straight ahead and did not see McCallan. At the front of the church, he genuflected and took a seat by the aisle with his head bent in prayer.

McCallan stood slowly and walked towards him, his thick rubber soles squeaking on the polished stone floor.

'Mr Keane?'

He was about seventy and he looked grey and weary. There was no lustre in his eyes and the skin around them sagged.

'Who are you?' he asked, stiffening, in a voice that was deep and strong. He would have carried his authority with ease in the classroom and the school corridor.

'My name is Jack McCallan.'

Eamonn Keane's shoulders slackened. He slumped forward and put his head in his hands.

Chapter Thirty

The back road was not all that good. It was winding and hilly and not built for speed but there was comparatively little traffic and it would save him time. Toner reckoned somehow that he did not have a lot of that. He was by-passing more than the city. He was ignoring all normal reporting procedures and going straight to where his information was needed most. There was no other way.

The Police Service headquarters was at Knock, in Belfast's well-kept eastern suburbs, and he kept the siren on right up until the moment he reached the gates. There were extra guards, he noted, officers in flak jackets and carrying rifles, but the urgency of his arrival got him in without any trouble.

He parked quickly and dashed into the security hut, flashing his warrant card. 'I'm Inspector Toner from Lisburn,' he said. 'My boss is at a meeting with the Deputy Chief and I've got something for him. Where would they be?'

'You need to go up to the main office,' the guard told him. 'Somebody up there will direct you.'

With the video clutched in his hand, he ran out and up the steps to the headquarters building. There was a reception area where a uniformed sergeant sat behind a glass screen. Toner showed his card again.

'You seem to be in a big hurry, sir.' The sergeant was not impressed; he was not going anywhere.

'I've got something for Mr McIvor, the Head of the Regional

Crime Squad from Lisburn. He's at the big meeting. Do you know where it is?'

'It's in the Chief's conference room.'

'Where's that?'

'Up the stairs and along the corridor. It's a bit hard to find if you don't know where you're going. If you hold on, I'll ring up and get someone to come down for you. What did you say the name was?'

'Toner. Inspector Toner.' He couldn't hang around here waiting. 'Look, don't worry. I'll find it.'

He turned and ran up the stairs, having no idea where he was going. There was noise and bustle. People were hurrying along the corridors, in and out of offices. Some were in uniform, some in plainclothes. They looked tense, preoccupied, and no one gave him a second glance. The whole place felt out of control. A girl emerged from an office in front of him and he almost knocked her over.

'Sorry,' he said. 'Listen. The Chief Constable's conference room. Do you know where it is?'

She pointed. 'Through those big double doors. Then go left.'

He found it. Clutches of men in uniform were pacing about outside, fidgety, talking to each other in snatched, urgent whispers. Occasionally, someone with a piece of paper would hurry down the corridor and enter the room. A young man with a dark suit and a folder in his hand was about to go in. Toner stepped in front of him.

'Excuse me, is this where Mr O'Brien's having his meeting?'

'Yes, who are you?'

'I'm sorry. I'm Inspector Barry Toner from Lisburn. Mr McIvor, my boss, is in there. I need to talk to him very urgently. Would you tell him I'm here? It really is important. I've got new information about—' he waved his hand in the direction of the door – 'all this.'

'In that case, wait here.'

Toner waited for a minute, then the door opened and McIvor came out. He glared.

'Toner. What the blazes are you doing here?' It was the nearest he ever came to a full-blown swear word. The other men in the corridor turned to look.

Toner held up the video. 'I found this in McCallan's house. I think you need to see it.'

'What are you talking about? You were taken off that case. What do you think you're playing at?'

'I know – but you've got to see this. Mr O'Brien should see it, too.'

McIvor grabbed the video and read the label. 'So what's this got to do with anything?'

'When you see what's on it—'

'Look, get out of here, Toner. I'll look at this later. I haven't time to waste with it now. There's a major crisis going on here or maybe it's escaped your notice. I'll deal with you when I get back to Lisburn.'

He started to turn but Toner grabbed his arm.

'Get your hands off me,' McIvor said.

'Look, sir, I'm sorry, but if you don't take this in with you I'm going to have to go in there myself.'

Their voices were raised. Everyone was looking. The door opened and they saw a tall, gaunt man in a dark uniform.

'McIvor,' Peter O'Brien said. 'Have we got a problem?'

Some time later, Sir Iain Crichton's car swung through the side entrance which led to Stormont. The correct address was Parliament Buildings but everyone knew it simply as Stormont after the hill to the east of Belfast on which it stood, an enormous pillared structure in white stone, looking haughtily down a mile-long drive with sweeping lawns on either side and evoking all the bygone grandeur of the empire. It was an imposing presence in anyone's language, even if you hated what it had once stood for, which a lot of people in Northern Ireland still did.

It was here that the various incarnations of the Northern Ireland Parliament had sat, ruling with Unionist certainty until the Troubles had forced Westminster to put Stormont into suspended animation, and it was here that the Northern Ireland Commission now met, as it had since shortly after the Troubles ceased two decades ago. It would be meeting in special session tonight to discuss how the bombing at the hotel, the murder of the Chief Constable and now the rioting in West Belfast could be prevented from burning through the thin fabric of peace.

The Secretary of State was very quiet. Sitting beside him, Miles Beardsley was silent too. Neither man felt much like speaking. They had gone straight to the hotel after their plane had touched down and had been horrified by what they had seen. In the confined space, the destruction had been appalling. The side of the building was a gaping hole and the walls and the floor immediately above had collapsed in an avalanche of rubble. The injured and the dead, what was left of some of them, had been taken away but it was the odd little things which remained that you noticed. An empty wine bottle, miraculously unbroken. Dust-covered carnations blowing in the wind. A bloodstained copy of the menu. Then, as Crichton looked on, a policeman had spotted a man's shoe under some of the rubble and tried to lift it clear. When it resisted, he had tugged and found himself holding both the shoe and the foot that was still in it.

Crichton tried to shake the image from his mind and he was glad the cameras had not witnessed it. For the moment, while the scene was still being examined, they were being kept at a distance, filming with telephoto lenses and growing in number as the foreign crews began to arrive. They would be allowed in eventually and, worse, before tonight's meeting of the Commission, he and the Deputy Chief Constable, Peter O'Brien, would have to give a news conference. He had no earthly idea what he was going to say.

They drove past the front of the building, circling the

roundabout, now unadorned, but where the statue of Lord Carson, the Unionist leader, had once pointed defiantly to heaven. He was still pointing but from a different location these days. The statue was one of the many Ulster landmarks which had symbolised communal division, like the gable wall in the Bogside which had proclaimed itself proudly as Free Derry corner. Some years before, a selection of such historical artefacts had been moved intact to the vast open acreage of the Ulster Folk Museum, where farms, schools, even whole streets, had been brought from their original locations to be restored and preserved. It was there that Carson now stood firm, eyed with mild curiosity by passing tourists.

Just down the hill a little from the roundabout was Stormont Castle, its pretentious turrets showing above the trees which shielded it, and it was in this building that Crichton and his officials were based. O'Brien would be arriving there soon. Crichton had been about to summon him to give a progress report when he himself had called to say that he wished to brief the Secretary of State about a possible new development.

Crichton hoped it was something positive. He contemplated the news conference and tonight's meeting of the Commission with little relish. In addition, the Cabinet in Dublin had already held an emergency meeting and that little twerp of a Minister for Foreign Affairs, with a Kerry accent he could barely understand, was on his way to see him. He would arrive within the hour and would no doubt berate him with his government's concern about the way all this was developing. Crichton had to concede they had a point but he would not do so to the Minister's face.

He got out of the car and strode up the steps into the building. He was a florid man in his late fifties with unkempt hair straggling over the edge of his ears like ivy on a garden wall. He nodded a response to the greetings of the security staff. He was still dressed for rural Gloucestershire, cords and brown brogues and a tweed jacket camouflaging the dandruff which always decorated his shoulders. He would have to change into something more appropriately muted but he would see O'Brien first.

His office was spacious but dreary, with a couple of dark landscapes and the obligatory photograph of the King on the walls. The carpet around the big oak desk had once looked expensive but it had gradually become worn and colourless. The castle heating was erratic and long in need of being replaced although, thoughtfully, someone had lit a fire in the deep hearth in case the room would be chilly. Crichton, however, was not in much of a mood to appreciate it.

He had the easy assurance which came with having great private wealth but his confidence was being tested now. He had an agreement with the Prime Minister, personal, nothing in writing, that he would stay in this post for another few months and then there would be a task more pleasant and less demanding for him, a commissioner's job in Europe, perhaps, something like that, but he did not want to leave the Northern Ireland Office as the man who let the whole thing come apart. He tried to push the thought out of his mind as the door opened and an aide told him that the Deputy Chief Constable had arrived.

O'Brien was pale and a little breathless. He carried his cap and something in an envelope. 'Secretary of State, I've got—'

'Mr O'Brien,' Crichton interrupted, 'what's the situation in West Belfast?'

O'Brien coughed. 'Improving, sir. I think we're getting things under control now.'

'I should bloody well hope so. As if the bombing wasn't bad enough, now there's trouble on the streets. Good God, how did you let that happen?'

'All a bit unfortunate, sir, I have to admit. If it hadn't been for the incident with that little girl—'

'If it hadn't been for you sending your people in there in the first place like it was the bloody Normandy landings. What the hell were you thinking of? Why wasn't I consulted?'

'It was an operational matter. We had to move quickly, sir,' O'Brien protested. 'Surely you can acknowledge that? Our first thought was the gangland leaders, the godfathers. Grab them before they could disappear.'

'But for heaven's sake, man, if they were behind it, you didn't expect them to be sitting around waiting for you to drop in? And a couple of Sinn Fein councillors as well? Pensioners? Why were they picked up?'

O'Brien was beginning to perspire. He twisted the envelope in his hand. 'I'm afraid that was a bit over-zealous on the part of some people on the ground. The matter's been dealt with. As for the known criminals we picked up, we're still holding one or two but everyone else has been released now.'

'Yes,' said Crichton, looking to Beardsley for endorsement, 'when the damage has been done. Half the television crews in the world are descending on this place. They'll be describing it as Internment all over again.' He sighed. 'All right, we'll leave that for the moment. What's this development you want to tell me about?'

O'Brien brightened. He opened the envelope, slipped a slim video box out and held it up, almost waving it. 'This is it. It came to light a couple of hours ago and we believe it may be the key. The murders in Dromore, everything. I felt it was crucial that you see it so that you know what we may be dealing with.'

Beardsley came forward and took the video from him. He went to where a television monitor and player were mounted on a bracket in a corner of the room and slotted it in. First the screen showed a black and white clock counting the seconds down. Three, two, one. Then came the opening images. It was a funeral. The shots were of a hearse with a long line of mourners coming behind it, many of them, Crichton could see, in the uniform of the old RUC.

'This is twenty years ago, the funeral of a man called George Miller,' O'Brien said, and then he told the full story of Miller's death and its aftermath. They played the video through several times as he explained how it had been found and what Barry Toner believed it meant.

Crichton asked Beardsley to turn the sound down; he did not need to hear the reporter's melodramatic script again. There was a close-up shot of a woman in a dark coat, walking unsteadily and weeping. Someone's arms were around her, the arms of a tall girl in a dark school uniform. She had long auburn hair being tossed wildly by the wind, almost obscuring her face as she bent forward towards her mother. She raised one hand and brushed it back.

'There,' O'Brien said. Beardsley hit the 'pause' button.

'Is he absolutely sure?' Crichton asked.

The girl's gesture with her hair had revealed her face clearly, although only very briefly, before it was concealed again, which was why Toner had not noticed the first time he had played the video through. It was a face that was angular, perhaps a little thinner than the face it would become, but just as distinctive.

It was not a face that meant anything to Crichton, O'Brien or Beardsley but it meant a lot to Barry Toner.

It was the face of Ann Reilly.

'A hundred per cent,' O'Brien said.

He pointed to the frozen image on the screen. 'The girl you're looking at is Laura Miller, the daughter of George Miller. She's about fifteen here, still at school, as you can see. But our man Toner is convinced this is the same woman, grown up now, of course, who's been living out at Dromore in an old farmhouse owned by the late Bob McCallan. The same Bob McCallan who was a close friend of Dorothy Taylor. The same Bob McCallan whose house her two dead staff officers were found in. The same Bob McCallan whose son has now disappeared. And the people at Ulster Television have confirmed that a man answering Jack McCallan's description bought this video from their archive department yesterday.'

He was pleased with himself and he paused for effect.

The Secretary of State turned to Beardsley. 'I think someone else ought to see this, don't you?' The younger man nodded and left the room.

O'Brien frowned. 'What—?'

'In a moment,' Crichton said.

Beardsley came back. With him was a small, dapper man in a dark suit with a faint stripe. He wore glasses and he had silver hair which was carefully brushed and tended, unlike that of Crichton who stood to welcome him. He had arrived in Northern Ireland just an hour before. It was also his sixtieth birthday, a fact to which he did not propose to draw attention since it was a sensitive age and he did not want the people who ran him to start wondering about his continued effectiveness.

The Secretary of State gestured. 'Hugo Tarrant – I don't think you've met our Deputy Chief Constable, Peter O'Brien.'

The two men shook hands. 'I'm pleased to meet you,' Tarrant said. His voice was modulated and mellow. 'Although these are of course rather tragic circumstances under which to do so.'

O'Brien did not speak but tried not to look bewildered and overawed. He had never met the man before but he most certainly knew who he was. Tarrant was one of the most powerful people in Britain, the head of the National Security Service, the organisation which had been set up some years before to incorporate MI5, MI6 and various other secret agencies. Its main focus of attention had become the rise of organised crime and how to halt it, but security matters, espionage, mostly involving international trade and the economy, were still high on the agenda, not to mention world terrorism.

O'Brien found his voice. 'I'm sorry,' he said, 'I had no idea you were in the Province.' He turned to Crichton to seek explanation.

'Hugo has come at the personal direction of the Prime Minister.' His use of the first name was not lost on O'Brien.

'The PM wants results. He wants this business sorted out before it gets any worse and he will approve any action which we deem to be appropriate.'

O'Brien frowned. In spite of being in the presence of a legend, he was concerned to maintain his position and state it. 'But this is still a police investigation, of course. The Police Service must have primacy.'

'That is correct,' Crichton replied, 'but I don't think we can afford to stand on ceremony here. Hugo and his department have great expertise and we must make full use of it.'

O'Brien did not respond.

'That is the Prime Minister's express wish,' Crichton said emphatically.

Tarrant smiled at the Deputy Chief Constable. 'I believe you have a break?'

They played the video again. Tarrant sat deep in an armchair, watching and listening silently as O'Brien explained. His fingers were a steeple at his lips. Silver cufflinks gleamed. It took O'Brien about ten minutes to give the full picture, everything they had discovered and everything that had developed since the video had come to light. It was a story which included Alfie Hutchinson's death and Jack McCallan's possible connection with it.

Police activity in the past few hours had been intense. The files on the Miller case, as well as his career record, had been combed carefully and had shown that Miller, Taylor and Bob McCallan had all worked together at around the time of the terrorist assassinations. O'Brien took a photograph from the envelope and handed it to Crichton. It was the picture Toner had found at the house. Dorothy Taylor, Bob McCallan and George Miller. All of them were dead. Two had been murdered, Miller and Taylor, killings that were twenty years apart, and McCallan had died recently in an accident although now, O'Brien reported, there were some question marks over that. Traces of blood matching that of the dead man had just been found at the edge of the floor in his kitchen.

They had also begun to trace what had happened to Miller's widow. If they knew that, then they might find out something about the girl. They had been piecing together the details of Mrs Miller's life after her husband's death: her move with her daughter to the Republic of Ireland, her remarriage some time later to a headmaster called Eamonn Keane and her death six months ago from leukaemia. For the moment, that was it.

'Has there been any sign of this Ann Reilly?' Crichton asked.

'None,' O'Brien said. 'We've been to the farmhouse and it's completely empty. No sign of anyone living there at all. No clothes, no personal belongings, nothing. There's been a complete clear-out.'

The phone on Crichton's desk rang. Beardsley picked it up hurriedly, then handed it to O'Brien who scribbled on a pad while he listened.

'Thanks,' he said finally and rang off. He looked at them with a satisfied smile. 'Well, we know a bit more about the girl now.'

He consulted his notes, letting the others wait for a second. 'It seems that when her mother remarried, Laura changed her name as well and became Laura Keane. She also converted to the Catholic faith and finished her schooling at a convent just outside Dublin. We've discovered she won a scholarship to Trinity College where she graduated with an honours degree in law and then, would you believe, she was head-hunted.'

'By whom?' Tarrant asked.

'By the Dublin police.'

'For what purpose?' Crichton asked. 'Do we know?'

O'Brien nodded. 'Indeed we do. Their new drugs division. They've been running the unit for more than ten years now. They're very good but as we all know only too well, it's an uphill bloody struggle. They do a lot of undercover work, planting agents among the drug gangs, that sort of thing. Very dangerous. Anyway, the latest information is that Miss Miller or Miss Keane, as she is now, resigned from the unit rather abruptly, no explanation at all, at around the time of her mother's death. Nothing's been heard of her since. She had a flat in Dublin which she sold and there's no new address.'

'And you think she's taken a new identity, turned herself into this Ann Reilly?' Crichton asked.

'Inspector Toner thinks so. And it's certainly possible. The timing of the disappearance of the one and the appearance of the other would seem to coincide.'

Tarrant stood up. 'Would you excuse me for a moment?' he said and left the room. He was back in two minutes. 'It might be useful if you came with me,' he said. 'There's something I'd like you to see.'

The three men stood but Tarrant held his arm out with the palm upstretched like a traffic policeman and motioned Beardsley to stay. 'No need for you, I think.'

They walked down the corridor and opened the door to the smaller of the castle's two dining rooms. To O'Brien's surprise, it had been turned into some kind of an operations area. There were five people in the room, four men and a woman, and they had set computer equipment up on the long formal table with modems which linked them to the outside world. Crichton winced slightly when he noticed a scratch on the surface but he let it pass.

O'Brien took in the scene, feeling increasingly indignant as he realised that the security chief had not come to Northern Ireland alone. Tarrant put his hand on the woman's shoulder. 'Any joy?'

'Just getting it now,' she said without looking up, as her fingers tapped on the keyboard. 'There we go.'

Crichton and O'Brien stared at what began to unroll on the computer screen.

'What's this?' Crichton said.

'Laura Keane's file,' Tarrant explained.

'How did you get this?' O'Brien wanted to know.

'In ways that I'm afraid you couldn't without your colleagues across the border wondering why you wanted it,'

Tarrant said with a colourless smile. 'I must say you've done very well with your inquiries so far, very impressive, but we operate rather differently. We have friends in Dublin, you see, people in well-placed positions who help us discreetly and allow us to get into things. No one will know we have this.'

The three men began to read over the woman's shoulder but the information was already being printed out for them. It was an impressive litany of successful operations. There were flattering appraisals from Laura Keane's superiors about her coolness and resolve, her skill and determination.

'Quite outstanding,' Crichton said. He went to the window, looking up to the darkening sky. There was not much of a view, just the rhododendron bushes crowding against the building. In their shelter, a mistle thrush stabbed at the soft earth.

He turned to O'Brien. 'Could she have carried out the bombing?'

The Deputy Chief Constable frowned. 'I'd prefer to answer that in private, sir, if you don't mind.'

Crichton stared at him in irritation for a moment. 'Back to my office,' he said and led the way.

Once inside, he swung round. 'Have you a problem, O'Brien?'

The Deputy Chief Constable gestured to the door behind him. 'Look, those people – what's going on here? I didn't know about any of this. We can't have two investigations, one being run by the police and another clandestine affair going on up here. I can't operate like this.'

'That's up to you,' the Secretary of State said and sat down firmly behind his desk. Tarrant slipped into the armchair he had recently vacated, leaving O'Brien standing alone and on the spot in the centre of the room. He knew he was beaten. He could protest some more, which would not get him anywhere, or he could resign, which would be utterly self-destructive. Crichton had made the terms clear enough: he was not in the driving seat.

Keith Baker

The Secretary of State broke the silence. 'Sit down,' he said gruffly. 'There isn't time for any of this. I asked you a question. Could Laura Keane have carried out the bombing?'

O'Brien sat, as he had been told, but he was silent for a few seconds. 'Yes, she could,' he said eventually. His voice was a little subdued. 'Some of the big drugs players in Dublin have used bombs to dispose of their business opponents. The old terrorist skills haven't gone to waste; they've just been handed down a generation. The Drugs Unit give their people a good grounding in bomb-making, the sort of devices which are used and what to watch out for. She could have picked it up from that.'

'Anyone can pick it up, really,' Tarrant added, 'if you know which lay-by on the information highway to stop off in.'

Crichton nodded. 'All right, let me try to review what we know so far and correct me if I get any of it wrong. I'm not the detective here. We believe, or at least we almost believe, that a person calling herself Ann Reilly and living out in County Down is in reality Laura Keane, or Laura Miller as she was originally, and that she's the daughter of George Miller, the detective who was murdered twenty years ago and implicated in the assassination of a lot of IRA activists. Right?'

O'Brien nodded.

'And now two of her father's former colleagues have been killed. One of them is the Chief Constable – and, God knows, the whole world is aware of what happened to her – and the other is a man called Bob McCallan from whom she has been renting a house. So what about the two dead policemen? All this surveillance activity they've been involved in? What's the connection there and where does McCallan's son fit in?'

O'Brien shook his head. 'We don't know any of that yet. We don't even know if this McCallan fellow is still alive.'

'If the Keane woman is behind it all, what's the motive?' Crichton asked.

'Retribution of some kind, most likely,' O'Brien said. 'Revenge. We don't know what's going on inside her head

284

but clearly Taylor and McCallan must have been targets somehow because of what happened to her father. If we find her, we'll know. That's if we get a chance to question her.' He gave Tarrant a glance but it was wasted because the other man was staring into the fire with evident lack of interest in the conversation.

'Are there any other likely targets?' Crichton asked.

'We've checked out the rest of the team who were in this particular anti-terrorist squad at the time. There were three others. One's been dead for several years, natural causes, as far as we know, another is in Canada and the third is living in retirement up in Ballymena. We're having people keep a discreet watch on him, just in case.'

The Secretary of State stood, then walked over to where Tarrant sat by the fire. He looked down at it with his arms stretched forward, warming the rough palms of his hands. For a few moments he seemed lost somewhere in the glow but then he spoke, quietly, without turning, and his words seemed to be meant for Tarrant more than for anyone else.

'We have a problem.'

'Indeed,' Tarrant acknowledged.

'If we find this woman and it comes out in the wash that there's even the faintest suspicion our beloved Chief Constable was anything less than totally squeaky clean, there'll be absolute hell to pay. What if we discover that Taylor was mixed up with this whole George Miller business somehow, a co-conspirator in the assassinations, perhaps? That would be wonderful, wouldn't it? So much for the reformed police force. Dublin would be on our necks again, all the old hatreds would be opened up. The Commission up there would collapse.'

He turned to face the room. 'God, it could set us back years. Look at what's happening out there already. We'd have a real war on our hands.'

There was a knock at the door and one of Tarrant's men came in carrying a yellow folder. Beardsley walked towards him but the security agent ignored him, gave it to his master, then left the room without a word. Tarrant opened the folder and began to read the photocopied sheets it contained.

'What's all this, Hugo?' Crichton asked.

'It's a copy of this chap McCallan's Army file. I just thought it might be useful to have a look at it.' He kept reading as he spoke. 'Indeed . . . yes. Interesting background. Special forces training, some experience in that kind of work. Explosives a part of it as well, apparently. Wounded in Africa, I see. Head injury, took some time to recover. Oh, and a bit of psychiatric care, too.'

He closed the folder and looked up. 'Who knows? Perhaps he hasn't been entirely stable. Look at the enormous trauma which the death of his father must have been for him, only child and all that sort of thing. I'm not a psychiatrist myself, of course, but could it be that the loss of his father triggered something, drove him over the edge, you know? Wouldn't it be a possibility that he might go on some sort of a killing spree?'

O'Brien began to speak. 'But surely—'

'Just a minute,' Crichton said. 'Let's think about this.' He knew what Tarrant was saying. The video had been found in McCallan's house which meant McCallan had come to the same conclusion about Ann Reilly. What if he had uncovered more? In that case, wherever he was, he was just as much a liability on the loose as the woman.

The world did not know about Laura Keane and would never do so if Tarrant and his people got to her first. There might be a problem with this man Toner, of course, although he was sure that could be handled somehow. But they would also set their sights on Jack McCallan. Find him. Take him out of the picture. Tarrant had the public explanation right. The work of an unstable man driven mad by grief. The past, George Miller, none of that need ever be opened up again.

He looked down at Tarrant and as their eyes met they knew they understood each other. O'Brien was a different story.

'What we need,' Tarrant said firmly, 'is what the Prime

Minister has demanded of us: a speedy end to this affair. And—' he paused and smiled: 'there will be considerable kudos for anyone who helps to settle it and get the right result. The wrong result, on the other hand, might do a lot of damage, as the Secretary of State has quite rightly pointed out. It could bring a lot of people down.'

He held out his hands with the palms upward, as if inviting them to take their pick.

'Jesus, I don't like any of this,' O'Brien gasped. 'You're talking about killing two people, just . . . just disposing of one of them and putting the blame on the other one because it will be less damaging.'

Tarrant shrugged although he did not disagree with O'Brien's analysis. 'It's a question of the most effective course of action to take. And, of course, as far as public perceptions are concerned, the Police Service is involved in a thorough and extensive and proper investigation. No one is asking you to get involved in the, shall we say, hands-on stuff. That's a matter for us. You can sit back and eventually take the credit for the efficiency of the force you have been commanding in extraordinarily difficult circumstances. Admirable position to be in, I'd say. Now I think we'd better find out a little more about Mr McCallan – how he earns a crust, who he sleeps with. The whole picture.'

The phone on Crichton's desk rang for O'Brien again. He listened intently for a few minutes.

'We've been interviewing some of the survivors, some of those who were at the hotel before the explosion,' he explained when he rang off, 'hotel staff, some of the television people, trying to see if anyone remembers anyone or anything unusual that might help us. Most of the people seem to have been accounted for in one way or another but at least two interviewees have mentioned a tall woman, dressed very casually, jeans, who seemed to have been part of the general crowd setting up microphones and all the camera gear. They've checked with the TV companies who were there, but no one appears to have a member of staff who fits that description.'

Crichton clapped his hands. 'Well, that's that, isn't it? What's the next step, Hugo?'

'Start from the source, I think. The Keane home.'

'How can you do that?' O'Brien asked. 'It's across the border.'

Tarrant's smile barely concealed the thinness of his patience. The man was so naïve.

'Bearing in mind the fact that most of our people are extremely used to operating across borders of one kind or another, I don't really think that's much of a problem, do you? But for your information, while my colleagues and I were flying to Belfast this afternoon, one or two others were flying to Dublin, just in case. They're at the British Embassy now, awaiting instructions.'

'What you must do,' Crichton said to O'Brien, 'is to steer your people away from the girl. Tell them there are sensitive security issues here that are being handled by the NSS and they're to forget about her for the time being. McCallan's the man to look for still. And keep Hugo closely informed if you manage to trace him. Then you can pull back and let events take their proper course, shall we say.'

He turned to Beardsley. 'Now, Miles, get our colleagues a drink while I go and change.'

Chapter Thirty-one

It was almost dark. There was just a glimmer left in the
east coast sky and the street lamps were on, casting a faint
light into the graveyard where McCallan and Eamonn Keane
stood. They were looking at a headstone.

'Eileen, dearly beloved wife of Eamonn Keane,' it read.
Below it were the dates of her earthly span.

There were tears on the old man's cheeks. 'But it's not
enough,' he was saying. 'It should also say that she was the
dearly beloved wife of George Miller – because she was. And
she was robbed of him. I wasn't the man in her life: he always
was, no matter how long we were together. I could never have
replaced him, never. I was just someone to listen when she
wanted to talk, someone to share her pain.'

They had sat together in the church while Keane had
recovered himself. It was a kind of relief, rather than alarm,
which had caused him to break down. In spite of anything
the police might say, he knew McCallan was no killer.

'If you're here, it must mean we both know the truth,' he
had said, wiping his nose on a tissue.

'Not all of it,' McCallan had replied. 'Not yet.'

When Keane had regained his composure, he had begun
to talk more. With everything that had happened he had not
known what to do except wait, certain that someone would
turn up, someone who had worked it all out, but he had
not known who it would be. For his part, McCallan had
told him everything that had happened since his father's

death, everything he had uncovered, including the gift of
£100,000.

At the graveside now, while he listened to the old man's
grief, McCallan reflected on the journey which had started
the day before and which had brought him to this place. God,
was it only yesterday? So much had happened since then, so
much had been changed forever.

It was the picture in the *Belfast Telegraph* that told him he
had gone beyond the point of no return. It was not the best of
photographs, the girl's face was partly hidden, but something
in the tilt of the head had suddenly made him think of Ann.
And so when he had left the newspaper offices, he had gone to
the British Telecom place in the city centre where they would
have telephone books.

First he had tried to locate the number of the International
Institute for Irish Studies, but neither the phone lists nor the
operator could help him. There was an Institute for Irish
Studies, right enough, without the 'international' a venerable
collaborative venture between Queen's University in Belfast
and Trinity College, Dublin, but no one he spoke to in either
establishment knew anything about anyone called Ann Reilly
or a project involving the jails.

Still, it might simply have meant he had been talking to the
wrong people. He had tried another avenue and had called
the Government information office at Stormont to find out
if they had a public relations department which dealt with
prisons. They had. He was trying to track down a friend,
he told the press officer eventually, someone who was doing
research out at Maghaberry. But the person he spoke to had no
knowledge of anyone carrying out an academic study like that
and certainly no one had either applied for or been granted
access to do it.

He had emerged from the Telecom office feeling a bit
shaken, trying to think, and had wandered the streets for a
while. Sitting in the cheery clamour of a twenty-four-hour
café almost opposite the Lomax building he had had another

idea which had taken him to the offices of Ulster Television. There he had gone to the video library and asked for a copy of the old news footage of the George Miller funeral. And then he had sat at the house and watched the truth unfold on the screen in front of him.

It was getting very cold in the graveyard. He put his hand gently on Eamonn Keane's shoulder and suggested he should drive him home. There was a lot he hoped Keane might tell him, things he might want to share.

It took them only a few minutes to get back. The street was dark and quiet. His was the only car moving on it, although there were two parked cars, outside their owners' houses, he presumed. It all seemed perfectly normal but he remembered another street, in another climate, in what now seemed like another lifetime. It had seemed perfectly normal, too.

He did not know if anyone could follow him here but he had to assume it was possible. He drove past Keane's house and round the corner.

'What are you doing?' Keane asked.

'Just being careful. Going round the block first. Those cars,' he said. 'Do you recognise them?'

Keane looked confused, wondering why he had asked. 'Well, yes. The green one belongs to young Fitzgerald who lives at number 27 and the black one . . . oh, that's Dermot Slavin's. He owns a grocery shop in the village. What's the problem?'

'Oh, probably nothing,' McCallan said. 'Just me being over-cautious.'

When he had done his circuit, he parked a little way from the house and they walked the few yards to it, going round the back and turning the key in the kitchen door. It seemed safe enough and he did not want to alarm Keane any more than was necessary.

'Sit down here,' McCallan said, pulling a stool out from the breakfast bar, 'and let me get you some tea. You look cold.'

He filled the kettle and while they waited for it to boil,

Keane guided him to where everything was kept. When he had made the tea, McCallan took a stool beside the old man, letting the steaming cup bring warmth back to his hands.

'Mr Keane,' he said calmly. 'I have to know the rest of it. I have to know why.'

Keane nodded slowly in agreement and his head seemed very heavy. 'It's a burden I have kept to myself. I don't want to do so any more. But there may be things which are hard for you to hear.'

'I know. I'm prepared for that,' McCallan told him, although he was not entirely sure that he was.

The old man began. First he told him about Laura growing up and the sensitive circumstances in which he had become her stepfather. She had been a bright girl but cold, always an observer, a bit apart, very strong academically. She had done well at school, adjusting with apparent dedication to the unfamiliar cultural environment of the convent, and she had gained very high marks in her university entrance exam.

'There weren't many men in her life,' Keane said, 'just the one real involvement, a lecturer. Her mother wasn't too happy about it, said he was too old for her, but if Laura set her mind on something, that was that.

'And then he got killed, stabbed to death by a drug addict. Imagine it – first her father and then this. She became very withdrawn after that and threw herself into her work. We were very surprised when the Drugs Unit thing came along and she took it but later I saw that it all made sense. It was a way of doing something about the problem that had killed the man she loved as well as making up for the disgrace she believed her father had brought.'

He rubbed his forehead as if to soothe away a pain. 'But then,' he said, 'then things changed. Just over a year ago she was home for the weekend. She had her own place in Dublin, a little flat, but she came home quite often. Her mother loved making Sunday lunch for her but she was quite ill by then, almost confined to bed, so Laura used to come and do the cooking. We knew Eileen wasn't going to get any better.'

He sipped his tea and then paused to put a little more milk in it. 'But this Sunday she'd got up for a while, managed to have something to eat with us but not much. She was hardly eating at all.

'I remember it all so well. We were sitting in the living room and I was reading the Sunday *Independent* and Laura was talking about some case she was working on. I remember thinking that was unusual because she rarely did. She knew her mother was a bit anxious about that side of things and that she worried about her safety.

'However, Laura started to tell us about this particular investigation – that an informant had tipped them off about some big drugs importer. She'd been digging into his background and had discovered he used to be a director of a company in the North, a company called LOC. She'd been checking on the other directors, who all seemed to be ordinary enough, but lo and behold, she'd come across a retired policeman, someone who used to be in the same unit as her father. A man called Robert McCallan.

'She'd begun to wonder if he could be involved, too. I could see what she was getting at. If her father had been up to no good then it was possible some of his old colleagues weren't averse to dubious activities either. She asked Eileen if the name meant anything to her.'

Keane shook his head in dismay at the memory. 'God, she just didn't know what she was saying, blurting it out like that. But how could she? It had all been kept from her. I looked at Eileen and she'd gone deathly white. I thought for a minute that she'd died. Laura was getting alarmed, asking her what was wrong, but Eileen couldn't answer – she just slumped back in her chair. She seemed to have gone off into another place altogether and there was something strange in her eyes. We got her to bed and sent for the doctor who said she showed all the signs of having suffered a severe shock, which was true. That was exactly what had happened to her.'

He gave McCallan a hard look, accusing. 'It was your father, of course, the very mention of him. That was what had done it. Bob McCallan was a name she had been trying to blot from her memory for twenty years and now all the horror associated with it had come flooding back in like some poisonous tide.'

McCallan tried to suppress the confusion of emotions he felt, resentment and hurt among them. He needed to hear it all.

'What did you tell Laura?'

'Well, obviously she wanted to know what was wrong, why her mother had suddenly reacted like that, but I couldn't explain. I knew the truth but I had promised Eileen I would keep it from her. I said it was the memory of her father and what had happened to him, that in her weakened state she couldn't take much stress because the leukaemia was getting worse. In fact, she began to deteriorate fairly steadily after that.'

He gave a wry smile. 'But by then, of course, we had rather unexpectedly come into some money and I was able to use it to provide the best care that I could for her. For a time at least. Only a few months later she was gone. Laura felt terrible about it, held herself responsible, even though I tried to reassure her. That was why I decided to tell her the truth. I knew it was against her mother's wishes but Eileen was dead and I really believed Laura should know. God, if only I'd realised. But I couldn't bear the thought that she would spend the rest of her life hating the father she should have loved.'

He paused and took a breath. 'George Miller went to his grave labelled as a sectarian killer, a rogue policeman who brought shame on himself and his family and the force. But that couldn't have been further from the truth. A short time before his death, he confided in Eileen about a secret investigation he was conducting, one that he'd embarked on himself, without anybody knowing. He told her he believed that Dorothy Taylor and your father were involved in the assassinations of those IRA people. He told her some of the detail – conversations overheard, security files missing for periods of time, and that he had a feeling they suspected he was on to them. They'd all been close colleagues once but he felt he was being frozen out. That was why he decided to talk to Eileen. In case anything ever happened to him, he wanted her to know the truth.'

'How did she take that?'

'Oh, she was petrified, of course. She urged him to go and talk about it to someone higher up but he refused. He told her he hadn't enough evidence to do that yet and he would do so as soon as he had. But he never got the chance. Only a couple of nights after they had that conversation he was dead.'

'Why didn't she go to someone then? Why didn't she tell what she knew?'

'Fear. Fear for herself but mostly for her daughter. And, anyway, what would it have sounded like? She had no evidence; it would just have been the ramblings of a woman stricken by grief. And she knew that there was the distinct possibility that someone would kill her to keep her quiet too. Then the gun was found in the car and there was the scandal and the shame of all of that, even though she knew perfectly well that it must have been planted there. So eventually she felt she had to move away and she came to live here, to try to find an escape from it all. And that was painful too because that was when Laura began to change.'

He lifted his cup to his lips but was disappointed to find he had finished the tea. McCallan got up and brought him some more.

'You see, after that, Laura turned her back on her father. She believed that everything in the papers, what people were saying, was true. All the evidence pointed to it, anyway. Eileen tried to tell her not to think badly of him but she couldn't convince the child without telling her the truth and she didn't want to do that. She just couldn't.'

'Why not?' McCallan asked.

'She still worried about putting her at risk. At risk from Taylor and your father and anyone else who was involved. She knew how like George she was – the same sense of purpose, the same determination to get where she was going, no matter how long it took. She worried what Laura might do some day if she found out. And, my God, she was right. Look what I did – what I unleashed – by telling her.'

As Keane talked on, he told McCallan of Miller's belief that his father and Taylor had not acted alone. They always had solid and separate alibis on the nights the murders took place and the killings themselves had been highly professional. Skills like that carried a high price tag and would have been expensive to fund.

Talk of money reminded McCallan of his father's gift. 'What did you think when you got the £100,000?'

Keane shrugged. 'It was presented to us in such a way that we weren't allowed to think, were we? I always knew it was bound to be some sort of pay-off from somewhere, someone's guilt, but I never dreamed for a moment that the donor wasn't actually dead. And I certainly didn't know until tonight that it was your father.'

McCallan stayed with Keane for another half-hour, hearing him out, every last detail. What remained of the £100,000 had been left to Laura. She would have used that to fund her plan, renting the farmhouse, for instance. He had no doubts now that whatever had happened to his father, it had not been an accident.

God, she had used his own money to help kill him.

And you – you have screwed her. He knew how exciting it had felt. The touch of her skin. Her scent. Her heat. Her mouth on him. But now there was the agony of his guilt stabbing inside, a knife being twisted. He remembered the incident in the car, too. She had been torturing him, playing with him, all part of the punishment.

But worse, damn it, worse than any of that was the knowledge that his father was a murderer. That was the hardest truth of all.

He listened to Keane in torment, consumed with shame and humiliation at what he was hearing. Everything that he had held dear throughout his life, right from childhood, had been stripped away. There were no certainties any more, no assumptions. Nothing was what it appeared to be; everything was a lie. He felt bereft all over again, as he had when his father had died, or when Julia had cut the cord. But with the sense of loss there was now anger and a burgeoning need for retribution.

Keane told him he did not know where Laura was and he had not seen her for months. She had left her job, simply handed in her resignation without any explanation and sold her flat at the same time. She would have that money as well, McCallan thought, enough financial resources to do whatever she wanted.

'She just vanished,' Keane said. 'And then I read about your father's death in an accident and I started wondering. But I couldn't . . . couldn't bear to think it could be anything, you know, to do with her. And then today – that explosion. Dorothy Taylor. And the two men in your house and everything . . . it all seemed so . . . so monstrous and all so connected and I couldn't dismiss the thought any longer and it frightened me. And then when you appeared at the church, I knew.'

McCallan looked at him. The man had lived with an enormous burden all these years, the knowledge of an awful truth, but he did not have to face any more of the nightmare on his own.

It was time to make a move but first he wanted to be sure the old man was safe. 'Listen, I've been thinking,' he said. 'Maybe it's a good idea if you didn't stay at home tonight.

People are looking for me and, you never know, they might be able to track my movements and end up here and I don't want you getting involved. God knows, you've had enough to cope with as it is. Is there anywhere you can go easily?'

'Well, yes,' he said as he wondered about it, 'there's my niece at Rathmines. But what would I tell her?'

'Tell her . . .' McCallan thought, 'tell her you're having some work done to the central heating before you sell the house and that it's out of commission and too cold to stay here.'

Keane listened, deciding, then nodded. 'OK, I can do that.'

'Have you got a car?'

'Yes, it's in the garage. I don't use it a lot.'

'Well, don't use it tonight either. Take a taxi. Oh, and don't let the ever-watchful eyes next door know where you're going.'

Keane smiled. 'Mrs Donovan. You've met her, then?'

'She told me where to find you. I wouldn't want her telling anyone else.'

The old man's smile faded and he looked anxious. 'Laura,' he said. 'Have you any idea where she might be?'

McCallan shook his head but he was beginning to believe that he did.

Chapter Thirty-two

The hub of the city was the Europa Hotel and the huge bus and rail terminus which sprawled in its shadow. The Europa towered over everything, a grid reference for the unfamiliar, a symbol of survival. It had once been known as the most bombed hotel in Western Europe, a peculiar title it could keep for itself since there had not exactly been a queue of rival establishments eager to claim it. But the hotel was still there, the best part of fifty years since the first time they tried to blow it up.

Often in that half century, it had stood almost derelict with windows which were boarded up or just blackened holes. Tonight, as McCallan stepped from his bus on to the pavement in front of it, it was brash and brassy, ablaze with light, looking as if it would have been just as much at home on the strip in Las Vegas as in Great Victoria Street in Belfast.

He felt emotionally drained and in need of sleep but the Europa was not where he would be laying his head. He stood for a moment and looked around, feeling as if he might as well have a placard around his neck announcing that he was the man everyone was looking for. On the radio in the car, before he ditched it, he had heard the Secretary of State and the Deputy Chief Constable giving a press conference, saying they were following a definite line of inquiry that connected all the killings and that they were still most anxious to trace the whereabouts of Mr Jack McCallan.

It was time he put that theory to rest, whatever the risks, and, while driving, he had worked out what he should do. The more he thought about it, the more he was certain he knew what Laura's next move was. She had not finished killing. Not yet.

When he had got as far as Drogheda, he had pulled into a car park, locked the car and dropped the keys into a litter bin. The garage owner's son would get it back eventually. Then he had found a telephone and called Grace Walker. She had not been at home but the call had been redirected to her mobile. When he finally reached her she had been relieved to hear he was all right. She was also anxious to help, thank goodness.

When he had finished explaining what he wanted her to do, he had walked through Drogheda to the railway station and waited for the next train to Dundalk. From there he had taken a bus to Newry, a service with which he was becoming familiar now, and in Newry he had hopped on to the last express bus to Belfast.

He turned from the bus station and began to walk towards the city centre.

There were two policemen coming slowly towards him.

His heart was in his throat. He could not turn now; it was too late and they would wonder why.

Calm, keep calm. The trick was to look just as preoccupied and distant as any other passerby on the street. The trouble was, there were not many of them and none of them was a man walking alone. But surely no one would expect to meet Jack McCallan here, just strolling through Belfast like this; they would imagine he was in hiding somewhere, armed to the teeth.

Don't make eye contact but don't avoid looking at them. If he did either, they might notice and think quickly and he would have had it.

They were about twenty yards away now. His mouth was dry and he was not sure that his knees would hold out.

A car passed him swiftly and pulled into the kerb ahead.

There was a blue police sign on its roof. The two officers moved towards it with a greeting and in a second he was past them, turning sharply left into the Grosvenor Road, and heading in the direction of the Falls.

Mrs Donovan heard the car doors slamming and went to the window to see what it was all about. There had been people coming and going all day, the young priest first of all. He and Mr Keane had come back to the house and then the priest had left but about an hour ago, she had heard a car hooting its horn and looked out to see Mr Keane getting into a taxi. He seemed to have a little suitcase with him, too. What on earth was going on?

It was after seven, dark now and harder to see through the curtains so she pulled them aside to get a better look. There were two men walking up the path and looking right at her. She dropped the curtains abruptly and stepped back into the darkness of the room. She could not see their faces, not in this light, but there was something she did not like about them.

She waited for a minute. There was no sound at all. When she went to the window again, there was no sign of anyone but the car was still there at the gate. She walked down the hall to her front door and peered out. Where had they gone? The house beside her was in darkness.

Suddenly its door opened and the two men emerged. She turned quickly to go back in but they had seen her.

'Good evening,' one of them said. His accent sounded English. He was smiling as he stood in the path looking over at her. The other man carried a briefcase and said nothing.

'I hope we didn't startle you,' the smiling man said. 'We're from the estate agents. We came to check a few things in the house on our way home but Mr Keane doesn't appear to be about.'

'How did you get in?' Mrs Donovan asked.

'Oh, we have our own key.' He held up a bunch and jangled them. 'It's so we can show people around when he's not here. You've no idea where he might be, have you?'

She shook her head. He seemed like a nice man. The estate agents. Of course. Stupid of her to have been suspicious.

'He left about an hour ago,' she said. 'A taxi came for him.'

'I see. You don't know where he went?'

'Haven't an earthly notion.'

'Was there anyone with him?'

'No, he was by himself. The young priest left a bit before that.'

'A priest?'

'Yes. The young fellow who came this afternoon. Said he was from England. Didn't know Mrs Keane was dead.'

'What did he look like?'

'I don't know.' She shrugged. 'He was a priest, that's all. Dark clothing.'

The man turned and whispered something to his colleague. 'Oh well,' he said, 'not to worry. We'll catch up with Mr Keane again.'

The car engine started and she suddenly realised there was another man in it, a driver. The smiling man turned back to her as he opened the passenger door.

'Sorry to have bothered you,' he said.

As she watched them drive off, she wondered why estate agents would ask questions like that.

The massive gates opened to the fortress that was Lisburn regional police headquarters and the patrol car drove in. Constable Gary Irvine was at the wheel with his partner half-slumbering beside him. It had been a long day and boring as hell.

It had been eventful enough, that was true. Christ, you could say that again. Eventful? Unbelievable. But Gary Irvine's part in it, sitting out there in the cold in Dromore for hours on end and then helping them search that old barn where the dead men's car was found, had not exactly been historic, had it? Still, it was over now.

He parked in the bay which had his vehicle's number painted on it and got out and stretched. He felt very stiff. Days like this made you weary. He would unwind with a cup of tea in the canteen. With any luck, the new WPC from juvenile crime might be there. She had smiled at him the other day.

He opened the rear passenger door to get his cap. There were three letters on the seat under it. For a fraction of a second he was puzzled and then he remembered.

The road block. The postman. The television crew coming up the road.

Jesus, he had completely forgotten.

McCallan sat in the back of a black taxi heading into Andersonstown. He was not alone; no one ever was on these journeys. He sat on one of the cab's folding seats with his back to the driver, facing three dead-eyed children and a large woman who watched him suspiciously from behind a bank of carrier bags resting on her knee.

The West Belfast taxi service had begun in the early days of the Troubles, taking the place of public transport which had been suspended because buses were being hijacked and burned. When the conflict had stopped, the taxis had not. Now they were legal, licensed and insured, operating alongside the official bus service, using the same stops.

Tonight, however, the buses were not running. Tonight was like old times, which was why McCallan figured that West Belfast would be a good place in which to lie low. In spite of his English education, he could still manage a believable Ulster accent, but it was a gamble, he knew.

When he had got to the taxi rank at the top of the Grosvenor Road where it met the Falls, he had asked one of the drivers if he knew a decent guest house where he could book in for the night. The driver was a pudgy man with a cap. He had scrutinised McCallan with narrow eyes.

'What's wrong with a hotel?'

McCallan had screwed up his nose and shaken his head. 'Nah. Don't think so.' He had noticed the man studying him a bit differently now, wondering if he was hiding from something.

'You look like a peeler.'

McCallan had laughed. 'Someone else told me I looked like a priest.'

'Get in,' the driver had said. 'There's a place up the road.'

They had collected the other passengers along the way. For about five minutes the journey was silent and sullen but suddenly the taxi jerked to a halt, pitching McCallan out of his seat and on to his knees, with his head in the fat woman's lap. The bags collapsed on top of the children.

'Watch what you're fucking doing!' the woman said.

McCallan scrambled back to his seat, hearing raised voices outside shouting instructions. There were faces looking in, excited young eyes above handkerchiefs tied around mouths and noses. He saw baseball bats being carried.

Someone slapped the side of the taxi. 'OK,' a voice said, 'away you go.'

They moved off slowly and McCallan could feel heat on his face all of a sudden and then there was a blaze of light to go with it as they weaved around the burning hulk of a bus which had been overturned in the middle of the road. A vision of the remains of his father's caravan flashed through his consciousness. The taxi picked up pace again. From the window, McCallan could see groups of restless youths at street corners. Tape players were blasting. A screaming police car roared past in the direction from which they had come and in a few moments there were cheers and the smashing of glass.

They went round a roundabout. 'Here you are, mate,' the driver said and pulled up. McCallan scrambled out past the glowering woman and her brood. They were parked outside a house with double bay windows and a bed and breakfast sign in one of them. When he had paid the driver and the taxi had driven off, he looked across the road and saw that the kerbstones were in green, white and gold, the colours of the Irish national flag, and that the street sign on the gable wall was written in Gaelic. Even though Northern Ireland was still technically British, this corner of it had long ago donated itself to the Republic.

He did not have a clue where he was. He stood there alone with his bag in his hand, unsafe and unsure, feeling like an alien in a strange land.

Barry Toner walked into his office and slammed the door behind him. He took his raincoat off and threw it on a chair. Then, as he walked behind his desk, he caught his foot in the telephone lead and the receiver came crashing to the floor.

'Shit,' Toner said. He picked the phone up. Part of its casing had come unstuck and he tried to put it together again but he had trouble getting it to fit. Not the only bloody thing that did not seem to fit around here.

He had just had another spat with McIvor. After he had discovered the video, he had fully expected that they would have been forced to bring him back into the case. He had been right, although his renewed involvement had not exactly been what he had anticipated. For the past couple of hours he had been farting about in the wet and the cold on the farm where Mattheson and Tweed's car had been uncovered and interviewing the old bugger who had found it.

Why in the name of Christ was he doing that? The farmer had nothing left to say. Toner was convinced it was just a device to get him offside. Why, though? What were they doing about the video?

It was hours since he had found it and since then he had not heard a thing. Worse, he had caught a bit of the Secretary of State's news conference on the radio and discovered that they were still talking about Jack McCallan. No mention of the girl at all. There was something bloody funny about all of this, which was why he had gone over everyone else's head yet again and burst in on McIvor, only to be told that he was to keep out of it, that there were security implications and that the NSS were involved and if he was not careful he would find himself suspended.

He had left McIvor's office feeling angry and distinctly uneasy. He was going to find himself out of a job if he was not careful. But the NSS? What was going on here?

The phone casing clicked into place at last and there was a timid knock at the door.

'Yes?' he snapped.

Constable Gary Irvine was there. What did he want? He had just left him, for God's sake.

'Irvine? I thought I'd seen the last of you for the day.'

'I'm sorry, sir. I really am.' He had some letters in his hand. 'I should have given you these earlier. I simply forgot.'

Puzzled, Toner took the letters. It was the big envelope, the one with Jack McCallan's name scrawled on it, that caught his attention. He was about to ask where they had come from when the phone rang. It was still working, at any rate. He flicked it on to loudspeaker.

'Toner,' he said.

'Sorry to bother you, sir. It's the front desk. There's someone here who insists on seeing you, says it's very important.'

'Who is it?'

'It's a woman by the name of Grace Walker.'

Chapter Thirty-three

The landlady was wary of him and he could not blame her. He stood at her doorstep, lit by the lamp in the hall, while behind him they could hear the sound of madness out there in the dark. She was in her sixties with a flowered apron which he felt must be a permanent feature.

'It's just for the one night,' he said. 'I'll be away again in the morning.'

'Who told you to come here?'

'One of the taxi boys. I met him down the town. He said you would put me up.'

She was still not sure. She did not like it when she was in the house on her own. She had her regulars, lorry drivers a lot of them, a couple of reps, the odd student in the summer. But none of them was around tonight. She eyed McCallan again. He did not look like a murderer, come to strangle her in her bed, maybe worse, then take the tin she kept hidden in a cupboard under the sink. But he looked like he could handle himself and maybe it would do no harm to have someone like that about, especially on a night like this.

'I'll pay you cash, of course,' he said. 'Give it to you straight away.'

She appraised him again for another couple of seconds and then she nodded.

'You'd better come in.'

He counted out the money while she told him the rules. No drink on the premises, no women, the door locked at midnight, breakfast between seven and eight. He said that was fine. He was going to go out for a little while but he planned to have an early night.

'Where are you going tonight? Sure they're murdering each other out there.'

'Just got someone to see. Won't take me very long.'

She was wondering if she had done the right thing. She looked at his hold-all. What had he in it? Guns? A knife? Maybe he was one of these drugs boys. The young fellows around here were up to their eyeballs in it, out of their minds half of them. Could that be his game?'

'Can I see the room?'

'Oh . . . right. Yes.'

She led the way up the stairs, waiting for the knife to plunge between her shoulder blades, but by the time they got to the top she found to her surprise that she was still alive.

'This rioting's terrible,' he said. 'Where's it all going to end?'

'Haven't seen anything like it for years. Not since the Troubles.'

'Were you around then?'

'Oh, aye. All my life. Wouldn't move from here. No place like it.'

She showed him into a front room. There was a thin single bed under a picture of the Virgin Mary. A wardrobe with the varnish peeling from it stood against one wall and a small chest of drawers cowered in a corner.

'This is great,' he said. 'It'll do the job well.'

The bathroom was along the landing and the toilet was separate. He was very complimentary about how clean and tidy everything was. She had warmed to him again.

'Would you like a cup of tea or anything?'

'No, it's fine, thanks. I'll nip out now, if you don't mind. Won't be very long.'

She would be watching him from the window so he pretended he knew where he was going, striding away confidently down the hill until he was out of sight. He needed to find a phone. There was one in the house but he could not use that. He did not want her to overhear what he was saying or for the call to be traced there.

When he reached the main road it was noisy, a bizarre mixture of people up to no good and life going on as if nothing had happened, like the elderly man walking his dog on the other side of the street. A cider bottle smashed on the pavement ahead, thrown from a car which sped past, then wheeled with a screech in the centre of the road and rocketed back the way it had come. It was full of youngsters, some of whom were no more than thirteen.

A hand came out of the rear passenger window. There was a gun in it.

McCallan ducked into a shop doorway just before the first shot. Two women further along the road began to scream. The windows in a parked car shattered as the bullets hit it and there were whoops of delight from the joyriders as they disappeared into the night. McCallan came out of the darkness and hurried on.

Everywhere seemed closed, with shutters up to keep the trouble out, but he found a Chinese takeaway that was still functioning normally. Amazingly, so was its public telephone. The place was bedlam. Laughter erupted from a television set behind the counter while music blasted from a radio and orders were bellowed in Cantonese to the kitchen for the drunks and delinquents getting gravy and chips. None of this oriental muck for them.

He checked his watch. He knew Toner would still be in his office, waiting for the call. Grace would have been to see him by now to tell him. But he could not stay here long, a stranger attracting attention. He dialled and got through quickly. When he heard Toner's voice he gave him the message clearly and as quietly as the background noise would allow. Then he hung up.

As he left, a man watched him from the counter, waiting

for his battered sausages to arrive. Unlike the other customers, he was not drunk and he was wondering if he had picked up a snatch of an English accent amid the din.

McCallan had not noticed him and would not have recognised him anyway without the cap. It was outside in the taxi.

The street with the guest house was quiet, removed from the mayhem, a row of semis trying to be normal. The landlady seemed glad to see him back and sat him down in the living room with a cup of tea, a plate of biscuits and the evening paper. He told her about the joyriders with the gun and she said he should watch himself. All these drug gangs. They ran the place, did what they liked.

He watched television for a bit, then he went upstairs and lay down on the bed for a moment, listening in the darkness of the room to the wail of police sirens and the occasional crack of gunshots not so very far away.

He did not know what had woken him.

He sat up, alert, blinking, trying to think what it was. A sound of some sort. In the house or outside? He looked at his watch: 2 a.m. He must have fallen asleep hours ago. The night was quieter as he listened but then he heard something again. Whispers. A gate. He got off the bed and went to the window. The curtains were still open and he stood back from it to look out.

A black taxi was sitting down there. Someone was at the wheel and in the light from a street lamp he could see the outline of a man's cap.

Damn. Stupid, so stupid. How had he been so naïve as to think he could just blend in here, that no one would take any notice? There was anarchy in the air tonight, a savagery. They would be interested in strangers. But who did they think he was? The taxi-driver had said he looked like a policeman. If they thought he was an undercover agent of some sort, then he was dead. He thought of Barry Toner's father, what had happened to him. It was not the IRA out there now but the justice of the gangs would be as bad, not to mention the interrogation.

He opened the bedroom door and stepped on to the landing, listening. They had gone round the side of the house and he could hear scratching noises at the back door. He hurried along to the bathroom, went in and locked it. The window shelf was an array of small ornaments, a basket of soaps and jars of bath oil. He took a towel and swept them all into it, then opened the window.

The bathroom was at the side of the house, just above the garage. The roof was metal and it would make a hell of a noise when he jumped on to it but it was the only way he was going to get out of here. He climbed on to the shelf, crouched at the open window and waited.

The kitchen door caved in with a crash and the smashing of glass and excited yelling. There was the pounding of feet on the stairs and in her room the landlady began to scream.

He jumped, landing neatly and without too much noise, then he dropped from the garage to the ground. But he had not been totally silent. As he straightened, a figure came round the side of the house with some kind of weapon in his hand. He raised it to strike and McCallan kicked him in the stomach, then in the face when he doubled up.

He picked up the weapon. It was a curved bat, like a hockey stick. A hurley stick, that was it. The Irish version.

They were going crazy in the house and he wondered how many of them there were. Enough to fill a black taxi anyway. Things were being smashed and he heard the bathroom door give way and their shouted curses when they saw the open window.

He ran down the path towards the cab. The driver was getting out to see what was happening but he met McCallan in full flight with the hurley stick. He hit the man across the collarbone with it and he fell forward with a whimper against the open door, then slid to the ground.

McCallan tried to step over him to get into the vehicle but there were running feet behind him now and he knew he would not get the cab going in time, never mind working out how to drive it.

There was a shot and the whine of a bullet hitting metal and he began to run. He had to put as much distance between him and them as possible. And as quickly as possible. If they kept sight of him, they had him.

He sprinted with his head down as he heard more shots. Behind, they were shouting and then he heard a throaty roar as the engine was revved to the limits of its capability.

He was at the main road.

Right? Left? Go right. Across and up the other side.

He could see a turning and he might just be able to disappear into it before they saw where he was going.

No chance. The taxi was almost on him. But he would get to the corner first.

He found himself running down an avenue with a sharp dip.

He could smell the petrol before he saw the lorry.

It was blocking the narrow road, the letters BP emblazoned on its side. A gang of boys of about fourteen had opened its tanks and were filling crates of bottles, stuffing rags into the necks.

The taxi careered round the corner on two wheels and the boys turned and froze as its lights caught them. McCallan could see in their eyes that they knew what was going to happen.

He dived over a hedge into someone's front garden but that would not be safe enough. He picked himself up and ran on, round the back. There was a wooden fence to climb. Dogs were barking.

The driver stood on the brakes, a hysterical screech of rubber that brought them skidding through a wash of petrol into the side of the tanker.

The ground shook like an earthquake and a great, billowing

sail of flame soared into the sky, turning it from night into a burning daylight. Even though he was shielded behind the house, McCallan felt the incredible blast of heat and the reverberations of the shock wave. Hedges and trees began to blaze and one of the houses caught fire.

He did turn to look at the inferno but kept on going.

Chapter Thirty-four

'Can I get you anything else?'

The waitress's tousled hair was like a field of exotic crops, bright orange and black at the roots where the rinse was growing out. She cleared away the plate on which she had served him his bacon sandwich. McCallan had disposed of it swiftly and his stomach felt warm with food inside it. There had not been much time for eating in the past twenty-four hours.

'I wouldn't mind another cup of tea,' he said and she went to fetch it.

It was 7.15 a.m. and he was in the twenty-four-hour café along the waterfront. He still felt weak and shaky after everything that had happened but the food was helping. After the tanker explosion he had headed towards the city, hiding from passing police patrols, watching the fire tenders scream by. He had made his way to the ferry terminal where he had sat and dozed unnoticed in among the drivers waiting for the first sailing and at six thirty he had walked in here.

There were only two other customers, a couple of men wearing luminous yellow jackets with black lettering announcing that they were from the Department of the Environment water service. The waitress had the radio on and they listened intently to reports of the fire. A disaster, they were calling it. The reports said there were at least seven people dead but it was difficult to get an accurate count because the bodies had been so badly burned.

He had never seen his father's body. The police in Donegal had not been at all suspicious, just careless and a bit lazy, not wanting any fuss, and they had not felt the need to examine the charred corpse for any other cause of death. How had she killed him, he wondered, and where?

He sipped the hot, fresh tea that had been placed before him and waited, facing the window which looked on to the street outside. A dark saloon drove up slowly, crossed his vision and passed from view. After a moment, the door of the café opened and a man in a raincoat walked in. He ordered a cup of tea at the counter and then sat with it at McCallan's table.

'We did promise ourselves we'd have a drink some time,' Barry Toner said. 'I hadn't quite meant this.'

McCallan managed a smile. It looked as if Toner had come alone, as requested, unless there were SWAT teams swarming all over the street outside. He doubted it. He had taken a chance but it seemed as if his instincts about the man were right.

'You're on your own, then?'

'Almost,' Toner said. 'Just a driver. Someone to keep an ear on the radio in case things get busy.'

He looked at McCallan, taking in the sunken eyes, the pale, unshaven cheeks.

'You've had an interesting couple of days,' he said. 'I hear you've had an injury.'

McCallan patted his side where the improvised bandage was still wrapped. His adventures in the night had put it under some strain but the bleeding had not begun again.

'It's getting better. Could have been worse.'

'Yeah, you could have been dead.' He stirred his cup. 'Your friend Grace is an impressive person.'

'Yes, she is. I couldn't have managed without her. But I haven't told her too much about what I've found out. I wanted to talk to you, someone I might be able to trust. God knows, they've been in short supply lately. That's why I sent her to tell you I would phone. I wanted to make sure you'd be waiting.'

'She told me about you turning up at her house and everything that happened afterwards. Seems to put you in the clear, all right, although a lot of the people I know would like to get their hands on you, nevertheless. I could have talked to you for a bit longer last night myself.'

'I had to keep it short.'

'Why – was your takeaway ready?'

McCallan looked surprised.

Toner laughed. 'You forget that calls are easily traced these days. Anyone can do it. But you picked a good spot. I had no intention of trawling the streets of Andersonstown looking for you, not in the present circumstances. Jesus, that was a mess last night.'

'I know,' McCallan said and then told him what had happened.

'Christ almighty! How do you get into these scrapes? You're lucky to be alive.'

'So people keep telling me. I'm beginning to agree with them.'

'There'll be a lot of questions.'

'So you're going to take me in? There's still unfinished business.'

'You don't know the half of it. I won't bring you in just yet, though. They don't know I'm here. They think I'm still waiting for another call from you.'

'I don't understand,' McCallan said. 'Why have you taken a chance like that? It'll land you in trouble.'

'Don't worry, I'm well in it already. Now listen: there are a lot of funny things going on, a lot of things about this investigation that I don't like. For a start, the National Security Service are in on it. Creepy lot, keen on making little problems disappear, if you know what I mean, good at getting rid of people who know things they're not supposed to. We wouldn't want you becoming another George Miller.'

It was McCallan's turn to be startled at the mention of the name.

'What do you know about George Miller?' he asked.

317

Toner told him about finding the video in the house and taking it to the Deputy Chief Constable. He told him what McCallan had already guessed, that it was Mattheson and Tweed who had been listening in on his calls, no doubt following Dorothy Taylor's instructions. And he told him quietly and with care, because he knew it would be painful, about the death of Alfie Hutchinson who had been shot in the head after being beaten and mutilated.

McCallan went pale and closed his eyes.

'Oh my God. That poor, poor man. What have I done?'

Finally, Toner told him about the traces of his father's blood that the forensics people had found in the kitchen.

'Something happened in that house before the fire in Donegal,' he said.

It came back to McCallan, the sharp smell of disinfectant he had noticed when he first walked in, how pristine the kitchen had been. He told Toner and then he described his visit to Eamonn Keane and what he had learned.

The policeman took a bulky envelope from his coat pocket and handed it to him.

'What's this?'

'Read it. As you can see, it's addressed to you.'

McCallan looked at it. 'Somebody's opened it.'

'Yes, me. But whoever posted it to you read it first.'

There was a smaller envelope inside and from it he took five sheets of A4 paper in what he recognised straight away as his father's writing.

Alfie. This was what he had found and it was why he had been killed.

They had not been able to find it because he had posted it. McCallan looked at the name and address, just a scrawl, the stamp stuck crookedly in the corner. He must have bought an envelope somewhere on the way home from the Masonic hall and dropped it into a letter box. But in the end he would have told them where he had sent it; he would not have been able to stand the agony.

He shared the thought with Toner who nodded. 'That was why Mattheson and Tweed went back to your house. Their plan would have been to kill you, leave your body somewhere where you wouldn't be found for a while, and then go back and wait for the postman. They had to get this letter. And even though you'd managed to get away from them, it was something they still had to do. It was too important to leave lying around. And then our friend Miss Keane came into the picture.'

'So what was she doing there?'

'Oh, I'd have thought she was trying to kill you. You were a loose end to tidy up before she went off to blow the Chief Constable away. She might even have planned to make it look like suicide, who knows, using your father's gun.

'You wouldn't have been on her original list but she would have made up her mind to kill you anyway. Don't forget it wouldn't exactly have been part of her consideration for you to benefit from your father's death, inheriting all that wealth. She would have hated that idea all right. But then when she came to the house and found Mattheson and Tweed waiting, it gave her a different opportunity. Why not kill them and make it look as if you did it?'

McCallan turned to the pages in his hand. He read quickly, gripped by it. There was no doubt now, no lingering hope. It was a complete admission, a full account of the murders, how they were planned, who was involved, the hate that had driven them.

And in it he saw something else, something which had already been unveiled to him by Eamonn Keane: the story of one man's greed.

The final page of the confession was about George Miller.

It wasn't my wish that George should die, although there's no point in protesting about that now. I was just as much involved as the others, every bit as responsible, and I cannot deny that. If only he had looked the other way, taken no notice, it would have stopped soon anyway. We had done what we set out to do. But once we knew that he was suspicious of us, he left us no choice.

I suggested talking to him, perhaps trying to get him in with us. He was no different. He hated the IRA just as much, he felt the same frustrations about the security policy, but Dorothy wouldn't hear of that. It was too much of a risk and she insisted that George had to be taken out of the way.

I'll never forget the way she said it. She frightened me. Me, for goodness sake. God, I wished then that I'd never become involved with her. I knew then that whatever there had been between us before, it could never happen again.

I think George knew we were on to him. We'd been friends, the three of us, but the chumminess had stopped. There's a pub out in the country at Aghalee, not used much, the sort of place where you're not noticed. When I drove out there one night George followed me. But Dorothy had decided to keep on eye on him, do a bit of shadowing herself. She saw him taking pictures of us in the car park, knew he'd seen everything. So that was that.

We stole the camera out of George's car. God, the poor man must have been petrified when he found it gone. He must have known his number was up. He had this Loyalist grass who used to give him a lot of information, a fellow called Gillespie. We put the elbow on him about a couple of things, scared the shit out of him, and got him to ring George and say he knew where the camera was.

'That was how we did it. It was a set-up. George got hit in the car, Gillespie too. The other gun was left where it would be found and we knew George would get the blame for the whole thing.

'I don't know how I feel now that I've written this down. I expected to feel some sort of relief, I suppose, but that hasn't happened. It doesn't mean we didn't do those things, didn't kill those people. Sometimes I tell myself that the end justified the means. There's peace now and what we did brought it a bit nearer. But the guilt I feel, the remorse, has been getting worse since Jack's life was spared. I thank God for him every day and I ask for forgiveness for what I've done.'

There were tears in McCallan's eyes and he could not read on.

'What . . . what will happen when this gets out? It'll be the end of this place.'

'Which is why I think it never will get out,' Toner said. 'They won't want to risk seeing Northern Ireland going back to the way it was. Jesus, it's bad enough at the minute. But the Chief Constable involved in a private campaign of murder? No way. This will have to be kept quiet. Some other explanation will have to be found for everything that's happened over the last few days.'

'Like what?'

'Just now I'm not so sure. You see, you would have been a convenient scapegoat for a while. Every one of the deaths has your name in it somewhere. It wouldn't have been hard to, shall we say, remove you from the picture and then concoct a theory to explain why you did it. But they would have had to find Laura quietly and dispose of her as well. And all that's going to be difficult, if not impossible, now that you've emerged into plain view.

'They'll have been following their own leads since I gave them the video. Whatever the NSS may be, they're not slow.' He tapped the envelope on the table. 'But they won't have this kind of detail, this gold dust, although they'll have worked out some sort of version and they'll have been looking for Miss Keane. And not to bring her to trial either.'

McCallan looked at the letter and then at Toner. 'What about me? I know what's in here. I know the truth and so do you.'

Toner smiled. 'Insurance, perhaps? Something to lock away where it can't be found unless you want it to be. I'm the only one who knows you have this but when they interview you, you might want to drop hints about the document's existence. You can guarantee that the acting Chief Constable and the Secretary of State and whoever else is running this show will get to hear about it. I can look after the letter for a while. Letter? What letter? And then you can hide it away.

'Even though it's not witnessed, it's signed and it can easily be proved to be your father's writing. And with all the stuff that's in there, an enterprising journalist or an interested MP would have a field day. No, Jack, while you've got this, you've got a guarantee of a long and, I hope, peaceful life.'

McCallan studied him. 'Why are you doing all this?'

'You remember when we met, I told you why I'd joined the police? Well, I didn't join a force that has people killed conveniently. At the same time, I don't want to see the country going bad again. Maybe it's better that this doesn't get out, you know? But without anybody else having to die.'

McCallan lifted the envelope and handed it to Toner.

'Eamonn Keane told me the story from Miller's point of view,' he said, 'the way he had told it to his wife before they killed him. Miller knew my father and Taylor weren't pulling the trigger themselves. Someone else was doing it for them but it would be costing money to hire the sort of person they needed, so where were they getting it?

'Miller had a feeling he knew although he couldn't prove it. The night he followed my father up to Lough Neagh, he saw him park and get into a Range Rover that was already there. He had the camera and he managed to get into a position from where he could take pictures without being seen – except, as we know now, he was being watched all the time.

'He saw three people: my father, a tall man who was in shadow so he didn't get a very good look, but he did see who was driving the Range Rover.'

Toner nodded. 'Henry Lomax.'

'Yes, Henry Lomax. Uncle Henry.'

It was different, more real in a way, now that he had said it rather than simply thinking it. But the hurt and the sense of betrayal were just as deep. His face began to flush with anger. He saw everything with different eyes. Words echoed in his ears with a different sound, a different meaning. There was

Lomax's defence over dinner of what he had assumed was Miller's handiwork. But it had not been Miller he had been defending at all: it had been his own actions and those of his fellow murderers that he had been attempting to justify.

All his life he had heard Lomax's point of view, the Protestant bigotry that was never far below the surface. He had always tolerated it – it was only Henry giving off – and it had even been amusing at times, like black humour, but not any more. Hatred and greed were a potent combination which had produced desperate measures.

He thought of how much Lomax had profited from the peace. There were the derelict inner city sites bought for a song and now worth a fortune. There were the land development deals, the companies bought and sold, all of it symbolised by the glass monument on the other side of the road, the celebration of a prosperity that Lomax must have feared would never last.

It was worse to think that what they had done had worked, that it had helped bring about a turning point. In the tide of peace, Lomax had become even richer and in the slipstream his father had grown wealthy, too. And now that wealth, created from so much spilled blood, was his.

'There have been people in there all night,' Toner said, inclining his head in the direction of the Lomax building. 'Police search teams have been through the whole place. When you phoned and said you believed Lomax was the next target, I had to do something about it. I couldn't just wait to see if you were right – I had to pass the message on. And,' he smiled with some irony, 'they had to listen to me. But I managed to check before I got here. They haven't found anything.'

'Does Henry know any of this?'

'No, nor do any of the other people with offices in there. We've kept it discreet so as not to cause too much alarm or scare her off, just in case you were right.'

'Damn it, I know I'm right. She's bound to be getting desperate now and she's frustrated that it hasn't all gone exactly to plan. Just think about it. She worked it out meticulously. My father first, getting close to him, getting to know him – it would have been easy. Then there's the bomb. That was meant to kill Henry as well as Dorothy Taylor, except he was ill and wasn't there and that leaves the job unfinished. So where's her next opportunity to get him? Where might he be exposed and vulnerable? Right here, this morning.'

He looked at his watch. 'And that's in ten minutes, at eight o'clock, when he announces that LOC's been sold and introduces the new owners, just in time for the opening of the markets.'

'What if he couldn't make it? He was sick yesterday, after all.'

'That was always a possibility. But after I called you last night I saw a piece in the paper with a statement from him, saying that in spite of everything he was going ahead with a news conference this morning at which he would reveal a big new business development. Besides, I stood over there an hour ago and watched him drive in.'

'It's a good theory,' Toner said, 'but I'm happy to say that I think we may have got in just ahead of the posse this time. The building would seem to be as clean as a whistle and any strange woman who looks remotely like her will be scooped if she gets within a mile of the place. No, I think Henry Lomax will survive this one.'

He stood up from the table. 'But I think it's about time we ambled over there and looked him in the eye. I'm sure you'd like to see the look on his face.'

In the street outside, Toner's driver was getting out of the car.

'Bit of news,' he said. 'A young policewoman's been murdered. Body found in the back of one of those Japanese four-wheel-drive things somewhere in East Belfast. Bloody terrible. She'd been stripped and tied up and gagged and then shot in the back of the head. Her uniform's missing, too.'

McCallan and Toner looked at each other, then began to run in the direction of the Lomax building.

Lomax was sitting behind the desk in his huge office. It was a corner location which gave him two walls of glass and made people gasp when they walked in for the first time. It was like being on a cloud. Far below, the commuter traffic on the bridges was becoming noisier and more dense but he was too well insulated to hear any of it, nor, at this moment, did he seem to notice anything at all of the world outside his transparent kingdom.

His face was grey as he looked at the piece of paper in his hand. Three dark-suited young men with document cases sat across the desk from him, watching him silently, noticing that he did not appear to be reading the note any more but just staring at it absently. For the past few minutes they had waited for the sort of ferocious outburst with which they were horribly familiar but it had not come. Maybe it was something to do with the other man, whose presence Mr Lomax had not bothered to explain to them, the man sitting over in the corner.

Gavin Pierce sat watching them and at the same time he kept an eye on the door.

The piece of paper in Lomax's hand had been received a short time before by electronic mail. It was from the American buyers and it told him that, regretfully, they would be unable to complete the deal today. Indeed, they would be unable to complete it any day and were withdrawing their offer for the company. There had already been a phone call from another Lomax employee who had seen them in the departure lounge at the airport, waiting for the Heathrow shuttle.

Lomax was having trouble breathing. His chest hurt and he felt his mouth dry. In truth, he could not blame them. Look what had happened. Two policemen found murdered in the home of one of LOC's directors, who has also died in strange circumstances. Not much point, as it turned out, in covering up poor Bob's murder, was there? All that business with the caravan. He had hated that. His old friend should have been afforded more dignity. But the deal had to be protected.

He laughed suddenly, alarming his young men. Pierce gave him a dry glance. Protecting the deal. Jesus, there would not be too many deals now, not now that half the bloody business community had been blown away, along with the Chief Constable. Looting and rioting in the streets all over the television screens. Who would want to bother?

This was just the sort of thing they had tried to stop all those years ago. Look at the prosperity they had brought. A few Provos had been topped – so what? It had worked and the place had taken off as a result. Now people were getting killed again and he was afraid of being next.

He put the paper down and turned to the window. The pain in his chest was sharper. There was someone out there waiting to murder him and he had no idea who it was, no idea at all. But Bob had gone. And Dorothy. Mattheson and Tweed, too. Jack was being fingered for that, wherever he was. They had let him get away, the stupid bastards, but Pierce would find him. He was uncomfortable with the thought of Jack being killed but it had to happen. Anyway, Bob was dead and it did not really matter a damn now.

Pierce would look after it all. He would keep an eye on him and find out who was behind it. Christ, he was an expensive bodyguard. A million, it was costing, paid up front. That was Pierce sticking the arm in because he had been screwed on the shares. The bloody shares. They would be worth fuck all now.

He would get through this morning somehow and get away, far away, and he would leave Pierce to clean things up. He had done it before. George Miller and the other man and all those Provos. Pierce had done a great job, no loose ends. He had already done the wee policeman, Hutchinson. But in the meantime, there were people down on the next floor waiting for him to start a press conference. God, what was he going to say?

★   ★   ★

McCallan was fitter and faster, although Toner was doing a good job keeping up. It was early but a lot of people had already arrived for work and there were quite a few vehicles in the Lomax car park.

They were half-way across it when the car bomb went off.

There was an enormous orange flash against the wall of the building, then the deafening blast and the tremor of the explosion. They ducked instinctively, then threw themselves to the ground as pieces of hot metal began to land around them. There were women screaming, alarms jangling, when they got to their feet again.

McCallan could see bits of the vehicle still blazing and there were flames in the windows of the ground-floor offices. Policemen in black combat clothing and carrying short machineguns had appeared and people were yelling and running in panic away from the building.

The first of them had reached the entrance to the car park when the second car went up.

It was a dark Ford saloon placed where people would have been bound to run past it. It exploded with an enormous roar and the blast sprayed metal and flame and pieces of flesh and clothing into the air, to fall like an infernal rain.

People were running in all directions now, not knowing which way was safe, which way to go. But a tall woman in a police uniform seemed to, hurrying round the back of the building, her pistol in her hand, to where there was a private executive entrance. Two dazed and bewildered security men unlocked the glass door as she hammered on it.

'There's been some sort of a bomb attack,' she said breathlessly. 'We've got to get everybody out of here. There's a private lift, isn't there?'

One of the security men nodded.

'Do you know the code for it?'

He nodded again. Shock had robbed him of speech.

'Then come with me and help me bring Mr Lomax and the others down. Come on! Hurry!'

Her urgency woke them up and they bustled ahead of her and round a corner to the narrow elevator door. There was a key pad beside it and one of the men punched in the code. The lift reached them in seconds and the doors eased open.

One of the men turned for a moment, just as Laura raised her gun and fired. The bullet went through his eye and he fell inside, his body propping the door open. Her second shot entered the back of his partner's head and he folded sideways to the floor. She jammed the gun back into her belt and grabbed the first man's legs, hauling him out of the lift, then she stepped inside and pressed the button she wanted.

High upstairs Lomax was now undeniably alert to the world outside. He and Pierce looked down towards the car park, seeing the flames and the panic and the pall of black smoke rising towards them. There were horns going off in the corridors and an emotionless computer voice.

'There is an emergency situation . . . Please evacuate the building by the nearest exit . . . There is an emergency . . .'

'What's the quickest way out of here?' Pierce asked.

'There's the executive lift,' Lomax said, 'just down the corridor.'

'Right then. Let's go.' He turned to the three young executives standing like frightened rabbits in the centre of the room, waiting for someone to tell them what to do. 'I'm looking after Mr Lomax,' he said. 'You better find your own way out.'

It was only when they had fled from the room that one of them realised he had a gun in his hand.

In the car park, McCallan was on his feet again, unhurt and feeling surprisingly clear-headed amid the chaos, although he thought Toner might be dead. It did not look good at all. He was on his back and he was not moving. A piece of shrapnel had hit him in the head and his right eye appeared to have gone. Blood gushed from the wound on to the surface of the car park.

There was nothing anyone could do until the ambulances arrived. McCallan felt a rush of anger as he opened Toner's coat and took his pistol from the holster on his belt. He knew what this was about. It was a diversion, pure and simple, brutal but brilliant. She did not care how many she killed to get the one she wanted.

There had been enough slaughter. It had to stop now and there was only one way it could: he had to kill her. She was here somewhere, the woman who had done all this, who had murdered his father and would have killed him, too. He felt a surge of excitement. She was so deadly. And so close.

He began to run towards the building, sprinting against the tide of panic.

His father's letter. It had been in Toner's pocket. But he could not waste time going back to look for it.

At the main door, he forced his way through into the marbled entrance hall, skidding along the polished floor towards where he knew the lifts were. He looked at the lights on the number board. The first lift was ten floors up, on its way down. What about the second? Three floors to go. He would just have to wait for it. Lomax was on the eighteenth floor and that meant the stairs were out of the question.

The doors opened and three well-dressed young men tumbled out. McCallan grabbed one of them by the shoulder as he tried to rush past.

'Do you know where Lomax is?' McCallan yelled into his face.

'In his office,' the man gasped, his eyes widening in terror as he spotted the gun. 'There's a man with him . . . a man . . . with a gun!' He stared at it again.

McCallan jumped into the lift.

'They're going down in the private elevator at the back,' the man shouted as the door closed but McCallan caught the words too late. He had already hit 18 and the non-stop button.

Lomax and Pierce were in the corridor but they were not

in the lift yet. The horns were still sounding, the robot voice insisting that they leave the building by the nearest exit. Lomax was in pain and sweating and he turned back to the office to get his heart tablets. Maybe they would ease this agony. Pierce hurried on to call the lift.

It was already coming up and he wondered why.

There was a faint noise behind him and he turned to see a man pushing through the corridor door. Whoever he was, he was carrying a gun, so he fired twice at him but McCallan had seen him for just the fraction of a second it took to dive out of the way. Pierce's bullets splintered the polished woodwork of the door.

Lomax came out of his office as McCallan and Pierce both raised their guns. He was right in the line of fire. No one moved.

With an efficient executive swish, the doors of the private lift opened.

Too late, Pierce turned.

Laura stood there, legs apart, gun in both hands, and shot him twice in the chest. He fell back with a soft grunt as if he had been winded.

Lomax lurched to his left through a door that led on to the back stairs.

Now Laura saw McCallan, stretched on the floor in an aiming position, and she hit the lift buttons as he fired. Three bullets made a neat grouping in the metalwork and then he was on his feet, running towards the stairs. As he ran, he looked at the lift numbers and saw that it stopped only at the three Lomax executive floors, 16, 17 and 18. Laura could not have gone far and he wondered if any of his shots had hit her.

Once through the door and on to the stairs, past the gunman's body, he saw Lomax almost at the floor below, doubled over the metal banister and clutching his chest.

As McCallan reached him, he heard a door bang open against a wall somewhere further down and he looked over the edge of the stairs to find Laura staring up. For a moment he was shaken. Her green eyes held him with a fierceness, like that morning in bed. Then he fired. His bullets chipped concrete off the wall and she ducked back through the door.

He prised Lomax off the stair rail and began to help him back up. He struggled with the old man's awkward weight and helped him down the corridor as quickly as he could, shuffling backwards with his gun in his right hand and supporting Lomax with his left arm. She would follow Lomax to wherever he was. Out here, exposed, he was vulnerable but once McCallan got him into the office, he had a better chance of taking her by surprise.

He lowered Lomax on to a chocolate leather settee. But not quickly enough.

When he heard the sound of feet running along the soft carpet of the corridor, his back was to the door.

As Laura burst into the room, he managed to turn and throw himself quickly to one side, trying to get some kind of aim as he did so, but she got her shot in first, although it was off centre and hit him in the left shoulder instead of the chest, knocking him backwards across an upright chair and into a heavy bookcase. There was a brief moment of blackness and he felt sure he had broken something but it did not matter now because he had lost his gun and she would finish him.

He was wrong. Instead, she walked towards where Lomax was lying and raised her gun, pointing it at his head. His eyes were closed and he was groaning.

'Open your eyes, you bastard,' she said, her voice even and calm. 'Open your eyes. I want you to see this.'

Lomax turned painfully and looked up at her, seeing a face that meant nothing to him, wondering why.

She took aim but her back was to the corridor, as McCallan's had been, when she sensed that someone was there.

She swung round to see the bloodied figure of Pierce propped against the doorway with his gun levelled at her chest.

He fired five times in rapid succession and the shots hit her with a force that lifted her off her feet and into the sheer glass just behind her. It shattered into huge, razor shards which slashed her as she went through it, falling down, far down, her arms trying to catch hold of the air, to the river flowing below.

Someone, somewhere turned the alarm system off.

Chapter Thirty-five

Laura's shot had taken a chip out of his collarbone and he spent a night in hospital before being released into the care of the police with his shoulder strapped up and his arm in a sling. He was with them all that day, being interviewed by men who did not identify themselves, while others watched sullenly and took notes, and then, when they told him he could go for the time being, he called Grace. He did not want to have to go back to his own house.

Toner was not dead but he had lost an eye and his days in the Police Service were over. Grace took him to the hospital. Toner was in a secluded side ward, sleeping, his head swathed in bandages and his wife was with him, holding his hand. She was a dark-eyed woman who had been crying. Two bemused children stood beside the bed.

McCallan introduced himself and she shook his hand. She looked dazed and he felt a dreadful guilt. He did not want to ask but he had to and so he wondered if among her husband's things there had been a letter in a big envelope. She shook her head. No, there had been nothing like that but there had been some plainclothes officers around who had helped the nurses pack his clothes away. She did not know who they were, she had not spoken to them, but perhaps they had retrieved it.

He left the hospital feeling drained. It was gone. They had it. He did not think Toner had made a copy either. Outside a couple of men were waiting with a black Rover and the message that the Secretary of State would like to see him.

An aide opened the door and showed him in. Crichton came forward, beaming, his arms outstretched like a hotel manager greeting a well-heeled guest.

'My goodness,' he said. 'You've certainly been in the wars.'

McCallan looked at the other two people in the room as Crichton introduced them. One was a man called Hugo Tarrant. He had heard the name before, read it in the papers often enough, and the other was the acting Chief Constable, Peter O'Brien. Tarrant smiled and offered his hand and for a moment McCallan thought about refusing it. After all, this was a man who would have had him murdered. But he took it and smiled back, playing their game.

Crichton beckoned him to sit. 'It's been an appalling ordeal for you, and for the whole community indeed, but it's over now, thank goodness.'

McCallan raised an eyebrow. 'But it's not quite, is it, Secretary of State? There are a few loose ends, surely? Henry Lomax, for instance?'

Crichton's smile was still there but the thin coating of charm was cracking.

'Ah, yes, Henry Lomax. Mr Lomax is in a private hospital in the south of England where he's recovering from his heart attack. He's well enough to talk now and he has been putting people in the picture, shall we say.'

He looked towards Tarrant who nodded as if giving permission and then he went on.

'Including the details of what really happened to your father,' he said.

Crichton spared him nothing, knowing full well the effect it would have. He told him of all the horror that Beth Benson had found in the kitchen and how she had been murdered so that Mattheson and Tweed could conceal it. McCallan listened in an agonised silence.

'Let me make something very clear,' Crichton said, following through. 'I have the well-being of Northern Ireland to take care of. It is my number one priority. And I do not think any useful purpose will be served by the public exposure of a litany of revelations and allegations about wrongdoing in the past.'

He raised his arm in a dismissive gesture. 'Twenty years ago, for goodness sake. Things have moved on, progressed so much since then. We've seen how thin the fabric of this place is, how easily that can be damaged. It is a delicate equilibrium and we cannot allow Northern Ireland and its future prosperity to be affected any further. God knows, it will take long enough to pick up the pieces from the past few days.'

'A cover-up,' McCallan said. 'That's what you mean.'

Crichton reacted as if there were suddenly a nasty smell in the room. 'My dear Mr McCallan, these are cheap terms, journalistic clichés. What we are talking about is a pragmatic imperative in the interests of the greater good. I cannot imagine, for example, that you would seriously consider telling your friend Grace Walker what really happened to her sister.'

McCallan was stung. He was right. Grace did not need any more suffering.

'What about the woman?' he asked. 'Is there still no sign of her body?'

'None.' It was O'Brien who spoke. 'The river's been dragged thoroughly but there's been nothing. She must have been carried out to sea and if that's the case there's no guarantee that she'll ever turn up.'

He wondered if O'Brien was telling the truth or whether this was just another lie. If there was no body, then an embarrassing identification could be avoided. Very convenient.

'I doubt if her identity will ever really be known,' Tarrant said.

McCallan looked at him but his face had all the human response of a mask. This was not opinion he was expressing; it was policy.

'Indeed,' Crichton said. 'We've already told the world that we've no idea who this woman was but that it certainly seems as if she was acting alone. If you've studied the papers, you'll see there are all sorts of theories now, that she was some sort of psychopath, a mad anarchist perhaps, with a hatred of the state, the police, capitalism, God knows what. I think it will go down as an extraordinary and unexplained episode, like an earthquake or a flood, unpredictable and unrepeatable, one of life's mysteries. We've instituted an inquiry, of course, but it's unlikely to achieve very much.'

'And George Miller?' McCallan asked.

'History can't be rewritten,' Crichton said. 'Dorothy Taylor's reputation cannot be tarnished – too much is at stake – but I'm afraid that, regrettably, Mr Miller's will not be restored.'

'My father's letter—' he began.

'A very interesting document,' Tarrant said. 'Lomax made us aware of its existence, said he and Dorothy Taylor had been most anxious to get hold of it. We tried to work out where it might be and eventually we retrieved it from your friend, Inspector Toner. I think it's best if I hang on to it now.'

McCallan felt beaten. He asked about Pierce, whose identity he had learned from the police who had questioned him. Gavin Pierce. The man named in his father's letter as the assassin. Lomax would have told Tarrant's people about him, too.

'A business associate of Henry Lomax,' Crichton said, 'who was unfortunate enough to have become an innocent victim. It's as simple as that. All this has been very distressing for Lomax, of course, on top of a rather serious illness. He has decided that when he has recovered – and apparently there's every indication that he will – he is going to retire from business. I understand that he's got a little place in the Channel Islands and he's going to live there. Lucky man.'

McCallan's eyes flicked from Crichton to Tarrant to O'Brien. They were all watching him, waiting to see how he would respond. But there was one loose end they had not mentioned.

'Eamonn Keane,' McCallan said.

Tarrant smiled. 'Very nice man, I'm told. Sends you his regards.'

They had fixed him, too. There were rumours, quite unfounded, of course, Tarrant acknowledged, about his days as a teacher and his relationships with certain of the boys in his care, but rumours, nevertheless, which would be dreadfully painful and damaging if they were to resurface.

'Anyway,' Tarrant said, 'our recent difficulties are likely to disappear from the headlines quite soon. I understand that tomorrow's papers will have their hands full. Apparently, a French magazine is publishing a story this evening alleging that the Irish Prime Minister, that paragon of family values, is having a homosexual affair.'

There was nothing McCallan could say. They had it all sewn up.

Tarrant saw the distaste and the defeat and he smiled.

'We've been taking a keen interest in you in the past few days, as you can imagine, finding out rather a lot about you. Life will move on, Mr McCallan. You'll find new preoccupations. For a start, you might like to know that a rather close friend of yours is coming home tomorrow.'

Somewhere over the west coast of Ireland, the stewardesses handed out a light snack on a tray as the flight from Kennedy made its descent towards Heathrow, but the silent group in the front of economy were not interested. There were five of them, three men and two women, and when the aircraft touched down, they were ushered off first and steered through Customs and Immigration.

The others had dozed on the flight, even her husband, but she had not. She had too much on her mind. She had felt elation at first that it was all over but now she was nervous, wondering where Jack was. She still felt the agony of the call she had made that Sunday morning. It would have destroyed him. But had Brian managed to explain?

Daniel Shriver's suit was badly crumpled. He was unshaven

and without a tie and his head was bowed as he walked handcuffed to one of the two policemen who had sat with him. Behind him Julia walked with a policewoman, dark glasses concealing her tired eyes. They had questioned her in New York but it was only a formality because it was Daniel they wanted. They would spend a long time talking to him.

Two police cars were outside and they sped off to the police station in West London. There, Julia stood and allowed the tension to slip from her as she watched her husband being taken away. He turned once and she saw the helpless look in his eyes but she felt nothing.

They made her wait in an interview room for a while. It was bare and dirty with an ashtray that no one had bothered to empty. She wanted to go home. She had to try to reach him.

The door opened and a policewoman came in.

'Right, Mrs Shriver. You're free to go.'

'Great.' Julia followed her in a hurry. 'Can I call a taxi from here?'

'It's OK. I've already got one.'

Her heart leapt and she swung round towards the sound of his voice. His left arm was in a sling and she wondered if he had had an accident.

Epilogue

Brittany had just gone through one of its tempestuous periods, thunderous skies and deluges of warm rain that washed away everything in its path. Now the July skies were cloudless and dazzling but there was a brisk breeze that was deceptive and on the beaches the unwary would burn and feel ill if they stayed out too long.

Henry Lomax was not one of those. He came up from below where he had slept deeply after a lunch which had involved far too much wine. He put on his white skipper's cap and his dark glasses and watched his crew of one take the big motor cruiser into the little harbour, elbowing its way among the elegant yachts like a prizefighter muscling in on a troupe of ballerinas.

'Oh, we're here, then?' a woman's voice said.

'Yes, we're here,' he sighed with little tolerance.

She was his next door neighbour in Jersey, a widow spending the fruits of her husband's achievements without much difficulty. She was good fun at a barbecue or a party by the pool but Lomax regretted the moment of liquid weakness in which he had asked her to come on this trip with him. Still, he had brought plenty of drink and it helped to blot her out of his consciousness.

He wished that was the case with the other woman, Laura Keane. She haunted him. He saw her face everywhere, in shops, restaurants, walking on the street. He was imagining things, of course. People who had been shot five times and then fallen from a multi-storey building did not tend to survive the experience. Still, her body had never been found, or so they said. Maybe that was just a story and they had recovered it after all, getting rid of it quietly so that there would be no questions asked about her. But buried secrets had a habit of working their way back up to the surface, as well he knew.

They had stopped now and lines had been tied. She wanted to see the shops. He would find the nearest bar and sit outside it until she came back.

People had gathered at the harbour rail, as they always did, to see who was coming in and going out. Lomax's boat was attracting a lot of attention and he looked up at the faces gathered above.

Was she there, waiting among them? He felt the beginning of a cold sweat in spite of the heat of the day and he told himself not to be so stupid.

The woman began the steep climb up the rusting iron ladder mounted against the wall. 'Don't let me fall, Henry, will you?' she called out over her shoulder. One or two of the people watching began to laugh at her awkward progress. Lomax glared indignantly and began his own climb, his eyes trying to seek out the offenders.

He was about half-way up the ladder when his chest felt as if someone had hit him a blow with an enormous, heavy hammer. He gasped and lost his grip and began to fall back on to the deck.

The faces on the harbour wall looked down at him as he died. One was a woman, slim features, auburn hair.

It was probably her imagination but she could have sworn he had been staring right at her.

THE 13th JUROR

The compelling thriller from the author of
HARD EVIDENCE

JOHN T. LESCROART

'A heart-pounding page-turner . . . *The Thirteenth Juror*
is courtroom drama at its best' *Playboy*

Jennifer Witt is a woman who has suffered. Virtually
every man in her life has abused her, so who would
blame her if one day she struck back? Killed her doctor
husband Larry whose strictures and punishments have
made her life a living hell . . . But when Larry is shot
dead Jennifer, suspect number one, denies she was ever
beaten and consistently refuses to admit she killed him.
Dismas Hardy, agreeing to undertake her defence, tends
to believe her, especially since her seven-year-old son,
the apparent centre of her life, was also killed . . .

But as Jennifer's trial – a capital case – continues and
Dismas watches his own family life disintegrate under
the pressure of her defence, he begins to wonder if his
judgement has let him down. And if Jennifer Witt is a
cold-blooded childkiller . . .

'Unusual in his ability to combine courthouse scenes
with action sequences, judicial puzzles and dimensional
people, Mr Lescroart produces a full house of well-drawn
characters . . . A fast-paced text that sustains interest to
the very end' *Wall Street Journal*

'Engaging characters and a riveting plot that fans of
Scott Turow and John Grisham will love; recommended'
Library Journal

FICTION / THRILLER 0 7472 4760 9

STEVE MARTINI

PRIME WITNESS

'MR MARTINI WRITES WITH THE AGILE EPISODIC STYLE OF A LAWYER QUICK ON HIS FEET' John Grisham

'Steve Martini seems to have hit the nail right on the head'
Irish Times

'A real page turner' *Sunday Telegraph*

PRIME WITNESS

In the space of five days the rural college town of Davenport is rocked by four brutal murders: two couples – undergraduates – whose bodies are found tied and staked out on the banks of Putah Creek. Then two more bodies are discovered. This time the victims are Abbott Scofield, a distinguished member of the university faculty, and his former wife Karen.

The police suspect Andre Iganovich, a Russian immigrant and part-time security guard, but Paul Madriani, hot-shot Capitol City lawyer, thinks there is more to the case than meets the eye.

Forensic reports on the physical evidence suggest lingering questions about the Russian's involvement in the Scofield killings, and Paul becomes increasingly convinced that the second murders are the product of some copy-cat killer – a cold and calculating murderer who has taken the lives of the Scofields for reasons that Paul is determined to uncover . . .

'Prime is indeed the word for this involving read'
Publishers Weekly

'Nice insider touches, and a hard-punching climax'
The Times

FICTION / THRILLER 0 7472 4164 3

A selection of bestsellers from Headline

BODY OF A CRIME	Michael C. Eberhardt	£5.99	☐
TESTIMONY	Craig A. Lewis	£5.99	☐
LIFE PENALTY	Joy Fielding	£5.99	☐
SLAYGROUND	Philip Caveney	£5.99	☐
BURN OUT	Alan Scholefield	£4.99	☐
SPECIAL VICTIMS	Nick Gaitano	£4.99	☐
DESPERATE MEASURES	David Morrell	£5.99	☐
JUDGMENT HOUR	Stephen Smoke	£5.99	☐
DEEP PURSUIT	Geoffrey Norman	£4.99	☐
THE CHIMNEY SWEEPER	John Peyton Cooke	£4.99	☐
TRAP DOOR	Deanie Francis Mills	£5.99	☐
VANISHING ACT	Thomas Perry	£4.99	☐

All Headline books are available at your local bookshop or newsagent, or can be ordered direct from the publisher. Just tick the titles you want and fill in the form below. Prices and availability subject to change without notice.

Headline Book Publishing, Cash Sales Department, Bookpoint, 39 Milton Park, Abingdon, OXON, OX14 4TD, UK. If you have a credit card you may order by telephone – 01235 400400.

Please enclose a cheque or postal order made payable to Bookpoint Ltd to the value of the cover price and allow the following for postage and packing:

UK & BFPO: £1.00 for the first book, 50p for the second book and 30p for each additional book ordered up to a maximum charge of £3.00.
OVERSEAS & EIRE: £2.00 for the first book, £1.00 for the second book and 50p for each additional book.

Name ....

Address ....

....

....

If you would prefer to pay by credit card, please complete:
Please debit my Visa/Access/Diner's Card/American Express (delete as applicable) card no:

Signature .... Expiry Date ....